Indomitus Oriens

Book Three of The Fovean Chronicles

---

by Robert W. Brady, Jr.

The horse that you love the best, will be the one that hurts you worst.

The Fovean Chronicles
Book Three: Indomitus Oriens

ISBN: 978-0-9793679-3-9

Cover art: Boris Vallejo

Third Printing

10 9 8 7 6 5 4 3 2 1

Dedicated to Ann Brady

Whose steadfast acceptance of this life as it came inspired this book, even before I realized it myself

Dabar ji sėdi Dievo dešinėje!

The Map of Fovea

Prologue

A Story About a Nice Girl

A girl woke up in a dirty bed, its gray sheets sticking to her skin. Red dots on her legs and arms showed where fleas had bitten her in her sleep. She'd matted down her black hair with her own sweat; the t-shirt she slept in stank of her own perspiration.

Hazy light filtered through a dirty window onto a carpet that stank of mold. She could see fleas hopping in it in the weak sunshine. The room had a dirty little bathroom attached, with a toilet bearing the stain of a lifetime of 'near misses.'

What could anyone expect from a $25/night room?

She rose, the inside of her left leg sticky, her cheeks feeling chapped from the tears that had dried on them. Her stomach ached from hunger but she didn't want to eat, didn't want to speak, didn't want to do anything but take a shower. She'd been denied that last night because the water wasn't working. She prayed that it did now.

Last night, she had done it. Last night she had crossed the line. Last night, for a measly fifty dollars, she had bent over for a man in an alley and let him pull her panties down, and pretended to moan with pleasure when he entered her.

Afterwards he tried to tell her how good she made him feel, how pretty she was, how much he enjoyed it. Couldn't he just shut up? Couldn't he just pay the money and leave? Did he have to be nice to her? Did he have to try and make her feel a connection to him, and have to remind herself she was just a whore?

A whore. She was a whore now.

She entered the bathroom and she turned the knob in the shower. A noise like steel cockroaches running up and down the pipes greeted her. The shower head jumped, and jumped again, and did a little shimmy, then a trickle of water leaked out of it, then the trickle strengthened to a flow.

"Yes!" she said. Her own voice surprised her, loud in the dismal room, too bright for the morning, too young for the million and one years she felt she'd aged.

She shucked the t-shirt and stepped into the shower. The water felt tepid and smelled of sulfur. A bar of Ivory sat on a scummy shelf. She had to pick the wrapper off of it but at least she could rub it on her body.

She scrubbed her breasts, where his hands had been. She scrubbed her backside, where he had gripped her, and up and down the inside of her leg, where he made a mess taking the condom off.

The water wasn't hot, but it burned her skin like fire, and she scrubbed herself red. She used the last of the soap on her underarms and then scrubbed her hair as hard as she could with her fingernails to get it clean.

She stepped into the stream and let the water envelope her. The rotten-egg smell made her gag, but it was better than the alternative – what had been left on her from the night before.

Sex had been love to her. Sex had been the special gift she gave to Mike--her commitment to him. Mike who held her, kissed her and took her for her very first time. She had kept his house, his company, and his bed. She had been everything but a wife to him, and that only because he hadn't asked her.

The man last night had left her with a wink and an awkward smile, in an alley where the garbage smelt of rot and pee, holding fifty dollars in her hand and knowing this reflected her worth in the world.

Mike had left her less. Mike had just walked out with the rent money, lacking the courage even to say good-bye to her, to give her another chance, even to cry in front of him.

Mike had been the first steps on the path that brought her here.

When she couldn't stand the sulfur smell anymore she stepped out and realized there were no towels. She didn't want to, but she used the bed sheet, imagining the creepy-crawlies that hid in there and that had returned to her skin. She did her best not to think about it as she dressed back in the clothes she'd worn last night. She had a simple mini and a tube top; she tied her hair up in a ponytail with her one and only scrunchy. She looked in the mirror and felt thankful she had the kind of face that didn't need makeup.

She'd never had much, but this was the first time she'd had nothing. She'd had a daddy, a sister, a mom. She'd lost them all. She'd had a college career, and A's in biology and chemistry. She'd lost that, too. She had done worse than lose Mike—he had deserted her. Now she had given up her dignity, and couldn't help wondering what more she had, and if she was destined to lose that, too.

She left the cheap hotel room and she went to a diner where she could eat. She wanted a real breakfast with waffles and bacon and a cup of coffee. She had taken up smoking for Mike, and she looked forward to a Marlboro, if she could get a pack.

She sat down at the counter, because she liked the stools. Her dad had taken her to breakfast at a place similar to this on Sundays, when they still went to church. She would sit on the stool at the counter, and she would hold her back straight and pretend she was an important woman who was just taking time out of her busy schedule for a quick bite. Her father, once he knew the game, would call her, "Ma'am", and ask for her advice on stocks, or what she thought of the news, and she would give him her sage advice, woman of the world that she was.

Now she placed her order and paid up front, because she didn't look like the kind of person who had $4.50.

She stared into the dark depths of her coffee, and wondered what had become of her life.

Lysette, her younger sister, had called the game stupid. Lysette would kick her feet to scuff her paten leathers, and complain the food was cold, the milk was warm and the air was smoky. When their mother had died, Lysette had found a new thing to hate about her world every day and acted on it.

"If that isn't the saddest face on a pretty girl."

She turned to her left and saw an old woman with silver hair, wrinkled skin, dressed in a yellow sundress and white shoes. She smelled of Sunflowers perfume.

"I guess it's a pretty bad morning," she said.

"Lose your best fella?" the woman asked.

"Oh, he is long gone," she said. "He is the reason I am up here, I guess."

"Up from where?"

"Portland," she said, pronouncing it *Powat*-land, as any Mainer would.

"Been here long?"

"Just a day."

"And what are you going to do here in Augusta?"

The girl thought about that. She really didn't know.

"Eat breakfast, I guess, ma'am," she said. "Look for work, and a place to live."

"Ya got no place to live, girl?" the woman seemed halfway between sympathy and making fun of her.

"No, ma'am," she said. She looked back into her coffee. This was becoming very depressing.

"And you got no money, I gather," she said.

She shook her head.

"Well, ya got a name?" the old lady asked. "You must have a name. You can't be that bad off and not have a name for it."

"Oh, leave her be, Eve," the waitress said. She poured a little more coffee in the girl's cup. "Your breakfast be out in justa minute, hun," she said, and patted her hand.

Eve looked back to her own business, which seemed to be nursing her own cup of coffee.

"Melissa," the girl said. She looked back to her right, to the old woman, and met her sea-green eyes, and said, "My name is Melissa, ma'am."

And for the life of her, and despite her best efforts, she burst into tears and fell into Eve's arms, because she'd done a bad thing, and she was a *nice* girl, and she shouldn't be a whore.

"Oh, there, there," Eve said, and rocked her, staring down

onlookers over her shoulder. “You jes git it all out now. You’re in a room full of strangers, and don’t you nevermind what they think.

“It’s a big a world and sometimes a body jes needs to cry.”

The waitress dropped a plate with waffles and eggs in front of Melissa’s stool, and refreshed her coffee as Eve pushed her away.

“Now, you eat, girl, and you tell me about what ails you,” Eve prompted. “Sometimes when you air out dirty laundry, you put it away smelling fresh.

Melissa hesitated. There was something about Eve, so motherly to a girl who barely remembered her own. With some difficulty, she decided to start there.

“My mom died when I was ten,” she said. She looked down and took a sip of coffee. The waffles smelled of home as she preferred to remember it, earthy and good.

“She was really, like, hard on me,” she continued. “I used to hate it when she told me, ‘Put your knees together,’ ‘Sit up straight,’ and all that crap.”

“It’s a mother’s job to raise her daughter up proper,” Eve said.

Melissa cut a piece from her waffle. “Yeah, I s’pose,” she said. “Didn’t make me hate her less. I couldn’t do anything right for her. Then with no notice, she was gone. She went to the hospital and she never came back.”

“Accident?” Eve asked.

Melissa shook her head. “Cancer. Wasn’t caught in time. I didn’t know that then. All I knew is that my dad was drinking a pint of Jack a night and if you talked to him too long, he started crying.”

“Oh, dear,” Eve said.

“I took over,” she said. “I don’t think I knew it then. I knew that if I did chores, then it was like, you know, doing it for mom?”

Eve gave a sympathetic laugh. “When my mother died, I went and cleaned her headstone every Sunday for two years,” she admitted.

Melissa took a bite and chewed. She had never been to her mother’s headstone. Her dad never brought her.

"Lysette was the problem," she said. "My younger sister. She says she doesn't remember mom at all, but I think she does."

"She in Portland?"

Melissa shook her head. "She's in Warren," she admitted.

Eve touched her hand and looked into her eyes. "Prison?"

Melissa nodded as she chewed. "Robbed a liquor store with her loser boyfriend. He turned her in when the cops caught him."

"Goodness!"

She nodded. "She liked 'em like that. Tattoos, a record, whatever pissed off daddy most. He'd yell at her and she'd just get worse. Then, when she got busted, he spent all of his money on her lawyer. Not that it mattered or helped. She did it."

"That's hard on a family," Eve said.

"It was on me," Melissa said. "He spent my college-fund, so I had to drop out. That's when I met Mike and ended up in Portland."

Melissa took another bite and shook her head. This was a bad idea. Why was she spilling her guts to this woman? She couldn't help. She was an old biddy using her to kill time.

"He that fella' you mentioned?"

She nodded. She got that hot feeling you get in the back of your throat when you wanted to cry but couldn't let yourself.

"Took everything? Left you flat?"

Through sheer will she swallowed her mouthful. She put the knife and fork down, and laid her hands in her lap, on her napkin.

She felt the tears in her eyes, her vision becoming blurry. She looked back at Eve, who had drawn all this out of her.

"He—he—he," she said, and sniffed. She took a moment, started again, looking down at her sneakers.

"He said he loved me," she said. "I gave him everything—*everything*—and after a year together, I come home and there isn't even a note. Like, thanks for the sex, slut! Next thing I know, the freaking landlord is telling me get out by tomorrow because the rent hasn't been paid and we're evicted. And there is Melly on her own, no money, no job, hitchhiking to Augusta to start again."

"Your dad couldn't help you?"

She shook her head.

Eve reached out and took Melissa by the chin, turned her face to look at her, and looked into her eyes.

"Where did you sleep last night, girl?" she asked.

"The Cityside," she said.

"And how did you do that, if you didn't have money?"

The waitress nearly dropped her pot of coffee, eavesdropping on that answer.

"Oh, now you know better than *that*," Eve said.

"I know, ma'am," she said. "I hate it. I should have just stayed up all night, or—"

"Oh, and you know better than that, too," Eve scolded her. "If you could go undo the past, do you really think you would pick last night to change? I don't think so, young lady."

No, Melissa agreed. Last night was a symptom of the problem, with the sickness being the way she ran her life.

"You're a very nice girl hoeing a very hard row, and you are here blaming all the rocks. Well I tell you, and I am a Mainer, so as I know, that it ain't the soil's fault for being stony, it is the girl with the hoe," and she jabbed Melissa in the arm, "who don't know no better than to pick another spot for her garden."

"What?"

"You're in the wrong place, girl," Eve said. "You are a good girl in a location where she can't succeed, and all you're doin' is hoeing up rocks. You need to move your garden to a place where you can plant you some vegetables."

The woman clearly didn't know what ho' meant to a young girl, especially to Melissa this morning, but she got the message. She finished her meal with a last gulp of her coffee, and she left a dollar on the bar. She stood and kissed Eve on the cheek.

"You're a nice lady, Eve," she said, looking into her eyes.

"So you ain't gonna move your garden?" Eve said.

"I would if I had the money," Melissa said. "I would move the heck away from here. If I can get a job today then maybe I can start saving so I can jump on another bus and get to another city."

Eve poked Melissa right in the collarbone with a long, wrinkled finger. "Well, I hope you do," she said. "When you git you going, you go someplace rural. I don't mean start farming, but get the idea of big city life out of your head. Busses go to nice places, too."

Melissa nodded. Someplace where people had a stake in her maybe. Not a big city, but a nice town. Some place in the south.

"I will, ma'am," she said. "I promise."

"So where you off to?" Eve asked her, as the waitress cleared her plate.

Melissa chuckled. "You won't like this, but to get a pack of Marlboro's," she said. "Then to find a job."

Eve smiled, fished into her purse, and pulled out a pack. It had two missing, and she handed it to Melissa.

"Why wouldn't I like it," she said. "That's my brand, too. You keep the pack—mebbe it'll bring you some luck."

Her manners said refuse, but cigarettes were expensive. She gave the old lady a hug and a kiss, and she took the pack.

Outside, she opened it, and she noticed something in the wrapper—a green slip of paper.

She pulled it out and found four, one hundred dollar bills. Sometimes people put their change in their wrapper, but that wasn't change.

She turned back to the diner. It didn't even occur to her to take off with the money. Even if it was a gift, the woman had to be asked if she meant to give it.

Melissa just didn't have it in her to steal, and old people lived on fixed incomes. This could be her rent money.

She went in and the place was packed. Her seat was taken, and Eve's as well. She went to the counter waitress and she waved.

"Yeah?" the overworked counter waitress asked her.

"What happened to the old lady I was talking to?" she asked.

"Who?"

"The old lady—you know, the one—"

"Hun, I don't know any old lady's and I don't have time to kid around. If you want something, order. If not, get out."

She turned and left her standing with her mouth open.

* * *

In another reality, Adriam the All-Father held the perfect wife, Eveave, in his infinite arms.

"This one?" he asked her.

"She is perfect," Eveave informed him.

"There is nothing in this one," he argued.

Eveave's lips remained in the grim line of balance. In glee she saw sadness, in hate she saw love. She knew the place between success and failure. Only in Adriam's arms did she know peace.

"This one is more than we could imagine," she informed him.

"The instrument of War is strong," Adriam said, "as is Power's. We have Life's help, but the Almadain cannot fight the tide."

"No one can fight the tide, husband," Eveave said.

"The machinations of War already shake the face of Earth," Adriam said. "Your instrument must stop the flood, hold back the tide."

Eveave heard the love in the All-Father's voice—love for his children, even the errant Power and War.

And it was War's nature to destroy.

"My instrument fights for the balance," Eveave told him. "The take and give. The balance *is*, my husband. Where the instrument of War devours, do not counter him with another who would take more.

"Whoever fights the tide will drown. Ride the tide, and then find the safety of the shore."

"And this one can ride the tide?" Adriam asked her.

She considered. What to her was a moment was to her champion a year. Time is immaterial to a god.

"This one can keep her head up," Eveave said, finally. "Sometimes she fights best who sees the balance, who raises not the sword but the heart of a man. My champion is my balance, my husband. My balance *is*.

"Let the tide be the tide."

Chapter One:

He Said, She Said

"Ma'am, can I have a moment of your time?"

"Sir, have you ever dreamed of making all of the money you can while working at home?"

"Are you happy with your current employment?"

"Can I interest you in a new life?"

"No," the woman told him, with some additional instruction on what he could do with his telephone.

She clearly had no concept of anatomy.

At least the call ended at spot-on 10:45am. Break time. Man, he was dying for a cigarette!

Bill stood up from his cubicle and stretched. All around him on the telesales floor: gray and off-white cubbies, with black computers and black, ergonomic chairs that made your back feel like there were knives sticking out of it. He shuffled down the row of agents, conscientious about his belly touching anyone. Some of them rose with him, some stayed on their phones, he left for the blessed exit and fifteen minutes of time that were not spent here.

* * *

Glynn Escaroth liked to think of the royal throne room of Outpost IX as a lesson in the Uman-Chi themselves. In her 167 years of life, as the sole surviving member of the House Escaroth, whose family had protected the southern towers of Outpost IX for centuries, she had reflected on this many times. White marble covered walls and the floor, simple and unadorned, polished and without veins. Grooved marble columns rose white to the height of more than ten Men, simple rings at their bases, to an arched ceiling, plain in construction, white with no frescoes, no murals, no chandeliers. It glowed a white light that filled the place with a ghostly radiance, making the people and the things here seem unreal.

She stood in the Circle of Judgment before the dais; twenty ringed steps flush against the white wall, rising higher than a tall Man's head, to a white marble throne, the seat of Angron Aurelias, her king.

The Circle, the only surface in the room that hadn't been polished, a woman's height in diameter, existed as a place for the penitent and the needy to stand. A bright red carpet ran like a rivulet of blood on a field of snow from its edge, covering more than two hundred paces from the polished oak double-doors bound with burnished brass that always stood open at the throne room's entrance.

Normally the solid oak gallery behind her to her right would have held hundreds of courtiers sitting for court. Thirty-two paces long, it remained draped in the banners of the great houses, the Proud Falcon of the Escaroths among them

An Uman-Chi with 167 year of age could barely be considered an adolescent among her people. She felt like a child now, playing dress-up in the white robes of a Caster, a part of her feeling foolish to speak before so many, another seeing what it meant to be grand, to be truly the noblest of all people.

To be Uman-Chi meant to be unadorned; to have one's grace and elegance be so simply stated as to be beyond question. It meant more to maintain it clean than to decorate it.

The Cheyak had built this place millennia before, and when the Cheyak had passed, it had come to the Uman-Chi to be the first among all Foveans; above Men, above Uman, above Dwarves and Scitai and Slee and Swamp Devils. Uman-Chi lives spanned centuries. Uman-Chi lived supreme.

Supreme among the supreme ruled Angron Aurelias, King of Trenbon. Great, wise eyes, long white hair brushed fine over his shoulders, dressed in the white robes of a Caster with the Royal Eagle upon his breast, he steepled his long, thin fingers before him, sitting on his throne, and took on the look of a predator. Even his bushy white eyebrows seemed to bristle at her temerity.

In the Circle of Judgment, a person may beg the King's favor. Most begged for wealth and power, some begged for advice, and many for direction.

Glynn Escaroth begged to sing.

* * *

Like a wave of pleasure washing over him, Bill exhaled two lungs full of smoke from his Lucky Strikes.

There had been a time when you could walk into any break room and just inhale to cash in on a good nicotine buzz. That era had passed. First the smokers had been given a few rooms, then fewer rooms, then a place outside by the door, then a smaller place, away from the door.

Now you went wherever you could get away from people. He leaned against the brick wall, the sun beating down on him, the sweat already running down his heavy jowls into the hair of his beard. Sweat soaked his temples, made a line down the back of his t-shirt, wet against his skin. He tilted his head back and pulled another sweet drag from the cigarette.

"Bum a butt?"

Bill looked to his left where one of the girls on his aisle stood, looking at him. He immediately classified her as one of the three types of telesales agents he'd become familiar with: young hotties who don't want real jobs but who do have debts to pay.

"Yeah, here," he said, pulling the pack from his shirt pocket. He deftly pushed a stick out from the pack in her direction.

She wrinkled her pert nose at him, its dusting of freckles peeking out from her make-up. Her pink top, made from the stretchy material that young girls liked, accentuated her tiny waist and over-large bosom. Her long, dark brown hair tumbled past her shoulders and framed her big, brown eyes. Legs like a fashion model were barely concealed by a short turquoise skirt.

The type of girl who did *not* waste her time talking to him.

"Ewww—Lucky's?" she complained.

"What I smoke," he said.

She looked him up and down. "No chance you'll switch to Marlboros?" she asked, and gave the eyes a bat.

That probably worked on the second type of telesales agents: the young guy whose real job doesn't pay too well, and who needs to make a car or rent payment fast. That guy would be skipping off to the cigarette machine in a lick to get her what she wanted, in hopes of getting her to go out with him.

"Nope," he said, and shook the pack. "Still want?"

"Sure," she reconciled herself. They were the only two out there. She picked the cig out from the pack with long, multi-colored nails. "Thanks."

"No problem," he said, and popped her a light from his Zippo. She leaned forward and sucked it lit.

Just amazing how hot the girls looked here. Not that it really mattered to him. He classified himself as the third type of telesales agent: old people no one else would hire.

At fifty years of age and, coincidentally, overweight by fifty pounds, he found himself doing a job anyone could do. He had a full head of gray and brown hair, and a scruffy gray and black beard.

When he had been young he would have gone for the hottie, and he wouldn't have had to fetch her cigarettes to get her. Back in his twenties, it had been a brave new world and he had been on top of it.

He checked his watch. Ten minutes left. He took another pull.

"Been here long?" she asked him.

That surprised him. Normally a girl like this would get what she wanted and go somewhere else

"A year," he said. "Been in sales more than twenty, though."

"Wow," she said. "That's a really long time. Did they do telemarketing back then?"

Oh, *man*! "Yes, but I sold switches."

"Like, light switches?"

Another drag. “Phone switches. Calls coming in and out.”

That had been so sweet for so long. Every big company had to have them. They were all unique, making it easy to say, “Mine handles more trunks and more lines,” and get a giant commission.

Years and years of sales and specialization, knowing his product, knowing his clients, and then the damn phone companies had surprised the world with the exact same features at a fraction of the price. Switches all became computerized and the industry had left him behind.

He had paid to put his kids through college, but they were done with college now and had their own lives with their own kids, in other parts of the country. He had been divorced for a decade and never bought a house, because he didn’t want to have to cut his own lawn.

She nodded. He had almost forgotten her standing there. “Don’t they have that here?” she asked.

“Not the same,” he said. “They’re computers now. Totally different sales.”

“So why not sell those?”

Another drag. She took one, too. “Totally different,” he repeated. “I don’t know anything about computers.”

She nodded, then giggled. “Me, neither,” she said. “You do okay here?”

“It pays my bills. Can’t beat the hours.”

“Yeah,” she agreed, and took a drag. “One of my girls works here and got me in. She got a hundred bucks for signing me up.”

“Had a payment to make?” he asked.

She nodded. “Car needs work.”

“Hate that,” he said. “Been taking a bike here lately. Trying to drop weight.”

She giggled again. He wished she would get to whatever she wanted, because he had a hard time not looking down her blouse.

“I’m Melissa,” she said, and stuck out her hand. “Pleased ta meetcha.”

“Bill,” he said. “Bill Howard.”

Her hand felt soft as silk. He held it maybe a second too long, but he couldn't help himself. She managed to stroke his thumb as she pulled her hand away.

"So, what do you do for fun, Bill?"

* * *

The song had come to Glynn in a dream six months before and burned itself into her memory. It had taken every fiber of her concentration and training not to burst out with it, every moment of the day, since then.

Had she been a normal Uman-Chi, if there were such a thing, she would have been unable, however Glynn had received Caster training from Chaheff Tamulin. Through her mind's focus and discipline she could command the control necessary to suppress the imperative, to hold back the tide, the power. With Chaheff to guide her, she had come before the King that first morning and begged to sing it.

His advisor, Avek Noir, also a Caster, had suggested they try to write it down. The letters scorched the parchment when they tried. Clearly this song came from Power, or Adriam, or one of the gods who imbued their minions with magic. This made the decision more serious.

Had Chaheff Tamulin himself been the recipient of the song, then there would be no question. House Tamulin were merchants, and Chaheff looked it, standing there in the throne room behind her, the fattest of all of the Uman-Chi. But Chaheff, a gifted Caster, had discovered *The Ultimate Truth of Things* before his two hundredth year. He could handle any ramifications of any song he voiced. Glynn Escaroth had come to that same truth at the impossibly young age of ninety-five. While her friends had been learning etiquette and discourse, she had been diverted to spell casting and donned the White Robe.

If she couldn't maintain control of the song then there could be no guarantee she wouldn't loose all the power of the spell on those around her. In Uman-Chi terms, less than seventy years was to have barely begun training.

Angron had decreed then that Glynn would not sing. That had been six months before this day. Now she returned, the song still burning in her mind.

"If the song will not depart your mind," Angron said, "then clearly you must sing. The question is where."

"I still advise against the casting," Avek Noir said. Glynn detested the Noirs, who had bought their way back into the King's favor after the sack of Outpost IX. "But I defer to the throne, and then advise a fast ship, a trip into Tren Bay, and there singing."

The King nodded. Glynn grudgingly agreed, much as she dreaded the water. She lowered her head in obeisance, her long green hair falling before her face. Eldadorian 'Sea Wolves' sailed in defiance of the Trenboni 'Tech Ship' on Tren Bay. Armed with 'Eldadorian Fire,' they'd become the scourge of the sea and a tremendous threat to all other ships.

"I disagree," D'gattis the Far Traveled said from the gallery. Also in the white robes of a Caster, his were adorned with a yellow mark down the front, something resembling a hook and a dot. D'gattis came from a family which had never produced anything but gifted Casters, himself no exception. As a member of the mercenary army, the 'Daff Kanaar,' D'gattis as an Uman-Chi was out of favor, Glynn knew.

D'gattis as a Caster was indomitable. Chaheff himself deferred to him. Angron summoned him here to advise because no one else had his knowledge.

"This is the place of power. *This* is where Uman-Chi and Cheyak wards protect us, not the Bay. If it is the will of the All-Father that we should be spared, then we will be spared, and if not then there is nothing we can do to prevent that.

"Pretending we can circumvent His will is as ill-advised as was not letting her sing six months ago."

"You speak plainly," Angron commented. "You amaze me, D'gattis, for your association with the Conqueror."

D'gattis inclined his head and spread his hands, palms up. "Your Majesty, if I am frank, then I am frank in deference to your time and your importance," he said. "The Emperor does not dictate to me. He is a Man, and his entire life is a blink of an eye."

"Perhaps he is the sliver in an Uman-Chi eye," Chaheff said. "Because this blink has pained us so."

"I must agree with D'gattis," Aniquen Demoran said.

Glynn controlled the smile that begged to cross her lips, her head still down. Aniquen was young and handsome, his house a high one, and he merely five decades her senior.

More importantly, Aniquen had *personally* crossed swords with the hated Conqueror and been beaten, but survived.

Glynn's mirth left her for melancholy. Her brother and her father had not been so lucky.

"Remain here," Aniquen said. "Remember that this is Adriam's month. There is no pleasure in being on Tren Bay now."

Angron actually smiled, an honor to them all. "It has been so long since I have been outside of the palace, that I forgot Adriam's month was cold. Yes, let it be here, then."

"Then allow me to summon the Casters, as many as we have," Avek said. Glynn looked up to see Noir's protective hand laid atop the royal throne. "If there must be a containment, let us be ready."

"One hundred or more Uman-Chi, each acting on behalf of his Majesty?" D'gattis asked the rest. "I think we would be safer if the Conqueror returned."

Angron held his mirth that time. The rest stayed quiet as well. Glynn looked from one set of eyes to the next, un-fooled by the silver-on-silver appearance. Uman-Chi saw eyes of green and blue and lovely violet, in a frequency other eyes could not see. Another sign that Uman-Chi were superior.

All of them shifted between D'gattis and Angron, to see if the bold one had lost more favor with the elder.

"You are right, and forthright, D'gattis," the King said. He turned to Noir. "You are my heir, bring me four more."

Then he turned to Chaheff, and said, "You are her mentor, prepare her for containment, if it is needed. If she must give herself to her song, see that she knows how."

A lesser being would have shown her surprise. Glynn had the discipline of a Caster and a century in protocol training. Her first duty remained to her people. The Uman-Chi lived long and died rarely.

Rarely, and not lightly.

* * *

"For fun?" Bill repeated. "You mean, besides all of this?"

Melissa smiled. "Yeah."

What the hell did she even care for? Bill wondered. This reeked of scam and agenda.

"Not a lot," Bill said. "I'm not married; my kids don't live in-state. First thing you learn in sales is that you don't make the kind of friends you keep when you change jobs. It's no different from here. How many people have you made friends with here?"

"Other than you?" she said. "None."

Bill took another drag, held it, then exhaled. He hadn't missed the 'other than you.' "So other than the thrill of the kill here," he said. "Movies, football in season, I guess."

"I'm surprised," Melissa said. "I thought you would be hitting the clubs, some nice ride…"

"Yeah, right," Bill said. She might be looking for a sugar daddy or just making fun of him. Either way, he wasn't playing.

"Serious," she said.

He checked his watch. Two minutes left. Screw it. He flicked the butt and smiled. "Back to the salt mines," he said. "Good talking to you."

"Thanks for the cig," she said. "Think about those Marlboros."

Bill smiled. "You did okay with the Lucky's."

He was in the door as she smiled up at him.

* * *

The rest of the morning was like the start of the morning. Provocative questions to incite interest, interest means you have an opening, push the opening to get them a package out, get a committal statement to say that (a) they would read the package and (b) they would talk to you again when you called back.

You could be a robot. In fact, it surprised Bill that he hadn't already been replaced by one. The sorry part was he was capable of so much more. Bill knew he had a good resume as a sales person, but everyone thought a good sales person in his fifties was a manager by then. A good sales person in his fifties didn't have to sell any more, no matter how much he loved it, because he *was* that good.

Not Bill. It left him feeling depressed. When he tried to be unique and up his sales, he either ended up getting reamed by a boss or just embarrassing himself. Like they told him, "The program works. It works best if you just don't think about it."

Lunch rolled around from 12:00pm to either 12:30pm or, if you made your numbers, 1:00pm. He had made his numbers, so he logged out of his terminal and stood, planning to grab a sandwich and then listen to Rush Limbaugh for his first hour.

"Bill, can I see you?"

He turned and saw Eileen, the floor sup for his division. "It'll just take a minute."

He shrugged and followed her to her 'office,' a slightly larger cubicle at the end of Bill's row. She was a slight girl with small tits, kinky blonde hair and dancer's body, in tight black jeans and top.

She sat, he sat.

"Do you know Melissa?" she asked.

Bill's first thought was that he'd said or done something no longer considered 'PC,' and she'd taken offense at him.

"I know one who bummed a cig from me at break," he said.

"She's having a hard time selling," Eileen said. "And I was talking to her about it. I offered to set her up with someone to show her, and she asked for you."

Bill shook his head. "Eileen, I'm not a trainer."

"I know, but you could be," Eileen said. "You're really good—you always make your numbers. You aren't some young guy who is going to be looking down their blouses, and you aren't some young girl where they will be looking down yours."

Bill chuckled. This was as nice as he had seen Eileen. Usually she just bitched about how, when *she* was on the floor, she never had a hard time making her numbers.

"More work, less pay," Bill said. "And the first time one of them doesn't make their numbers, they're going to say I harassed them."

Eileen gave him her best solemn eyed look. She had *really* missed her calling selling used cars. "We lock your pay in at your average week for the last year," she said, "so you can never make less than you are, but you get another hundred a week and if you beat your average, then you just make more. No downside."

Bill did an impressed frown. That wasn't bad, actually, and the extra money would really help him. "And the other thing?"

Eileen leaned back. "Bill," she said, and reached out and touched the back of his hand, "even *I* have had to deal with it. Everyone knows it's crap. I won't lie—if you're ever seen with one of these kids outside of here, they are going to be able to get you fired, so don't party with them and you'll be fine."

Bill sighed. "Well, it isn't like I am hitting the discotheques."

She just laughed. "Actually, any place with a mirror ball, and you're safe."

"So when do I start?"

"You start now," Eileen said. "Take her to lunch; keep the receipt and the company pays for it. You get one lunch per trainee. Find out what her problem is and then haul her ass back here and let her watch you sell. Tomorrow you watch her sell. If she can do it, let her know and, if she can't, let *me* know."

Bill nodded. He stood, turned, and there stood Melissa waiting for him with big, watery doe eyes. Why she wanted some old fart baffled him—maybe he looked just like her dad or something.

But she had just made him five thousand dollars more per year, and for that she could count on a *hell* of a training.

* * *

Chaheff knelt before the altar of Adriam, the All-Father, first among the gods. Glynn knelt down beside him, before the goddess Eveave, the Taker and the Giver. Eveave taught the balance, and Glynn would need balance to survive the singing.

That is what Chaheff had told her, anyway.

They chose a simple room for their devotions, small with rough-cut stone walls and bare floors. They knelt before a simple altar of hand-carved wood, a statue of the austere Adriam upon it, and a similar one beside it for the goddess.

"Perhaps we should have Power here," Chaheff said.

Adriam, the All-Father, had come first among the gods. His first creation had been Eveave, the Taker and the Giver, his perfect match. He had educated her in every aspect of his divinity, and coupled with her.

The gods Earth and Water had sprung unexpected from Eveave's womb, and later Power and Desire. These four had lesser aspects of Adriam's might, and Adriam and Eveave had sought to teach them but failed. For all of their might, they were not wise like the All-Father or even-handed like the Taker and the Giver.

Power became a dark god who would work against the others when it suited him. "Why would we want to taint this place—?" she began.

"No god taints a place," Chaheff interrupted her. "Power exists as does every other god, and has his followers and his motives, just like any other god."

"Not like Chaos, Destruction and War," Glynn challenged him. The primary sin was laying on daughter by son, and Power and Desire, Earth and Water each had done this. Chaos, Destruction and War were the sons of Power and Desire, and in the history of all things, they had done nothing but cause heartache and woe.

Chaheff grinned. Glynn knew he tolerated her for her youth and temerity. Since the death of her father, he had tried in small ways to advise her, in ways beyond his requirements as a mentor.

"True," he said, "Chaos and War, as the scriptures tell us, brought about the end of the One Place, where the gods lived. And we know War encouraged the people of Fovea to nearly annihilate each other before the Uman-Chi created the Fovean High Council.

"But even his presence does not defile," he wagged a finger at his student. "People will defile themselves ultimately, and you know the Rule of the Gods."

Glynn nodded. When the One Place had been destroyed by Chaos, the goddess Water had been struck dumb. Earth, who loved her, had taken her to a burning remnant of the One Place to warm her, and bonded with her to sustain her, and to rock her from side to side.

Water had birthed Life in his embrace, and Life had spread all manner of living things upon Earth's divine body.

Eveave had stepped in by creating the 'Rule of the Gods,' which protected Life's children from the direct influence of the Gods.

However the gods found indirect ways…

They prayed together. Glynn ignored the hard stone that made her knees throb, the stiff posture that made her back ache. She ignored the dryness in her throat from taking no drink, and she prayed even until her voice cracked.

She knew the pain served its purpose. The discipline of enduring it, the suffering, brought one through to the other side and, there, to enlightenment.

After hours and hours, knowing the sun had not only set but had risen, Chaheff spoke the final prayer and they were done.

She stood smoothly and with decorum, the only hint of her discomfiture the smudge on her white robes around the knee.

Uman servants appeared as if from the stone walls with food and drink. Glynn took a goblet full of red wine and waited for her mentor to drink. When he did, then she sipped, the tart liquid soothing her raw throat.

She didn't thank the Uman. It wasn't their place to be thanked. They would serve, she would cast, that is what they did. You didn't thank the Caste of Warriors for killing, the Caste of Merchants for selling, or the Caste of Artisans for making these goblets every time you used them.

It was simple in its grace, and all parties understood it.

"Sore?" kindly old Chaheff asked her.

She bowed her head and smiled. "I persevere," she said. "It is a matter of the mind and what it will hear from the body."

"We are about to let you sing a song, Glynn." Chaheff's kindly brown eyes focused on Glynn's violet ones. "You were chosen to be a Caster, because you came to your father on your own, and like me with mine, you told him, 'The most powerful thing in the world is not a knife, or a sword, or a spell, or a god, but a thought.'"

"A song is a thought you sing out, in a way to get others to believe in it. Lose control of your thoughts, and you will unleash the most powerful thing there is, and be at its mercy."

"I can sing it out, my Lord teacher," Glynn promised him. She searched his eyes, silver on silver to anyone else and lovely violet to her. Even now, exhausted from the prayer, the song remained burning in her mind.

"I have no doubt you can," Chaheff squeezed her shoulder. "But what will you do with the thought?"

Chapter Two:

The Evolution of Woman and Man

Lunch on the company dime was at a sit-down restaurant—specialty burgers, curly fries and double-large sodas served in glasses, not paper cups.

They sat together on the outdoor porch, where they could smoke. Melissa had her Marlboros from her car.

"Stupid no smoking laws," Bill complained. "Like we aren't Americans."

"Tell me about it," Melissa said. She took a long, satisfying drag. Bill had learned she was twenty-four, dropped out of college, followed some band around for two years, ended up here for lack of a better place and lived with two roommates.

"This your only gig?" Bill asked.

She took another drag and exhaled it. "It is for now," she said. "I tried working in an office but I don't have the clothes."

"They can be pretty strict," Bill said.

"Yeah, they can," she said, accentuating the 'yeah.' "Like, show one bit of cleavage and it's, 'Adios, slut.' So I said, 'Screw that,' and came here."

"Never sold before?"

"Girl Scouts. Can you believe it? Me in one of those uniforms? My sister said I was a total geek and she wouldn't join."

"I don't know," Bill said. "I really love the cookies."

"Oh, I could kill for the cookies," Melissa said. She sat back in her chair and blew a puff of smoke in the air. "You know the thin mint ones? I think I went up a pants size on those things."

Bill prevented himself from looking at her middle. He still wasn't comfortable with the rules in the office; better to stay quiet.

"But you're not from here," he pressed. That was as personal as he dared get.

She took a drag and shook her head. "Nah," she said. "Main—ah, born and raised. I thought I would take a break from the northeast, from city life. I like it down here. It's nice. You know your neighbors; people come over to your house and say, 'Hi.'"

Bill grinned. He had no idea who lived next door to him at the apartment.

"So what's happening with sales for you?" Bill asked, as their meal arrived. "Are you following the steps?"

She nodded, reaching for her burger. She had a healthy appetite for a girl. Women Bill knew were either fat or sweating every calorie.

"It's like, I follow the steps, yanno," she said, "but then they ask some stupid question, like, 'How much money will I make in my first year?' and I am like, 'I don't know—a lot.'"

Bill choked on a mouthful of beef. He almost felt like he was shooting pieces out his nose. He chewed and swallowed, feeling like a horse at a trough, and finally said, "You said that?"

"Well, the stupid card didn't tell me what to say."

She was referring to their script cue cards. You had a pack of laminated cards with numbers on them, and you could shuffle through them by number, so that if you were on card seven, and a client answered a question one way, then you went to card ten or, another way, card fourteen.

Newbies always got the cards mixed up, or read them and didn't listen.

"I can show you a trick to that," Bill said. "I used to have the same problem with that question."

"Really?" she asked. The expression on her face seemed

so grateful, as if she had asked him to cure her father's cancer, and he'd just said he could. "That is nice. *Thanks*, Bill."

She smiled a giant smile, putting him right on his guard.

"Yeah, not a problem," Bill said.

They ate quietly for a while.

"So no kids, no woman, no fun—what's up with you, Bill?" she asked, taking a bite of her French fry. "You gotta have something going in your life."

"I do?" he asked. This had become way too personal, and he didn't like it. "Why is that?"

She shrugged. "I dunno," she said. "Cuz otherwise you live your life between commercials? What did you do at my age?"

"At your age?" Bill said. "I was at Woodstock, or telling everyone who would listen how great being at Woodstock was."

"Really?" she said. "You were there? That is *so* cool. Was it really all, like, drugs and sex and cool music?"

Bill laughed. "Maybe in some peoples' minds. It was mostly bad weather, too many people with too few facilities, and a bunch of people thinking they were going to save us. The music was good, though. That was the last time I saw 'The Who' live."

"Wuh—who?"

"*The* Who," Bill said. "Before your time."

"Guess so," she agreed. "Did you want to be a rock star?"

Bill laughed. "When I sing, wild dogs show up trying to mate. No, it made me want to hate the government and protest the war."

She nodded sagely. "Korea."

"Vietnam," he corrected her, angrily. "Cripes, what do they teach you kids in school?"

"Not a lot," she said. "Which is how I landed this great job. So, you can show me how to sell?"

"Yeah," Bill said.

"And can you tell me something else?" she asked.

She looked right into his eyes, and Bill thought, *Here it comes, oh, boy.* This is her whole angle.

"What?" he asked.

She looked down, and looked up, and said, "What is it we're selling? Because I have been selling it for three days now, and I have, like, no friggin' idea."

* * *

Glynn knelt alone at her personal altar, dedicated to Adriam.

Most Uman-Chi worshipped Adriam. Some preferred Eveave, and most of them were women. Glynn felt as if the god-mother forced justice on those who didn't need it. Most Casters were men, Uman-Chi men worshipped Adriam, and so did she.

"Oh, Adriam, who is great and wise," she intoned. "Clear my mind, my burdens and past. Give me the moment, that I might serve thee in it."

She spoke the litany, and imagined herself alongside a stream. Her mind became a pitcher, and she emptied it into the clear water. The thoughts became fish that swam away.

Out poured the worry that she was not up to her challenge. Out poured the male Casters who judged her. Out poured the thorny beast of a fish that was her hatred for the Conqueror. Out poured her longing for her father and her brother.

And in her stream, a great, white fish with jagged teeth and long, whale-like flippers devoured all the others, and looked up into her vessel, hungry for more.

And that was not good. If she could not clear the stream, then she could not have the moment. If she could not have the moment, then she could not cast.

In her mind's eye, she knelt by the stream, she lowered her top, and she leaned forward. Her breasts dragged the water, its cold embrace bringing rise to her nipples, and she nourished the white fish.

It looked hungrily to the pitcher and, seeing nothing, addressed her breast. She felt the pull within her as the beastly thing suckled, the pain of its teeth on her soft flesh.

Being an enchantress, a woman who cast spells, made Glynn rare in and of itself. With precious few women to learn from, Glynn's methods were, by necessity, mostly her own.

To create, she'd realized, a man gives from himself.

To create, a woman gives *of* herself.

She bore the pain. She nourished the fish and, when it had

its fill of her, it swam away without a backward glance. Her stream ran clear, sweet and free, and her mind reflected it.

Her non-corporeal energy floated out from her body, in her imaginary world and in her real one. She looked down upon her two selves, pristine in the dream and real in her little chapel, alongside her rooms in the royal palace.

She saw the little imperfection in the skin beneath her shoulder. She touched it, and connected her lifeline back to herself. She reached out with her power, into the cold air of a day in the month of Adriam, and wrapped the city in her ethereal self.

She would do this every day, many times a day, exhausting herself and, at the same time, defining her strength. Each day saw her a little stronger, a little better, a little more able to disperse herself.

When the time came, she would sing. If she lost the song, if she lost the thought, she would use this newfound power to dispense the energy she released. Giving of herself, she would save her people and her city.

Transitioning herself from caster to conduit, Glynn Escaroth of the Family Escaroth prepared herself for singing.

* * *

Melissa sat at her cubicle, squeezed in front of her work station. Her headset made her ear sweat, her top made her boobs sweat and Bill's hamburger-breath settled in her nose. She scrunched in between him and her desk, in a space too small for more than one. Bill's big ol' belly took up a lot of room—most of which she needed.

She felt frustrated. She did a job that seemed stupid to her, getting people to work from home selling 'products,' to other people who worked from home. Personally, she saw it as a sucker's bet, but people sure sold it and people sure bought it, and if they could do it, why couldn't she?

"Hello?"

Someone picking up the phone startled her back to reality.

"Hello, Sir," she said. The Teleminer program on her screen told her this was Edward Befram of Hershey, PA, that he was 35-50, and that he owned his own home. "Is this Edward?"

She girlied up her voice like Bill had shown her. She called him Edward, not Mr. Befram, so he would warm to her. What man didn't like a call from a girl?

"Yes."

She picked up the caution in his voice—already on to her. Bill raised his eyebrows, prompting her to move forward.

"I called because I heard you were looking for a change in your life?" she asked, making her 'provocative statement.' She had made that up on the spot. Bill grinned a wide, wolfish grin. She felt some of the anxiety drain out of her—she was doing OK.

"You heard that, huh?"

"Oh, yes," she said. Now she caught herself warming to this person, too. "I called because we don't have a rep in Pennsylvania, and if you're looking for a change, we're looking for a rep."

Bill nodded. The man seemed interested. She flashed through her cards, giving him little bits of information, making him ask for more. In five minutes he had asked her how he could get more information on this, and she set up the program to send him a mail packet while updating his contact. He wanted her to call him—this was a good lead.

She clicked off after her prospect did, and looked at Bill, feeling six feet tall and super-charged.

"See how easy?" he asked her.

She couldn't help herself—she hugged him. She felt his body go rigid like iron, but it didn't bother her. She pressed her cheek to his beard and her breast to his chest, and gave him a squeeze.

"Well, um, uh, good job," he said, when she let him go.

She adored the shyness, the gentle chivalry. A boy her age would have had his hand on her ass or worse—not Bill. He turned his body a little away from hers, not wanting for her to know she had excited him. Of course, she wouldn't have noticed otherwise—she wasn't a perv or anything. Now she warmed to him even more.

"Again?" she asked him.

His eyes widened. He thought she was going to hug him again. She found it so funny—he was so *cute*. Not Brad Pitt cute, but teddy bear cute.

Her teddy bear, at least so far as training went.

* * *

Glynn had always seen dinner at the Uman-Chi high court as a tedious but necessary part of her nobility. Sometimes she longed for the tables of Men and Uman, who fed at the board like pigs at a trough, cramming their faces and belching, then leaving every bit as quickly as they could.

Several hundred nobles attended, dressed in the white of Casters, the blue of Merchants, the red of Warriors and the green of Artisans. Protocols over half a millennium old dictated where they sat, each space defined by their favor in proximity to the King, who entered last, ate first, finished last and left first.

House Escaroth sat sixty-five seats to the right hand, a respectable accomplishment but not spectacular for a High House. The favor of the Escaroths came into question with the death of her father and her brother fifteen short years before. Her father had sat seven to the left—left-handed not being optimum but seven seats being very respectable.

House Escaroth boasted no males by birth now. This doomed the house unless a member of a high house changed his name.

Today she entered the banquet hall to see the entirely unacceptable Earl Vendan Yelf of the Inner City standing by the Escaroths' traditional chair. This man's house had been responsible for the area around the stadium for the Fovean High Council during the Conqueror's sack of Outpost IX—his earldom had become a shameless failure.

Even if she must be replaced, to be replaced by *that*!

But one place remained open, on the right, four seats away from the head of the table.

No! Impossible! Four seats?

She walked by the place setting, twirled elegantly, and took a glance at the symbol for the house assigned here.

The Proud Falcon, in the colors of the female. This place had been reserved for *her*.

Such honor stunned her speechless, even if her face

described none of it to her own Uman-Chi people. A Caster remains in control, she reminded herself, even when bone weary.

She took her place behind the seat. The other nobles chatted and danced, taking mincing steps and buzzing about her, her song, her preparations, her house. They floated before her eyes like a dream! Adriam had not simply smiled, he had positively beamed at her.

She spoke to none of them, but held her elegance simple, her chin and her dignity high. To her left at seat five was comfortable Chaheff, her mentor, ignoring her as he swelled with pride at her accomplishment.

Without flourish or preamble, in the nature of her people, his majesty Angron Aurelias entered with the royal train.

His heir, Avek Noir, followed on the right behind him. He would sit one seat to the right. Next came the former heir, Ancenon Aurelias, who would sit one seat to the left. Both wore the white robes of Casters, however like D'gattis, Ancenon's robe bore a strange hook symbol and a dot, his in purple.

The mark of the Daff Kanaar—mercenaries currently turning Fovea into a war zone.

Other members entered in the train, but they were lost on her. Angron wore the ceremonial Black Cloak of Change, reserved for funerals, weddings and those who changed house, but no one had died or would be marrying.

However Ancenon wore the Proud Falcon on the golden circlet that held back his hair, in the colors of the male.

The next hour passed as a blur. Servants piled food high before them; they picked their favorite portions from their favorite plates. Glynn was voracious; she had extemporized her being several times, and on the last effort Chaheff had spontaneously attacked her, forcing her to throw out his energy into the Bay, making the water boil and the fish die in Adriam.

"She is of a healthy appetite," Angron commented, having waited politely for her to swallow, that she could easily respond.

"She fills the air with her power," Ancenon commented before she could, the proximity of his chair making this his prerogative.

Now any other could answer, but did not, and so she did.

"I am honored," she began, in perfect etiquette, "and am graced," she added, in response to Ancenon, "and remark that the food is excellent. I have found the training exhilarating and uplifting under Chaheff's tutelage."

Angron nodded, and acknowledged her perfect manners.

Angron spoke no more to her during dinner, but from that point on she must consider Ancenon her brother, an Escaroth, and her house saved. Its prestige rose, her prestige rose, her whole life changed with the color of a cloak. Ancenon would address her at a time he deemed appropriate, probably after the meal.

She would sing and, in so doing, she might die. Ancenon's conversion ensured House Escaroth would live on. This told her much about his opinion of her chances and of her abilities.

A lot to digest with dinner.

* * *

The girls in the ladies room were giggling—well, like girls. Probably why Melissa hated that expression. However, they got quiet when she came in.

That meant she had to do mirror time before she peed. She did the obligatory primp and refresh to her own image, and then reached for a lipstick when she saw she was fading.

"So how's the archeology going?" one of the girls, Amanda, asked her.

Melissa threw her a dark look. "Digging the fossil, you mean? Grow up."

"I dunno, Melly," Trina, one of her girls, said. Trina was a leggy Spanish girl who always had ponytail hair. They shared rent, but she could still be mean if she wanted. "Spending a lot of time with that guy."

"Yep, sure am," she said. She put down the lipstick and checked her lips. They were good. She turned back to the three girls.

"He's nice," she said, lowering her chin in challenge. "He helps people here, which is pretty cool of him."

"Well, yeah, seeing as he gets paid for it," Amanda said.

The third girl, 'lexis, chimed in, "Doesn't explain you chasing him out to the smokers' lot."

“I’m sorry, ‘lexis,” Melissa squared off on her, faking real concern, “where were your numbers this week?”

“My numbers?” ‘lexis drew herself up to the challenge.

“On the board?” Melissa asked. “You know—the one you can’t make it on to?” She waved her hand. “What am I even wasting my time with you, bitch. They’re gonna *can* your sorry ass.”

Trina raised her eyebrows in surprise. “Whoa,” she said.

“Really,” Amanda added. “Like, chill out, girl.”

“Like, *no*, girl,” Melissa squared off on Amanda next. “You’re right after her. What are you, like, one sale for the week? I probably made that while I was in here.”

Trina put her hand on Melissa’s forearm. “Really, girl, what’s with you?”

Melissa turned to her. “Well, these bitches piss me off,” she said. “What do they care if I learn from Bill—are they learning from anyone? Can they even *make* it here?”

“So, you’re just learning from him,” Amanda backed down. Melissa had a lot of friends here. She went to The Mill three happy hours a week, with and without her girls, and the boys lined up to talk to her. Amanda must have thought to get her props by teasing her and now felt worried she’d find herself on the outside for going too far.

“I am *not* just learning from him,” Melissa pushed right back in her face, surprising herself with how angry they’d made her. It had occurred to her this would get back to Bill, and then Bill would get shy, start being afraid of her, and she wouldn’t be able to talk to him anymore.

So better to address it now, and let the right word get around.

“He’s my *friend*,” she said. “I like Bill, and the person who ruins that, I am *not* going to like—I’m not going to like that person a *lot*, bitch.”

She stabbed Amanda right in the collar bone with her right index fingernail, literally driving the point home.

“Do the math, ‘manda,” she said, looking right into her eyes.

Trina immediately changed sides, turning her body to be

shoulder-to-shoulder with Melissa. Trina could be mean, but not stupid. She had also learned a lot from Bill, and she probably liked how easy paying the rent had become.

"If you were smart, you would be listenin' girl," she said. Her Spanish accent usually presented itself when she was angry, and it did now. "Bill puts people on the board. Don't be messin' with my meal ticket, 'neither."

Melissa gave Amanda a last look, turned and headed for the stalls. She could retreat, after a few grace-saving comments to her friends, with most of her dignity intact.

Which was good, because Melissa felt the tears coming on, and she didn't need anyone to see it, hear it or be a part of it.

Melissa's mother had died when she had been a little girl. Her father didn't know how to raise a daughter, and didn't have a lot of places to turn.

It galled him to buy pads, or any of the other things girls needed. She had to learn how to put on lipstick from a cosmetics girl at Sears. Her monthly cycle had been a trial and miss nightmare. She had no idea how to date.

In the middle of college her sister got busted and her father pillaged her college fund to pay for her defense. Lysette got five-to-twelve in Warren Correctional Institute and Melissa got to learn how to wait tables.

That's when she met Mike. He looked so handsome it almost made him beautiful, with a line so smooth she'd been hooked before she knew it. They went from dating to living together to moving to Portland in record time, he pursuing his career and she pursuing him.

Mike had been her first love, which was the only thing they had in common. He cared about himself alone and, when he couldn't make it in Portland, he bailed with all of their money, and not so much as a good-bye.

She'd had to do some things she wasn't proud of after that, before she turned her life around and come here. Three years had passed since then, and she still didn't trust handsome or young men.

When she was pretty sure that the ladies room was empty, she got up and left the stall. Who stood at the counter checking her makeup but Eileen?

"You okay?" she asked.

She took a look in the mirror, her mascara a disaster. She sighed and got out her compact.

"I'm okay," she said.

"If that's an allergic reaction to Old Spice," Eileen told her, touching up her curly hair with her fingernails, "you better stay away from Bill."

Melissa laughed despite herself, wiping away the streaked mascara.

"I noticed he was wearing it," she admitted.

"I know you did," Eileen said. She took a sideways glance at the younger girl, one that Melissa didn't miss. "He is doing a lot of things different. Eating with people, eating better, I think he lost a few pounds thanks to the salads."

"Well, you shouldn't let a man eat the crap he eats," Melissa said, then caught herself.

She had cared for her dad that way, while she could.

She looked at Eileen, and Eileen focused right on her.

"I'm not going to tell you how to live your life," Eileen said, which of course meant that was exactly what she wanted to do. "But keep in mind that men get funky as they get old."

Melissa got her eyeliner right and looked at Eileen. "Funky?"

Eileen nodded, and washed her hands. "Men get a strange idea about what their chances are and who loves them. A man over forty-five is one hundred times worse than a boy under seventeen."

"Oh," Melissa said. "You mean crushes and junk?"

Eileen nodded. "Be careful," she said. "He's a good guy, and he is scared to death he is going to be made fun of or worse by you kids."

Melissa knew what she meant. "I just like him for a friend," Melissa said. Well, it might not be a complete lie.

"Uh, huh," Eileen said. She dried her hands on a paper towel and tossed it into the receptacle.

"Make sure he knows it," Eileen warned, and left it at that.

* * *

Ancenon Escaroth had been born Ancenon Evoprosee, of a respected house, where he as third son had a brilliant career ahead of him as a hanger on, had he wanted it.

He had not.

When his older brother Haldan had joined the Casters, and his next older brother the Merchants, Ancenon had taken it on himself to join the priesthood of Adriam, a rare and usually ignominious destiny, as priests did not normally seek more power than that of a god.

In the priesthood Ancenon had come to the *Ultimate Truth*, and then combined the power of a Caster with his existing teachings to make himself a rarity among a rare people, the only priest and Caster among them.

From there, he'd been adopted by the King himself and married to the King's daughter, taking on the name Aurelias and enjoying the title of Heir for more than 100 years.

Then had come the Conqueror, and the Daff Kanaar, and a fall from favor that cost him his title of Heir, his prestige among his people and the favor of his own wife, who in his absence laid shamelessly with their Uman servants. It had been a matter of time before another, with an infusion of gold which Ancenon knew well had come from Outpost V's hidden treasury, had replaced him, and Ancenon had become an Aurelias in name only.

Today Ancenon lost that name, and became an 'Escaroth,' the sole male of a dying house responsible, at least, for a portion of the city wall. His new 'Proud Falcon' could be seen from Outpost IX's southern towers.

Contagious in the Conqueror's weird sense of humor, he allowed himself a smile as he contemplated flying the purple hook of the Daff Kanaar beneath it. Walking beside him through the stone halls of Outpost IX, to those southern towers, his new sister took note.

She raised her left hand and turned her wrist out in the form of the Inquisitive Relative, and said, "You are in good spirit, Lord Brother."

He nodded and, still walking, put his knuckles to his hips and informed her, "I was considering my house."

For every condition, etiquette defined over centuries by the Uman-Chi, shared only among themselves, differentiating them from lesser races, lesser species, persons to whom form was barely more than excusing their own farts in public.

"Are you familiar with our proud history, brother?" Glynn asked him, placing her left hand in her right palm at her waist before her, in the position of the Eager Teacher, Supplicating.

He nodded. He'd studied their scrolls. "My concern for you, sister, is more for your future than your past."

She smiled, and returned her hands to her side. "My song?" she asked him.

"I regret I cannot hear you sing it," he said, "however my cousin, D'gattis, will attend in my stead, as I am unavoidably detained."

Glynn extruded her lower lip for just a moment—an actual younger sister deprived of an older brother's approval. He extended her his elbow, to walk beside him as Equal Companion, all he could offer her at this time.

Because of my ambition, your father and your brother were killed, he thought to himself, walking beside her. *Both were friends of mine. In penance for that ambition, I take their names now, and extend their house's life.*

She took his arm, this young girl, so promising, so full of Life among the Uman-Chi. Every one among them knew Glynn, the youngest of the Casters. Her father, of the Caste of Warriors, had been *so proud* to claim her and her extraordinary abilities.

Some among them thought her the answer to the Conqueror's wife, Shela Mordetur. Ancenon knew better. He'd never seen Power represented so clearly in another. Shela wielded a magic Uman-Chi had no answer for. Power where their grace could be overwhelmed completely by her raw might.

Ancenon's ambition had cost him much, and rewarded him much more. Angron ruled Trenbon but, with his companions beside him, Ancenon could actually buy it out from under him, or take it by force. Ancenon had incurred great debts along his path, and the lives of the Escaroths were high among them.

He would do a lot of things to repay that debt, however watching Glynn Escaroth die was not one of them.

* * *

By the end of week two as Trainer: Bill Howard, the other employees just assumed they could go anywhere with him, ask him for advice on any topic, and that he would answer any personal question about his past life, having kids, why guys were horny jerks or how to close a sale, including what it was okay to say.

Melissa praised his wisdom, kept him at arm's reach at all times and kept the number in their new-formed clique increasing. The answer to any question became either, "Bill said," or "You should ask Bill." Of course there followed a steady stream of advice on his clothes, his hairstyle and his beard, which his new friends alternately hated or needed to manicure in a different way. When Melissa found out he bought his trousers at Target, Bill thought for a moment she would cry.

He impressed himself by wearing cologne for the first time in five years. By that second Saturday, however, he'd been properly groomed, manicured and styled, and left no question in anyone's mind that he had graduated from trainer to 'pet,' mostly Melissa's.

Chapter Three:

The Song in Her Heart

The day had come.

Angron had decreed the time for the event. Her new brother had apparently spoken with their King before leaving the Silent Isle.

Glynn donned the beautiful white robes of a Caster. In the two weeks since she had been given permission to sing, she'd had a new robe commissioned for her, just to be worn this one time. She wished only that her father had lived to see it, or her natural brother.

The cotton felt like a dream to wear. She cinched the belt tight on her trim waist. Its touch made her alabaster skin tingle, light and secure, properly demure and yet deliciously naked in the way it let her move beneath it. It imbued her with the power of her station, a Caster—the ruling elite of the Uman-Chi.

Finally, to *sing*! Even if she died this day, she died on a high note seldom felt by others.

Well, perhaps not. She drifted back to reality, and let her toes touch the ground. A good enchantress doesn't build bridges from twigs and muck. She might sing that the next harvest would be dismal, or that the herds were palsied.

She straightened her back and set her jaw, then with a wave of her hand had the Uman servants open her chamber door for her. No, she assured herself. She had not spent these days in deep training with a Master like Chaheff, learning how to focus great energy, to give crop or weather reports. This would be whatever the gods decreed it, certainly, but no less than it would be.

Glynn glided in the manner of Uman-Chi Casters, maintaining the hem of her robe equidistant to the floor. This discipline prepared her mind for the song, and for the sacrifice she might have to make. She maintained it until she entered the throne room. Ten other Uman-Chi, all in the white robes of Casters, waited for her there in the gallery. D'gattis, with the yellow mark on his robes, stood closest to the throne where she would be, as her brother had promised.

They'd drawn a chain of thirteen circles, each interlocking, on the white marble around the Circle of Judgment before the throne. The priest of a different god had consecrated each one of them. Glynn took her place within it, and D'gattis and Avek sealed her with a spell. If she should lose control, then that would be the first line of defense against the unleashed power.

Her heart raced, her mind swam with the song, its imperative, its *power*. Her years of discipline in the art of casting barely kept her from fidgeting. The time had finally come!

Glynn inhaled, exhaled, and looked to her wise King.

* * *

Lunch rolled around and for once Bill found himself alone. The timing couldn't be better—he had driven and he *really* wanted to listen to Rush on the car radio.

That wishful thinking lasted until he saw them all in the parking lot by his car. He sighed and grumbled to himself—he didn't always want to talk and answer questions at lunch. Bill shook his head and let the door swing shut behind him. As he started down the office steps he saw the hood up on Melissa's car, and realized they were looking at that.

And there stood that sweet, friendly girl, bent over her engine with a guy he knew as Roy standing next to her, and one of her teenybopper friends trying to crank the car over.

"Stop!" he shouted. Melissa, Roy and most of the others jumped like so many kids stealing cookies from a jar. He ran the short distance to them, his belly jouncing up and down over his belt.

"Dude, like, what's up?" Roy challenged him.

"If you're going to look at the engine, tie back your hair," Bill scolded them, ignoring Roy. He came to a stop, already sweating, next to Melissa. He took her by the shoulders and pulled her from the engine compartment. "Your hair was right in that engine, Melissa."

The girl in the car cranked again, and the engine roared into life. Melissa jumped again, but she didn't pull herself away.

"See that?" Bill asked her, letting go of her and pointing at the fan belt. "Melissa, your hair was *right there*. You'd be dead now."

Her eyes widened and she looked to her peer group for support.

"He's right, Mel," one of the girls said. "There's even grease on your tips."

Melissa grabbed the ends of her long black hair and held them in front of her eyes. Sure enough, some were sticking together, black with grease.

"Wow, Bill," she said, looking up at him. For a second he thought she would cry. "I, you know, like, I am so sorry."

He shook his head. "Don't be sorry, just tie your hair back," he said. "My dad got pulled into the block of his Chevy that way, by his tie. It didn't kill him but I saw the bones in his chest where—"

He looked around, and they were staring at him like he was the messiah or something.

"What?"

"Dude, that was, like, so cool of you," Roy said.

"What?"

"Yanno," the girl who started the car said, Spanish by the look of her. "All Sir Lancelot to save her." She looked at Melissa, and said, "Girl, you've *got* to buy him drinks tonight."

"Oh, yeah," Melissa said. "We're like, going to the Mill tonight."

Bill took a step back. "Oh, kids, um—I don't think we should—I mean, you don't want an old fart like me—"

The look in Melissa's eyes burned with excitement, and then faded as he watched them.

Bill immediately felt every second of his fifty years of age. In one sentence he had reminded them he was older than most of their parents, and he just couldn't play with them.

His heart slowed down, and only then did he realize it had been pounding.

"Come on," he said, "you kids don't want some old guy slowing you down."

"You're not so old," Melissa said, her eyes on the ground.

"And who cares if you are," Roy said, and actually put his hand on Bill's shoulder. "Dude, you know how much I'm making here, 'cuz of you?"

"Me, too," one of the girls that he hadn't trained said. "Just talking to you, listening to what you tell the other people to do, I made more sales this week than I did last week, and I still have Thursday and Friday to go."

"We, like, owe you," another of Melissa's girls said. "So come out with us." She waved a hand at him. "You don't want to make Melly cry, do you?"

It looked to Bill like Melly *was* going to cry. She wouldn't look at him now, focused on the tips of her hair in her hand, and her shoes, apparently.

Every bone in Bill's body melted. Even as the words came out of his mouth, he knew that he was screwing up.

"Okay, the Mill tonight," he said. Melissa looked up like she had just got 'Bingo'. "What time?"

"We meet at six for happy hour," she said. She turned to her friend and continued, "This is great, and I've got this new top I want to wear."

"The pink one?"

"No, the blue one with the sparkles that I got at Bealls."

"Oh, I *love* that one!"

And off they went to lunch, where they would only let him get a salad, and of course Rush Limbaugh was on his own.

* * *

"By the power of Adriam, we do invoke thee," the

combined Casters intoned.

"Praise to the All-Father," Glynn answered.

"By the power of Eveave, we do invoke thee."

"Praise to the Taker and the Giver."

Throughout the list of gods, they invoked the protection they would need for the song. Finally they came to Steel, who was only half of a god, a child of Earth and a woman, who had emerged from Water to be among them, and be the One who could touch Adriam's creation directly.

"In the name of Steel, we invoke thee," the Casters intoned.

"Praise be to Steel, who is the Savior," Glynn said.

The power boiled in her throat. Tears ran down her cheeks, from the effort to contain it. She could see the words before her in her mind, becoming more imperative, letting her know they needed to be spoken.

This preparation went on for grueling hours.

"Commence your song," Angron commanded from his throne.

And Glynn sang:

"Fovea, oh Fovea, beloved of the gods,
Of Earth and Water's coupling
Were we among them born.
We walk upon the fertile Earth
'Mongst seeds already laid,
Six heroes brought forth by the One
Await the coming day."

"The day, the day, there comes the day.
The day, the day is near.
The day, the day, here comes the day.
The time of War is here.

"From Fovea, from Fovea, the Cheyak, they are gone,
Struck down for their failing,
To make way for the One.

The One, who walks upon the Earth
The One, who is of War.
The One, who others wait upon
To fight forever more."

"The day, the day, there comes the day.
The day, the day is near.
The day, the day, here comes the day.
The time of War is here."

"To Fovea, to Fovea, a champion is called.
Summoned on these very words
To witness rise and fall
They will fall, who walk with her
They will fall, who oppose her
They will fall, for the power
Of the goddess, who chose her."

"The day, the day, there comes the day.
The day, the day is near.
The day, the day, here comes the day.
The time of War is here."

"On Fovea, on Fovea, seek a noble young and old,
A foreigner among his kind
A hero, fate foretold
One who fights as does the Sun
Waits in a sacred place
A guardian will bring you there
With a devil born and raised"

"Through Fovea, through Fovea, over you shall watch
One who eludes prying eyes,
With one who can't be touched.
So shall they come together
Heroes of the land
Together to oppose the One

While all apart they stand."

"The day, the day, there comes the day.
The day, the day is near.
The day, the day, here comes the day.
The time of War is here."

"For Fovea, Fovea, then must they live and die.
Fight the battle from within
With a champion from outside.
You shall be the weapons
The tools of men and gods
Who come too late for victory
And win despite these odds.

"The day, the day, there comes the day.
The day, the day is near.
The day, the day, here comes the day.
The time of War is here."

As the last note died, the thirteen circles burst into flame and burned themselves into the floor, one at a time, as the magic released fought for a way out. A moment later all of the fires died down together, and Glynn flew from their midst down the center of the throne room, more like a rag doll than a Caster, to bounce from the polished surface of the double doors and to fall unconscious on the carpet in a heap.

* * *

The bar was smoky, crowded and reeked of beer and aftershave. Bill showed up after he ate, lots of starches, so he wouldn't get drunk. Whatever happened, he wouldn't compound it with a DUI.

He found them all sitting at the bar, all smoking and each with a drink. They were clearly waiting for him, and the stool next to Melissa had been left empty.

"Hey, there he is," Roy said.

"There I am," Bill said. He sat next to Melissa on the stool, and she kissed him on the cheek.

"Thanks for coming," she said, probably to cover his embarrassment, rubbing off her lipstick with her thumb right after.

"What are you drinkin'?" one of the bartenders asked him. There were at least four of them. If he went out at all, Bill usually went to the sort of place that had one person behind the bar.

"Bud," he said.

"Uck, beer," Chelsea, one of Melissa's girlfriends, said. "Half the alcohol at ten times the calories."

"You mean I might lose my girlish figure?" Bill said, taking a stab at being funny at his own expense.

That got an 'Ohhhhh,' from the girls and a few smiles. The bartender poured a one-pint bar glass and Melissa pushed a five in front of Bill.

"You don't have to pay," he said.

"Nope, you're mine for the night," she said. "Deal's a deal."

"Yeah, but that's not right," Bill said.

"Check out Galahad," the girl who had tried to start Melissa's car said.

"I thought I was Lancelot?" Bill said, not knowing if he should be offended.

Melissa smiled at him. "You're both," she said. "I think it's sweet. Boys don't know how to act these days."

"Well, how are *we* supposed to know?" Roy protested. "You want us to open doors but you go racing through them ahead of us, then you smack us down for being sexist."

"I got smack down for ordering for a date, once," another of the hanger-on guys said. "Said I did it to make her feel stupid."

"Uff—I hate it when guys order," Chelsea said. "They always get it wrong."

"Then you have to choke down a steak and potatoes when you wanted chicken," Melissa said.

"Or lobster," another of the girls said.

"Slut," Chelsea commented, smacking lobster-girl's hand on the bar. All of the girls smiled, though Bill didn't get it.

"Well," the girl said, "the first part of hitting pay dirt is *pay*."

"Wow," Roy said to Bill.

Bill just shook his head and took a sip from his beer.

"I thought I was being cool showing up with flowers," another of the guys said.

"Oh, you *have* to show up with flowers," Bill said.

All of the girls laughed. "No one does that," Melissa said.

"They should," Bill said.

"I did once," Roy said. "The girl said I was playing her."

"Were you?" Bill asked.

He at least had the class to say, "Yeah, but I was doing it with *flowers*."

They all laughed. Little by little, Bill began to think this would be nothing more than the first fun night out in a year.

* * *

"She lives," the Uman-Chi healer said. Glynn recognized him as a priest of Adriam from his yellow robe.

Glynn lay on her back in her own bed, in her suite of rooms. Avek, D'gattis and Chaheff attended her, their white robes covered in soot.

"Where…what?" she asked.

"You are in your suite in the palace," D'gattis said. "Your song burned a hole in the floor and then fired you like a crossbow bolt down the throne room.

"Is anyone hurt?" she asked.

"Only you," the priest said. She recognized Taffer Roo, whose people had been Adriam's beloved for as long as Uman-Chi could remember. Angron claimed a Roo had helped bring him into this world.

"Am I…" she began to ask, and then her courage failed her.

Taffer smiled. "You are well, just exhausted," he said. "Still the same fingers, the same toes, and all of your hair still attached."

She ran a hand reflexively through her green locks.

"When can she cast again?" Avek asked.

"Avek, please," Chaheff said.

"The matter *is* somewhat pressing," D'gattis said.

"What is?" Glynn asked.

They looked at each other, then at her. Finally, Taffer said, "Well, it seems that, since you cast your spell, there is a vortex in the throne room we can't close."

Her head buzzed like there were bees in it, but Glynn tried to sit up. The bedclothes fell to the floor, revealing her naked beneath. Her knees and elbows felt as weak as a newborn colt's.

"You must be still now," Taffer told her, as he pressed his hand between her naked breasts.

His hand felt as smooth as the silks she wore to bed. Healers' hands, sensitive and loving. 'The wife of a healer knows contentment,' it had been said, and she knew why.

Power radiated silently from him, refreshing her body. She took a breath of air and the energy she breathed in amazed her.

"She is ready?" Avek demanded.

Avek enjoyed no great power, so he didn't understand being strong and then being weakened. Her power already exceeded his, centuries her senior. He demanded that she rise to a challenge he could never hope to equal.

Protocol allowed her no alternative but to wave a weary hand and to acknowledge him. "I am well," she lied. "Let us to the King."

She dressed in her whites, now scorched and frayed and nowhere near as good as before. With Chaheff helping her, first to dress, then holding her elbow, Glynn returned to the throne room.

She made no effort to glide this time—she couldn't have done it, had she tried. She felt relieved merely that her knees didn't buckle.

***

A multi-colored whorl sat at the base of the throne now.

"Angron first tried to dispel it," Avek informed her, wringing his hands. "Then he tried to move it so he could depart his throne. Finally we tried to rally the Casters in a joint effort to terminate the thing."

"Nothing worked," D'gattis interrupted him. His contempt was clear. "Now Angron seeks your counsel."

Glynn stepped into the throne room and almost tiptoed

down the long, red carpet. She felt no rush of air from the vortex, no roar of great energies, no sound at all, in fact. The room had become velvety quiet, the other Casters standing like white crows at the vortex's edge, all in contemplation of whatever this could be.

"I am amazed," Glynn admitted.

"Yes," Chaheff agreed, "we all are. This is an anomaly and we cannot dislodge it. There are spells which, once cast, cannot be undone except by the caster, and we are in hope now that this is one."

"It is not," Angron said. They all looked up at him, still pristine and white and ancient upon his throne.

"It is an opening, and we do not know to where," he continued. "We dropped an orb into it, and it rolled across the surface. We wait in contemplation of this thing, for what comes out."

"What comes out?" Glynn asked.

D'gattis clicked his tongue. "Surely, girl, you must understand that, if nothing can go in, then something must need to come out."

"Then what use have you for me?" she asked. She felt weary on her feet, even from the short walk.

"In fact, our need for you has grown," Aniquen said.

"It is my opinion that you are ill-advising our monarch," D'gattis said.

"I believe I am not," Aniquen said.

"And I am swayed by him," Avek said. "As is Angron."

"In what?" Glynn asked, thinking she must already know the answer.

And they confirmed it. "That you should sing, of course," Aniquen said. "You have sung something halfway here, clearly you must sing it the rest of the way."

"My song is sung," Glynn said. It was true—she no longer felt the need, although the words now were burned upon her memory.

"I have tried to sing a portion of your song," Avek said, "and I cannot. Nor can any other, and that is strange, because you are not the greatest among us, Glynn Escaroth. Some here,

Aniquen for example, could not hear your song, which speaks for its power. We believe that this is your destiny, and you must continue in it with your own voice."

Chaheff nudged her elbow where he held it. "Do not sing your song at first," he said. "Sing something sweet, as you might use to coax a horse from a barn."

Glynn nodded. She thought this made sense. If something *was* trying to come through, it might be lost because it sought her voice.

She opened her mouth, and she inhaled.

This would be disaster; or her greatest moment yet.

* * *

Bill, in his day, had been a power drinker. He could pound it with any client like he had a hollow leg. It was a matter of pacing, even if you were pounding; little sips instead of a few big gulps, and of course eat before, during and after.

Bill wasn't pounding on Melissa's bar tab, but the rest of these kids were on their own, and that made him really nervous because drunks don't always remember things very accurately.

"So, yanno," Melissa said, with her tiny hand on his shoulder, "how did you get so good at sales and stuff?"

"Stuff?" he asked. Her breath smelled like a brewery. Roy and another hanger-on had been trying to get her attention and shoehorn in between them all night, but Melissa would have none of it. She was entirely focused on Bill. She'd made him her mission apparently.

"Yanno," she said. "Like, cars 'n co'puters and boys 'n stuff."

"Ah," he said sagely. "Well, by living it, I guess. Benefits of growing old, more memories than expectations."

"You say that too much," she said, and slapped his shoulder. "You aren't *that* old."

"Nah," Chelsea said. "You are totally middle aged."

"I would do you," another of the girls said, with a wicked grin.

"You would do anyone," Chelsea said.

"Except Roy," all of the girls said together, like some big

joke. Of course, Roy's chin hit the floor, as the girls went into gigglefest.

"But seriously," the girl who 'would do him,' said, "you're not old like grandpa-old. You're doing okay."

"Look at you, totally perving on him!" lobster girl said.

"Yeah," said Chelsea. "Melly's buying him beer; she is the only one who gets to perv on him tonight."

"And you girls say we're bad," one of the other guys said.

"Oh, we know *we're* bad," Chelsea said, and hooked pinkies with the girl next to her. "Buy me a shot and you'll see *how* bad."

The boys went for their wallets as one, then laughed.

Bill had been growing steadily crimson during the whole conversation. This was going somewhere he didn't want to go. Melissa was looking down at her tips again and smiling.

"I'll be right back," Bill said, and got up from the stool.

Roy leapt into it, and that was fine. A trip to the men's room and then he intended to beat a hasty retreat.

"Hey, can I ask you something?"

Bill turned as he pushed through the door with the 'man' symbol on it. He entered to find himself alone with one other guy in the Men's room. Strange for a place this crowded.

"Sure."

The guy looked to be in his twenties, tightish jeans, maroon business shirt open three buttons, nice shoes. He had a great head of hair, parted on the side and black as night with white highlights, brown eyes, and a black beard with the same white highlights.

"Is that your 'crew'?" his mouth smiled at Bill, his eyes didn't.

"No, they think it's funny to go out with dad," Bill said. "I give it a week before they're bored with me and do something else."

"So no interest in the long-haired one who can't get her eyes off of you?"

Bill laughed, and dried his hands with a paper towel. "She's younger than my daughters," he said.

The younger man laughed. Something didn't seem right,

whoever he was. He had a youthful face and old eyes, with a far-away look but no crow's feet.

"So you watch over her?" he asked Bill said finally.

Bill tossed the paper towel, looked at the guy a final time and said, "Look, she's a nice girl, so if you want to ask her out—"

The other man smiled. "I inquire of your interest, not mine."

Bill walked past him to the door, but the man put a hand on his shoulder. Bill turned and they looked into each other's eyes. He wanted to look away but couldn't.

"You have no feelings for this girl?" the man asked.

"Of course I do," Bill said. The truth had to be wrung out of him and he didn't like it. "Who wouldn't? But I'm not kidding myself. It wouldn't be fair to either of us."

"All I wanted to know," the guy said, releasing Bills shoulder. Bill walked out the bathroom door without looking back, so he didn't see the crowded Men's room and the two men sharing a laugh over the old guy who walked through the whole place talking to himself.

* * *

Uman wives sang a simple song when their husbands left for the bay. Thanks to the Eldadorian Sea Wolves, that had grown a lot more dangerous than it used to be. Glynn sang that now, calling through the vortex for whatever might be lost within.

It was a song of summoning, a yearning for one close, to draw the heart in closer.

* * *

"I'm sorry for that," Melissa said.

Bill almost ran her over before he saw her, where she must have been waiting for him at the Men's room door.

"No problem," he said, smiling down at her.

"This was supposed to show you we're your friends," she said. "And now it looks like we were just baiting you."

"I never thought that," Bill lied.

She looked down, then looked up at him. "Do you want to go somewhere else?" she asked him, eyes wide and innocent, just like when she'd asked him for Marlboros instead of Luckys that first time she met him.

Oh, for the love of God, won't this end? Bill asked himself. This was a pretty girl. This was a girl who should be out dancing and smoking and looking for a nice guy, not some old fart with no future.

"Yeah, sure," he heard himself say. "You alright to drive?"

"No," she smiled up at him. "You better take me."

They were out the door before he realized it, the knowing eyes of the girls and the jealous glares of the boys burning into his back.

Stupid, stupid, stupid, he thought.

He didn't kid himself on what she was offering. Her hand felt as fragile as the petals of a flower in his, as she led him to his own car. She looked up at him and her eyes told him she knew where she wanted to go. For her it would be different. For her, it would be love and babies and dressing him up in clothes and taking him to places to show her friends.

Neither noticed the car they were walking toward glowed brighter than the space around it.

"What are you thinking?" Melissa asked him, as she planted her butt on his fender, and took both of his hands in hers.

"Why you want an old fart like me," he said, honestly.

"You are *not* old," she said.

He just looked at her. She sounded so sincere. She wanted this, God knows why.

"Am I older than your parents?" he asked.

She looked away, and looked back at him. Her eyes were shimmering from the tears she held back. He wanted so badly to hold her, comfort her, tell her something funny to keep her from crying.

"I don't really see my parents anymore, Bill. My mother died when I was real young, and my dad never got over it."

"Oh," he had stepped in it. He saw her clearly, saw the sparkle of the light on her sequined top, saw the makeup that highlighted her eyes and her cheeks, and the redness of the lips he wanted to be kissing.

"That music is nice," she said, changing the subject.

He looked around. He didn't recognize the tune.

"Is it a full moon tonight?" he asked.

* * *

Glynn sang the song's refrain, and already she sensed something in the void. She probed it with her mind, as she'd learned to try to sense a bear in a cave, to see what she might be drawing out.

* * *

"What song is that?" Melissa asked him.

"I don't know," Bill admitted. "It doesn't really have any melody."

"And there is no band, just the singer. And where is that light coming from?"

She looked at his chest, then at his face, then at his chest again. He looked down and saw her shadow on him.

They looked behind her, and saw the hood of the car pulsing. She leapt from the fender and crashed into him. Her tiny hands took his upper arm in a death-grip. Even with the shock of seeing his car turning into a Vegas sideshow, he found himself amazed by the strength in her fingers.

"Bill?" she asked him. She wasn't thinking about sex, she just wanted his arms around her.

"What the hell is that?"

Chapter Four:

Down With The Sickness

Glynn ended her song. They could all hear the grumblings of something in the whorl now. The Casters steeled themselves. Angron stood up upon his throne, his white hair standing out from his body as he let his power swell.

The Uman-Chi would be ready, come sweet greetings or bloody war.

"Come to me, traveler," Glynn commanded.

* * *

"Did you hear that?" Melissa asked.

"What is this, close encounters?"

"No, it is not."

Both turned and there was the guy from the bathroom. Same shirt, same hair, same too-tight jeans. He walked right toward them, his eyes focused on them.

"Who? What?" Bill couldn't frame a thought.

"You said your intentions were true," the guy accused him.

"What the—"

Melissa looked up at him, fear and suspicion on her face now.

"What are you doing?" she demanded.

He looked down at her. "I have no clue what is going on."

"Then know this," the guy said. "You are guardian protector, Bill Howard. Stand beside her and give her what she needs. She cannot stand alone."

And he put a hand on each of their breasts, and shoved.

The car they should have fallen against shimmered, flashed, and became normal once again, alone in the parking lot. The man smiled to himself, contemplated the empty scene for a few moments, and then vanished.

* * *

From the whorl, two beings emerged, stumbling onto the white marble floor.

Men, Glynn noticed. A male and a female. The song spoke of Men, of Uman and of Uman-Chi.

They dressed strangely, one the size a giant with the look of age, the other a woman, and by her dress of low birth.

Strange visitors to be traveling between places in a whorl, Glynn couldn't help thinking.

The whorl collapsed into nothing. The room fell silent but for the crackling of power from the Uman-Chi.

The female cowered against the male. No surprise. Men were aggressive; look no further than the Conqueror to know that.

But the Bitch of Eldador came of the race of Men, and she hid behind no man. Arguably, she was not of low birth.

Arguably.

Avek stepped forward. "I greet thee, travelers, in the name of the Silent Isle, to the land of Fovea."

The male regarded him suspiciously, aged eyes squinting. The female held him by his right upper arm, her eyes moist. Her lower lip trembled, her eyes stood wide as saucers. There were points of moisture on the male's sleeves, at her fingertips, that could be blood. She didn't know better than to cling to his sword arm, however he bore no weapon, Glynn noted. This was not a warrior. He might be a fellow Caster.

He growled like a bear and looked like one. He might be communicating in some manner to Avek, but Avek knew nothing of it.

The female tried to draw away from him, growling as she

did, gesticulating wildly. He barked something at her, and she defied him. His voice changed from bark to roar—another trait of Men. What they can't attract, they attack.

Angron surprised them all. He said something in some gruff tone, and the male looked up at him, relieved.

At least he knew greatness when it came to him.

* * *

"Who the hell are you people?" Bill demanded.

The thing in front of them sang something in its fluty voice.

'Thing' being the best word. It couldn't be human. These things had pointed ears, green and violet and white hair, alabaster skin, and strange faces. The whole room had been built in some kind of glowing white marble, with a throne behind them and something sitting on top of it.

Clearly, they had been abducted by aliens.

"Bill, where are we?" Melissa started to cry. He could feel her fingernails in his arm, so tight his fingers were tingling.

"You are guardian protector, Bill Howard. Stand beside her and give her what she needs. She cannot stand alone."

Bill's heart stirred and he laid a hand on her shoulder. Whatever the hell this weirdness was, or whatever these people wanted, it would have to come through him to get to her.

In his twenties he would have already hit. Three decades later, he had enough sense to know getting his ass kicked wouldn't help anyone.

"I can't understand you," he told it. It looked puzzled then looked at the others of its kind.

In her twenties, Melissa had no such self-control.

"Bill, we have to get out of here."

He looked down at her. The tears had started. Her lower lip trembled and there was blood on his upper arm.

"We have to find out where we are first," he said.

"No, we have to *go*!"

"Go where, exactly?" he threw the question back at her. "We have to be calm—"

"Be *calm*?" she released him. She teetered halfway

between attacking him and bolting. “Be calm? Are you challenged? Do you not know what’s going on?”

“Yes, Melissa, I do not know what’s going on!” he roared. This was stupid. He couldn’t help her if she wouldn’t let him.

From on top of a dais of some kind, one of them with white hair said, “Perhaps I help you with that?”

Bill’s head spun around. It spoke English. Badly accented English, but still English. Some of them spoke English.

What should have comforted Melissa made the whole situation worse. “Oh, no!” she said, shaking her head and stepping backwards, away from Bill.

“Melissa, what are you doing?” Bill asked her.

“He freakin’ knows you,” she said. She began moving down the carpet, toward the door. Bill saw two of these frail creatures moving between her and her goal. One might be a female, if females here were built like humans.

“That guy in the parking lot knew you,” she said. “That guy up there knows you. You are in on this, aren’t you?”

“Don’t be ridiculous,” Bill said, and took a step forward.

That did it—she bolted. She spun and crashed into the two creatures that had moved behind her, knocking one on its ass and the other back two feet. Her sandals flew off in two different directions as she sprinted for the door.

She didn’t get far.

* * *

D’gattis looked up from the floor at the fleeing female.

Typical Man-child. Where did she think she was going? Through the palace, into the city of Outpost IX, out the gate, through the market, and then perhaps to leap into the harbor for a winter swim in Tren Bay to the nation of Volkhydro?

He raised his hand and closed it. She fell to the floor. Not dead, which would have been his first choice, but weakened, to the point where her legs would not support her.

To his surprise she rose and fell, not once but twice. Volkhydran warriors had fallen, gentle as babes, with less effort by him.

* * *

Bill saw her fall, try to get up, and fall again. He took a step forward and felt a gentle hand on his shoulder. He turned to see the old man from the top of the dais, amazingly now at his side.

He dressed all in white, except for a picture of a shield and an eagle on his breast in red and black and gold. His hair stood out, but his face remained bland, almost kindly. His eyes were like mystical orbs, looking through him as if he were too small to see.

It struck him suddenly, their eyes were all silver. No pupil, no cornea, no iris. He couldn't tell where they were looking, or if they saw him at all.

"You cannot go to her," the old man said.

"I am her protector," Bill said.

The old man nodded. "We will bring her to you. She is not harmed. She is simply too weak to stand, and will recover."

Already the male and the female were at her side, and lifting her from the floor. They struggled with her weight, lifting her by her upper arms and dragging her back to Bill. Her head hung down, her hair dragging the floor.

"We are the Uman-Chi," the old man said. "I am Angron Aurelias, their King. I am perhaps the only one here who speaks this language."

"Why did you come to our planet?" Bill asked.

The man seemed puzzled.

* * *

"He is not from this world," Angron said to Avek, in the language of Uman-Chi.

The Heir stepped up to D'gattis and Glynn, helping them to lay the female at the feet of the male. Her eyelids were closed, her cheeks wet. Some black fluid leaked from the corners of her eyes.

Glynn stood back in disgust. She knew something of the concept of stars and worlds—this idea that they hung in a great, dark arena, and everything revolved around everything else.

What strange sickness could they bring with them, which made their very eyes run black?

The King looked directly at D'gattis. "You have injured her," he accused.

D'gattis shook his head. "With respect, your Majesty, I did not. And I detect no illness in her. What runs from her eyes may well be natural in her species, whatever that may be."

* * *

Bill knelt at Melissa's side. She was whimpering, but he couldn't make it out. He pulled a handkerchief from his pocket and wiped the mascara from her cheeks. She tried to lift her hands to his, but they fell limp back to her sides.

He looked into her eyes. "You don't worry, hun," he said. "He said this isn't going to last. I don't know what they did, but it isn't permanent and you are going to be fine. You lay there and get your strength back.

"Is she injured?" Angron asked him in English.

He looked up at the old man. "You said she wasn't," Bill accused him. "You tell me."

"We do not know this thing that makes her eyes run black," the King said.

Bill smiled despite himself. "It is called 'mascara,'" he said. "It is—um—it is a decoration women wear for the face. It won't hurt her."

Angron seemed relieved.

"Are we on your space ship?" Bill asked him.

Angron looked puzzled again. "I do not know this word."

"Look around you," Bill said. "This is a vessel that flies through space."

"I must confess, I do not know what you speak of," Angron told him.

"How did you get to our planet?" Bill asked.

"This is no sort of ship," Angron said

He stepped away from Bill, and to his own people. They in turn bowed and backed away. He counted eight of them, only one a female—the one he had seen before. She looked younger than Melissa.

"You are in the royal palace of Outpost IX," Angron said. "In a place known as Fovea."

"How did you bring us here?" Bill asked.

The man stopped and looked puzzled. “You did not come of your own accord?”

“We were pushed into my car by a man with black and white hair,” Bill said.

“I do not know the word, ‘car,’” Angron said, turning finally so he faced Bill, three feet away, his ‘Uman-Chi’ forming a ring behind them. He was a fleck of a man, a foot shorter than Bill and a third his weight. Still, he had such bearing; Bill didn’t think he could bring himself to raise a hand against this ‘King.’

Melissa seemed to be stirring at Bill’s side. She raised her hand, and rubbed a knuckle clumsily against her eye.

“Automobile?” Bill said. “Vehicle? It has a motor, we move around in them, very fast?”

“A wagon?” Angron asked.

“It is similar,” Bill said. “A self-propelled wagon.”

“We have no such thing here,” Angron said.

“If you didn’t bring us, how did we come here?” Bill asked.

Angron looked at the female, then at Bill. He said something in their song-language, then the woman said something back

* * *

“Your majesty,” Glynn said. “I cannot say. The song makes no mention—”

“It certainly does,” D’gattis said. They all turned to him.

“‘Fight the battle from within, with a champion from outside’, you sang,” he continued. “If your battle is within Fovea, then these are from outside.”

“Yet there are two,” Avek said.

“One is brought by the other,” Aniquen said. “His concubine, apparently.”

“If he is the one,” Glynn said. They all turned to her.

“She is a slip of a girl, clearly a sexual toy,” Avek said.

“However, the song mentions ‘she’,” Glynn said.

“He calls himself her protector,” Angron said. They all fell quiet to hear him. “If he is that, then I think we must assume it is she who is the champion.”

The male clearly tended the female. She acted terrified, he more wary. He protected her, clearly, but if he filled that role, then what might she be?

"Already she recovers from your spell," Chaheff noted to D'gattis. "I would have thought she would be done for this day."

"I note," D'gattis said, nodding, then turned to Angron. "May I inquire, your Majesty, as to their language?"

"It is called *Anglesh*, the language of the North," the King said. "And it was spoken by a Man from the North when I was just a child, and the mark of the Uman-Chi was not upon the land."

"The Emperor claims to be from the North," D'gattis noted.

"Perhaps another of the questionable truths about him," Aniquen said.

"Shall we ask them, then?" Avek said.

* * *

"What are they doing?" Melissa asked.

"Talking about us," Bill said. At least the Uman-Chi didn't lie. She could already take his hand, already move her head to look him in the face. "I don't think they know why we're here."

"Who was that guy who pushed us?"

"I have no idea," Bill said. "He talked to me in the Men's room and wanted to know what my intentions were with you."

"Oh?" her expression still showed skepticism.

"I thought he wanted to ask you out," Bill said. "And was making sure I wasn't in the way."

"He didn't act like he wanted to ask me out," Melissa said. "He sounded like he was trying to hook us up."

Bill thought for a moment.

"That sounds more like it now," he lied. In fact, it sounded more to Bill like he wanted to make sure they *wouldn't* hook up.

"Well, I did ask you to take me somewhere else," she said.

She was actually smiling. He smiled back at her, impressed that she could collect herself so fast. She was a fighter, this girl.

The King turned to them, and asked, "Which of you

leads?"

"Leads?" Bill asked.

"Surely, one of you is responsible for the other," he said.

"You are guardian protector, Bill Howard. Stand beside her and give her what she needs. She cannot stand alone."

"I am her guardian protector," Bill told him again.

Melissa looked up at him with a tough little smile on her lips.

"So, in fact, she leads?" Angron said.

"I don't lead, no," Melissa said. "Our society isn't like that."

"Neither leads, but you are guardian protector," Angron said, his eyes unreadable. "Why do you need a guardian protector, then?"

Bill looked down at Melissa. She shrugged.

Why not tell the truth? Bill looked at the King and said, "We were told I am her guardian protector by the man who pushed us into the car and sent us here."

"And he did not say why?"

"I am sorry, no," Bill said.

* * *

"He is her guardian protector," Angron said to his Uman-Chi, in their own language.

"However, she does not lead," he continued. "It appears that other forces are at work here, and these Men do not control them. If there is a 'champion,' it is the female."

"Already, she speaks," Glynn noted.

"I would think that rather obvious observation beneath you, Glynn Escaroth," D'gattis said to her, his chin up.

Glynn wanted to whither, Chaheff straightened. "Were that you were so strict in your personal discipline as you are with hers," he noted.

"Enough," Angron ordered them. They quieted. He, too, had been impressed. He had smelled the very power when D'gattis cast. The girl should be paralyzed until sunrise.

"What shall we do with them, your Majesty?" Avek asked, attempting to divert the argument.

Angron considered.

"She sang of a hungry one," D'gattis said, "and of a fight, and that the fighters against the hungry one are already doomed to lose, because they are too late."

Angron nodded. "I think we need to delve deeper into the words," he said. "However, it does not bode well, and I find myself concluding that, if this girl is the one from outside, then she should have some ability to aid us. We must derive what it is."

They all looked at the two visitors. The male was helping the female to sit up. No one needed to reiterate that her resolve was amazing. As they watched, the male looked up at them.

"What?" Bill said.

* * *

Avek Noir sat in his personal chambers, in a tower just within the main gates to Outpost IX. These were the traditional quarters of the family Noir, who had held the gates to Outpost IX for centuries.

Avek's rooms seemed lavish for a Caster. Padded furniture, thick pile carpets, a gigantic bed of four posts with a canopy and a desk and chair in the bedroom, a sitting room with lush couches and what the Conqueror called 'kaw-fee' tables, which were good for drinks and feet, and a study packed with lore.

He spent most of his time here, and so D'gattis found him.

D'gattis could be considered haughty even for an Uman-Chi. His power rivaled Chaheff's. Uman-Chi considered him the leading expert in the world on Cheyak lore. However, Avek had been in the vaults of Outpost V, and D'gattis could make no such claim.

D'gattis entered in his white robes, the strange yellow symbol on the front of them. It marked him as a member of a group of mercenaries called the Daff Kanaar, the most feared warriors in Fovea, after the Conqeror's *Wolf Soldiers*. They turned battles; they defeated many times their number in enemy troops of all races. They were for hire to whomever could afford them. D'gattis' skills had been for hire. There had been a time when a Man could barely sell a duchy for the price of an Uman-Chi's services, especially a Caster's.

Avek had been for hire once. He had been a Wolf Soldier himself, after Lupus the Conqueror had sacked the city of Outpost IX, pushing past Noir guards like they weren't there, leaving them dead in the streets.

Avek Noir had sought to redeem his honor by pursuing the Wolf Soldier ships as they fled the City for Tren Bay. He had failed in that, too. The Conqueror had managed to sink his ships, and Avek had returned to Trenbon in a lifeboat.

Angron had suggested that a nice, safe knighthood in Outpost VII would be more fitting for the Noir's. Rather than accept that shame, Avek Noir had sailed to Thera and bent his knee to the one who had shamed him, and become a Wolf Soldier, of the Mage Corps.

Uman-Chi seemed to be becoming a commodity.

"I greet thee, House of Noir," D'gattis said, spreading both hands and rolling his wrists in the traditional greeting of equals.

"I welcome thee, D'gattis of the Daff Kanaar."

They weren't friends. They weren't actually friendly, but they had something in common, and that seemed most likely to bring D'gattis to his door. Avek would have gone to him otherwise.

Avek assumed the friendly, receptive posture, and inclined his head in the respectful gesture due a Caster like D'gattis.

"Our mutual friend must be informed of this," D'gattis said.

That was it.

"I concur," he said. "And I am suspicious, as I believe you are as well."

"That we have in some way discovered the home of the homeless Conqueror?"

"Verily."

"These two Men look like him," Avek said. "The male is a giant, with those heavy bones of Lupus' people. His hair is gone gray, as the old among Men do."

Avek nodded.

"A gray-haired Man is a gaffer with no teeth," D'gattis said. "Have you looked in the mouth of the Conqueror?"

"In fact I have, in his service," Avek said. "Steel implants in the teeth."

"Why anyone would do that baffles me," D'gattis said, and suppressed a shudder. "But they melt silver into their teeth. These two have it as well, although it is a white material more difficult to see. I saw it as the female reclined."

"That cannot be a coincidence," Avek said.

"I agree," D'gattis said. "We must convince Angron to summon Lupus the Conqueror to meet these two."

"I think that will never happen," Avek said. "And I think you know why."

Avek indicated with a turn of his wrist D'gattis could seat himself. D'gattis delicately lifted a pile of scrolls from a hassock to a table, and did so. He looked directly into Avek's eyes, and assumed the posture of assertiveness. Avek himself turned his toes outward where he sat, showing a receptive stance.

"You were in the Emperor's hire," he said.

Lupus the Conqueror hadn't been an Emperor for that long. He hadn't even been a noble for that long—barely more than a decade. In the 83rd year of the reign of the Fovean High Council, King Glennen had died and been replaced by his self-appointed Heir, Duke Rancor Mordetur of Thera, known best throughout Fovea as Lupus the Conqueror.

Lupus the Conqueror had been king for less than a month before he marched on Andoron and annexed a tribe he called the Wolf Riders, and staked out the junction of the Safe and the Great Mid Rivers as their tribal home. Eldador went immediately from Kingdom to Empire, and His Majesty became His Imperial Majesty.

Lupus the Conqueror had purchased Avek's fealty long before that with Cheyak gold. He had gotten it from Uman City, which he had needed to conquer on behalf of Eldador when its Duke, Yerel, had attempted to secede.

He'd revealed Uman City as the forgotten Cheyak Outpost V. Lupus the Conqueror in his short years had uncovered what Uman-Chi expending every resource available to them for centuries had failed to do.

That gold had purchased Avek as the Emperor's eyes and

ears in Trenbon. He reported back regularly.

Avek knew full well Angron was too wise to fool, so he hadn't tried. Trenbon needed to not be the target of this new Eldadorian Empire, which could sack Outpost IX. Maintaining Avek as Heir kept his most dire enemy close, without having to smell his breath.

"That is well known," Avek said.

"And Lupus gave you the gold to supplant Ancenon as Heir," D'gattis continued. "The gold from the treasury at Outpost V."

"You know of Outpost V?" Avek was stunned. He leaned forward, as if afraid his words would betray them if the other Uman-Chi didn't breathe them in. "How long have you known?"

D'gattis snorted in an un-Uman-Chi way. "He is a Man, Avek," he said. "He has no secrets from me, whether he thinks he does or not."

Avek hadn't found the Emperor so transparent, but said nothing.

"In light of Lupus knowing where the Outposts are, and Angron not knowing, I have had time to reflect on this song of young Glynn's as well," D'gattis said.

"And you know what that means, then," Avek said.

"I think we both do."

Chapter Five:

A Bold, New World

They were led by the female Uman-Chi through a maze of halls and passageways, Bill supporting Melissa until she could finally walk with just a hand on his arm. Eventually the Uman-Chi pushed open a door to a room paneled in green, with varnished wood floors and a wooden table in the center with a red marble top. Polished rosewood cabinets lined the walls, with shelves full of bottles and urns behind glass doors. The female guided them inside, closed the door behind them all, and had handed them each robes. They looked at each other, then at her, and blushed crimson. Finally she sighed and turned around.

"They want us to put the robes on," Melissa said.

"Yep."

She looked at him, looked down, and looked at him, still blushing.

"Hell," she said finally, and pulled her top off. She wasn't wearing a bra. Her breasts, pert and pink and perfect, bobbed free. She looked into his eyes.

"Start strippin', stud," she said. "You were going to see it tonight anyway."

He started unbuttoning his shirt. "Yeah?"

She smiled, turning her skirt on her hips so she could unfasten it, and kicking off her heels. "Oh, yeah," she said. "It was your lucky night."

He pulled the shirt off, then the t-shirt. His belly felt like it had more bounce than her breasts, the skin hidden under a mat of hair. He kicked off his shoes as well.

"When did you decide that?"

She pulled the skirt off and was naked in front of him. She had shaved her pubic hair away except for a heart, just above her lips. He had never seen that before and caught himself staring. Then he realized she hadn't put her robe on.

"I can turn around if you want," she said.

"You don't have to."

She turned, put her hands on the marble table, and arched her back. *This was better than cable,* he thought. He wanted so bad to touch her right then, as he pulled off his pants and his desire betrayed him.

She turned around, then reached for the robe. It wasn't silk or rayon, but it was something soft like that.

She looked at him and said, "I would ask if you liked it, but I already know the answer."

He smiled as he slipped his drawers off. He was fat. He knew it, but he still felt self-conscious about it, especially with her fashion-model looks. She seemed to sense this and she laughed.

"More salads for you, Bill," she said. "I am going to work that belly off."

He peeled off his socks. "Really?"

"Yeah."

He slipped the robe on, and he tapped the alien girl on the shoulder. She turned around and reached for their clothing.

"Man!" Melissa said. "I hope I'm getting that top back. I just got that."

"I think those drawers are older than you are," Bill said.

Melissa laughed out loud, startling the alien girl. She pushed the clothing into a cloth bag of some kind, and pointed to the table. She waited for them to climb up onto it, and then she left without a word to them.

"You didn't answer me," Bill said, when the woman left.

"Sure did," Melissa said.

"Did not."

"About what?"

"When you decided."

"Oh, that."

She didn't continue and he sighed.

"Why are you fighting me off so hard," she said finally. "I thought you would like me."

"I think you're a great gal," Bill said. "But you're younger than my daughter."

It was out of his mouth before he remembered about her parents, probably a sore spot for her.

"You know what I need right now?" Melissa asked him.

His heart skipped a beat. She saw his expression and smacked him.

"A cigarette, you dog."

"Oh, don't remind me," Bill said. "I've been dying. And you know they aren't going to have them here."

"*What?*"

"Dorothy, we aren't in Kansas anymore," Bill said. "I thought they were space aliens, but this is a whole other world, if these people are to be believed."

"Do you think they *can* be believed?"

Bill shrugged. "That tunnel between there and here would be quite a trick," he said. "And their language isn't like how people speak. It sounds more like whistling."

"It was like a flute playing," Melissa said.

"I can't think of any language that is like that, and I used to work in communications, so I've heard a lot. Languages obey certain rules based on the noises people can make. And those didn't look like people."

"You could see better aliens on Star Trek," Melissa said.

"Yeah, but you can always see the makeup lines up close," he said. "Those weren't masks, those people look that way. Those eyes are definitely real."

"So, some kind of worm hole, star gate, watcha-ma-call-it," Melissa said.

"I think so."

"And we have to wait for them to let us go," she said. "Except they don't seem to know how we got here."

“Yeah,” Bill said. “I don’t like that much.”

She looked down at her feet kicking, then back at him.

“Take care of me, okay?” he saw tears in her eyes.

“Of course I will,” he said.

“No, I mean it,” Melissa took his hand and held it in her lap. “Be there for me, do the Lancelot thing, guardian protector, whatever the hell. Will you?”

He squeezed her hand. “I will Melissa,” he promised. “I am right here for you.”

She worried about having bolted, he knew. She either blamed herself or him, and either way she expected him to handle it.

In his heart, he knew he would—somehow.

Their hosts made a liar out of him almost immediately. An older Uman-Chi came into the room, and the first thing he wanted to do was separate them.

Melissa took a death grip on Bill’s upper arm. The older man tried to guide her away by her elbow. That failing, he took a firm grip of her shoulder and pulled.

Bill straightened and pulled back on Melissa. The Uman-Chi gave a prolonged whistle and four men came in wearing metal armor and carrying long knives, not quite Bowie knives and not quite swords.

They wore an armor of rings connected to other rings, like what had seen in movies about knights and such. The long knives sat ready in their hands.

They looked like Uman-Chi but Bill could see the differences. They were darker. They didn’t have the silver eyes, and they clearly deferred to this older man. Their eyebrows grew pencil thin and sat raised in arches high above their eyes. Their ears seemed more human and less pointed, and yet had no lobes.

They indicated the girl, and Bill stepped in front of them.

Overpowering one would be easy. He probably had a hundred pounds on the largest of them. From there, if he could get a knife, he had a chance.

With no warning his feet affixed themselves to the floor and his arms to his side. He tried to pull against his own limbs, to work his muscles and defend her, but Bill remained as still as a statue. He did nothing but watch as two of them took Melissa, one by either arm, out the door and away from him. To her credit she kicked and screamed and looked to him to intervene, but he couldn't even wave good-bye.

The moment she left the room, he could move. At first he thought to charge after her, but the old man, the Uman-Chi, raised a threatening hand.

The old man could do something to immobilize him. He wouldn't hesitate to use it, and he'd been wise enough to leave two of these other beings behind with their swords out. Bill would have had his hands on the man's neck otherwise.

Bill sat up on the table again. The man looked into his mouth, under his robe, and at the soles of his feet. He took a sample of hair, and he talked to him the whole while, although Bill couldn't understand it.

Finally the Uman-Chi Angron entered, and the old man bowed to him. Angron waved him off and looked at Bill.

"You resisted our taking your female," he said.

"Yes, I did," Bill said. "Where is she?"

His eyebrows rose. Probably a King wasn't used to being talked to that way. Well, Bill didn't know a lot of Kings.

"She is well," Angron said. "We are interested in your health and your nature. And we wanted to talk to you separately."

"To make sure our stories match," Bill said.

He nodded. "And so," he said. "When you have answered me, then you will be reunited."

Bill nodded and waited.

"You have no nobility where you are from?" Angron asked.

"I wouldn't say we are animals," Bill countered.

Angron thought for a moment, then nodded and said, "I meant you have no King."

"Some do, my people don't," Bill said.

"Where are your lands?"

"A planet called 'Earth,'" Bill said, looking for some emotion in the silver-on-silver eyes. "Does that mean anything to you?"

"Earth is one of the Fallen Gods. Is that what you mean?"

Bill shook his head. “God is different from Earth, at least for my people,” he said. “There are some people who think that God is in the Earth, but not most.”

“Here, we know Earth is a god, and that we live upon and are of Him, and his mate, Water.”

Well, that seemed weird, but he didn’t say anything about it.

“You do not know how you came here?”

“I have no idea,” Bill admitted.

“How old are you?”

“Fifty,” Bill said. He almost lied.

The King looked shocked. “In truth?”

Bill nodded.

“Do most people look like you?” Angron asked. “Are you common for your people?”

Bill shrugged. “I don’t know what you mean by common. On my world, most people are Chinese. They have black hair, yellow skin and are shorter. In my nation, most people look like me, except not so fat.”

“What do you eat?”

“Meat, beef and chicken and fish,” Bill said. “Do you have those?”

Angron nodded.

“We eat vegetables. Some people eat all vegetables, but they aren’t the norm.”

“Do you know a man named Lupus?”

“Most people have two names,” Bill said. “But I don’t know anyone by that name at all.”

“Rancor Mordetur?”

He was leaning forward slightly. The salesman in Bill told him that this question had been what he really wanted.

“Rancor is a word that means ‘anger,’” Bill said. “Mordetur means ‘death.’ I think in Latin or Greek.”

Angron smiled. “So you know these words.”

“I know Lupus, too, as a word,” Bill said. “It means ‘wolf.’”

Now Angron *really* started smiling. “So although these are not names, you know these words,” he said.

Bill nodded.

"Do you know 'ercher nomics'?"

"Ergonomics, or economics?" Bill asked.

"What of chem—stree?" the old Uman-Chi asked. His eyes, though silver-on-silver, seemed more intent by the set of his eyebrows. This was a question he *really* wanted to know the answer to.

"If you mean 'chemistry,' I studied it a long time ago," he said.

Angron turned and left. The doctor came back and looked at him some more, then left as well.

Sitting alone, he wondered at what he might have just learned.

* * *

They wrestled Melissa down a passage, dimly lit with torches, the walls gray and rough, to another room like the one she had left. They tossed her inside and closed the door.

She found the first breakable she could, a ceramic urn, and whipped it at the wall. It smashed into bits. She followed it with other breakables, glass and ceramic. Finally she had to hop up on the table for fear of cutting up her feet.

She felt humiliated. She had been ripped from her home, she had been ripped from Bill, they had done something to her once that made her weak as a kitten, and they would likely do it again.

Already she felt stupid for trashing the room. She was about to actually get up and start cleaning it when the door open and the old man from the first room entered.

He looked around the room, then at her, and didn't try to hide the disgust on his face. The silver-on-sliver eyes only made it more obvious. He whistled something and those men who had dragged her in here entered after him. They looked around the room once, one said something that she couldn't understand, and both left. The older man crunched over to her and pushed her shoulders back onto the table.

She inhaled but controlled herself. Just get through it, she thought. Just let it go.

He touched her. She bit her lip to keep from crying. He looked in her mouth. She made fists of her hands, the nails sinking into her palms. He took some of her hair and peeled off one of her press-on nails. She thought it might be over, that she had survived it, when he looked at the bottoms of her feet, but then he moved to push her robe open. She wore nothing under her robe.

She smacked his hands away and leapt off of the table. He whistled something and he pointed to its surface, but she hugged the front of her robe and shook her head.

No way. No way in hell.

He whistled loudly and the two armored men reentered.

Her eyes widened. She didn't know what she expected, but she didn't think it would be armed guards—not for this sort of examination.

The older Uman-Chi shoved her brusquely toward the table and she slapped him. The surprised look might have been gratifying, but she didn't get to enjoy it long. The three men approached her, all frowning, reaching for her arms.

She kicked at them and they grabbed her ankles, but not before she caught one of the goons in the thigh with her heel. She clawed at them and they grabbed her wrists, their skin collecting under her fingernails. She bit and they bled, and as a last resort she spat at them.

"Get away from me," she demanded, feeling stupid and scared and angry all at the same time, because she knew they couldn't understand her and she knew they would do it anyway if they could.

They tossed her onto the table and they flipped her onto her stomach. She screamed her lungs out as the old man did the inspection that he wanted to do. She swore at them, she threatened them, but their hands felt strong as steel on her wrists and ankles. She had never felt as helpless or as violated. The old man ignored her and did what he wanted. When he finished they pushed her back to the table like they might have done to an animal.

She leapt from the table and out the door in a shot, naked as the day she was born, crashing right into Angron as she fled.

"Stop!" he commanded her.

To her own surprise, she obeyed him.

"They will do you no harm," he told her.

"Little late for that, asshole," she informed him. "Your old man already got his jollies and his two goons helped him out."

She stood there, naked, her skin wet, out of breath, half-turned to face him or to run, whichever she needed.

She could still feel that bastard's fingers.

"If you are offended, then I apologize on behalf of the nation of Trenbon," Angron said. "You must understand—"

"Where's Bill?" she interrupted him.

The King didn't hide his shock at being spoken to so commonly.

"Well?" she demanded.

The old man came out of the room, crunching through the broken glass, her robe in his hand. The two goons followed him.

Angron whistled to him, to the two goons, and then left without another glance at her. The old man threw her the robe.

* * *

Bill waited for half an hour before Melissa returned to him, and then she flew into his arms.

He just held her. When she had cried herself out, she sat up next to him on the table. She didn't talk to him, just pressed her cheek to his upper arm. She finally managed a weak smile at a few stupid jokes.

Bill wanted to ask her what had happened, but he could guess.

* * *

Outpost IX had already been ancient when the Uman-Chi occupied it, designed by the Cheyak before the Blast. It had rooms for everything imaginable, and the King took one of these to meet with his advisors.

Angron sat in a windowless chamber, at the head of a wooden table, under a glass orb enchanted by him to provide them with light.

To his left sat D'gattis and Avek. To his right, Aniquen and Chaheff, and at the other end of the table, Taffer Roo, who had examined these new-comers.

"They are Men," Roo said. "Although they are larger than any Men I have ever seen, and longer-lived. The male is fifty. The female is twenty-four. They have white metal implants in their teeth, but they have all of them. The male has hair like a mule, and could probably still pull like one.

"They are aggressive. The male had to be restrained when we took the female. He made her pose for him when she undressed, so we can assume they are mated. The female lacks the hymen human females lose with intercourse."

"Spare us," D'gattis said.

"My apologies," Roo said. "Their bones are heavy. The old one is probably still a match to wrestle any of our Uman guard. The female destroyed a laboratory and required two Uman to hold her while I examined her."

"I think we all have one question," Chaheff said. "Are these the Conqueror's people?"

"I cannot tell that," Roo said. "I can say they look more like him than Men that we know."

"They know words that he knows," Angron said. All eyes were immediately on him. "I know now that Rancor means 'Anger', Mordetur 'Death' and Lupus 'Wolf'."

"And thus, Wolf Soldiers," Chaheff said.

"It is too large a coincidence," Angron said. "They claim to be from Earth, but they think Earth is not a god. In fact, they believe in one God."

"One?" D'gattis scoffed.

"Barbaric," Avek said.

"Indeed," Angron said. "The one they claim has sent them here sounds suspiciously like Steel, the Savior."

"Could Steel leave Fovea?" Avek asked.

"Steel is born *of* the god Earth," Angron said, "and hence does not leave Fovea. Could Steel fetch Men from the lands of the Conqueror? I think so."

"This could be where War went to fetch His instrument," Avek said.

"If Lupus is War's instrument," Taffer Roo said, "and Lupus is not of Fovea, then War is not bound by the Rule of the Gods."

"War could speak to him directly," Angron said. "And War could affect him."

"And then any god could affect these two," D'gattis said, "if they have not already."

They all sat quiet for several minutes in contemplation. Finally, Avek spoke.

"I should like to hear Glynn's song again," he said.

"It is too dangerous to sing," Chaheff said. "We might reopen the whorl."

"I think that this is exactly what we should do," Taffer Roo said. "And if possible, send these back."

"I agree," Aniquen said. "One Lupus changed our whole way of living. Three could reap even more havoc."

"Or two could counter the one," Angron said.

"Or six could conquer the one," D'gattis said. "And we have either one or two of them now."

Again, they sat quiet.

"Find a noble young and old," Avek said. "Our Glynn, young by our standards, old by those of Men and Uman."

"Clearly," Angron said. "The others are a mystery to me, however. I have tried to divine them."

"Can we assume that these two shall lead us to the rest?" D'gattis asked.

"Can we assume that Lupus is the One?" Avek asked.

"I think we must," Taffer Roo said. "And if that is true, then Fovea is on the brink of a bloody, painful war."

"A war that it is already too late to win," Angron said, "quite possibly because of my own decision to wait."

"In that case," Aniquen said, "and I am loathe to state this, but the best thing we can do is tell the Emperor everything we know, and ally ourselves with him."

Again, they all sat quiet. Avek and D'gattis looked at each other, then at Angron.

"Speak, both of you," Angron said.

"I know Lupus better than any Uman-Chi," D'gattis said. "Perhaps as well as anyone living. I know his methods, his thoughts, and his mind.

"I think that, with the resources of Eldador and the years

he has had to control them, Lupus the Conqueror probably already has an army that could march on Trenbon and overwhelm it.

"I know the woman Shela, and I believe that together we could defeat her, if we knew she was coming. However, Lupus will ensure that, as before, we have no idea when she is coming, and that before we can match the Bitch of Eldador, she will have destroyed most of us.

"And I know that, with Trenbon under his control, there will be no stopping Eldador from controlling Tren Bay, and the combined armies of Fovea will fall to him. Even if we were to march against him now, Sea Wolves using his Eldadorian Fire will defeat our navy as they have before, isolate us here and neutralize Trenbon, so he can pluck us at his leisure."

"I think that the expense of managing a completely conquered nation would be overwhelming for Eldador or for any other nation," Chaheff commented.

Angron shook his head. "I should have brought a Merchant here for this conference," he said. "And if I did, he would tell you Eldador is a juggernaut producing gold. Taxing less, they make more, a science that still baffles our shrewdest counters. Eldador produces more grain than she can eat, more iron than she can smelt, more ships than she can sail and more warriors to man them than people the Silent Isle."

"And let us not forget, when he invaded," D'gattis added, "that our own Scitai subjects helped him. This was an act we have been unable to punish—in fact have rewarded, in that we sold to them disputed plains which they now farm."

They were quiet again, then Angron turned to Avek.

He looked at the table, collecting his thoughts. He knew what he wanted to say, and what he had to say, and what his King needed to hear. In the end, he sidestepped it all and spoke from his heart.

"You know I was a Wolf Soldier," he said. "I believe I am Heir in part because of that. It is my place in life to know the Emperor's mind, and I do."

He thought for a moment, looked right into his King's eyes and said, "Your Majesty, I cannot lie to you. Our supremacy on Fovea is ended. We were too dependent on our walls, our magic and our influence with the High Council. Lupus has answers for it all.

"Give him the strangers, tell him what we know. If the gods wished for us to act, they planned poorly for our success by their own admission. The best we can hope for now is to survive until the next prophesy."

They were quiet together. Fourteen years is the blink of an eye to an Uman-Chi, and in that time they had reverted from the virtual rulers of their known world, to the vassals of Men, a race barely more than animals.

"Better to suffer the fate of the Cheyak," Aniquen said.

"No," Angron said. "For them, there is no hope. For us, there is much. Remember every person here will outlive the Conqueror. There is nothing to say his successor shall be anything like him. We who live our lives by centuries, not months, can bend the knee for a decade.

"In humility, let us find strength. And as tame as sheep, let us summon the Wolf."

* * *

In her personal chambers, Glynn knelt in prayer, in humble thanks to the All-Father, and to the Taker and the Giver, who looked out for her and who protected her in this trial.

In her heart, she knew who had touched her. It was the god-mother. She simply knew it, as one knows yellow is not red or sugar tastes sweet, she knew she had sung Eveave's words.

Right now Uman-Chi males, like Angron and Aniquen and D'gattis, debated the meaning of her song. She had worshipped them just a day before, but they seemed smaller to her now. They remained her people, however she didn't worship them. Gods had spoken through her, and these males were not they.

It became difficult to clear her thoughts, so many were they. She poured them like fish into a stream, and this time the great white one she had nourished did not come to devour them. The fish swam around her in the stream, but the current didn't sweep them away.

Had she become dependent on it? Perhaps.

She saw the fish for what they symbolized. One

represented the thought of the newcomers, another the truth of the song. She saw the worry she hadn't been invited to the meeting of the King's advisors, and several regarding her new brother.

In her mind's eye, she knelt by the stream, and watched them. They turned their wide eyes up toward her expectantly, fish-eyes oddly sentient in regarding her.

She willed them away, and they scattered, but returned to her again. She could not nurse them, she could not nourish them—how would she scatter what had never been meant to stay?

Then it occurred to her—she could not. These thoughts belonged to her, and remained real. Where she had scattered them once before, or nourished and cultivated them, or absorbed them in the greater worry of her song, now she had them here, and they had nowhere to go.

Instead, in her minds eye, she shed her garment, and she leapt into the icy stream. The strong current, the icy water swept her away, leaving these thoughts and worries to swim behind her.

Immersed in the water, she accepted its cold, its pain, and let it numb her and batter her, accepting that she had no strength to fight it.

She swept down the stream, past rocks and fish and curious things without end, growing ever colder, numbed and battered thoroughly.

As she departed her unreal body this time, leaving it to the water and the rocks, she saw it ruined and broken in the stream. Her real body remained relatively pristine and perfect. She again identified the tiny imperfection on her real shoulder, and she connected her lifeline to it.

She arose before the city of Outpost IX, this time not as a thin sheet but a fog, a pulsing mass, wet and invisible, radiating thundering power as she had never done before and should not do now, exhausted as she found herself.

In the city, she identified a young tree with no bark, its leaves springing green in the coldest months. She caressed its trunk with her ethereal fingers, feeling ghostly smooth. She pressed her ethereal lips to it, and tasted its woody purity.

When she withdrew from it, she saw herself in its bole, not as a woman but as a jewel, and had to wonder at what that meant.

* * *

The armored guards brought them to their own room in a tower in the palace. They saw a gigantic bed, thick carpets, another room to sit down in, a table for eating, even a canvas and paints where they could indulge their creative needs if they wanted to, and a gigantic window to look out onto the city, supposedly for inspiration.

From the window they looked out onto a bustling place where people in robes and dresses, pants and armor, on foot and in wagons and on horseback, moved from here to there by torch and lamp light. A plain white moon hung over the horizon, casting its reflection on the water past the city walls.

"It's an island," Melissa commented.

"They seem to be in the Middle Ages," Bill said.

"Like, King Arthur?" she said.

"Yeah. Those men who came to get you wore armor and had some kind of swords. There are some more like them down there."

"I see a few on horseback, but I don't see any cars," Melissa said.

"I am having serious doubts about their ability to get us back from here," Bill said.

She walked away from the window and back to the one bed. Apparently, they assumed the two were a package.

Someone had piled the mattresses and quilts up so high that Melissa actually had to jump to get up on it. When she did, she sank back down another foot into its softness. "Whoa, wow!"

"Is that a feather bed?" Bill asked, following her.

"I dunno," she said. She lay back, threw back her arms and spread her legs. Her robe flew open and exposed her from stem to stern.

Bill turned away politely. She didn't need to look up to know he did it. She sighed.

"You've already seen it," she said.

"I know."

"You don't like it?"

"Didn't say that."

"You gay?"

"*What*?"

She laughed, pulled her arms out of the sleeves of her robe, and rolled over, raising a leg up. "There," she said. "Look at my butt. You like my butt."

She heard him sigh, then felt the bed shift as he crawled in next to her.

She had had enough of being out of control, of being victim-girl, of being 'Melly.' He hadn't asked what happened to her, and she hadn't told him. He couldn't fix it for her, and she didn't want his sympathy, didn't want to look in his eyes and see pity.

"Wow, this *is* a goose down mattress," he said.

He settled in a polite foot from her. The mattress dipped toward him, and she let herself roll toward him.

"Whoops," he said, as her breasts rolled over his arm, and she pinned his hand under her belly.

"Deal with it," she said, wryly.

She hadn't chosen to be here, she hadn't chosen to be touched, paralyzed, stripped and dragged around. *This*, she chose.

He looked into her face, then leaned back and closed his eyes.

"You don't want me?"

"Of course I want you," he said. "Its just that—"

"You are sweet," she said. She laid her head on his shoulder, and turned so he could get a better look at her.

Sometimes she just enjoyed teasing him. He was a nice guy. He might be older, but her track record with boys her own age hadn't been that great. Bill respected women. She could look in his eyes and saw the tenderness there. Those eyes held no harm for her, no cruelty. Bill had love to give to her, she could see it in almost everything he did.

What did a few years matter for a man with love to give?

"What do you think?"

"I think I am having a nic' fit so bad, I could bite the top off of a beer bottle, and I bet they don't have that here, either."

She laughed. "I am right behind you," she said, laying her hand on his chest. "I would dry a butt from a wet ashtray right now."

"The only butt I've seen around here is yours," he joked.

She looked up at him, a wide grin on her face. "Why Bill, are you flirting?"

He screwed up his face and considered. "That could be flirting," he said, nodding.

She reached inside of his robe. "Well, then, why don't you come on?" she said. "It isn't too late for you to have your lucky night?"

"Don't you want to order lobster first?"

She reached up and kissed him. His beard was rough on her lips. She pushed her tongue into his mouth and opened her eyes to see the surprise on his face. She grinned and pulled back, letting him press her, tasting his mouth on hers. She surprised him again by sucking on his invading tongue, then giving it a gentle bite.

A younger man would have tried to clean her tonsils, drooled all over her and made her jaw sore. Bill seemed more interested in her enjoying it. The hand beneath her turned and found her breast, the free one found her back, and traveled between her shoulder and her upper thigh. She stood just over five feet tall, he could reach all of her with his long arms.

His fingers reminded her of the old Uman-Chi. She fought the memory. Bill felt her tense up, and broke the kiss to look in her eyes. She took his beard between her thumb and forefinger, and pulled his lips back to hers. She forced the thought to the edge of her mind, because she hadn't had enough time to force it away.

The kissing kept on going, until she felt good and ready for the next part. Again, she took the lead, pushing his shoulders back, getting him ready with her mouth first, then getting up on top of him. He was too big to lay on her, but she found herself athletic enough to make it work from on top. He watched her, wanting to put his hands everywhere at the same time, to squeeze and tickle, to nibble her breasts when she leaned forward, and to gently tug her hair as she leaned back.

Bill counted as her third time, but she knew what she was about. She made it all happen for herself. It turned out wonderful, just what she hoped for. He didn't rock her world—but he got the job done. Afterward he held her, safe in his arms, his breath on her, his heart beating under her ear, until she felt safe and she fell asleep. Not since she had been rocked in her daddy's arms had she known that contentment in her life, and that had happened a long, long time ago.

Chapter Six:

The New Kids on the Block

They spent their days trying to learn the language. They spent their nights in each other's arms. They were cared for and fed, and it all made Melissa feel like a pet—one whose cage was too small.

Human throats just couldn't utter the sounds made by Uman-Chi, but the others, the servant race that called themselves Uman—their language could be spoken. Melissa learned that, slowly picking out the nouns and vowels, and the differences between 'I am hungry' and 'I am hunger.'

They found Men who worked within the palace. Bill greeted them like lost relatives, but they seemed standoffish. He towered over all of them, heavier than the biggest of them and older than any two of them combined. They spoke a language that Bill said sounded a lot like Polish, which his grandmother had taught him as a boy. He picked that up, moving a lot faster than Melissa could.

All of the local humans, who called themselves Men as a race (and didn't that get Melissa's feminist dander rising!) were servants, just like the Uman. That made them hard to engage. If Melissa tried to speak with them, they immediately assumed she wanted something, and then were very focused on how to get it for her. Once they figured out that she wanted to talk, to learn their languages, they usually just gave short answers to questions, pretended not to or actually couldn't understand anything too deep, and excused themselves as soon as they could.

"You're too used to being free," Bill informed her one day, in their rooms, two weeks after coming here. It was evening and they'd been served their evening meal—steaming platters of meat and roots like potatoes and carrots laid out between them with pitchers of milk and clean water. In Fovea, or at least among the Uman-Chi, you weren't served directly—food was laid out communally and you grabbed what you wanted from a pile.

Melissa had tried to get the Uman servants to stay and eat with them, and they'd gone wide-eyed when they'd realized what she wanted, and fled.

"Everyone should be free," Melissa argued, sitting across from him in a padded, wooden chair at a little round table by their one window. Their room faced south, and when the sun went down they were treated to an excellent view of the city, all with lit lanterns and little houses, smoke rising from chimneys here and there, and people walking down immaculate cobblestone streets. There were trees and flower beds here and there and, if you looked long enough, you'd often see men and women walking side-by-side, holding hands or being trailed by their children.

"Everyone should be," Bill agreed, "but in fact not everyone is, even where we're from. This place is more like the Middle Ages, and these people are vassals to their lords."

Melissa reached out to a platter with a two-pronged fork and pulled a red strip of beef onto her plate. Here they *never* used the fork to eat with—that was the purpose of your knife, which had a wide, curved end almost like a flat spoon. You fetched your food with your fork or held it while you cut it with your knife, and then you used your knife to put it into your mouth. That actually made more sense when you considered this fork was going to touch food on a platter that other people might want.

"Vessels?" she asked Bill. He was dressed in an evening robe—they changed clothes like three times a day here. You had your morning wear and your day way, and then something blousy and comfortable for the evening.

They also went commando—no underwear. Women in their cycle would wear something almost like a diaper, but they wore such giant, full skirts that it was impossible to tell.

"Vassals," Bill corrected her. He spoke around a piece of meat he was chewing. Melissa took some as well, with a smashed piece of potato—it was *amazing*. Bill had called it 'farm fresh' but she didn't know what that meant, other than to say it had more flavor than anything she'd ever had from a restaurant or from a supermarket.

"People who are literally owned by their noble lords, like property," he continued. "They exist to serve their so-called betters, people of higher birth. All of the betters here are Uman-Chi."

Melissa felt her eyebrows knit. "Like—slaves?" she asked.

Bill shook his head. "Serfs, not slaves," he said. He took a big gulp of milk, then continued with a little of it hanging on the end of his moustache. "They can't be bought or sold—they have some rights, but they live to serve.

"Believe it or not," he continued, poking at his meat, "that's been the human experience for most of our history. People have only started to be born common *and* free for a few hundred years."

Melissa thought about those old Errol Flynn movies she'd watched as a kid, before cable. Those times of men with swords and peasants in Sherwood Forrest had seemed very romantic to her at the time.

She had been an enthusiastic student in college, but not on topics like this. She'd excelled at the physical sciences, chemistry and biology, but found it difficult to connect with the social ones.

People here were more beaten down—they were actually afraid to talk to her. On the other hand, the Uman-Chi had violated her privacy and thought nothing of it. Angron had seemed to apologize, but in fact he was clearly surprised by it bothering her.

In fact they hadn't seen Angron again, but the female, whose name they learned was, 'Glynn,' had become their constant companion. She directed Uman servants to make them clothing, a set of dresses with billowy skirts with hems down to her ankles for Melissa. They preferred tight waists and uplifting bodices that flattered her figure. Bill was measured for pants and long robes of red, blue and green, and blousy shirts that opened at the chest.

Glynn arrived early the following morning, knocking at their door after they'd finished their breakfast. They didn't have coffee here (this bothered Bill but Melissa could live without it) but they did have a very heady tea with caffeine in it. They were drinking that when the Uman-Chi girl walked in.

"Good morning to you, my lord and lady," Glynn said, smiling brightly to both of them. She'd dressed in the single white robe she always wore—Bill had guessed that it marked her station, but they hadn't asked how.

"And to you, my Lady," Bill said to her, smiling, in the language of Men. "May I pour some tea on you?"

Glynn smiled and corrected his grammar. In the language of Men, you could change the meaning of a sentence just by your inflection, and Bill was having trouble getting it right.

She accepted some tea from him and sipped it, sitting with them. She gazed out the window for a moment, clearly collecting her thoughts, and then without looking at either of them said, "I received a rather disturbing report that you invited your servants to eat with you."

Melissa frowned. "Is that not allowed?" she asked in the Uman language. Bill shot her a warning look but she ignored it, focused on Glynn.

"It isn't fair to the Uman," Glynn said, gently chiding her. "They are not—" and then some word she didn't understand.

Melissa repeated the word. Glynn tried again—this could be very frustrating some times, especially in a case like this when there wasn't something to point to and say, "That thing right there—this is a word for that."

Glynn patiently pointed out words to them at every opportunity, both in the languages of Man and Uman. She never became frustrated, she never seemed to mind repeating herself. Melissa couldn't imagine how a girl who couldn't be more than fifteen could be so even-tempered and patient, but apparently that was a big part of being an Uman-Chi.

"Today we do something good," Glynn informed them, abandoning the word she'd been trying to teach Melissa. "I have horses for us to ride."

The grin that split Bill's face took thirty years off of him, Melissa thought. She'd seen him staring longingly after the horses they'd seen from their window. He hadn't said anything to her, but she'd have to be blind to miss it.

"Where we ride?" he asked her.

"Where *do* we ride?" she corrected him. "There is a <some word> in the palace where we can <some other word>."

Normally Bill would be all over learning the word he didn't know—now he clearly didn't care. Glynn stood and asked them to dress, and Bill was already tearing his clothes off.

That was *another* thing about the Fovean—they had about zero modesty. Glynn would stand right there while they changed, and she wouldn't think twice about shucking her robe and squatting over a chamber pot if she needed to. Melissa hailed from New England, where it was unheard of to wear jeans to work.

They kept their clothes in an armoire—a big, wooden container with intricately-carved doors that opened out into the room. She pulled those open and stepped within their confines, dropping her robes and her simple dress and looking for something more appropriate for riding.

They'd made her high-topped boots as soft as leather could be, but no pants at all. She thought to ask Glynn but felt she knew what the answer would be: ladies do *not* wear pants here. She sighed and pulled out the lightest dress she could find.

Bill was already dressed out in chocolate brown leather pants, boots and a white pull-over cotton shirt that was open at his neck, with a wide black belt around his middle, by the time Melissa was ready. Glynn approached her and turned her around, cinched up the laces in the dress' back and then turned her around, smiling.

Melissa painted on a smile. It could sometimes suck to be a girl.

* * *

Melissa hadn't sat on horseback for ten years. Bill had apparently ridden for a big part of his life but hadn't done so recently. They put him up on a big bay gelding, and found her a gentle palfrey with a sidesaddle.

She'd never seen a side-saddle before—it bore two stirrups on the left, one shorter than the other, on an otherwise normal saddle with a saddle horn and a high back. The Uman servant in the stable, dressed in brown pants and a white shirt buttoned to his collarbone and a red ascot, his green hair loose around his shoulders, walked the gentle mare to a mounting block—three steps that would take her almost to the horse's height.

She guessed she was supposed to plant her butt on that.

"Can I get…" she began, but she didn't know how to say, 'normal' or 'saddle.'

Glynn frowned. "Afraid?" she asked.

Melissa shook her head. She climbed to the top of the mounting block and tapped the saddle, and asked 'What is the word for this?' in Uman.

"Shedell," Glynn informed her.

She pointed at the saddle on Bill's horse. Bill was still playing around with the cinch that held the saddle to the horse's back—he'd already adjusted the stirrups. The Uman who attended him, dressed the same but older and with white hair, was speaking to him in the language of Men.

"What is the word for this?" she asked.

Glynn gave her the word for horse, but she shook her head. She pointed at the saddle, said, "Shedell," and then she pointed at Bill's saddle and said "Shedell-na."

'Different saddle.'

Glynn nodded, and pointed to hers. "Agla-def," she said.

"For women."

Melissa pointed to Bill's saddle and said, "Melissa-def."

"For Melissa."

Glynn frowned more deeply, and pointed at Melissa's saddle. "A woman must protect her—" and then a word she didn't know but could easily guess at.

Glynn knew they slept together, so it couldn't be virginity. *Waddaya think, sister?* she couldn't help thinking, "*It's gonna rub off?*"

She sighed and planted her butt gently on the saddle. Her

feet found the two stirrups and she would have pushed herself off backwards on the other side if she hadn't been able to grab the saddle horn. The Uman raised a hand and lowered the stirrups for her, and that made balancing easier.

She wanted a cigarette so bad she was ready to bite someone's head off. Still, she smiled at the Uman, who smiled back up at her and led her horse out of the stables into the bright, sunny day outside.

Bill trotted out behind her on the gelding. The air was brisk but not too horribly cold—it must be near the start of spring here, she thought. Another Uman opened a gate outside of the stable entryway and the two of them rode into a covered arena lined by a wooden fence. There were other Uman in there, working other horses, some with ropes and long-handled whips teaching the horses to walk or trot properly, others riding on soft sand that seemed a good four inches deep. Before the Uman at the gate could close it, Glynn charged out of the stable on a little white mare with pink, flaring nostrils and blue eyes, also riding a side-saddle.

Glynn held her reins in one hand and placed the other on her hip, keeping her back straight. She circled once around the arena while Melissa watched her.

Bill, of course, was right behind Glynn, a huge grin on his face. The horse trotted for about half the way, then Bill kicked him up into a canter, a three-step lope that was the horse's travelling speed. The horse raised his black tail high and Bill straightened his back.

Glynn reined in beside Melissa, already breathing a little heavy. Riding wasn't quite the horse doing all of the work, and balancing on a side-saddle wasn't easy. The smile on Glynn's face told Melissa she loved to do this.

"He is good," Glynn said to her, in the Uman language. "He has a good," and then some word she didn't know.

Melissa repeated the unknown word.

Glynn frowned. She sat up very proper in her saddle and held the reins before her.

He has a good seat, Melissa thought, *or something like it.* She nodded.

"He's good man," Melissa said.

"You—some word—him?" Glynn asked.

Here, when they asked a question, they lowered their voice at the end of the sentence, not raised it. That took her two days to figure out. Bill said Europeans spoke the same way.

Melissa repeated the word as a question.

Glynn wrapped her arms around herself, laid her head to one side and rocked herself.

Love.

Mike had been her last love, and had done her *so* wrong. Bill treated her with a lot more caring. He far exceeded Mike as a lover—if not with enthusiasm then with caring. He always made sure she got hers, and that had been every night so far. More importantly to Melissa, he held her after. She would place a hand on his belly, he would wrap her in his bear arms, and he would give her little kisses on the top of her head, her forehead and her ears. Already, she couldn't imagine falling asleep anywhere but in his arms.

As she watched him, his head came up, he scanned the faces around him until he found her, and he smiled. His whole face lit up, then he went back to his riding once she smiled at him.

He did that. He'd be doing what he was doing, then realize he hadn't seen her in a while. He'd make sure of Melissa's safety, make eye contact, and then go back to what he was doing.

She was *his girl*. He was her guardian protector.

She got that little glow back again.

"Yes," she informed Glynn. "Love him."

Between the nic-fit and the saddle and the whole, "I'm not on my home planet anymore" loneliness, she felt herself wanting to tear up, and she shook the reins for the palfrey to move forward.

It obliged her at a fast walk. She started around the inside of the wooden arena fence. It wasn't long before Bill was approaching her from behind, getting ready to pass her.

"Take a firm hold on her," he said in English.

She half-turned in the saddle, almost lost her balance and then righted herself. "What?" she asked.

Bill slowed to a trot. Already the horse and he seemed to

have reached some understanding. "Take a hold of her," he said. "I'm going to pass you and some horses will go charging after another if they—"

By then Bill was trotting past her, and didn't that gentle palfrey get it into her head that she should trot right behind the gelding?

A trot is bouncy and actually more work for the horse than a canter. If she'd had a leg on either side of the mare, she'd have been able to stay on, but instead her first instinct was to grab for the saddle horn and dig in her feet. That propelled her right off of the horse's side and head first into the fence.

Her world exploded in an aurora of stars, and she faintly heard Bill call her name.

* * *

She found herself back in Augusta, Maine, in front of that diner she'd gone to for breakfast when she could afford it.

This wasn't right, she couldn't help thinking. She'd left this place years ago. She'd gotten a cleaning job and she'd pocketed her money until she could afford to move to Florida.

The smell of breakfast—waffles and eggs and coffee—poured out of the glass front door to the place. She could see inside to the white counter with stainless-steel bar stools and red cushions, the sugar jars and menu-holders lined up neatly in front of them. There was only one person at the counter, her back to the door.

Melissa walked up to the door and opened it. A bell jingled on the door's corner. A few heads turned but the woman at the counter remained still, smoking a cigarette.

She wore a yellow dress and had white hair, done up in some old-lady style. Melissa walked past her and sat on one of the stools at the counter.

She smelled Sunflowers perfume. No one wore that anymore.

The old woman turned to her at the counter and smiled, then nodded in greeting. Melissa smiled back.

"You were a long time coming," the old woman said.

"Wh—what?" Melissa stammered.

The woman took a drag off of her cigarette, then stubbed it

out in an ash tray in front of her.

"Wish I had another one," she said, then turned again and looked Melissa in the eye, "but I gaved you my pack."

Melissa felt her heart constrict in her chest. She knew who this woman was!

* * *

Bill paced alongside the giant bed in their rooms, where Uman servants had carried Melissa on a litter.

An Uman-Chi whom they called Lord Roo was seeing to the tiny girl's limp body. Glynn was standing behind him, her one hand holding the other before her at her waist, looking as concerned as someone with pure-silver eyes can look.

Dammit, he swore to himself. His fault. He hadn't ridden in more than a decade, and he'd been so excited to get a horse between his legs that he'd simply not cared that maybe Melissa didn't have his experience. He'd grown up around Appaloosas when he'd been a kid, but the ones here were so well trained he could just *think* of doing something, and they did it.

Apparently that little sorrel they'd given to Melissa had thought about trotting, but had forgot to tell her rider.

Roo said something to Glynn, who smiled, looked across the bed at Bill and nodded. "She's only sleeping," Glynn said in the language of Men. "She will arise when she's ready—there is no real injury and no—some word he didn't know—broken."

He repeated the word. Glynn ran her fingers down her arm.

Bones. No bones broken. Bill sighed his relief.

The door opened behind him and Roo and Glynn's eyes widened, then both lowered their heads. Bill turned and found himself face-to-face once again with King Angron.

He lowered his head. "My Lord, your Majesty," he said, as they'd taught him.

"Bill," he said, meaning Bill could raise his head now. The two Uman-Chi did the same. "How is your lovely lady?"

"She's well, my Lord," he said. He didn't like all of this deference to nobility. Some people thought nobles were impressive somehow, but Bill had always had the 'we broke away from this' attitude toward so-called royals that many Americans felt.

"Thank Adriam," Angron said, "and, of course, Taffer Roo, Adriam's priest."

The old healer nodded in deference to the King's praise and did something with his hands Bill didn't understand. Glynn remained quiet.

"Sirrah," Angron said, turning his attention back to Bill, "I need to speak with you."

"I'm at your service, your Majesty," Bill said.

Angron led Bill out of the room, his Uman guards joining them and one of them shutting the door behind them. They walked down a dimly lit hall past several wooden bound doors, to one no different than the others. Angron stood beside it and an Uman opened it for them.

Wow, Bill thought. *He doesn't even open his own doors when he's standing right there.* He walked through the door behind the King.

The room was like many others in the palace—stone walls, polished wood floors—this one had no windows and a round table at its center. Another Uman-Chi sat at it—a younger man by the look of him. His long green hair hung around his shoulders and he dressed in the white robes that some of them wore. His features were more aquiline and cunning than the King's, the eyes were the same silver-on-silver but the pencil-thin eyebrows lowered over them in a discerning squint as Bill entered the room. He didn't rise for the King, and that was strange.

The King sat and indicated a wooden chair with a cane seat and back, stained a deep walnut and polished to shining. The table between them also shone—Bill could see his reflection in the walnut finish.

"Bill," King Angron said, "this is Aniquen, a younger Uman-Chi but a trusted advisor of mine and a shining light amongst our people. He has some questions he would like to ask you."

Bill nodded and turned his attention to Aniquen.

"Sirrah," the younger Uman-Chi said, his voice almost an

alto

and much more like a singer than the King's, "I would like to ask you about chem-stree."

He spoke in English, which Bill found strange. Angron had said he was the only one who knew this language here.

Bill frowned. The King had brought this up as well. "Chemistry," he said. "The study of how the elements react."

Aniquen may have looked sideways at Angron—it was impossible to tell with the eyes, but the King straightened and said, "The four elements, you mean?"

Bill shook his head. "There are hundreds of elements," he informed them.

Aniquen snickered. It seemed almost contemptuous.

"There is Earth, Wind, Water and Fire," he said. "Two of these are gods, one the province of the goddess Weather, and then Fire which is independent of the gods."

"Ah, Okay," Bill nodded. "Well, I guess those are elements, but I'm speaking of things like oxygen and iron, how they can mix to form ferrous-oxide, which you'd call rust."

Aniquen shook his head. "I do not know your 'oxygen,'" he said. "But it is water that makes iron rust."

Bill had never been much of a student in school—which mostly explained why he'd gone into sales. He couldn't explain why rust was called ferrous-oxide, he just knew it was. He tried to explain how water could have salt in it, and how the salt could be taken out, but that fell flat as well.

"We know the Emperor can do this," Angron informed him, "but we believe this is with magic, not with your chem-stree."

Bill chuckled. "You believe in magic?" he asked them. "Seriously?"

"You've seen us use our magic," Aniquen said. "You were brought here with magic. I am a Caster—I am a man who manipulates the elements, who uses magic."

Bill smiled. "If you say so," he said.

Angron sighed. "You believe your chem-stree can remove the salt from water?" he said.

"On Ear—where I'm from," he said, remembering at the last second that they called this place 'Earth' as well, "we do it all the time."

"But you yourself do not do this?" Angron asked him.

"I'm sorry," he said, "but no. I was in sales—what you'd call a merchant."

The two Uman-Chi smiled as one. "Then perhaps you know the urcher-nom-echs," Angron said.

"Economics?" Bill asked, smiling. He was a die-hard student of the EIB Network. He knew a *lot* about economics.

"What do you want to know?"

"How can you tax your peasants less, but then have more money?" Aniquen asked. "We have seen this, but it makes no sense. When we've tried it ourselves it has been an expensive undertaking and, when it failed and the peasants were returned to their normal taxes, they were very upset."

Bill chuckled. "Well, first of all, it's not going to work with peasants," he said. He leaned forward—now he felt like he had some solid footing.

"What do you mean?" Aniquen demanded. "We have peasants, the Emperor has peasants—the Emperor taxes only tiny fraction of his peasants' earnings, and yet his coffers swell."

"I don't know who this Emperor is," Bill said, "but when you have high taxes on your citizens—your peasants—you take away their willingness to work hard. That is called their 'productivity,' how much they can create, based on how much work they're willing to do."

Angron shook his head. "This makes no sense," he said. "A farmer has a field. He sews his crops, the land produces a bounty and he reaps it. No matter how much you take, the land is the same, the crop the same. Leave him all of his crop and he'll eat what he needs, sell what he doesn't and then spend the rest."

"Take the excess for the state," Aniquen continued, leaning forward, "and put it to the common good, and then all peasants live better, live safer, with better roads, more soldiers to protect them, and all of the things that the state can provide."

Bill had heard this all before. The debate was probably thousands of years old. He argued that when the peasants could keep more of their money, they would find new ways to be productive and increase their wealth. The increase in wealth led to more taxes for the state.

The Uman-Chi argued it was no different if the state took the money—the gold was all the same. If the farmer couldn't get to market then he couldn't sell his wares.

They reached an impasse. The Uman-Chi just didn't believe him and they claimed their own experiments proved they were right. However, they kept mentioning some Emperor who was making it work, and were demanding that Bill justify how.

Finally they thanked him and sent him on his way. He returned to his rooms with Melissa, and found her sleeping alone. He passed up on dinner and slid into bed next to her, and wondered at a place so alien, and what he'd found and what he'd left behind.

Chapter Seven:

Being Good Pets

They were another month in Outpost IX. In that time they spent their days learning Uman and the language of Men (of Volkhydrans, they were told, although they'd never met one or really heard of them), learning to ride, and answering the questions put to them by Angron and Aniquen, who spoke to them together or, more rarely, individually, about what they called 'chem-stree' and 'ech-nomics.'

In the evenings they were encouraged to occupy their own time. Bill tried to learn to fight with a sword but he wasn't very good at it. Melissa fought more with a paint brush, first on her own and then with a tutor once Glynn had seen her work. She would sit on a stool before an easel, her dark hair framing her frowning face as she chewed the end of a brush and gazed out their one window. Although she saw the hills and homes and blue water of Tren Bay before her, she painted these intense abstracts, auroras of color and altered perception the likes of which the young Uman-Chi Caster had never seen before.

"And you think this means she has the skill?" Chaheff asked her at their morning devotions.

Glynn lowered her head before the image of the goddess Eveave, standing in a long dress as a piece of white marble on a wooden shrine before her. Her knees felt every grain of dust the servants had missed on the floor, her back ached for the posture she kept. Her power might be growing but her body wearied of the intensive training.

"It is not uncommon for Men to exhibit artistic skills as an indicator of the gift," she informed Chaheff, as if he didn't know this. "We know the Emperor is strange in his thinking—we have no reason not to believe his kinsmen would be as well."

"The Emperor does not have the gift," Chaheff stated, flatly. He knelt beside her, before a marble cast of Adriam, the All-Father. His breathing was labored—mostly due to his weight, Glynn imagined.

She'd worn a new white robe cut a little too large for her, and she'd caught him admiring her breasts. Chaheff already shared his life with an Uman-Chi woman whose family protected the stables in the palace, so Glynn couldn't imagine that he'd want a new wife. However that woman, of a median house, had given him no children.

These thoughts made Glynn testy. In fact she was of an age where her brother should be seeking out a mate for her, and she knew Ancenon had not interested himself. In fact, he had not returned to the Silent Isle even once since their last conversation.

Now she was occupied with training and with managing these new-comers, mostly it seemed because she was blamed for bringing them here. She didn't find that fair and she admitted to herself she'd like nothing better than to find someone else to provide a reason to monitor them.

"In fact," she said, "we know only that we have no record of the Emperor *using* the gift. He is the only person of the race of Men who speaks both Uman-Chi and Cheyak, and the latter better than most of us. It has been conjectured that he may be *barely gifted.*"

Chaheff smiled. "He might need to go to his own schools," he said.

Glynn allowed herself a reciprocating smile. Years ago, the Emperor of Eldador had begun schools for those persons of all races who had minor magical abilities, but not the skill to master them. Such people were previously prevented from studying the craft and, in fact, were stripped of their power if it was possible. These unfortunate souls usually ended up trying to teach themselves and inevitably suffered for it.

Now they filled a thousand roles throughout Fovea, either as truth sayers, or as messengers or helping repairmen, working as healers or studying crops and livestock. They were taught to be happy to use just the tiny sparkle of the power Adriam had granted them, and to make their way in the world accordingly.

It had caused even more people to flock to Eldador, not that most Foveans needed a reason. Now every nation—even Volkhydro, which had very few gifted persons—had these same schools, and made use of the barely-gifted.

"If he does, I'm sure he'll either dominate it or kill everyone in it—that is the way of the Eldadorian Emperor," Glynn assured him.

She had her own reasons to hate this Man.

"If your Melissa has the gifts, then she has them," Chaheff informed her. "Let us close our prayers and move on to other things."

They incanted the closing together, with the proper form and intonations, learned by each of them over decades and, in Chaheff's case, centuries.

Rising after, Uman servants approached them with libations—fruit juice for Glynn and milk for Chaheff. The two Uman-Chi accepted the drinks without comment and the Uman withdrew.

"As for another matter, it has finally been agreed that you are the noble, young and old, from your poem," Chaheff commented.

He stepped back as he said this, dropping one arm in the posture of the friendly messenger. Glynn straightened and raised her left hand elegantly as the interested host.

"I thought as much," she informed him.

"As such, you must reassert yourself to the ultimate meaning of this champion," Chaheff said. "While some great minds work together to decipher the song, none have your intimate knowledge of the woman, Melissa. As well, you *are* our only female Caster and, as such, may have insights we lack."

Why did males always assume that women shared some common bond? Glynn asked herself. However she smiled politely and took on a receptive stance.

"If I can decipher them, then I will," she promised. "However these two come with strange minds and wild ideas. I cannot promise more than to try."

"Trying is all we ask of you,"

* * *

One thing that had come to bother Melissa in the later years of her life was any inability to do anything. It just *bugged* her. Perhaps because she'd lost so much, or perhaps because she wanted so much, if there was a task at hand, and she couldn't overcome it, then it would drive her crazy, and she'd throw herself at it over and over again until finally she overcame the thing she couldn't do.

Because of that, she'd spent a month of evenings in the stables where the horses were kept, riding the horses there until she was confident she wouldn't fall again.

At first she'd been met with resistance by sleepy-eyed Uman servants whom, once the horses were fed and stalled for the night were welcome then to enjoy their lives as their assets let them. One had even complained to Glynn, not that it did him any good. To Glynn, the stablemen were servants like any other, they lived to serve and if service was required of them then, come day or night, that was what they needed to do.

Melissa, however, treated the ones who stayed to help her with such appreciation and respect that the Uman servants couldn't help but find an affection for her, even the old stablemaster, Geflain, who had complained about her. It was he who, more than any other, stayed in the early evening to teach her and to coach her in her learning to ride.

"The side saddle is a test of your balance," he'd informed her. "It's like a lesson in life to a young lady. Keep your balance, keep your poise, and no harm will come to you."

"A lot you know about it," Melissa had groused at him. "You get to hold on with both legs, not perch your butt on half a seat."

With that he'd helped her down from the palfrey she'd been practicing on, leapt up into the side saddle and commenced to ride the horse no less daintily than Melissa had seen of Glynn.

"This sort of riding," he informed Melissa as he trotted the horse around the enclosed arena, "is for a proper lady. Perhaps you'll find that in you and be able to imitate it, if not embrace it?"

That had been all it took for Melissa. A month later she could canter even one of the more aggressive Andaron horses in the side saddle. She found it invigorating and enlightening. Two weeks later Bill was commenting on the difference in how she moved, how she presented herself. At the end of that month she was noticing the same thing herself. Riding came not as a challenge or an imperative but as a natural motion. As she'd seen with Bill, the horse became an extension of herself. She felt its strength flow up into her, and she began to accept its grace.

Geflain, she'd realized, had been right. The side-saddle wasn't some kind of oppression by males. It taught her a discipline in poise and balance. It began to change her outlook on life.

Bill went looking for Melissa that night and found her where he expected to find her, riding another horse in the royal stables. He didn't understand her passion even though he shared it. Ben Franklin had said once, "What's outside of a horse is good for what's inside of a man," or something similar and he'd seen the change riding had wrought in Melissa.

Watching her riding a muscled gelding in the arena, turning left and right between poles that had been set up for her, he thought both, 'Wow, she's getting really good,' and 'Wow, I want a cigarette so bad, I'd cut off a lock of Melissa's hair and smoke it, if she would let me.'

The thought made him smile, and that's when she saw him. She smiled back and rode the gelding up to where he watched her, leaning against the rails of the arena wall.

"Where do you even come *up* with an idea like that?" she asked him, when he shared that second thought with her.

"Something from my sordid past," he confessed. "Girls smoking their braids. I don't know if it works."

She kicked her feet free of the stirrups and leapt off the horse. Smelling of the animal's natural musk, she threw her arms around Bill's neck and shoved her tongue into his mouth.

Her hand was on him. They'd been going hot and heavy

since they'd been brought here, with the exception of the three days of her last cycle, last week.

He reached for her. She giggled and ran her fingers up his sides.

"You're doing really well with that gelding," he commented to her after she broke the kiss.

She smiled and cocked her head to one side. "Maybe I'm ready for a stallion," she informed him.

He chuckled. "A stallion is a precarious beast," he informed her.

She smiled and kissed him again. "Don't I know it?" she informed him.

She'd been doing this, Bill thought to himself. He had a hard time keeping up with this girl. He thought it was a big deal when he lasted a whole minute against one of their warriors with a sword in his hand. She went out and conquered her fear of riding. He learned a little of the language of Men, she mastered Uman *and* learned to paint.

In his whole life, he'd never had regular sex more than twice a week. She left him feeling like she needed more than what he was giving her.

He could be falling in love, and in the back of his mind he couldn't stop thinking he was too old for falling in love.

"You're amazing, you know that?" he asked her.

She reached up and bit the end of his chin, through his beard. He tried to pull back but she held him for a moment.

He relaxed and she let him go. He turned his face down and looked into her eyes again.

"Want to go back to bed?" she asked him. "I think I'm ready to ride that stallion."

Bill took her in his arms and kissed her. She did this, too. She called the shots as to when and how. Usually it was her on top, because she didn't like his weight on her. She'd maneuver herself around his belly.

One thing Bill had never been was a kept man, and he'd been feeling more and more like one since he came here. They let him have what he wanted, but they made him ask for it. They fed him. They had him in a nice room, but he didn't own any of the things in it.

Sometimes, a man needs to demonstrate a little rebellion, if only to remind himself that he could rebel.

He reached his fingers up the sides of her body and past her shoulders, up her neck and into her long, black hair. She broke the kiss and looked up into his eyes, smiling and dreamy-eyed. He could feel her breath on his face, smell the horse's funk on her, filling his senses.

Melissa was an amazing beauty and, at least for now, all his. She was one part of his life that no one else dictated for him—except, of course, that these Uman-Chi had assumed they were a couple and paired them together.

What if they were trying to breed them? The thought rattled around in the back of Bill's mind.

His fingers reached into her hair.

"Wuh—Bill?" she gasped, breaking the kiss.

He looked into her deep, brown eyes and felt the smile cross his lips. Behind them, the old Uman stablemaster took the gelding's reins and led him from the arena, leaving them alone.

"Here?" Melissa's eyes flickered from the left to the right, even as her hand slipped into his trousers.

"You'd like that, wouldn't you?" he asked her.

She giggled, looked away, and then back up at him, her eyes flickering from left to right, searching his.

"You know," she said, and she bit her bottom lip, "I think I would."

"Such a bad little girl," he admonished her, and pushed her against the fence rails. Her fingers were fiddling with the drawstrings on the front of his trousers, but that wasn't fast enough.

He took the front of her dress in both hands and ripped open the bodice. Her breasts bobbed free, a thin sheen of sweat on them.

"What are you—*Bill*! We're going to get *caught!*" she hissed at him.

He turned her around and placed her dainty hands on the upper rail. She flipped her hair and turned her face up toward him, a cautious smile on her lips. "We'll—we'll get *caught*, Bill," she repeated. "They don't *do* this here."

"Royals have been screwing in front of the servants for hundreds of years," Bill informed her.

"We *aren't* royals," she protested.

The protest turned into a moan as his hands ran up the insides of thighs, then took her cheeks between thumbs and forefingers.

"*Bill!*"

He rubbed her, first with his fingers and then with his thumbs. She began to move her hips, the musk rising from her overwhelming the scent of the horse she'd been riding. Bill felt his need rising and pulled his right hand away from her to push down the front of his trousers. He leaned forward and rubbed her anew.

Her eyes widened, and he grinned, more to himself than to her. In the back of his mind, he thought to himself, "Has to be the sea air," as delivered a full-handed smack to her behind.

"Oh, *Bill*," she gasped.

He did it again. She shuddered in his grip, her heat easy to detect against him now. This had been a good idea.

Or it would have been, if he hadn't looked up from her exposed backside to see squad of Uman guards approaching them from the open stable doors.

"Oh, *dammit*," he swore.

Her head came up and she saw what he saw. She instinctively tried to stand and fell back against him, her dress slipping down her arms and midsection. She reached for her bodice and stumbled on the hem of her dress. Bill stepped forward, trying to put an arm around her, stepping on the hem of her dress as well.

The two fell in a tangle. The squad of Uman soldiers double-timed it to the fence and then came to a dead stop when they saw the two half-naked representatives of another planet struggling to get their own clothes on.

The disapproving look from the Uman guard spoke volumes. He said something in the Uman language, which Melissa had spent more time learning than Bill.

"What does he want?" Bill asked.

"For us to go with them," she said, her head peeking up comically from a bird's nest of her own hair. She clutched her bodice closed with her left hand, but Bill had done a good job ripping it and her ample bosom kept poking free.

"Where?" Bill asked.

She relayed the question, but they both hear the one-word answer.

"Lupus."

Chapter Eight:

Messages from Home

Court at night might be rare for the Uman-Chi, but not unheard of. This became necessary because the Eldadorian Sea Wolf, *The Bitch of Eldador*, had just pulled into port.

She was the flagship of the Eldadorian fleet, and brought with her the Imperial Couple, Rancor and Shela Mordetur, as well as an honor guard of two hundred Wolf Soldiers. Her sister ships, *She Runs Swiftly* and *The Pride of Eldador* berthed next to her with equal compliments.

As an added insult, the notorious thief, Karel of Stone, perhaps the most hated man on the Silent Isle after the Emperor himself, had joined the Imperial train.

Glynn had been invited to the royal court. She stood apart from the other Casters who advised the King. The King himself attended, with a gallery full of nobility, as could be roused from their homes at such a late hour.

The last time Karel had come here, he had left with a portion of the treasury, and on that same occasion Lupus the Conqueror had sacked the city and destroyed the main gates. It counted as Karel's third robbing of the treasury. Most suspected the Conqueror hadn't planned the robbery as a part in his retribution.

Glynn had been responsible for watching the two visitors. She had clothed them, fed them, and tutored them in Uman and in the language of Men. Of course, the moment she turned her back on them, they thanked her by getting caught rutting by the Royal Guard. This made for an incredible embarrassment for her. The race of Men behaved barely better than animals.

And here came its favorite son to tell them what it would take not to be conquered by their kind.

Glynn's Caster training couldn't quell her anxiety. Angron Aurelias sat implacable in white on his throne, but even he drummed his ancient fingers. Avek chewed his lower lip, D'gattis looked almost bored, the Conqueror's ally with no fear of him. Aniquen actually shifted from foot to foot—he had dueled with the Conqueror and lost, then visited him and been humiliated twice. Chaheff had been bested by Shela in the Sack of Outpost IX and now checked and rechecked with his fellow Casters to ensure they would be ready in the event of an attack.

Glynn owed this man a blood debt. Lupus the Conqueror, before becoming an Emperor, had personally cut her father's head from his shoulders in the market outside of the gates. His lancers had run down her brother.

And here she stood, waiting politely to turn over his rutting kinsmen to him.

She disagreed with this plan, but her King had spoken. She would not sway him. For his centuries, he did not have her vision, had not seen the prophecy in song from the inside, as she had. Knowing he would become the ally of the Emperor, she could not tell the ancient Uman-Chi what she knew.

"Who comes?" Bill asked her, in the language of Men.

She sighed. She didn't hide her disgust with them. They both dressed in blue, her in a dress and he in a robe, both in sandals. Blue for the eyes of the Conqueror, they being a gift to him.

Not in her riding apparel, of course, because he'd shredded that before trying to rut with her in the open arena.

"Lupus."

"Not know Lupus."

She turned her face up towards the old giant, his body thinner than it once had been, thanks to the superior medicine of the Uman-Chi, no doubt. Certainly he had the energy for his young wife now. She doubted he had the intellect to understand what he saw.

"Lupus is your friend."

He looked confused.

"You are from Earth?" Glynn asked. They called their home 'Earth,' similar to the name of the god whose face all Foveans lived on. The coincidence across an entire reality boggled the mind.

He nodded.

"Lupus is from Earth."

He looked very excited then, and growled something at his mate, who as well became very excited. She growled something and then both looked at her.

It was *so* tiresome.

The great doors opened and rescued her, admitting the Conqueror, this time by the invitation of Angron Aurelias.

* * *

"Are you sure?"

"That's what she said."

"How does she know?"

"I don't know."

"Well ask her," Melissa insisted.

The doors to the throne room opened, just before Bill could ask Glynn his questions.

The Man who walked in wore armor, corrugated all over, a black question mark turned upside-down upon its breast. He stood tall, taller than Bill, his blond hair past his shoulders. Bill noticed his striking blue eyes first, the angry look of a determined man, accentuated by a scar down the left side of his face, under his eye. He had a wry grin on his lips—almost as if he laughed at his hosts.

Beside him walked a beauty in a red dress, tan and buxom with thick, black hair down to her butt. She came up almost to his shoulder, as tall as an average woman but still shorter than this man or Bill, and taller than Melissa or Glynn.

He wore a long, red cape that dragged the floor behind him. The leather-wrapped handle of a sword showed over his left shoulder. He moved easily for wearing so much armor, he would have to be in good shape—a warrior of some kind.

As he approached, Bill picked out better details. The set of his jaw, the eyebrows made him Irish—Irish and something. New England Irish, that rare breed that made Kennedy's. The way he walked, the way he moved, his heel coming down to strike the floor, identified him for Bill as an athlete or a military man.

Behind him walked a tiny man and a giant, one in leather and the other in a heavy breastplate, both with swords. Behind them in ranks of four marched rows of men in light and dark gray uniforms, with a Wolf's head symbol on their breasts. No, he corrected himself—four, then three, then three, then the whole pattern again. As he walked down the center of the throne room on its red carpet, they fanned out and walked alongside, their cleats clacking on the marble floor in these groups of ten.

Angron had asked him about 'Lupus' and 'Rancor' and killing. They'd grilled him on chemistry and economics.

What could he be looking at now?

* * *

Angron Aurelias, an Uman-Chi with nearly 1,000 years behind him, sat on his throne and watched his palace violated by the marching army of an inferior Man and his inferior minions.

'Come to me, Lupus,' he thought to himself.

Men were barely more than animals, and yet here came one who had beaten him. Lupus had defied his assassins, his armies, his ships, and his mages. The King's own heir had become this man's puppet. In his entire lifetime, Angron Aurelias had not found one of the lost Outposts, and this one had found two. Angron Aurelias had taken over 100 years to design the laws of the Fovean High Council, and in three this one had made it irrelevant.

Uman trained for three years before they donned the tabard of the Trenboni High Guard, and Wolf Soldiers could train for eight weeks and defeat them in *their own city*. Outpost IX had been invincible for centuries before this one attacked and routed it.

This Lupus took impossible steps in logic with the inferior mind of Men. Avek alluded to the fact he knew the Ultimate Truth, and the nature of the universe—concepts Angron himself had taken centuries to grasp.

Lupus the Conqueror clanged down *his* throne room, insulting him by bringing forty squads of warriors with him. His wife who had humbled Uman-Chi Casters, and his ally Karel of Stone who had violated the royal treasury not once, not twice, but thrice, followed him.

She stopped at the Circle of Judgment, where a circle of thirteen interlocked circles had been burned into the white marble floor, and stepped fearlessly inside it, looking up at him as the first Cheyak must have looked up into Adriam's eyes.

He marched through the circle, and put a foot on the first step of the dais, clearly and intentionally violating protocol.

He raised his chin and looked Angron in the eye, and placed a hand on his own knee.

"I have arrived!" he said.

* * *

"You are welcome here," Angron said.

Glynn watched them, her charges quiet, enraptured by the Conqueror like the rest of them.

"I am glad I can come as a friend, your Majesty," the Emperor said, in flawless Uman-Chi. "I had despaired that Eldador and Trenbon would find no peace."

"And yet, you bring so many to protect you," Angron noted.

Lupus grinned, and answered, "One for each assassination attempt by the Trenboni crown."

His wife behind him grinned evilly.

Angron smiled, and Glynn did not feel honored. "Surely, not so many," he said.

"It feels like more, when you target my friends and family."

So be it. Angron moved on, and with a graceful turn of his

withered hand indicated the two Men at the base of his throne, beside Glynn, fifteen feet to the Conqueror's left.

"I present these, the two from the song," he said.

Glynn's heart skipped a beat.

* * *

This 'Lupus' spoke to the Uman-Chi in their own language, something Bill wouldn't have thought possible. He must have been here a long time.

"Look at how afraid they all are," Melissa said into his ear.

Bill had already noticed. In the gallery, the Uman-Chi fidgeted like crazy. Glynn kept unconsciously wetting her lips. Angron, who looked imperious and bold all the time, kept grinning and bowing his head. The one Uman-Chi who always stayed near him had a death grip on the top of Angron's throne.

When Angron gestured toward the three of them, Glynn actually jumped. Lupus and the woman next to him took a few steps in their direction, and he said something in the fluty language.

"I don't understand you," Bill said.

Lupus' face showed surprise. He recovered himself and smiled a wide, genuine smile. He extended his hand and Bill took it in his own, a firm grip with strong fingers.

"They call me Lupus here," he said, in English. No mistaking that distinct Connecticut accent. "Before you answer, you don't want to tell anyone your real name."

"What?" Bill hadn't expected that.

"If you already did, don't worry about it, but in this place you don't want to tell people your real name."

Bill looked at Melissa, then looked at him. "We already told them our first names. Not our full names," she said.

"That shouldn't be too bad," he said. He indicated the woman next to him. "This is my wife, Shela. She is from here, a nation called Andoron."

"Bill," Bill said, and they broke the handshake. "This is Melissa. We are from—"

"Let me guess," Lupus said. He looked them up and down.

"Well, you're a Mainer," he said to Melissa, grinning. "No

mistaking that accent."

"You got me," she said, smiling, and shook his hand.

"You're harder, bet you live in Florida, they have that 'I am from all over,' accent. I think I hear some…Massachusetts?"

"Pennsylvania," Bill said. "But I lived there for a few years."

"That's all it takes," Lupus said. "I'm told they brought you here by accident, and they don't know how or why."

"That's what they tell us," Melissa said.

"Well, they'll lie," Lupus said. "Uman-Chi love their secrets."

"Um—Angron can understand you," Bill warned him.

Lupus looked up at the throne, then back at Bill. "You're sure of that?" he asked.

"I have spoken to him in English," he said. "He said he learned it as a boy. Later there was another who could speak it—some Aniquen."

Lupus smiled, and said something to Shela, who looked up at Angron, then back at him and shrugged. She said something to him, and then he looked back at Bill and Melissa.

"If Angron learned our language as a boy, that was about a thousand years ago," Lupus said. "Did they tell you that?"

"No," Melissa gasped. "Really?"

"Yep," he said. "Uman-Chi live a long time. That girl standing next to you is one hundred and sixty-seven."

They looked at Glynn. Her face was turned to them.

"She is like a teenager to them," he said. "She wouldn't be here at all, except she sang the song that brought you here."

"She *did*?" Bill asked.

"See what I mean?" he said. "Look, I want to have them make her sing her song again. Sometimes I can hear things they can't. They won't like it, but they'll do what they're told."

"It seems like they do whatever they want here," Melissa said.

Lupus grinned. "I'll fill you in on that later."

* * *

Angron followed the conversation as best he could. They

spoke fast and softly, and his hearing was not what it once had been.

He heard Bill betray him to the Conqueror; another advantage compromised in this political game. He caught that Lupus would want Glynn to sing.

As Lupus informed them, he would cooperate. They summoned him because of it; of course Lupus would want to hear the song. As Lupus marched back to the Circle, Angron summoned Glynn up onto the steps without being asked.

"Sing for him," he commanded her.

"Your Majesty?" she asked. For her Caster self-control, her surprise and her fear were clear on her face.

"Sing," he said again. "Worry not, but have faith in Adriam."

Adriam would hopefully be most attentive, because the last time she sang she had ripped the fabric of the universe.

She inhaled, she held her hands before her, and she sang.

The words sounded sweet, and once heard were not easily forgotten. This time he felt no swelling of power and saw no opening of vortices. She merely sang, and she finished.

He watched the listeners. As before, some heard the song, such as Lupus and Shela, and some heard nothing, such as Karel and Lupus' Wolf Soldier guard. When the King's attention was drawn to the two visitors, their eyes betrayed them. By whatever power or whatever design, they followed the song and they reacted to it.

They growled to each other and they commented excitedly. Any doubt that they were both involved in this was gone right then.

Angron had to suppress a smile. These events were fortuitous, if unexpected. He had laid his plans so well that even this unforeseen event expanded his power.

* * *

The beating of Glynn's heart became so profound as to make her robes move. Beyond the terror of singing her song unprepared hovered the idea she would be turned over to the Emperor with her charges. Angron had not said, "I present the two from your homeland," he had offered him "the two from the song." That meant her and this female.

She waited, bold and patient, her head held high, a Caster.

Lupus looked up at her, then at Angron, then at his two countrymen, and back to her.

"Which god sends this to you," he asked her.

"I cannot be sure."

"Guess."

She lowered her head, then raised it, and looked into his eyes.

"Adriam," she said.

"She lies," Shela scoffed. She heard a stirring in the gallery, and Glynn knew that the King moved behind her.

"Speak true, daughter," Angron said.

She didn't turn. "Eveave, I think," she said.

Lupus nodded up at her. He looked back to his countrymen, then back to her.

"Which do you think they are?" he asked.

"He identifies himself as her guardian protector," Glynn said. "She, we believe, is the 'champion.' We believe I am the 'noble young and old.' The words bind me even as I sing them again."

"The first time tore reality and brought them here?" he asked.

"Yes," Glynn answered, and on her own initiative, asked, "was it thus for you?"

The entire throne room went quiet. The Conqueror *never* answered personal questions. Most considered it a coupe by D'gattis that he had tricked the Conqueror on the day of King Glennen's burying to admit his people voted on their leaders.

Lupus smiled, clearly amused with her temerity. She knew his weakness: his pride. He had to take the challenge.

"Yes," he said. "There was no singing, though. I was here one moment after I was there."

He flickered on the edge of a lie. Glynn didn't need a spell to know it. He told *a* truth, not *the* truth.

He looked up at King Angron and he said, "I will claim the three of them in the name of the Eldadorian Empire, if you will part with them."

Again, Glynn's heart skipped a beat.

"You intend to find those mentioned in the song?" Angron asked.

"I do."

"You must guarantee the safety of this Uman-Chi daughter," he said. "She will be treated as no less than a political hostage."

Lupus looked at her, then at Angron. "What title does she hold here?" he asked.

"She would be the Lady Escaroth of the Southern Towers," Angron said. "Her brother, your good friend and ally, Ancenon Escaroth, is Duke of the Southern Towers."

"I know him as an Aurelias," Lupus pressed the King, "so I will assume she will have no titles, except through marriage."

"And so," the King said.

"Then I shall grant her hereditary title of Baroness in Eldador, and make of her one of the court Barony in *Galnesh* Eldador. Let her have legal rights within the Empire."

"What lands?" Angron leaned forward.

"Britt," Lupus said, "on the Eldadorian peninsula. It is the closest part of Eldador to her homeland, and its Barons historically live in Eldador the Port."

"Historically?" Angron leaned back, grinning shrewdly.

Lupus grinned. "As of now."

"Done," Angron said.

Glynn saw herself transferred like so much merchandise. At least she hadn't missed that Angron had entirely disposed himself of the two Men.

She would be surprised if they lived until the War months.

Chapter Nine:

Interview With a Wolf

A suite of rooms had been set-aside for the Emperor and his party. The Wolf Soldiers quit the city and built their *jess doonar* on the plains, tearing up soil and cutting up trees, making themselves a 'little city,' supposedly to keep the troops sharp.

The stakes around their perimeter were sharp enough, that much seemed certain. Their commander, a Major in the Wolf Soldier guard, challenged the Duke General of the Trenboni High Guard to war games, at an insulting disadvantage of ten to one.

Angron saw the insult of the challenge exacerbated by its refusal for fear of losing. Fifteen Uman soldiers deserted upon the announcement, terrified the Wolf Soldiers would take offense and overrun the city.

"We paid a high price," Aniquen informed him.

Angron nodded. "We did, in fact, risk worse."

They sat with D'gattis, Chaheff and Avek in the King's meeting room as they had before, around a single table. An Uman servant poured them a deep, red wine. D'gattis was already tasting his, not waiting for his king to drink first. Avek clearly chaffed to be with the Emperor.

"He has warmed to his kinsmen," Chaheff noted.

"And to our Glynn," D'gattis noted, dryly.

"I will rely upon you to advise her brother," Angron informed him. "Ancenon should take responsibility for her safety, as a comrade of the Emperor."

"I think she will be safe," Chaheff assured them. "She is a competent enchantress; she has a good intellect, and the advantage of her birth."

"And I think she will pursue her prophecy the moment she believes she can do so safely," Aniquen said.

Chaheff smiled to himself, D'gattis as well. Angron shook his head.

"She will wait," he said.

"I agree," Avek said.

"Imagine my surprise," D'gattis added, drolly.

Avek shot him a sideway glance.

Angron knew he had to rally them. He quelled his own rage at the Emperor's insult. There were plans in play, and plans within those plans. Things that must be known, disguising what must *never* be known. The Emperor had made a fatal flaw, and Angron had found a fortuitous way to exploit it here.

"She is a Caster, an Uman-Chi, and an ideologue," Angron informed them. "She will let the Conqueror hunt down the others she seeks, and then she will try to unite them and fight the fight she feels is her destiny."

They exchanged glances around the table, then turned to Angron.

"I trust D'gattis will watch this happen without comment," Angron said. "I know his nature. D'gattis will remain aloof and aware, watch matters unfold and measure his loyalties."

"He is my ally," D'gattis said, "but I have no love for Lupus the Conqueror. In fact, I advised Ancenon Escaroth more than once that he should have been done away with, before our alliance made that impossible.

"He is, simply, the most creative military mind of our time, combined with an uncanny command of commerce that baffles us, even when we see it. That he took a backwater like Eldador and made it the economic and cultural center of Fovea demonstrates this is not a Man to be taken lightly.

"I believe, and Avek with me, that by empowering him

now, we shall let him reunite Fovea under his banner and, when he is gone, then we shall step back into our rightful place through his successors, and in fact be more powerful than ever we were before."

Aniquen slammed his hand down on the table before him. "We are Uman-Chi," he demanded. "We have the wisdom of centuries—"

"And not a moment of it will dull the point of a sword," D'gattis commented in his usual, dry tone.

This one is almost too intelligent to bear, Angron thought to himself. *He is to other Uman-Chi what we are to Men, and yet Men now can command Uman-Chi.*

"He is right," Chaheff said. "We shall cooperate and work with the Empire while it lasts, and we will be pushed, but only to a degree."

His steely gaze swept the group. "Only to a degree."

* * *

Melissa gripped Bill's upper arm as they walked to the Emperor's suite of rooms. She still wore her blue dress; he still wore his blue robe. They had been summoned; grim-faced Uman guards in the service of the King brought them to Lupus' chambers.

"What do you think he wants?" Melissa asked.

Bill shrugged. The guards made no secret of their exasperation at their slow pace, but he couldn't make his feet go faster. Every step took twice as long on his way to the blond man with the scowling face. "Probably to find out why we're here."

"We don't know that."

"Would you believe that, if you were him?"

Melissa stayed quiet for a moment.

"How do you think he learned Uman-Chi?" Melissa asked.

"Probably the same way he learned to make them so afraid of them," Bill commented.

She looked up at him. "You're in a bad mood."

Bill sighed, looked down at her, then focused on the backs of their two Uman guards. "I'm tired," he said. "It's late, I'm dying for a cig' and I just got traded to my countryman. If I met another American here, I'd have thought he'd try to help us out, not buy us."

"He might have done both," Melissa said.

Bill shook his head. "I saw them when he claimed us," he said. "I couldn't speak the words, but the body language looked pretty clear. And did you see the look on Glynn's face when she saw she was going? That was fear, Melissa. I *know* fear."

"Hey, I'm not sweating it. I have my own guardian protector," she said, and gave his arm a squeeze.

She looked up at him and saw the smile on his lips. He worried for her but he couldn't do a thing for her now. Not guard, not protect, just watch and wonder.

* * *

Finally, they stood at the door to the Emperor's suites. The Uman guard knocked once, and Uman Wolf Soldiers opened them. The five from Eldador shot a contemptuous look at the two Trenboni, nodded and waved the two from Earth in.

The suites had to be magnificent. Trenbon had provided a formal sitting room with rich tapestries and deep-pile rugs, couches and hand-carved chairs, as well as a circular table stacked with books. Cases of books and exquisite paintings lined the walls. Oil lamps hung from the ceiling and a window opened out onto the city with its flying bridges and bustling people.

To the left, an open double-door showed a massive canopied bed and more couches. To the right, another double door opened to a formal dining room with seating for twelve

The Emperor, Lupus, sat on a couch with his bare feet up on a coffee table, dressed in leather pants and a white cotton shirt. His wife, Shela, had changed into a black leather halter-top and short leather skirt, sitting at the table with the books, a pen in her teeth, giving them the side-view of her breasts and flat stomach.

She was beautiful, Melissa thought, and she knew it. She dressed to accentuate her features. Her belly said she had had babies, but Melissa didn't see them. She seemed too young for them to be too old.

The blue of Lupus' eyes seemed so distinct as to make them almost painful to look at. He wore his hair back and up, with no bangs. He had it tied up in a ponytail now, and it still went past his armpit. His shirt opened at his chest to expose a dusting of fine hair. He wore no jewelry other than a red ruby ring on his middle finger.

"Welcome," he said in English, not rising. "Take a seat on the couch, if you would."

"Thank you, your—um—Majesty?" Bill said, speaking for both of them.

He waved the attempt off. "Please," he said. "When we're alone, we're Americans. Americans don't call anyone 'Majesty'."

Bill smiled as they sat. "Lupus, then?"

"That's fine," he said. "I managed never to speak my name here, so I'm not going to start now."

"See dat you don't," Shela said, not looking up from her work. Her English had a strange accent, as if her language was more guttural. "And you two, do not say you name no more. You make up dey name for you, like effy-one elt."

Melissa looked from Shela to Lupus, seeing if they were kidding. "Really?"

"Oh, yeah," Lupus said. "Your name is power over you here. Death spells, summonings, location spells all require your real name."

"Spells," Bill said, skeptically.

"You are with the Uman-Chi for—what—eight weeks, and you haven't figured out yet that magic works here?" Lupus asked them, a skeptical look on his face and the scar on his face twitching.

"Oh, come on," Bill said.

"How do you think you got here?" Lupus asked.

Bill looked at Melissa, Melissa looked at Lupus.

"We thought it was, like, a black hole or something," she said.

He laughed. "A black hole would have ripped you apart," he said. "That girl, Glynn, who has been keeping after you, woke up with a song in her head, sang it and then poof—here you were."

"Back home we were in Titusville, Florida, and a guy with black and white hair pushed us into the fender of my car," Bill said. "My car was glowing, and we kind of fell into it."

"Magic," Lupus said, and leaned forward. "I need to ask you two some personal questions."

Bill answered for them, "We expected you would."

"What did you two do for a living?"

Bill and Melissa looked at each other, then at Lupus. "We worked together at a telesales agency," Bill said. Melissa just nodded, and added, "When they took us we were on our first date."

"Yeah?" Lupus smiled knowingly. Melissa risked a glance and saw that Shela watched them speculatively.

"Well, out for drinks with people after work," Bill said.

"It was a *date*," Melissa insisted. He just kept breaking her heart with that crap. Not enough that she slept with him, that she supported him, deferred to him? What more did he need?

"Easy there," Lupus said. "From what I'm told, you are an old married couple now, so no matter what it was, it seems to have worked out for you."

"Married?" Bill said.

"I guess she was dressed kinda skimpy when she arrived," Lupus said. "So they thought you were a—um—well, you were dressed kinda skimpy."

Melissa reddened. They'd mistaken her for a hooker. She did *not* dress like a hooker. That thought brought with it other memories that she didn't like to dredge up, and which had caused her a lot of pain in her earlier life.

"She was fashionable," Bill said, defensively.

"Dey Uman-Chi, dey tink you either a princess or a whore," Shela said. She stood, walked to her husband's side, and sat down at his feet, her head on his knee. He stroked her hair absently. "Me, when dey Lupus come, he take me as his slave girl. I wear less dan diss den. His Uman-Chi friend, dey look down dare noses."

Lupus chuckled. "And she whipped them up one side and down the other," he said. "One of the Uman-Chi you saw tonight, D'gattis—he has a yellow question-mark, turned upside-down on his robes—was there, and he made the mistake of challenging her."

"I teach him dey different between dey wizard and dey sorceress," Shela said.

"You are a sorceress?" Bill asked her, leaning forward.

Melissa found herself studying this woman. Shela really, totally loved Lupus. Melissa had never known a woman who would just sit at her man's feet like that, but she *had* thought of what it would be like to do it—to have a man who made her want it. Bill would freak if she tried anything like that. It would make him feel even more like a grandpa.

Lupus raised his eyebrows like he couldn't believe what he had just heard. Shela smiled, looked around the room, and pointed at a snifter, half full of some golden liquid.

The glass container flew from where it sat to in front of her. Four glasses appeared, the snifter filled them all, then dropped to the coffee table with a thud as the four glasses flew to the four of them.

"Uman-Chi brandy," Lupus said. "If it is less than four hundred years old, I think they use it to wash the dishes."

Melissa took the glass from mid air, and took a sip of the liquid. It tickled her tongue and burned it at the same time. It warmed her all the way to her belly and she shuddered.

Bill held his glass and looking at it like it had become a spider.

"Wow," she said.

Lupus nodded. "Good, isn't it?"

"Yeah," Melissa said.

Shela looked at Melissa and said, "You got bebe?"

"I'm sorry?" she asked.

"Are you pregnant?" Lupus asked her. "She is concerned about you drinking."

Melissa looked at Shela. "Um, no, but thank you."

"You sure?" she said. "I can tell you, if you want to know."

"You can?"

Shela closed her eyes, held a hand out toward Melissa, and hummed. Melissa felt a tickle go through her, like someone ran a feather down her spine.

"It you time, but you not pregnant," she said. "I think you

not want to get pregnant for a little while."

"So try and control yourself," Lupus said to Bill, who finally grinned and took a sip of the brandy. "They don't do a lot of telesales here, with the not having any phones and all. You might want to see what the future holds before you go adding people to it."

"What kind of society is this?" Bill asked him. Melissa felt thankful he steered the conversation away from her prospective motherhood.

She found herself oddly relieved to know she wasn't pregnant. She didn't have a regular cycle. No matter how she felt about Bill, the fact remained he had more than twenty years on her and he already had kids. He might not be looking for more. She would ease into that conversation very gently, and with no one else around.

Lupus took another sip and nodded. "Think of King Arthur, except Merlin is real, and there is more than one of him."

"You did okay for yourself, then" Bill said.

Lupus nodded. "I had a lot of help, mostly from Shela here."

"You not listen when he say dat," Shela warned them. "He very smart, does a lot of tings. He know dey erck-nomics, he know dey mil'tary. His Wolf Soldiers, the toughest killers dey is."

Bill smiled. "You brought them gun powder, didn't you," he said.

Lupus frowned, leaned forward, and said, "Do you know how to make gun powder?" His scar twitched again.

"I do," Melissa said. It wasn't rocket science.

Bill grinned. "I saw it on Star Trek," he said. "The episode—"

"With the Gorn," Lupus said, sat back and laughed. "Oh, that was the best show *ever*."

"You miss TV?" Bill asked him.

"I miss coffee," Lupus said. Still leaning back, he looked at them. "I drink strong tea here, it is *not* the same."

"No, I agree," Bill said. "We used to smoke. I don't suppose-"

Lupus shook his head. Melissa sighed.

Lupus leaned forward again. "You don't want to tell anyone here about gun powder," he told them.

That put Melissa right on her toes. The one octave drop in his voice, the slight narrowing of his eyes.

Not advice, a warning.

"You didn't develop it?" Bill asked.

Lupus shook his head.

"Why?" he asked. "Your armies would be—"

"What?" Lupus demanded, and his eyebrows dropped in anger. "Invincible? They already are."

"But with gunpowder…"

Lupus shook his head. "You think that if I had that, then I would roll over all resistance and sweep all before me," he said.

"Well—yeah."

"And who on Earth did that?" Lupus asked him, and Melissa clearly saw the anger now. Suddenly he seemed to be speaking to a stupid child who refused to admit that one and one made two.

"Well, Napolean—"

"Defeated."

"Okay, Hitler—"

"Defeated."

"England overran a good part of France—"

"France took it back."

"Okay—America," Bill said. "We kicked Indian ass from coast to coast."

"And what did the Indians do about that?" Lupus pressed him.

Bill thought for a moment, opened his mouth, closed it, then leaned back and took a sip of brandy and admitted, "They got guns."

"Exactly," Lupus said, and he leaned back again. "All of them, in the end, get guns. Why? Because when you base your military on superior technology, the first battle you lose, you lose the technology, too. The Chinese developed gunpowder—they didn't conquer the world with it. Kublai Khan had it, and he didn't conquer the world, because he gave the secret to people like Marco Polo. Then the Europeans all had it, then it was irrelevant.

"The conquerors, like Genghis Khan, Alexander, Julius Caesar, Attila—they didn't have gunpowder and, once conquerors did, they stopped being able to *be* conquerors."

"So, no gunpowder," Bill said.

Lupus looked skeptical, "You didn't already tell them?"

"Why would we?" Bill asked.

"No, we didn't," Melissa reassured him. Bill might have been missing this, but she didn't.

This man wanted to conquer. He knew it, and apparently the Uman-Chi did, too, and if she could judge people at all, she knew that the Uman-Chi had decided they couldn't stop him, so instead they tried to suck up to him by giving him…them.

Why?

"Why do you want us?" she blurted out. Even Bill looked shocked. Shela grinned this really scary grin, and Lupus smiled to himself and leaned back again.

"Why do you think?" Lupus asked. Not good.

"Well, she sang that song in English—but Angron speaks English, so they know what it says," she began.

"Dat song was in Andaron," Shela said.

"I heard it in English," Lupus said. "But I happen to know that they heard it in Uman-Chi, and the Uman and the Men among the Wolf Soldiers didn't hear it at all."

"No?" Bill asked.

Lupus shook his head.

"So…magic?"

"Yep," Lupus said. He just watched them now, his blue eyes hopping from one to the other, waiting to see what they said.

"Well," Melissa said. "The prophecy calls together six heroes and a champion to fight this 'One'. It sounds like they came too late."

"Okay," Lupus said. "And what does that tell you?"

"Well," she continued, "both of us are from outside."

"You dey one from outside," Shela said. "He dey guardian—he can't be dey one."

She didn't mention the champion was also a 'She.'

"Something will bring them together," Lupus said. "Do you have any feeling as to where they are?"

Melissa looked at Bill, who looked at her, then at Lupus. She shook her head.

"Maybe if I saw a map?" she said.

"So, Glynn doesn't spark anything in you?" Lupus said.

Melissa thought for a moment. "No, not at all."

Lupus turned to Shela, who looked at him.

"Well, they seem to think she's the noble, young and old," Lupus said.

She shrugged. It didn't make her feel anything. She thought about Glynn—she was Glynn, nothing more.

"Sorry," she said.

Shela said something to him in another language, he responded in it, then turned back to them.

"I am going to be honest with you," he said, "although I think you are smart people and you know what is going on already.

"It is pretty clear that I am the 'One who is of War,' and that the prophecy is a warning against me."

He regarded them both, leaned forward again, and took a sip of his brandy, then said, "The Uman-Chi have been called upon by the goddess Eveave to stop me, however, Eveave warns that they are already too late."

"Das tricky, doh," Shela said. "Eveave dey Taker and dey Giver. Eveave gwon give you tom'ting, she gwon take tom'ting. So, she tell you what gwon happen, she gwon take back you advantage."

"But not necessarily leave you behind," Lupus said. "I think we are, right now, neck-and-neck with the forces that will oppose us, when we move on the Fovean nations. And I think, as well, the Uman-Chi believe they can't win by opposing me, so they are picking our side."

"And you are taking us to make sure those forces don't oppose you?" Bill asked him.

Somehow, Melissa didn't think that would do it.

* * *

Shela watched them all, following the conversation in the difficult ang-lesh, which her *Yonega Waya* had taught her over the last few years.

She could see how he enjoyed them, speaking in their language, sharing perspective that only people of the same tribe felt.

The Yonega Waya, her White Wolf, came from a vast tribe. Now she knew he didn't come from the north, or even from this planet. Now she knew how he understood things differently.

He hadn't even confided this to her. That hurt, but she understood, too. Men had their secrets, just as women had theirs. It was part of the way of things.

This new comer had her more concerned. Yonega Waya never wanted more than one wife, but this girl could be her sister. She had a young, strong body, not changed by childbirth. If any had a chance to be a concubine, it would be her.

When Shela felt sure this girl had no power to detect the other members of the prophecy, she offered to bring them out to the stables and do away with them. Lupus had forbidden her. They had agreed that any threat to him must be extinguished, but he felt certain, as well, that they needed more time to know what that threat may be.

She couldn't help but believe he simply felt lonely for them. He shouldn't be. He had a new life now. Anyone would be fulfilled by it. He had three strong children. It should be enough for him.

She should be enough for him.

Shela had indulged these feelings before. In leaving her life as his slave girl and becoming his Empress, she'd forced him to push the way people thought here, not just in one country but in three. Rather than let him take a wife and she herself become a concubine, she'd almost touched off a war that would have shaken Fovea.

She doubted her own jealousy. She knew what she was capable of to protect and to keep her man. What she hadn't expected is what she'd turn that man into to please her.

Yonega Waya had killed thousands for her. He'd risked everything he'd accomplished, he'd even jeopardized their children, born and unborn, to please her.

"You are wondering if we are your enemies," Bill said.

The question roused Shela from her musings and she considered him.

He was old, Shela thought. He should be a gaffer with grandchildren at his feet, learning from him. Avek had told them he'd seen fifty summers—and yet he moved easily and had all of his teeth. This spoke well for Yonega Waya, much older than she. She felt reassured she would enjoy him for a long time.

"Frankly, it appears you are, no matter what I wonder," White Wolf said. "I don't hold it against you; I know what it is to be wrapped up in a god's plans."

"You do?" Bill asked him.

"Somewhat," Yonega Waya said, waving off the question. "It doesn't make you a bad person, and it doesn't mean I necessarily have to fear you. Do you know why they bring in people from another world, yet?"

"No," Bill said.

"Think about it," Yonega Waya said, cryptically. "But, if you stay close and stay good, and help me, we can defeat this thing. It doesn't say you will actually beat me, you know. It says you will find people who will be weapons. I would like to find a way to keep you, like the Uman-Chi, on my side. The longer you are here, the more advantages you will see that we have over these people."

The two of them nodded. What choice did they have?

As she had done repeatedly throughout the evening, she released her energy into the air around her, and sensed the presences of the Uman-Chi wizards. They occupied the rooms below her, outside in the courtyard, and surrounding their King, of course. Glynn's special presence could be felt in the next suite of rooms. That one she could touch without thinking.

She raised her head, and her man immediately became attentive to her. His hand went from her hair to her shoulder; she gripped his shin and focused. Shela knew of many who criticized her husband for the way he treated her but his arms held her all night long, and she knew the rhythm of his heartbeat better than she knew her own name.

The second she alerted, he knew it, his connection to her working faster than words or thoughts. His scar wrinkled on his beautiful face, his blue eyes told her that he would do anything to protect her. She knew there were soul mates, and she'd found hers.

Now someone watched them—someone close. She only had to think of it, and he knew.

* * *

Xinto of the Woods had a reputation for a lot of things, not all of them nice. This included acting as an ambassador between rival nations. He had a skill for ending wars and finding common ground. Since the Daff Kanaar had become a presence in Fovea, he'd found this a very lucrative trade to be in.

He also acted as a spy, for sale to the highest bidder. That bid right now came from Conflu.

Conflu had an emperor, just like Eldador. Trenbon had summoned one emperor to see something it had found. The other emperor wanted to know what—especially considering what usually went on between two emperors.

He had listened to Glynn Escaroth's song, nonsense as it might seem. Now, from a chink in the stone wall within the palace of Outpost IX, crouched in one of the many air ducts that ran through the building, Xinto listened to the blatherings of Men in a language he didn't know, which seemed strange because he understood them all.

He had understood clearly when Shela had offered to kill them both, but that had been spoken in Andaron, and either these other two Men didn't understand that, or they had nerves of steel.

When the conversation suddenly stopped and Xinto felt a tingle in his gray beard, he knew the Empress had figured out that he watched her, and the time had come to go.

He had enough to report. He started to scoot backwards through the air duct, to a linen closet where a different passage would take him to the exterior wall.

Or would have, had not Karel of Stone stood in that closet waiting for him, with a self-satisfied grin on his face.

Xinto was a Scitai—Scitai are the smallest of the races, few being over three feet tall. Scitai were born in two places. Most came from Trenbon or, more specifically, the Silent Isle.

Xinto didn't hail from that part like Karel of Stone.

"My lord ambassador," Karel said, his sword in his hand and the silver hook symbol prominent on his bearskin outer-garment.

Xinto had a dagger out in a second. The flat of Karel's sword smacked the heel of Xinto's hand and disarmed him, leaving his right arm numb from the elbow to the fingertips.

"Do that again and I will take that hand," Karel warned him. "I don't feel any allegiance to you."

Where Xinto's features looked swarthy, with a gray beard and brown hair, a cloak full of pockets and a cap with a rakish orange feather always on his head, Karel appeared as the opposite. Dressed in bear skins, impossible blue eyes much like the Emperor's, brown hair and clean-shaven with milky skin.

"Cut off my hand," Xinto said. "Compared to what the Bitch of Eldador will do to me, it would be a blessing."

Karel grinned a wicked grin. The Bounty Hunter's Guild had labeled Shela Mordetur as 'the Bitch of Eldador' when she had killed one of theirs in the Eldadorian court in defense of her mate.

Xinto had given them the reason to want him dead, and he felt quite sure the Emperor knew it.

"You're an ambassador," Karel said, indicating the door. "Talk your way out of it."

He sighed and opened the door. He could reach the knob—not always true in this world of giants. In a fair fight, he didn't think he could defeat Karel of Stone, who made his living by his sword, so he resolved not to fight fair.

"Don't think that I won't," he said, as the door swung open.

And there he stood, tall as a mountain, angry as a storm, in his bare feet and leggings, as blond and stupid as when Xinto had met him on the streets of Outpost IX.

"Xinto of the Woods," he growled in Scitai.

"Your Imperial Majesty," Xinto said, shocked. Had Shela turned the whole house out?

The fist felt like an anvil as it took him in the side of his head.

* * *

They were comical little men, Melissa thought.

One had that upside-down question mark symbol on his chest, in silver. He called himself 'Karel.' He took her hand and kissed it, and told her in Uman she was a pretty picture to see.

They called the other Xinto. He looked smaller than Karel, and wore a lumpy gray cloak that they took from him. They tied him to a chair with some twine Karel had.

For her benefit, they spoke Uman. She interpreted for Bill as best she could. It seemed to her that Xinto had betrayed Lupus somehow. Now Shela had caught him spying on them.

Lupus seemed upset about it, but Shela acted just spitting mad. Lupus, to Melissa's surprise, turned Shela around and gave her bottom a good, hard smack when she kept going near the bound and unconscious Xinto. That actually quieted her down, and she sat on the corner of the coffee table and glared at the little man.

Bill just watched everything. She saw him mouthing words, so he must be trying to pick up the language.

Melissa sat down next to Shela and put a hand on her thigh.

"Does he hit you often?" she asked Shela in English.

"He hit one time," Shela said. "He haf strong hand."

"No," Melissa said. "Does he usually hit you?"

Shela gave her a funny look, then she seemed to get it.

"He hit me when a wife need to be hit," she said.

Melissa bristled. "You allow this?"

She shrugged. "I his woman," she said. "He tell me no talk, I talk, he hit. Is what a good husband do."

Yikes! Melissa took a sip of brandy just to quiet herself.

Oh, God—they hit their wives?

It dawned on her—she'd found herself in a feudal society. Women had been voting in America for less than 100 years.

Who did you call to report the Emperor, especially when you didn't have phones?

"He not hit you?"

That roused her. "Bill?" she asked. "Bill not hit me, no."

She nodded. "He old," she said.

"No," Melissa was almost offended by it. "He's not old, he loves me." She felt glad she had learned the word.

"What he do when you a bad wife?" Shela asked, and seemed to be uniquely interested in the answer.

Melissa shook her head. "I don't know," she said, "but not hit. Yell, talk, not hit."

Shela shook her head. "He learn," she said. "Young wife, lot of trouble. Need to know who husband is."

So she *believed* a wife needed to be hit, Melissa thought. On the other side of the room, Xinto seemed to be returning to consciousness. Shela stood, and waited. Finally Lupus turned to her and beckoned. She went right to his side, her hand on the small of his back.

He hit her, and she loved him for it, Melissa thought. What made it worse, he hit her in front of other people, and she expected it.

Where the hell did she find herself?

Chapter Ten:

A Key to a Kingdom

Xinto woke up to pain in his wrists, his head, his ankles, his arms and his back.

And his neck—oooh, his neck! This didn't seem fair—he didn't even know where he had woken up!

Yes, he did—he'd been in the royal palace of Outpost IX, spying on Rancor Mordetur, and he'd been caught.

He raised his head, and there he stood—the Conqueror himself.

He didn't look happy, but Shela looked uniquely angry, sitting on the corner of a caw-fee table with a girl who could be her twin.

Lupus stood in front of him with his arms crossed over his chest. Next to him stood that old giant the Uman-Chi had pulled out of oblivion, the thief Karel of Stone, and an Uman-Chi he had met in court named Glynn Escaroth.

"My lady," he said to Shela directly.

"Speak to my husband, you scum," she hissed at him. He hadn't seen hatred like that in his life before, and he had seen a lot. "If he lets me, I will dip you in honey and bury you in an ant hill. I will use my power to keep you alive until the youngest Uman-Chi are old."

Xinto raised an eyebrow and looked to the Conqueror. "I think it best I speak to you, your Imperial Majesty."

"I think it best you take this a lot more seriously than you are," Lupus said. He spoke in Uman, probably so these newcomers could understand him. That struck him odd, seeing as they were Men. However, when he had spoken to Xinto before, it had been in Trenboni Scitai.

"You have a blood debt to this one, *Yonega Waya*," Shela said in Uman, mixing in the Andaron for 'White Wolf.' "He confessed you to the Bounty Hunters. It took years before they gave up on trying to kill us. They even attempted to kill Lee."

"No attempt was ever made on the Princess," Xinto argued. Out of the blue, the Emperor backhanded him.

He tasted the salt taste of blood in his mouth. "Liar," Lupus hissed. "I bought you dinners, Xinto. I called you friend."

"You invoked the Guild," Xinto demanded, angry despite himself, his lip already swelling.

"I didn't know any better," he said. "I'd only just come here."

"And if we had done nothing?" Xinto asked. "Would you have kept doing it? Would you have continued to call yourself 'Bounty Hunter?'

"I *did* continue to call myself 'Bounty Hunter,'" Lupus said, and smacked him again.

There he told the truth, sadly enough, and the Bounty Hunter's Guild that killed kings and nobles and powerful merchants, peasants and holy men, had failed uncounted times to pay him back for it. In his home, in the Eldadorian throne room, in other cities, at his inauguration, on the sea, through his food—nothing worked. He detected poisons, killed assassins, turned out operatives and tortured them. Finally, the Emperor had sent a message:

"Come up with a solution you can live with, or I'll come up with one that kills all of you."

A threat like that would normally have been laughed off by the Guild, but this came from the Man who'd sacked Outpost IX. They reached a compromise. Lupus could be admitted to the Guild and his crimes would be made moot. You can call yourself a member if you are one.

"As a fellow member of my Guild, then," Xinto said, blood flowing in a trickle from his lip to his beard, "I call on Guild Sanctuary."

"The Guild does not spy on the Guild," Lupus said, surprising him. He hadn't thought the Emperor would bother to read the Guild Charter.

He should have known better.

"Then I call for a trial of three Masters," Xinto demanded. He had this right. They would kill him for spying on a member of the Guild, but more mercifully than Shela would have done, if allowed.

"I will turn you over to the local authority instead," Lupus said, grinning fiercely. "I am sure Angron will be impressed with having you."

The Uman-Chi would never invoke the wrath of the Guild from the precarious spot they currently found themselves in. Lupus would know that—he bluffed to see if Xinto had any fear of them.

He would turn the tables and see how much the Emperor trusted these new allies.

"What makes you think he doesn't know I'm here?"

Lupus turned on Glynn with an unpleasant expression. The Emperor acted as a force of nature - get him going in the right direction and he leveled everything in his way.

"I don't pretend to know the King's mind," Glynn said. "However I see no reason to bring you here, give you these advantages, and then betray you."

"Unless he wanted to know if it worked," Lupus countered.

"How else would I know of her song?" Xinto pressed him.

"What?" Glynn demanded.

Lupus and Glynn looked at each other, then at Xinto.

"Did you hear her sing tonight?" Lupus demanded.

"What of it?"

"Did you?"

He opened his mouth to sing a few words of it, but couldn't. It felt as if his throat closed.

"He heard it," Glynn said to Lupus, in Uman-Chi.

"He can't sing it—only you can, but he's trying," Lupus said.

The giant asked Lupus a question in their language, and the Emperor answered it. His female stood and approached them, bent over and looked in his face, her pendulous breasts hanging sweetly under the neckline of her blue dress.

She looked back to Lupus and Glynn, and said in Uman, "I do not know him."

"It seems you do not need to," Lupus said.

Glynn looked skeptical. "Which would he be?"

"We should kill him," Shela insisted, in Andaron.

"No," Lupus said. "We'll keep him. Let's see if more are drawn to us. It would be nice if they all just turned up together."

He looked at Xinto. Lupus didn't have his sword, he wasn't wearing his armor, but he looked no less threatening for it.

"Consider yourself a prisoner of the Eldadorian Empire," Lupus said to him, and he didn't make any effort to hide how glad he was to say it.

"I don't mind waiting to dispatch this one."

* * *

The Eldadorian Empire took Xinto of the Woods into custody, meaning they took him in chains to the hold of *The Bitch of Eldador* and locked him in a cage barely large enough for him to turn around. Bill and Melissa returned to their rooms and Glynn to hers. It was impossible to miss the contempt the Uman-Chi caster regarded her charges with, and in fact Shela tended to notice things like that.

She could like that girl, she thought. If this dark-haired, younger woman kept her focus on this older man, then she could be a good friend.

Friends were rare for the Empress of Eldador. She herself had been the confidant of the previous Queen of Eldador - Alekanna. That sweet woman had cherished their time because Shela sought nothing from her.

She'd died horribly and it had destroyed Glennen, the former King. Her Yonega Waya had sacked Outpost IX in retaliation.

Shela missed that friendship. Now it was she whose favor others curried, to whom they listened with glazed-over eyes, waiting for the proper moment to ask for something, to suggest something, to do whatever it was they wanted to do to further their position.

The next morning, sitting in the captain's cabin of *The Bitch of Eldador* on a swaying deck while the three Sea Wolves pushed south, Shela listened to her husband and these outsiders, and thought these thoughts and wondered at the prophecy she'd heard.

They will fall, who walk with her
They will fall, who oppose her
They will fall, for the power
Of the goddess, who chose her."

One thing was certain in Shela Mordetur's mind: whether they walked with this champion or opposed her, no matter what it took, they would *not* fall.

* * *

"Have you ever heard of Greek or Byzantine Fire?" Lupus asked them.

They sat in the captain's cabin of the *Bitch of Eldador*, the flagship of the Eldadorian fleet. The deck swayed beneath them. It bothered Bill, but Melissa loved it.

"No," Bill said, and suppressed a burp.

"Yes," Melissa said. "It was a chemical that burned in air, lighter than water, and was used by the Byzantines to keep their remnants of the Roman Empire alive. Even now, no one knows how they made it. Some say only Constantine and his descendants knew."

Lupus grinned. He was still in his leather pants and white shirt, but now he dressed in leather boots as well, with a chain over the instep like a biker, and kept a sword over his left shoulder.

Melissa and Bill sat with Glynn. She'd traded in her white

robes for a grey travel dress and bound her green hair back. Xinto in a brown travel cloak and Karel, in his bearskins were seated on short stools opposite the room's one door, under a sealed, circular window less than a foot across. The ship was a three-master with square sales, and it plowed the waves southeast, from Trenbon to what they called 'Galnesh' Eldador, meaning 'the Port of Eldador.' The sailors seemed to be all grim-faced Wolf Soldiers. A huge funnel ran from the ship's stern to its bow, where it described an arc ten feet ahead of the ship.

"It wasn't hard to figure out," Lupus said. "Once you think about it."

"It has baffled every scientist for centuries," Melissa argued.

"Did it?" Lupus asked. "Or did they realize how simple it was, and keep their mouths shut? It burns hot enough to warp steel, you know. In the modern Navy, you still wouldn't want to be hit by Eldadorian Fire."

"Eldadorian Fire?" Bill asked.

"The same thing," Lupus said. "Spray it on the water and you better not run your ship through it. Spray it on your ship, and all you can do is jump off. It spreads faster if you throw water on it."

"Because it is lighter than water," Melissa said.

"Exactly," Lupus said.

"And this technology?" Bill said. "If your enemies have it?"

Lupus grinned. "Right you are," he said. "But it isn't good enough to have Eldadorian Fire. If you open the vats to study it, they have this irritating tendency to start burning."

"Ah," Melissa said. "White phosphorous is one of the ingredients."

"You're a chemist?" Lupus asked her, leaning forward.

"Two years—University of Maine," she said. "Got A's, though."

Lupus frowned appreciatively and nodded. "You know I interrogated someone with Nitrous Oxide once?"

"You made Nitrous?" she admitted being intrigued.

He grinned a very satisfied grin and informed her of his

brilliance.

He's vain, Melissa knew of him. He felt very pleased with himself that he could get away with the things he did. His constant warnings and sudden, serious inquiries into their knowledge told her he was also terrified of someone coming to take it away from him. He hadn't impressed the locals with his skills and rose to lead them, he'd taken out anyone in his way. After talking to him for two days and listening to his stories, she knew that he didn't care what he had to do or whom he had to hurt to get what he wanted. In every one of his stories he boasted about how he screwed someone whom he felt deserved it.

He used the tactics of military geniuses and passed them off as his own. He used Economics 101 to run his whole nation and then entrepreneurs made him fantastically wealthy, because he let them.

The trip to Galnesh Eldador took only three days, and by that third day, she hated him.

On that third day Glynn came to their door and summoned them from the relative warmth of the cabin to the weather deck. Melissa and Lupus wrapped themselves in furs left by the cabin's tiny stove while Bill sat on a stool too small for him and held his stomach.

The decks had become icy and slippery in an early spring freeze. Men and Uman scrambled across it in bare feet, just the sight of them made Melissa's own soles ache. She clutched her furs closer and stepped out upon the swaying deck behind Lupus.

"We are here already?" Glynn seemed amazed. They found her on the forecastle, the sea spray on their faces. The wind blew cold above decks from a frigid north wind. Ice clung to the bowlines, and fell like little missiles from the snapping sails. Every swell showed her how close the cold sea came to them as the ship tilted.

"Sea Wolves are much faster than your Tech Ships," he informed her. "Sleeker hulls, more canvas to the wind."

She nodded and looked out past the rigging to the land.

"That is the Eldadorian Peninsula," she said.

He smiled and looked at her.

"My lands?" she asked him.

He nodded.

She wrinkled her nose. “Barren rock, the land fouled by the sea,” she said. “No farming, perhaps a tower for my studies.”

“What ever you desire, and can get your subjects to build for you,” Lupus told her.

They spoke in Uman, Melissa getting most of the words now. The syntax proved difficult—you had to totally change a word sometimes when you spoke of the future or of the past, but it didn’t seem that bad. Xinto had started her on Scitai as well. She could say simple greetings, thank-you’s and ask “Where is the handsome man with the beard?” which he assured her would get her to him, wherever she might go.

“I already have a handsome man with a beard,” she had informed him.

When Bill could stop barfing he buddied up to this Emperor. Probably a good idea, because the looks she got from Glynn said she worried about her own affairs now and not theirs. As prisoners of the new guy, they ate and slept as well as they had with the old guy, but one day there would come a time when he said, “Thanks for all your help,” and it would be a lot better to have a barony somewhere than to be out on the street or worse.

Melissa herself had cozied up to Shela. They seemed close in age, in look, and they both found themselves the women of Earth men, so they shared some common ground.

She stood on the forecastle as well, wrapped in shaggy furs of her own. Melissa’s lower lip trembled and, when Shela saw it, she let hers tremble too, and they laughed at each other.

“Oh, I hate the sea,” Shela confessed to her in Uman. They always tried to improve her understanding of it.

“I like sea,” Melissa said. “Hate spray. Hard to get out hair.”

Shela looked to her hair and nodded. Then she looked at her husband. “He likes the cold, likes to be in the cold.”

“He is from the cold place,” Melissa said.

“Yes?”

Lupus hadn’t shared his past with Shela, so she decided to use this to increase her own value. “His home is called ‘Connecticut.’”

"Conn ecky cut," Shela said.

"Very good," Melissa smiled. "In the winter, very cold. Kill you outside at night."

"So he lived in a house?" she asked. Melissa nodded.

"Andoron is warm. We sleep outside most nights," Shela told her. "Our first time—he took me on the plains, on the ground, under a sky full of stars."

"Ooooo," Melissa said, appreciatively.

"I wanted so much to give him a son from that," she said. "I was his slave, but his sons would have been born free. You should see how he loves his children."

"How many?"

She smiled—a mother's smile. Melissa knew it, having seen it herself. "Three. Lee, the oldest. A Sorceress, like me. Then a son—we call him Vulpe. His sister will help him choose a man's name when it's time. And then my youngest—my heart yearns for her now. She has an Andaron name—Chawnaluh Nanahee Nudageehay. In the language of Men, that means, "Angry at the Sun."

"Angry at the Sun?"

"She sees it, and she screams," Shela shook her head. "We worried that she was sick somehow—so many babies die. But she is well, and simply doesn't like the light."

"I have sister, no brothers," Melissa said.

Shela looked at her. "Your mother died?"

Melissa was stunned. "How you know?"

"What man stops before he has a son?"

Melissa shook her head. She wanted to argue, but it didn't seem worth it. She hadn't come here to bring feminism to the masses, much less the nobility.

"Your man, he hasn't—" and then some word she didn't know.

She squinted at Shela. Shela made a gesture with her hands.

Sex.

"Too many people to hear," she said.

"Not what Glynn says," Shela said.

"What?"

"She said you were even caught by your guards."

Melissa blushed crimson as she recalled that night.

"She told you that?"

"You embarrassed her very much," Shela said. "I think Uman-Chi put pants on the stallions. But she was supposed to—" some word "—and then you did that."

"Supposed to what?"

She thought for a moment. "Like a mother with her babies."

"Ah."

"My babies never did that!" Shela had a good laugh.

Melissa felt mortified. Glynn walked by her, then the Emperor. Lupus gave her a perfunctory smile, Glynn walked past as if she didn't see her standing there.

Melissa called her a bitch under her breath, and moved to follow, but Shela made it clear she wanted to stay. Melissa pulled her furs closer around her, and kept looking off the side of the ship.

"I want you to tell me something, and be honest," Shela said. "If you lie, I will know."

Melissa nodded.

Shela didn't look at her, but said, "Are you happy with your man, or are you going to leave him for another?"

She felt stunned. Leave Bill? What the hell?

"I think I love him, Shela," she said. "I think I really do."

"That's good," Shela looked at her, and caught the tears on her face. She stroked one away and looked into her eyes.

"I see he doesn't—" and a word she didn't know.

"What?"

She sighed. "Hold you, kiss you, stroke your hair."

"I usually begin it," she said. "Everything."

She nodded. "I think that is these men from Conn ecky cut. Lupus is no different."

"No?"

She sighed. "He traded for me," she said. "He has a stallion that is very rare. So, my tribe, my father, bred it to a mare, for me."

Melissa's eyes widened. "So you were traded for, um—"

she didn't know the word, so she made the motion.

"Yes," Shela wouldn't look at her now. "And we had to trick him to do that. He didn't want me."

"You so pretty though," Melissa said. "You love so much."

Shela turned her face out to the bay. "You know, that doesn't matter to a man," she said. "You think it does, but then you think of all the girls, very pretty, very—" some word, but she was sure it meant loving.

"And they all tell a story of a broken heart," she finished.

Melissa thought about that. "Mine was Mike."

"He broke your heart?"

"Oh, so much, Shela," she said. "And left me with nothing. I met his mom, I gave him my—um—first time."

"No!"

Melissa nodded. "He promised stay with me."

She didn't say marriage, because she didn't know the word, but she got through it with some help from Shela.

"Someone did that to me, my father would tie him to five horses," Shela said.

"Five?"

Shela looked at her, and she got it.

"First Lupus didn't want me," she said. "Then he get the sex, and I know, I am just the sex for him."

"Oh," Melissa said.

Shela shrugged. "I was a slave," she said. "A slave is for sex. Have to be stupid, not to know that."

"Okay."

"But then, one day, a very cold day, we came to Eldador the Port, and went to the stables, very late at night."

She was looking off into space now, her face so serene. Melissa had no doubt this was some pivotal point in her life.

"We are "—some word—"the horses, and I remember I was brushing my horse's back, and Yonega Waya said to me, 'Look, I am so dirty!'

"Yonega Waya?" she asked.

Shela smiled. "His Andaron name—it means 'White Wolf.'

"And I say, 'Look—that is a horse, and you are—" the word again.

Melissa repeated the word. It turned out to be putting the horse up, brushing it down, making sure it was dry.

"Anyway," Shela said, and she threw an angry glance at Melissa for interrupting, "I say this, and he tells me I am dirty and must have a bath, and I say, 'No,' and that is disrespectful even for a wife, so for a slave—whew!—that was bad, and I was thinking, 'What is he going to do?'"

"What did he do?"

"Smack," she said, and clapped her hands together. "Right in the mouth, told me not to disrespect him."

"Wow," Melissa said.

"Turned me around," she said. "And then you know, he threatened to do it again, and then he washed me, right there, like you wash a dog with fleas."

"In the stable in the cold?"

Shela nodded, and her eyes glowed from the memory of it.

"Were there people there?"

"One boy, who set it up with him," she said.

"Set it up?"

Shela nodded. "This was all a plan to give me my first dress ever," she said, and she sighed. "So beautiful, that red dress. I have it—it is old, I don't care. I put that dress on; I am just his slave girl again."

"So, the dress—"

Shela shook her head, stroked Melissa's cheek, looked at her. "Oh, it's not the dress," she said. "He messed that up. He spent all this money, all this time, gets the dress, forgets the shoes. Thinks I am going to wear boots with a dress like that."

Melissa still felt pretty shocked at all of this, but she couldn't help but giggle. So typical of a man to forget the shoes.

"He put me right in my place that night," Shela said. "I never forgot that, not ever. When you are a slave, your Master can sell you, he can beat you, he can kill you if he wants to. You are nothing.

"Your man," she said, and her voice was breathless, "he goes out of his way to plan something like that, takes the time to learn your ways, put you in your place. You know you *have* a place, with him, in his heart. He thought I died once, you know what he did?"

Melissa shook her head.

"He charged his stallion alone into a Conflu army," she said. She said some word, then "warriors."

"How many?"

She sighed and she held up her fingers, and said some word that she didn't know.

Melissa shook her head. "In English?" she said.

Shela thought for a moment, then said, "You know, ten?"

"Yes."

"And ten ten is hundred?"

"Yes."

"Ten, ten, ten, ten men."

"Ten thousand?" Melissa gasped in English. "He charged ten *thousand* men?"

"He charged them," she continued in English, "he go through them, he come out dey udder side, and find me, and he cry."

"No!"

"Two weeks, he not leave me," she said, still in English. "I sleeping, he not care. Anudder army coming, he not care. I wake up, he dey first thing I see, and den he cry for me again."

"Wow."

"Battle of Tamaran Glen," she said. "No one not know dat story."

"Really?"

"Uh, huh," she said. "Very important battle. I pregnant with Lee."

"You were pregnant?"

Shela nodded. "When he get his hands on me, when I all better, whoo! He took a belt to me!"

"While pregnant?"

"Not hit dey stomach, hit dey butt, dey legs. Hurt so bad, I back in bed two days."

Feminist bile rose in Melissa's throat. What kind of man was this? He'd throw himself into an impossible battle to die at her side and then, surviving it, he beats her.

"So, he hits you, and that's love for you," she said, slowly, looking for the Empress' reaction.

"Oh, don't be stupid," Shela said, with a wave of her hand. "You sound like Uman-Chi now."

"No, I just don't get it," Melissa said. "And I want to, Shela. I want to understand."

She turned and faced Melissa directly, looked right into her eyes. "He loves me," she said, still in English. "He know he does, I know he does. You know, that not good enough. Keep a flower in a chest, flower dies, yes?"

"Yes," Melissa said. That she got.

"We in the stable, he try to show me that he know me, he know my ways, he know what I like, to give gift to me, express it," Shela said.

"Yes," Melissa said. "I see that."

"I smart mouth, he hit me, he tell me I have to be good slave. He show I can't push him, can't disobey him," she said. "He show, he strong. Strong for *me*. He not strong because he hit, he hit because he strong, good man. He know I Andaron woman. Andaron men, love dey horse, beat dey wife, yes?"

"What?"

She sighed, Melissa sighed. They didn't share enough common language to get this.

"You man, he tell you what to do?"

"Yes," she said. She took her lead from Bill. It didn't make her a slave, if that was what she was getting at.

"You talk back, smart mouth?" Shela asked her.

"No," she said. "He loves me, respects me, Bill is—"

Bam! She got it.

She looked into Shela's eyes.

"It is the thought that counts," she said. "It isn't the beating, it is that you can make him so mad, he hits you, not because he hates you, but because he couldn't stand it if you did the things that would ruin what you have."

"Yes!" Shela said, smiling and exciting.

"Because if he didn't love you, he wouldn't care what you did," Melissa said.

Melissa chewed on that, then looked at Shela.

"We chase that around," she said. "And how many of us even know it?"

"It funny what people don't know," Shela said.

"Well, what people don't think," Melissa said. "You can lead them to it, but they have to get over the threshold on their own."

"What you mean?" Shela asked her.

"You know," Melissa said. She shivered. The furs didn't keep her warm any more. "You hear the words, you see it, but you can still not get it. You have to work it out for yourself. You have to think it.

"The most powerful thing that there is, is a thought."

Shela's eyes widened, and she took Melissa by the shoulders. She looked her in the eyes, then she gave her a hug.

"I *knew* it!" Shela told her.

Chapter Eleven:

Glorious Rome

On the 6th day of the month of Weather, *The Bitch of Eldador* pulled quietly and safely back into Galnesh Eldador.

Glynn stood at the bow, wrapped in animal furs. The cold stung the end of her nose and the salty spray tugged at her green hair, pulling it back from her shoulders. The pain of exposure to the cold air made her eyes tear, but her training made her no stranger to pain.

They'd made her the baroness of a strip of rock, over hopeless peasants, in a land of inferiors that her nation hated. A far fall for the most promising enchantress in the history of the Uman-Chi, and a high price to sing one song.

The indignity almost exceeded suffering. Did it not play so readily into her hands, she might find it impossible to abide.

She sighed, her breath a cloud that blew past her. She had endured the pathetic ramblings of the Conqueror with all of the dignity and self-discipline that befit her people. She had listened to him pontificate on irrelevant stories of his conquests and the glory of Eldador. Behind it all, the thin veil of a threat: the knowledge that he would dispatch her if time proved her song could not be undone. She would be kept within reach until he decided whether or not she must die.

She would not be done in so easily! She was Uman-Chi. She was superior.

The smell of the docks came familiar to her. Slops and rot and things discarded into the waves, the pollution she associated with the race of Men. At least it seemed not so overpowering here as in a Volkhydran city. The Emperor saw the importance of discouraging the rats that made a filthy wharf their home. Still, by her own standards, the long wharves of Eldador ranked barely above a pigsty.

Her former charges, Melsa and Bill, approached her from behind. She ignored them, watching as barefooted sailors scurried across the decks, hurling lines to their counterparts on the docks, reefing sails and polling the gigantic *Bitch* into her mooring, outmost from the rest of the fleet, readiest to make way.

The tremendous leap in logic that had taken the Emperor from lateen rigged ships of half the size to these hulking, menacing battleships, sporting square sails and copper sides, spouting flame and carrying three times the cargo at half again the speed of Trenboni Tech Ships, stunned her. Fourteen years had passed since the day when the Eldadorian fleet had engaged the Trenboni at the Battle of the Deceptions, a fight for control of the Straights that separated Tren Bay from the ocean beyond. Even had Eldadorian Fire not devoured a third of the Trenboni ships present in the first minutes of the battle, Angron's best admirals admitted they would have lost. Eldadorian ships ran faster, meaner, better armed and stayed more resilient. They reduced the Trenboni to tinder in the waves.

This very ship had been there. The *Bitch* could be considered a blooded veteran.

"We go to Eldador now?" Melsa asked her in broken Uman.

She regarded the female down the length of her nose. What a painfully limited capacity to reason.

"Yes," she said, and smiled to reassure her. "Lupus will take care of you, I'm sure. He won't hurt you if you do what he says."

"You believe that?" Melsa asked her, looking into her eyes.

Of course I don't believe it, any more than you do, Glynn felt like saying. She just smiled and turned away, watching the sailors.

She had her own uses for these Men, after all.

* * *

Melissa turned back from Glynn to Bill and shrugged.

"She says we'll be fine," she said.

Bill grinned a wry grin. "Kind of hard to believe," he said.

Melissa nodded, and turned back to the port herself, pressing her body next to his, feeling his arm come around her shoulder.

She saw a tremendous city. Long, wooden docks pushed out into the Bay. They led into a market place of some kind, Men and Uman and even some Scitai like Xinto and Karel running between the ships to stalls, and from the stalls to the city gates, more than one hundred feet tall and imposing, framed by two towers in the city wall, half again as high.

Eldador sat on a plain framed by rolling hills. On one of these, facing out to the sea, she made out a monument of some kind, too far away to see clearly. The palace seemed to be central to the city. Its walls rose higher, probably because it had been built on one of those hills, although she couldn't tell for sure. Pennons snapped from her towers in the cold air. Shela had explained to her earlier that they were mostly decorative—not like in Trenbon where they marked the noble houses that were responsible for those parts of the city.

The smell coming off the place was bad, but she had been to Philadelphia and it smelled worse. She didn't know a lot about sailing but she had lived in Portland and been down to the Long Wharf. You couldn't escape some odors.

When the sailors made the ship fast to its mooring, Lupus and his wife climbed up on deck and watched their Wolf Soldier guard assemble smartly to escort them from here. A crowd of about twenty already waited for them on the wooden dock.

"You will come with us," Lupus informed the three of them in Uman, "and live in the palace with me. There is a lot to discuss."

He sounded stilted—trying to use words he knew they knew. Already she found herself thinking in Uman. Bill had picked up the language as well. They practiced with Xinto and Shela and occasionally with Wolf Soldiers when they could find one who felt like talking.

That rarely happened. They acted dour and mean. Their eyes stayed flat when they spoke and they looked at nothing, as if they considered some great injustice as they spoke. She'd been surprised to find out that they included men and women—with no differentiation between the sexes. She thought of Lupus as a sexist, and his being so cosmopolitan with his army surprised her.

She roused herself from day dreaming when Bill nudged her toward the ramp extending from the ship to the dock. Lupus and Shela and Glynn had already crossed it. She followed them, Bill behind her with a hand on her waist, being careful not to slip on its slick surface into the unforgiving water.

Below her, in the cold water, something swam quickly past. It moved like a snake, like a giant 'S' in the waves, but beneath them rather than on the surface. It looked up at her once with serpentine eyes, then it disappeared. There and not there in a moment.

"How do you like my *Bitch,*" Shela asked her in Uman, sidling up against her and smiling just as soon as she had achieved the relative safety of the dock.

"Your…?"

She laughed. "Yonega Waya named her after me, the flagship of the fleet."

She raised her eyebrows in surprise, part of her mind still focused on the thing she'd seen in the water. She couldn't help but look for him; courtiers talking rapidly in Uman and the language of Men surrounded Lupus. Bill stood uncomfortably on the outside of the group, Glynn next to him, ignoring them all.

"He calls you that?"

Shela shook her head. "No, when I saved him from the Bounty Hunter in Eldador, they called me 'The Bitch of Eldador,' they were so mad at me. Very soon that was my nickname. Lupus threw that back at them, showed them what it means to disrespect me."

Melissa nodded. The way Shela thought made sense to her now. People insulted her and, rather than take it to heart, she would have them face that insult in the form of the flagship of the fleet. She and Lupus told the world, "Call us what you will—we revel in it."

That seemed like both of them.

She followed the group down the wet wooden dock to the marketplace. First a squad of Wolf Soldiers, then Lupus and his courtiers, one of them a Wolf Soldier himself, then Bill, Glynn, herself and Shela, then Karel of Stone and Xinto with his hands tied behind his back, surrounded by Wolf Soldiers, then the rest of the Wolf Soldier guard, in order by their squads again, as she had seen them in the palace in Outpost IX.

"Where we go?" she asked Shela.

Shela's eyes almost glowed. She took in everything, the people, the smells, the sounds, the approaching city. She looked truly happy to be home, probably because she missed her babies, maybe for other reasons as well.

"My home, the palace," she said. "You will like it. I'm going to get you a good horse and take you for a ride, and show you the most powerful city in Fovea."

She nodded. She wondered if Shela also rode a side-saddle. It seemed to her an Empress would have to look a certain way, but Shela didn't seem the side-saddle kind.

"We walk now?" she asked.

Shela nodded. "Market is too close for the horses. It's easier to walk. And he likes to walk. 'Walk and talk,' he says, all the time."

Melissa just smiled.

The smell increased as she approached the city. Now she saw what looked like crude dumpsters overflowing with garbage, and all manner of things ending up in the waves. She looked to Shela, who suddenly started frowning.

"Meker," she said, and Melissa could hear the anger in her voice.

"M'lady," one of the Wolf Soldiers ran up from the ranks. He was an Uman, solid built, hair cut close to the scalp. He didn't bow, but he put his fist over his heart as she addressed him.

"The harbor master is letting the garbage overflow again," she said.

"I noticed that myself, m'lady," the Uman said. He was almost conversational with her. Melissa wondered if she knew him personally. After all, she knew his name.

"Take your squad to the harbor master's office, and let him know it is his last day," she said. "I think he has an assistant who has a year or two experience. Tell him this is his chance to impress me."

He lowered his head deferentially, then turned on his heel and called up his squad. They stepped to the side of the Imperial procession and marched double-time down the docks.

Lupus saw them and turned around.

"Something?" he asked in Uman.

"Firing the harbor master," she answered.

Lupus looked around him, then took a whiff, and smiled. "Just firing him, right?"

She grinned back. "He let the garbage overflow, he didn't kill anyone," she said.

"Yeah, I smell it," he said.

"I did as well," Glynn added, also in Uman. "I was hoping it wasn't the norm."

"Perhaps you want to be the new harbor mistress," Lupus asked her. He stopped, the rest of the entourage stumbling to a halt.

Glynn regarded him. Her eyes may have moved, but you couldn't tell looking at her. Her mouth was set in a thin line and she kept her back straight and proud.

"No, your Imperial Majesty," she said, "I do not wish it at all."

"Then you can keep your Uman-Chi attitude in check," Lupus said. You could tell exactly where his eyes focused, and their intensity made Melissa glad they didn't fall on her.

"I meant no offense," she said, and lowered her head.

"You meant not to be called on it, you mean," Lupus challenged her. He didn't move off of this point, as Melissa would have expected. He surprised her by becoming so angry so fast.

"I have no tolerance for it, Glynn Escaroth," he said.

"Ancenon and D'gattis and even Aniquen came here, and they showed their manners. I will have you in a peasant dress scrubbing those dumpsters you smell, if I need to in order to keep yours."

"I humbly beg your forgiveness, your Imperial Majesty," she said, her head still down. Melissa heard no trace of fear in her voice, but she didn't speak Uman well and the inflection might have been lost on her.

Without another word, Lupus turned on his heel and returned to talking to his courtiers, as if none of this had happened. The entourage scuttled up to keep pace.

"He do that all dey time," Shela said to Melissa in English.

"What?"

"He go from dey pissed off to dey happy," she said. "I know him, and I never unnerstan' that. He be so mad, and den it like he blow out dey candle."

"Quick to anger, quick to mend," Melissa said.

"What dat mean?"

"Something my grandmother used to say," Melissa said. "Men who are quick to be so angry are as quick to get over it."

"So dis like dey men from Conn eckky cut," she said.

Melissa smiled. "Well," she said, "it is like a few of them."

Shela nodded.

The market place at the landward end of the wharf consisted of a huge maze of stalls and tables, with hawkers selling wares of all sorts. She saw different foods, different types of cloth and skins. They saw weapons and wines, animals and ales, whatever came into her head, she didn't have to look too long before she saw it.

"Busy," she said to Shela in Uman.

"No, not at all," Shela said. She looked around the bustle. "It is early in the season. In Life, it will be ten times as busy. Look—you can walk between the stalls, there are so few."

"I am impressed," Bill said, dropping back to join their conversation.

Shela's nose wrinkled—a sign Melissa knew meant she felt annoyed. Melissa surmised Shela must not get much time with other women, especially one who could tell her about her man.

"The merchants come here, because they pay so little *shakun dhar*," she said.

"So little what?" Bill asked her.

"Shakun dhar," she repeated. "I don't know the anglesh word. You sell something, you pay some of what you make to the Duke or Baron, he pays that to the King."

"Tribute?" Melissa asked. Bill touched her shoulder.

"Taxes," he said in English, looking into her eyes. "Angron asked me about that—about economics. Lupus brought more business here by lowering taxes."

"Oh, for the love of God, he's a Republican," Melissa said. "No wonder he's so hot to go to war."

"Hey!" Bill protested. "I'm a Republican."

"What?"

"You knew I listened to Rush."

"I thought you liked old music," Melissa said. She shook her head and looked down. "I can't believe I put out for a Republican."

"You *what*?"

A wide smile crossed her face, she couldn't help it any more.

Bill shook his head. "You just…suck, you know that?"

"What a terrible thing for you to say," she goaded him.

"What you talking about," Shela asked in English.

"Shakun dhar," Melissa said. "And I was just giving Bill a hard time."

Shela winced. "I tell you, you not call him dat," she said. "Very dangerous, you use real name."

"Our names are our names," Melissa said. "I have no idea what else to—"

Shela held up her hand. They were coming to the city's gates. They were huge; timbers held together with huge bands of iron, attached to a tower on each side on some sort of hinge that lay hidden in the towers' stone walls.

They saw crows circling the gates. Occasionally one would swoop down and peck at the droppings from a horse, or at the wares of a merchant whose attention seemed diverted.

"What you call dat bird, in anglesh?" Shela asked Melissa.

"A crow, I think," she said. "Or a black bird, maybe. They are too small to be a raven."

"Raven," Shela repeated, nodding. "Dassa good name for you. We call you Raven from now on."

"And you," she said, looking at Bill. "You we call dey first word I learn in anglesh, 'Mountain.'"

"Mountain?" he said.

"You big, big like dey White Wolf. I almost call you dey old wolf, but day name gif you lotta trouble."

Melissa laughed. "It probably would."

"I guess I can be the Mountain," he said. They had just walked under the gates, and on the other side they saw a whole new crop of courtiers waiting for the Emperor, and even more Wolf Soldier guards to protect him from them.

"He is in his element, isn't he?" Bill said.

"In Uman," Shela reprimanded him. "Or in the language of Men. You will only learn them if you speak them."

Bill screwed his face up as he searched for the words.

"That is what he likes," he said, indicating the Emperor. He had no word for 'element.'

Shela smiled. "That is better," she said. "And yes, he likes it very much, but he complains about it all the time, too."

"Just like a man," Melissa said.

Shela laughed. Something caught her eye, and her face just opened up. Melissa followed her line of sight to two children running up the cobblestone street, followed by an older girl carrying a toddler.

Melissa didn't miss the Wolf Soldier guards double-timing around them, firmly moving pedestrians out of their way.

"There are my babies," she exclaimed, and squatted down with her arms open to receive them.

The oldest was a copy of her, somewhere in her early teens, her thick brown hair hanging down to her hips. The next one, a boy, stood almost as tall, his black hair cropped close to his head. The girl who followed them dressed in—of all things—a black leather bra and leather riding breaches, with knives on her upper arms and thighs and a bow over her shoulder. Her face looked almost as if she were surprised—the eyebrows perpetually arched – and framed in purple hair longer than Shela's, her skin ghostly pale. As she drew closer, Melissa could see her gray eyes, and the surprised look seemd to be her natural expression.

The purple-haired girl wore no furs despite the cold weather. Her flat stomach was exposed. The baby she held in the crook of her arm had her lower lip stuck out and knuckled her eyes, getting ready to scream her lungs out, Melissa felt sure.

The girl moved like a dancer, Melissa noted. She ran with a baby in her arms, no easy feat, but she kept the baby steady without slipping or stumbling. She kept her distance from the older children, not crowding them and not more than a leap away.

The older children hit Shela dead-on. They should have bowled her over but she held her ground. She plied their faces with kisses and they responded with giggles and one hundred questions.

"Are you well, mama?"

"Are you staying?"

"Who is that big man?"

"Is that girl your sister?"

"Cook caught Vulpe sneaking plums!"

Bill barked a laugh that even got the Emperor's attention.

"Just like my kids," he said. "Ten seconds before one is telling on the others."

"You have children?" Shela said, and looked at Melissa.

"I was married before," Bill said, struggling with the Uman language. "That was long ago."

"Your wife died, or you left her?" Shela asked, her arms still entangled in her children.

"She left me, actually," Bill admitted.

Shela nodded and returned her attention to her children.

* * *

Bill looked onto the scene longingly.

He had such great kids. Three of them, all girls; he had kidded his friends that he knew the gas station bathroom better than his own.

It just struck him then that he would never see his grandkids grow up. He wouldn't see his girls on Christmas; he wouldn't get to torment his sons-in-law during Thanksgiving football. He didn't see them much, but that didn't exactly mean never, either. If he ever managed to retire, he had hoped to go see all of them.

He felt a touch on his elbow, and he looked down to see the older children staring up at him with inquisitive brown eyes. Their mother now focused on the baby.

"Are you our grandfather?" the girl asked.

Bill couldn't keep the smile from his face. He squatted down to their level. "No," he said. "Don't you know your grandfather?"

They shook their heads. He could tell they were brother and sister. They had Lupus' Roman nose, the same eye set. They had Shela's features, her long fingers and her delicate jaw and cheekbones. They were both going to be tall—you could see it in them already, their long forearms and their gigantic feet.

"We never met them," Lee said. "Mama's mother died, papa's father lives a way away."

"A way away," the boy agreed. Melissa had told him their names. This was…Vulpe; Latin for fox.

"Well, I am not your grandfather," Bill said. "But I can do grandfather things for you."

"You can?" Their faces brightened.

He did the trick his own kids loved best. He put his hands together, then bent his left fore and middle finger over his left thumb and, pretending it was very painful, performed the illusion of pulling off his right thumb with his left hand.

They were appropriately amazed. Immediately they attacked his hand, trying to pull his thumb off themselves and, when that failed, insisting he do the trick again.

"Oh, it hurts so *bad*," Bill protested. "It was cut off in the war, you know."

"It *was*?" Vulpe immediately warmed to the violence. "Was it the Battle of the Deceptions?"

"Was it the Battle of Thera?" Lee asked.

"Was it the Battle of the Two Horses?" Vulpe asked.

Bill laughed. As much as he'd been suddenly melancholy, he warmed to these two immediately.

"Looks like you made new friends," Melissa said to him.

She stood next to Shela, watching him. The Empress held her youngest, and the girl with purple hair stood back from all of them, watching the crowd that moved past, looking through the Wolf Soldiers and into peoples' faces. She took in the rooftops, the city walls—she clearly protected the children as well as being their nanny.

"They are such well-behaved children," he said to Shela.

She inclined her head. "Their father has a way with them, this is true. And there is Nina—she never leaves them."

Nina, the girl with purple hair, looked Bill over once, then looked away again.

"I don't think anyone would cross that girl," Bill said, smiling.

"Not two times, no," Shela agreed. She looked at Nina. "Have you been bringing her outside? She is hardly crying."

"Every day," Nina said. Her voice sounded musical, not like the Uman-Chi, but as if she really sang her words. "She can tolerate it for an hour now. I ordered the closed carriage for the trip to the palace."

Bill marveled that he had gotten every word.

Six black horses pulled the closed carriage, and it approached even as she mentioned it. It looked large, but he didn't think it would be big enough for all of them. He opened his mouth to say something when Lupus turned around and saw him.

"Do you ride?" he asked, in Uman.

"Horses?" Bill said, then caught himself. Lupus probably didn't mean he had a Harley.

"Yes, your Imperial Majesty, I love to ride."

Lupus smiled. "Good," he said. "Because we are going to go exercise my stallion while the girls go back to the palace with Karel and Xinto."

Bill looked past the approaching wagon for another horse and didn't see one. He looked back at Lupus.

"Your stallion?"

Lupus smiled. "The grooms can't handle him," he said. "Watch this."

He put two fingers in his mouth, and he gave a very un-

Emperor-like whistle. Both the kids covered their ears and the baby screamed in anger at the sudden noise.

What could only have been a stallion's challenge answered him, and he heard a horrible crash from behind the wagon the team of six pulled. Then another, and another, and Bill took two steps to the side to see a smaller wagon behind the larger one, making great leaps as whatever it contained inside it tried to get out.

One more scream, one more crash, and two Uman groomsmen ran for their lives as the back door to the smaller wagon flew from its hinges. A massive white stallion immediately backed out and reared.

It stood bigger than a Clydesdale, built like an Arabian, with a huge barrel and powerful, blue-veined legs. Its iron-shod hooves actually made sparks on the cobblestones as it moved. Its scream might not be deafening but it sufficed to let you know an angry stallion made it. It dropped to all fours and raised and lowered its head several times, then drew a bead on Lupus and charged.

The Emperor stood his ground while the others around him scattered. The giant ran right up to him and immediately began to butt him with his head. The horse stood easily eighteen hands.

"Easy, oh," Lupus said to him in a low voice, rubbing the monster's neck and ears. The big stallion actually rubbed Lupus' face with his nose.

"What is *that*?" Bill asked.

"That's Blizzard," Vulpe informed him. "That is papa's horse."

"You can't touch him," Lee warned. "He will bite your arm off and *eat* it!"

"He will?" Bill couldn't be sure they were kidding.

"He does bite," Shela warned him. She took a step next to him, bouncing her whimpering baby, as the crowd of onlookers grew and the Emperor comforted his giant stallion.

"I have never seen a horse like that," Bill said.

"They do not have them where you are from?" Glynn asked him. She had been quiet since her confrontation with Lupus, and Bill had almost forgotten her.

"It looks like a warm blood mix," Bill said, in Uman. "It has the look of an Arabian to its head, but the thick legs and wide barrel of a draft—but, no, look at that tight middle!

"And you never see a warm blood all cuddly like that—but you say to anyone else, he's mean?"

"Blizzard loves him like I have never seen a horse love a man," Shela said. "No horse in Andoron would do what that horse does to be with him. And, yes, he hates everyone else. I can't even brush him if Yonega Waya isn't there."

"So they cart him out here for the Emperor to ride?" Bill asked.

"They have to," Shela said. "Yonega Waya, he built a thing called a winch, it pulls Blizzard on a chain into the cart. Then another horse pulls the cart. I think you will be riding that horse."

Bill saw that the groomsmen had returned and were removing the horse from the traces of the ruined cart. To its credit it had stood stock-still while Blizzard had snorted and reared.

"A—um, you want me to ride the draft?" Bill said.

Shela laughed. She rubbed her youngest daughter's nose with her own and was rewarded with a giggle. "That horse is 'Little Storm,'" she said. "Blizzard is his sire. He is like that. What you want him to do, he does, but nothing bothers him. He is not as big or as fast as Blizzard, but he is close."

"I want to go on Little Storm," Vulpe immediately demanded.

"I want to go on him, too," Lee said, not to be outdone by her brother.

Shela shook her head. "You will come with the women in the cart," she said. "Blizzard is going to want to run, and Little Storm is going to want to run with him."

"I'll sit with grandfather," Vulpe offered. He looked imploringly up at Bill. "I'll be good."

"I will be good, too!" Lee promised.

Shela looked into Bill's face. She raised an eyebrow in an expression of amusement and shrewd skepticism.

Bill knew full well the best way to make sure he didn't get executed would be to get the kids to love him. She must have known that, too.

"They asked if I was Lupus' father," Bill admitted. "I told them I was a grandfather, but not theirs."

"Papa can order him to be our grandfather," Lee said. "He can—" and then another word that Bill didn't know.

Bill found it frustrating.

"Your papa will not make a law that another man has to be your grandfather," Shela said, lowering her voice. "Now, if you won't do as you're told—"

"*Get in the wagon right* now!"

Lupus' voice thundered out as only a father's can. Bill had done it himself. Once you became a dad, you got *the voice*, that certain octave and decibel, that just scares the hell out of children.

They crashed into each other as they climbed into the covered wagon. Nina took up a position at the door, even the Wolf Soldiers deferring to her.

"I will see you at the palace," Melissa said to him, and reached up to kiss his cheek.

"Shela tells me there is no way you can outride Lupus," she whispered into his ear. "I think if you could, then he would have a lot of respect for you."

He gave her a hug, and surprised her with a pat on the behind. She giggled and jumped away, then followed the children up into the wagon, throwing a last, speculative look at him over her shoulder just before she disappeared inside.

"If you *can* outride him," Shela said, passing him, "then yes, he would respect you a lot. I think you might just want to do your best. Blizzard is very fast and Little Storm is very hard to ride."

Bill smiled and watched her go. Glynn followed both of them into the wagon without a word to him.

She had turned out to be quite a little pain in the ass, after all, Bill thought.

"Ready?" Lupus asked him.

Bill counted six horses there. Blizzard had already been saddled; Little Storm had just been cinched. Bill saw four mares between them; three had Wolf Soldier guards and one a plain looking Uman in a breast plate and a cloak. He had close-cropped hair and three scars in a line on his left cheek.

"This is J'her," Lupus introduced him. "J'her, this is—"

He knew better than to say Bill's name, but he didn't know what else to call him.

Bill stuck out his hand to the mounted man. "The Mountain," he said. Lupus laughed. "I am told it is a good name for me."

"I was told J'her was a good name for me," J'her said. "Then I found out it was a type of rock that you make fences with."

"Which makes it a good name for you," Lupus commented. "You are the most solid man I know."

"You are too kind, Lupus," J'her said.

"J'her is the Supreme Commander of the Wolf Soldier Guard," Lupus said. "Wolf Soldiers all call me by name, so don't be surprised when you hear it. That saved my life once."

J'her cleared his throat. "Your horse is stomping," he noted.

"He is," Lupus said, and reined him to the left. "Mount up, Mountain, or you will be late."

* * *

J'her watched the new man, this older version of Lupus himself, approach Little Storm, a horse very few people could ride.

He thought this a cruel trick, but then, the Emperor's judgment proved right more often than wrong. If he thought this an appropriate test of the newcomer, then J'her would support him in it. He would 'have his back,' as Lupus liked to say.

The Mountain stepped up to the horse and looked it in the eye. He rubbed its neck and ears and let it smell him. 'That is good; let the horse know him,' J'her thought. He had ridden, anyway. He had a chance to survive.

The wagon pulled away with the women inside, all of them but Nina, who leapt up to its roof, barely touching the side. The tiny thief, Karel of Stone, had already climbed up there. J'her had seen the little man bundle the other Scitai up to the top as well. If he recognized the legendary Xinto of the Woods, then it would be better not to have him occupy the same air space as the Empress.

J'her had been briefed before the flagship touched the outer docks. Imperial Wizards had spoken with the Empress while she sailed. They brought two more like Lupus, Men from the north. They would be treated like guests and guarded like hostages, to be considered important.

And this morning, the next message, "Have Blizzard and Little Storm ready for a turn around the city walls. Minimal guards."

J'her had become used to such sparse directives. Lupus played the world in close, giving his subordinates minimal information and expecting unquestioning loyalty. J'her smiled to himself. Absolute, unquestioned, unconsidered loyalty.

The new Man mounted Little Storm and the horse stood stock-still like it always did. Black like a shadow, still as a stone, Little Storm seemed an enigma until he decided to get going. Then you saw its sire in it. It had killed men who had fallen from it.

J'her had been in prison for multiple murders when Lupus had offered him a position in the Wolf Soldier guard over a decade ago. He had expected to die—he'd been a farmer. Better to die with the sun shining on his face than in the cold of the Steel City dungeons.

He had been one of fifty Wolf Soldier to survive the Battle of Tamaran Glen. He had seen Lupus turn the battle himself, charging the Confluni infantry with his sword and his horse, and nothing else. Terrified Free Legionnaire lancers had held to the trees until he shamed them with his bravery. When they engaged, the Hero—the Volkhydran warlord named Karl—had screamed, "Lupus!" and plunged into the fray, Wolf Soldiers at his back, and the Free Legion defenders had followed him.

The Confluni had fallen apart. Wolf Soldiers had turned the battle, and J'her knew right then he would be one for the rest of his days.

He remembered that day. He had never been so sure he would die, and he had never felt so alive, and afterwards, dripping from more wounds than he could count, seeing double from the pain, the blood of a score of men mixed with his own, he had never felt so proud, so powerful, so certain in his whole life.

So J'her, as he said, "Had Lupus' back." What other choice could there be?

Chapter Twelve:

A Race to the Finish

The wagon seemed dark as a tomb and didn't smell a lot better. It didn't seem close, but it had become musty, probably because they almost never used it.

Glynn sat prim and proper in a corner seat, her back to the front of the carriage, farthest from the door. The children avoided her; they had never liked Uman-Chi. Few Men did, in fact, and children usually had a good sense of people.

Now that they didn't have The Mountain to entertain them, they focused on the other newcomer, Raven. Shela forced herself to think of them in terms of their new names, put their old ones out of her head, with the discipline that came with being a sorceress.

Raven grinned ear-to-ear, answering the million questions a child has for every new situation. Was she their aunt? Was she Andaron? Was she a sorceress? Did she want to see Lee do a spell?

"You will *not*," Shela interjected. "And you will not make that offer again."

Lee lowered her head. "Yes, mama," she said.

"She did a spell the other day," Vulpe offered. He had the advantage on his sister now, so of course he immediately exploited it.

Lee glowered at him. “You’re a brat!” she hissed.

Vulpe didn’t care. He knew that if the tables should turn, then it would be his head on the chopping block. “She floated some plums from the larder and she ate them.”

“You ate them too!” Lee challenged him.

“After you made me sing for them!”

“So what we have here,” Shela interrupted them, “is a thief, and a liar. Not very much like the Prince and Princess of the realm.”

And then she invoked the words more powerful over her children than any spell, “I think your father needs to know about this.”

“No!” Their eyes went wide as gold Tabaars. They clung to her skirt and pleaded with her. “No, mama! You handle it! You handle it!”

Shela felt her heart swell with love for them. Another of her husband’s terms, ‘You handle it.’ They reminded her so much of him. Lee’s strength and determination, Vulpe’s eyes and nose, the way he held himself with perfect posture like Lupus, the way she dissected every situation and turned it to her advantage.

“In truth, does he sing?” Glynn asked them.

“He sings to us all the time,” Shela said. “He has a beautiful voice—I think it is Nina’s influence as much as any—”

She looked around the carriage and her heart froze. “Xinto!”

“On the top of the carriage,” Raven told her. She had seated herself in the opposite corner from Glynn, her hands in her lap, her blue dress billowed out around her legs. “I think they are keeping him away from you.”

“Karel of Stone is no fool,” Glynn commented.

The two women smiled at her expense. Shela felt her back straighten.

“I wouldn’t hurt him,” she said.

“I think Karel is afraid to take that chance,” Glynn pressed her. Yonega Waya had left Glynn to her care, encouraging Glynn to be bold again.

“Shela,” Raven said, and reached forward to touch the back of her hand, “let him freeze outside. Do you *want* him in here?"

"I don't," Shela admitted. "Karel probably did what was best."

"How does Nina stand the cold?" Raven asked her, leaning forward. The Trenboni dress shifted on her upper body, accentuating her figure as she moved. "I was freezing with furs."

"She is an Aschire witch, like Shela," Glynn interjected again. "If she wishes to she can be as warm as on a summer day."

"I think that the idea with the peasant dress is a good one for you, Baroness," Shela said. "Expect to have one in the morning."

"Your pardon?" Glynn said, lowering her chin, her eyes wide.

"Well, clearly you have no respect for me," Shela said. "Calling my trainee a witch, speaking familiar as you are. Humility makes kings of peasants, as my husband says.

"I think that Eldador shall make you a queen."

Raven actually had to bite her lower lip to control herself. Glynn sat back and glowered. The children remained quiet—they had dodged the arrow on the spell and the plums, they would be perfectly happy to see Glynn take their mother's attention for a while.

Shela pulled the laces of her bodice open, ignoring all of them. She had promised her husband she would have Angry at the Sun on solid food by the spring thaw, but this would be her gift to herself. Even through the pain of baby-sharp teeth on her nipple, she knew the comfort that belonged to her, and that only her child could give her.

She regarded Raven and asked, "How well does your man ride?"

* * *

Back outside of the gate, behind Lupus and J'her and in front of the three mounted Wolf Soldiers, Bill struggled with the reins and tried to guide the horse.

He had already made them stop once so he could shorten the stirrups. Little Storm was iron-mouthed; he would resist the bit and take the pain of the steel in his gums to do what he wanted to do.

What he wanted to do seemed to be to follow his sire and knock people and objects over, apparently in his own meanness. He didn't like heels in his sides, he didn't like direction, he had no idea what a knee pressed into his barrel meant, neither did he neck rein.

Bill saw Lupus and J'her had immersed themselves in some conversation, so instead he looked behind him for some help from the Wolf Soldier guards.

"Do you know this horse?" he asked them.

One of them, a Man, kicked his horse up alongside Bill and said, "I rode him once."

"How was he?"

"Rough," the Man said. "Mean. He takes the reins in his teeth—he has them there now."

Bill gave the reins a sharp tug and, sure enough, Little Storm snorted and turned his head, revealing the bit in his molars. No wonder he acted hard to maneuver!

"Your Imperial Majesty?" Bill called. The Wolf Soldier fell back. Lupus turned, making no effort to hide his exasperation.

"Yes?"

"He has the bit in his teeth—would you smack him for me?"

Lupus looked at Little Storm and smiled. "He's a bastard, isn't he?" He dropped back and whacked the stallion on his sensitive nose. The horse snorted and Bill pulled back on the reins, feeling the bit drop back in the horse's mouth.

Little Storm immediately arched his back and dropped his flank. He stepped back, bucked once and then crow-hopped, as Bill fought to keep his seat.

"Is he too much for you?" Lupus asked him, once Bill had settled the horse down. "Little Storm is from Blizzard out of what they call a dray mare here—a draft horse. I was hoping for something as powerful but more mellow than Blizzard, but I don't think I got it."

Now it was Bill's turn to be exasperated. "He *is* a draft horse," he said in English.

"He's broken to the saddle."

Bill shook his head, pulled up on the reins and dismounted. He stepped to Little Storm's head and pulled the headstall from him.

Little Storm just stood there, looking at nothing, still as night.

"Is there a tack shop near here?" Bill asked.

"We're in the market," Lupus said. "What do you need?"

"I need a snaffle," he said. He showed the bit to Lupus. "This is a straight bit. I bet he throws riders all the time."

"He does," Lupus said. He ordered one of the Wolf Soldier guards to get him a new bit and tossed the man a bag. The warrior, an Uman, took off like a shot.

"You know your horses," J'her commented in Uman, while they waited.

"I was raised on a farm," Bill replied, also in Uman. "I had two Appaloosas growing up. The mare had to have a hackamore, a harness with no bit."

"How did you ride a horse with no bit?" J'her asked him. "She would never learn to turn."

"You teach her to go with your knees," Lupus said. "You've seen me do that with Blizzard."

"Blizzard has a bit, though," J'her protested.

"You just have to know her," Bill said. He straightened out Little Storm's mane with his fingers, pushing it to one side. It had been wild cut, too long for proper riding. If he had scissors and a brush he'd have taken six inches off and pulled half of it right there.

The Wolf Soldier returned with six different bits, all jointed, all about six inches wide. The harness had been designed well and Bill changed the bit out easily. He selected what he recognized as a 'Tom Thumb,' a jointed bit with extended trailers for the reins.

Little Storm looked like he would gag on that one, too, but accepted it. Bill watched to see if he would scoot it forward to his molars, but he left it. Bill remounted and took the reins two-handed.

They all moved. Little Storm rode like an entirely different horse now. What Bill had called meanness turned out to be his inability to decipher what Bill tried to tell him. The Tom Thumb let Bill take a better grip on Little Storm's head and communicate to him.

They found their way through the market and moved on to the plains. Radiating out no less than a mile from the city walls, Bill could see hard-packed earth full of the frozen prints of horses, wagons and men. Bill saw melt on some tracks around their edges, pearling as the sun rose, meaning mud and slop and all sorts of hazard here.

"Hya!" Lupus shouted, and Blizzard took off like a bullet.

"Hya!" Bill shouted, and Little Storm dropped his flank and leapt after him, leaving the others to catch up as they would.

It had been *so* long. The horse at Outpost IX had been so well trained, it reacted almost on thought. Bill didn't like that. No fun riding an animal with so little spirit. He wanted some fight.

Little Storm obliged him—his first goal being to challenge this older stallion. Bill stood up in the saddle just enough to pitch his weight forward and to take his ass out of the seat. He whipped the barrel of this young horse with the reins, spurring him on to challenge the older, larger horse.

The wind whipped his eyes and left them stinging. Reflexively he narrowed his eyelids and turned his head to one side, squinting through his lashes and blocking the brunt of the wind with the side of his face. They already approached one tower, where there would be a turn.

The turn lay in the shadow of the tower. The ground would be frozen hard still. "Hya, Little Storm!" Bill shouted, and pushed the horse ahead.

Lupus looked to his left in amusement as the black horse pulled up alongside him. Blizzard's great neck was bowed, the cheek like a great disk and the nose as small as a teacup bobbing as he ran. He might not be in his prime anymore, but he was still a healthy animal with many natural advantages, and Lupus certainly would use them all.

They took the turn. Lupus slowed, Bill passed him on the outside. Blizzard screamed in anger, Little Storm in challenge.

"Hya! Hya! Hya!" Both riders urged their mounts on into the straightaway to the next tower.

Turning on the big stallion made Bill feel like he was about to fly off sideways. His heart thrilled to the danger of it—that horse falling would be the death of him. Bill's legs and lower back had already begun stiffening. At fifty, he wasn't in the shape Lupus surely found himself, but he wanted this—he wanted to show the old man hadn't become useless, even if he had been treated like baggage since he got here.

Blizzard gained on him, still faster in the straightaway. Hooves beat the hard-packed earth like some mad drummer. Both stallions screamed as they approached the next tower and the next turn.

This time the sun beat right on the corner, the shadow from the tower painted the ground well before the turn. There would be slop. Bill urged his mount to the inside, forcing Little Storm's tail into Blizzard's path. The white horse had to slow and take the outside, coming up on the slop at a dead run.

At the last second Bill pulled up on the reins, slowing his horse in the shadow of the second tower. Blizzard shot past him, caught unawares in a wash of little mud puddles and loose earth. Bill and Little Storm took the turn at a respectable canter while Blizzard and Lupus went wide, sliding and flinging mud, Blizzard dropping to his flank in the slop. By the time they recovered, Bill and Little Storm were forty yards down the wall.

Bill held the lead through mud and slop as they pounded along the south wall, straining for the next tower and the next turn.

Damn! Bill swore to himself. Past the tower he saw the southern gate, and a line of people gathered before it. His advantage would be lost if he had to pick his way through, and he would just be clearing the way for Lupus and Blizzard to follow at a dead run.

When they drew nearer, Little Storm saw them, too, and screamed his challenge. Horses reared, people scattered. Wolf Soldier guards with pikes pushed the crowd back from the gates, as if they expected this to happen and knew what to do. This probably hadn't been Lupus' first race around the wall, Bill decided. But then, how could he be caught unawares by the slop?

Some animal like a goat or a large dog leapt into the path

that they cleared and laid down. Men and Uman shouted orders at it, then out ran a pair of children, who threw their bodies across it.

No way could Bill hope to stop in time. Bill bore down directly on them, kicked with his heels into Little Storm's barrel and yelled, "Hya!"

The horse leapt into the air and sailed over the three of them. He landed with a ball-jarring thud on the other side, the horse barely missing a step as it plunged on. Just seconds later, he heard another "Hya!" and a thud when Blizzard had to do the same thing.

Another corner tower came next, clear now over a mile from the gates. Bill didn't need to see it to guess it would be pure slop this time. The sun would be against the city walls. Little Storm had taken the last turn sound, Bill crouched down lower to the horse's neck, his cheek and eyes in the stallion's mane, and he gripped the reins close. Pressing to the inside and listening to the drum of hooves on the earth, he entered the sunshine by the tower, waiting for that steady, hollow thud of his horse's hooves to turn into more of a 'thunk,' when the soft earth changed to mud and slop.

The ground would be hardest by the wall, where fewer people would walk. Bill reined back just a little as he took the turn, Little Storm's hooves flinging mud and water, coating him in earth.

Little Storm finished the turn, Blizzard flying past him once again, breaking the turn out wide. Now Bill ran down the straightaway pounding down the length of the wall, to his west rolling hills stretching out to the horizon, blanketed in winter hay.

They ran for miles, Blizzard pressing Little Storm but not making the push that would give him the lead. Finally Bill saw another gate two thirds of the way down the wall, horses being exercised outside of it. The stables would be here. Lupus' cry of "Hya, Blizzard!" told him they'd come to the final stretch.

Bill whipped the horse's barrel with the reins. Little Storm screamed and pulled forward, pounding toward the stables. Bill bounced in the saddle, the pain in his back and shoulders, his feet and hamstrings extreme. "Come on, Little Storm!" he urged his mount, leaning into his neck, whispering into his ear. "Come on!

Run!"

Blizzard screamed his challenge. Little Storm lowered his head and bore down. The ground whipped past them in a swirl. The winter wind bit mercilessly at his face and eyes.

Men and horses scattered from before the gate. Two mares reared, the handlers struggling with their reins. Little Storm thundered on, Blizzard pulling up along side him.

They passed the gate together. Bill could argue he had beaten the Emperor, but he would never be sure, and that hadn't been the point of it. He sat back, the air cold on his face and beard. He'd been sweating like crazy in the cold. He knew he'd be sick tomorrow.

So worth it.

* * *

The wagon trundled into the royal stables. Melissa sat quiet, the older children at her feet, thinking her own thoughts while Shela nursed and Glynn pouted.

"This is a very smooth ride," she said, finally, in Uman.

She had been on a hayride. Even on asphalt the wood and steel wagon wheels amplified every bump and twig.

"Yonega Waya's invention," Shela said. "He calls it 'take the bumps,' a steel pipe inside another steel pipe, a spring inside of that."

"Shock absorber," Melissa said in English. She knew the term because they'd blown out in her wreck of a car. Then in Uman, she added, "That makes sense."

The wagon stopped, the door swung open. They all waited politely for Shela to be the first to leave.

"No, you go first," she said to Glynn. "I want to finish. The Emperor won't be long."

"M'lady," Glynn said formally. She rose and exited the wagon. The kids scrambled after her.

"I *hate* her," Shela said in English. "I can't stand Uman-Chi, but she is worse den most."

"They seem to think very highly of themselves," Melissa said. She didn't know how much was safe to say.

Shela nodded. "Dey used to run everything before my

husband came," she said. "Now dey just hate ever'thing."

Melissa nodded. It jibed with what they'd seen of them.

"Mama! Mama!" the two older children stuck their heads back into the wagon.

"Yes, my darlings," Shela said in Uman.

"Papa's coming, and grandfather is riding with him on Little Storm!" Lee said.

"They're coming *fast*, mama!" Vulpe said. "I think Little Storm is going to beat Blizzard."

Shela's eyes widened and she scrambled through the wagon door with a breast exposed, her baby almost forgotten in the crook of her arm. Melissa might be eager to see them, too, but she didn't intend to flash the world to do it.

She exited the wagon and Nina already held the whimpering Chawny. Shela fought her bodice closed and moved as fast as she could to the gates on the other side of the stables. The children already waited there, Glynn with them.

Vulpe and Lee leapt up and down with their little fists in front of them. Wolf Soldiers and Men and Uman in varying finery formed a circle near the children, wary not to step in their way. Some had already begun to shout.

"Bother!" Shela said, and stopped. She waved her hand in a wide sweep before her, and the air shimmered. The center of the city wall seemed to vanish, to be replaced by the image of Bill on black Little Storm and Lupus on white Blizzard.

Melissa ran up along side Shela, and helped her with the laces of her gown. They both watched the wall as the two men raced.

"I can't believe it," Nina said. "No horse is as fast as Blizzard."

Melissa knew what she saw, and that turned out to be Bill grinning like a ten year old, urging his mount on, and a look of determination on Lupus' as he raced to catch him.

"There, you see?" Shela said. "Blizzard is catching him. This will be very close."

"Very close," Melissa agreed, as they cinched up the last of Shela's laces.

"Your man keeps a nice seat," Shela said, nodding

appreciatively. "Keeps his arms in, leans forward. I think he is tired, though. See him bouncing?"

"Hasn't ridden in long time," Melissa said.

"Ah, look—Lupus catches him!" Shela announced. Melissa nodded. They ran neck and neck, Little Storm perhaps an inch or two ahead, as they vanished from Shela's image on the wall and raced past the gates.

The men roared a cheer, the children leaping in the air. Being males, they fell to the inevitable arguing and the exchange of bets.

And, past them, in the plains grass, did Melissa see those serpentine eyes again? Could it be a trick of the sun? She couldn't tell for sure. However, she saw a swish of grass where no wind blew, and she watched something like a whisper through the winter hay move away through the city. Once again, there and not there.

"Come with me," Shela ordered her absently, and lifted the front of her skirts up to race for the gates. Melissa shook her head to clear it and followed the Empress. They arrived just as the men turned their horses around.

* * *

"Wow," Lupus said. "You're in trouble, Mountain."

"I am?"

They trotted back to the gates, both horses snorting, their heads bobbing. Little Storm's whole body quivered—or could that be Bill's?

"You forget where my wife is from," Lupus said.

"Andoron, yes?" Bill said, ready for the bad news now.

"Yuh, huh!" Lupus said. "Do you know how I got her?"

"Melissa told—oh, I get it," Bill said.

Of course! They traded Shela to Lupus for Blizzard's stud service. "She is going to want this horse. Well, it is yours, after all."

"Where'd you get that idea?" Lupus asked him.

"What?"

Lupus smiled and looked forward. "Man needs a horse in this world," he said.

"Your Imperial—" Bill began.

"Skip it," Lupus said in English. He turned and looked at Bill. "You know how many couldn't tame that stallion? A lot, that's how many. I put you on him to see how long you would try to stay on. There you went and freaking solved the problem.

"That's your horse. You earned him."

Bill didn't know what to say. "Um—thanks," he said.

"You're welcome," Lupus said. "But don't go thanking me too soon. Everyone is going to want that horse now. I can breed more—rest assured, I will. Be a hell of a lot easier to take it from you than me."

Bill nodded. "Hey, while we're alone," he began.

"Kids calling you grandfather?" Lupus interrupted him.

"Yeah."

"Heard it. They are dying for grandparents. They can't have mine and barely see hers—that's a long story."

Bill nodded. "Okay," he said.

"Let them call you grandfather, alright?"

Bill nodded again. "I've been missing my grandkids, anyway,"

***

J'her and the three Wolf Soldiers rode up to the stable gate just as Lupus and the Mountain returned to it. The Empress and the new woman already waited there with Glynn and the royal family.

Karel of Stone remained on the back of the carriage with Xinto of the Woods. J'her sent the guards to take charge of Xinto, under direction of Karel.

Karel would know how to keep a man that dangerous.

"Don't tell me you won," J'her said to the Mountain.

The old Man smiled. He dismounted, wincing as his feet hit the ground, and J'her imagined he heard joints actually creaking.

"Tell you the truth, I think it was a draw," the Mountain said, as his woman ran to his side and give him a wet kiss.

"I guess that is one truth," Lupus said.

"You think you took me?" the Mountain asked him. He'd

become excited and forgotten whom he was talking to.

"It was a draw," Shela said. She already knelt in front of Little Storm, inspecting his fetlocks and hooves. As always, five minutes in the stables and she'd covered herself in horsehair.

"No, mama," Vulpe said. "Little Storm won. I *saw* it."

"Blizzard won," Lee said. Probably defending her father like a good daughter.

"Looked like a tie to me," the new female said, returning to the Empress' side. Seeing them together like that, J'her would have believed they could be sisters.

"If I may, Lord Emperor?" Glynn said to Lupus.

"Please," Lupus said, dismounting. "I can't think of any party more disinterested than the Uman-Chi."

She smiled politely. "And so," she said. "My interest aside, I think there is no doubt that Uman-Chi eyes are sharper than those of Men and Uman."

Many people nodded. J'her knew it to be true. Of course, you never knew where those eyes might be looking.

"If your mark is the beginning of the gate," Glynn said, "then the victory is to the black. If it is the gate's far side, well then the white finished victorious."

Lupus looked at the Mountain. "Well, we didn't say, now, did we?"

"I was only guessing we were racing here," the Mountain said in Uman. He had an odd accent but J'her could understand him.

"Call it a draw," Lupus said. "The Emperor has spoken."

There followed a good deal of swearing from those gathered outside of the royal party, the stable help being notorious gamblers.

"He is perfect," Shela announced. Even she wouldn't inspect Blizzard. And after a race like that, the stallion would be particularly excited. She went right up to the Mountain, the focus on her face almost terrible to those who knew what she was capable of. "How did you get him to do that?"

"Before you answer," Lupus said, placing a hand on the Mountain's shoulder. "An Andaron takes talk of horseflesh seriously.

"We will walk and talk," he added. "I am hungry and I am sick of Uman-Chi fare. I want steak and potatoes and plenty of beer."

"Uck!" Shela complained. "You eat like the wolf you are."

"Why change what works?" Lupus said.

"He had the wrong bit," the Mountain said.

J'her listened as he sent two Wolf Soldiers to alert the house staff. He sent two more to ready rooms for the Men, and walked up next to Glynn.

"Baroness," he said, "will you be shown to your rooms?"

"An it please you, Sirrah" she said. "I must meditate."

"Your brother is in the city," J'her informed her. "Ancenon now calls himself an Escaroth? He asked I let you know he'll meet with you."

Glynn nodded, her face expressionless.

A squad of ten escorted her. She left without a good-bye.

"Who had the wrong bit?" Shela demanded.

"Little Storm," Bill said. He picked up Vulpe and put him in the stallion's saddle. Lee immediately started bouncing up and down, and he reached for her beside him.

The Mountain didn't see the dagger appear in Nina's hand. J'her intervened discreetly, pulling the Aschire body guard back from the group and informing her of Lupus' orders. She just snarled. Even Wolf Soldiers didn't touch Lee without Nina's permission. Certainly no strange Men could be allowed.

Shela had the headstall off of Little Storm, and the Mountain guided the stallion by a fist full of mane. Little Storm stood almost as tall as Blizzard, and had that same arched neck, the difference being Little Storm didn't rip the Mountain's arm off at the shoulder for touching him.

"Draft horses use this bit," she said. "You can't control him with this, he won't know when to turn."

"I think he would prove you wrong," Lupus said. "We took three turns and he beat me every time."

"With this?" Shela's expression told J'her where this would end. He would have an Empress in bloomers and no top shortly.

"Get the Empress' riding gear, and double time," he told

Hennethen, an Uman Sergeant. Hennethen could run a daheer in four minutes. He left before J'her could explain why.

"He gagged on the straight bit," the Mountain said, "and took it in his teeth. I thought he was just mean, but he was confused by it."

"We want to ride him, mama," Vulpe said.

"I will be the next to ride him," Shela informed him.

"You better ask his owner first," Lupus said. That surprised even J'her. Lupus casually led Blizzard into his private stall, with the reinforced walls, and the ceiling high enough for him to rear, which he did frequently.

"What?"

"You were going to geld him," Lupus said. "The Mountain earned him. It's the Andaron way, and you know it."

"I'm the only Andaron here," Shela said. "I'll decide what—"

Lupus turned on his heel. He stared her down, his eyebrows knit in anger. She stopped as if she had been pole-axed.

"Was I unclear?" Lupus asked his wife.

"No, my Lord," she said, and lowered her head.

J'her had been married once. She'd left with his family. He had been married only four years, but he'd never struck her. Not so, Lupus the Conqueror. From a pat on the bottom to a backhand that spun her completely around, Lupus thought nothing of striking the Empress.

The Empress had blown the gates off of Outpost IX when Lupus had sacked the city—J'her had seen it with his own eyes. A Bounty Hunter had broken into the Imperial nursery and Shela had caught him. J'her had ordered the man cleaned up with a dustpan. If Shela didn't see eye-to-eye with Lupus, as he often put it, there wouldn't be enough left of the Emperor to bury.

But this one thing he wished Lupus didn't do.

* * *

"Bill, share," Melissa said, trying to make a joke of it.

Mike had never hit her, but Melissa knew it had been close. She had discussed this with Shela; she knew the Empress felt that Lupus not only had a right, but a responsibility to hit her.

Melissa still didn't want to see it.

Bill grinned, his beard bristling. He had just led Little Storm into a stall opposite Blizzard. The mood had gone quiet and everyone seemed uncomfortable.

"If it is my decision, your Imperial Majesty?" he said, deferring to Lupus. That was smart, Melissa thought. She would have just said, "Of course you can," and possibly made matters worse.

Lupus nodded to Bill and turned his back on all of them, unbuckling the cinch and pulling the saddle from Blizzard's back.

"Empress Shela," he said, "I ask that you please ride my horse, and give me your opinion, if and when it is convenient for you."

"I am hardly dressed for it," Shela said, and slapped at the skirt of her dress, already covered in horsehair. "Of course, it isn't like I am going to ruin this outfit."

"Your riding apparel is on its way, Empress," one of the Wolf Soldiers said; one so big and strong, he could almost be mistaken for a Man, Melissa thought. She'd seen him leave with Lupus and Bill.

"J'her, you know me well," Shela said, and smiled. Right on cue, another Wolf Soldier ran up to them all, made a fist over his heart, and handed the Empress a pile of neatly folded clothes, and boots.

"*He* didn't forget the shoes," Shela noted, looking pointedly at her husband.

"That's it," Lupus said, and reached for a riding crop in Blizzard's stall.

"No!" Shela protested and, grabbing her clothes from the Wolf Soldier, took off down the row of stalls, her husband right behind her.

Melissa could hear her giggling, even when she heard the crack of the crop.

Vulpe looked at Lee. "Do you think she's telling him about the plums," he asked.

"You're stupid," she answered.

"*You're* stupid," he countered.

"Enough," Bill said. Again, he reached for them, and again

they leapt into his arms, allowing themselves to be lowered to the ground.

"Stay away from behind him," Bill warned. "He's excited still. He might kick you."

"That is the second time you did that," Nina said, stepping up to face Bill.

"What?"

"Don't touch the Princess," she said, her eyes flat, looking right at Bill. She held Angry at the Sun in the crook of one arm, but left no doubt in Melissa's mind that Nina could have one of her daggers into Bill without dropping the baby.

"Nina," J'her said. "You may not touch him."

"No one touches the Princess," she said, and didn't take her eyes off of Bill. "I won't have it."

"Lupus asked me to treat them like my own grandchildren," he said. "Grandfathers pick kids up. You don't like that, take it up with him."

"Chose your words better, Mountain," J'her warned him.

"I'll take it up with the priest at your funeral," Nina said, and raised her left hand, glowing with some light that seemed to come from within it.

Without thinking, Melissa took her by her shoulder. She had meant to spin her around, to tell her to think, to ask her to let the Emperor handle it.

She had no idea what happened instead, but the glow died out of Nina's hand, and the young girl fell to her knees. J'her snatched the baby from her arm as she fell face-first into the straw.

They all stood there, stunned. Even the kids went quiet. Melissa's fingers tingled like her hand had fallen asleep. She stood there looking at her hand like it had done something and forgotten to tell her about it.

Shela emerged from a stall, dressed in brown leather riding pants, boots and a laced-front, red leather top. She had a grin on her face and a hand on her butt, accentuating her walk.

Everyone turned to look at the Imperial couple, except for Nina, who still lay face down on the floor.

"Now, what?" Lupus asked.

Chapter Thirteen:

A Hero, Fate Foretold

Ancenon Escaroth met with his new sister and his Daff Kanaar ally in the suites assigned to her. Glynn looked a little thinner but she'd been through much. Black Lupus looked like he always did.

"You're well, my sister?" he asked her.

"I am, brother," she informed him. She'd dressed in her white Caster robes to receive him. She forewent the usual Uman-Chi greetings—Lupus was abnormally aware of such things and no one wanted him affecting their traditions.

"His gracious Majesty has seen fit to bestow upon me the rank of Baroness, and the duties of a villain," she added.

Ancenon raised an eyebrow at the Emperor.

The latter's lips twitched in a smirk, the scar shifting under his eye. "Your sister - which I don't understand - decided to smart off to the Empress, so she'll be cleaning dumpsters tomorrow."

Ancenon sighed. "Black Lupus," he said, "this is intolerable."

The Emperor raised his hands, palms up, and said, "Take it up with my wife if you don't like it. She made the decree and I'm not going to undercut her."

"Surely you'd need not resort to violence," Ancenon argued.

Black Lupus sighed. Ancenon was familiar with the term, but it irritated Lupus no end when he made these comments and they were misunderstood, and Karel of Stone had affected the practice of tormenting him this way. Ancenon didn't care for Karel of Stone, but Lupus was due his share of unprovoked torment.

"Perhaps if we traded services…," Lupus said, turning his eyes to one side.

Eyes - the weakness of all other races. Ancenon knew that Uman-Chi eyes were unreadable to any but other Uman-Chi. The eyes of Men were emminently readable, however, and usually betrayed them. They did Lupus now.

"Which services?" Ancenon asked.

"First of all, for all who care to ask, she's out cleaning dumpsters tomorrow," Lupus said. He regarded Glynn, who stood by with her hands holding one-the-other at her waist. "However if only one Wolf Soldier guards her, then I don't imagine she'll get to very many."

"Very well," Ancenon informed them.

"Then, I ask you to recall a day, about fifteen years ago, in Outpost IX, when you and I and a Scitai named Xinto had a meal together."

Ancenon felt the smile cross his face. "Our first meeting," he said. "How could I forget?"

"Our second," Lupus corrected him. "You'd seen me two days before at the Fovean High Council."

Ancenon frowned, not liking to be corrected. "I won't argue that," he allowed the Man.

Lupus smiled. "Remember when you called me a Bounty Hunter?" he asked.

Ancenon thought about it. An hour out of forty-five decades didn't merit much space in one's memory.

"I could believe I called you that at the time," he said. "Your existence in Trenbon, your armor, your command of *many* languages, and your association…"

"My association with Xinto, whom you *knew* was a Bounty Hunter," Lupus pressed him.

Ancenon sighed. The Emperor had enjoyed more than his

share of the attentions of the Bounty Hunter's Guild after that night. Likely he wanted to know why Ancenon hadn't defended him more vigorously.

In fact, Ancenon had gone to great lengths to do just that. It was an incredible inconvenience to him to be associated with someone whose every third thought was either defending himself from or hunting down Bounty Hunters. However, he'd invoked the Guild, calling himself a Bounty Hunter for whatever bizarre reason, and touched off a war.

Despite the reasons, he'd walked away victorious.

"Then you remember my then informing you that I *wasn't* a Bounty Hunter," Black Lupus said.

Ancenon frowned and looked sideways at his adopted sister. "In fact, I do remember this," he said.

Lupus smiled even wider. "There's someone whom I'd like you to share that with," he said.

* * *

They served dinner in the palace hall. A gigantic bay window ran the length of the northern wall overlooking the city and Tren Bay beyond it. A long, heavy table set for dozens of people, all of whom apparently had decided to attend, ran down its center. Lupus sat at the table's head, his Empress to his left, a Man to his right, his children next to Shela and three old Men in white robes next to the Man.

The Man's name was Hectar Gelgelden, the Duke of Eldador the Port or, in the language of Uman, *Galnesh* Eldador, chief advisor to the Emperor, an elegant man with long gray hair and a widow's peak. They called the old men 'Shem Hannen;' Lupus called them, "Oligarchs" when he spoke English. They advised him as well.

Down the right side of the table sat what Lupus called, "Palace Barons," members of the nobility who held only title and no lands, and who mooched off the Eldadorian state. Lupus had informed Bill he considered them mostly useless, although once in a while they could surprise him.

Glynn sat among them now, frowning all around herself as greasy hands reached into platters stacked high with food. Meats and fish and bowls of cooked vegetables, pots of foamy ale and carafes of wine; Bill sampled from a wheel of cheese so sharp it made his eyes water, and the style for feeding appeared to be to just reach out and grab.

Bill could find himself remembering how thin he used to be when he got here, if he didn't control himself. He also knew how much he loved to eat. Instead, he leaned over to Melissa and gave her a gentle bite on the ear.

"You need to ride horseback more often," she said, kissing his cheek.

"Will you do something for me?" he asked.

"Right here?" She opened her eyes up wide and innocent, looking stunned for all the world.

"Goofball," he told her. "Fill my plate for me, okay?"

"Do what?" Her pretty eyebrows knit. "You mean, feed you?"

"Make sure I don't eat too much," he said. "You know how much weight I've lost here?"

"Yeah, in fact," she said. "I give myself a lot of credit for it."

Bill grinned an evil grin. "As do I," he said. "And I know if I take what I want, I am going to put it right back on."

"Say no more," she said, taking his plate from him. "I told you I was going to flatten that belly."

"What is this now?" Lupus said. They had spoken in English. He had apparently been listening.

"She doesn't want him to get fat," Shela said in Uman. "He needs to lose weight so he can race you and win."

"Ho, ho! I heard of this," Hectar said, stabbing into a pile of pork with a long, two-pronged fork. "Seems to me Blizzard's ready for the pasture."

"Not likely," Lupus said. He turned his attention to J'her, eating on the side of the table opposite the palace barons. "Lord Supreme Commander, when did you lose sight of Blizzard?"

"At the first tower, Lupus," he said.

"And when did you see him again?"

"At the stables."

Lupus turned back to the Duke. "Faster than fast, your

Grace," he said. "Doesn't mean anything about Blizzard."

"I can't believe I didn't just change bits on him," Shela said. "That should have been the first thing I did."

"Well, not the first thing," Bill said, watching Melissa. "I would have reshod him first, then looked to the person who broke him to the saddle. I didn't pick up on the bit until one of the Wolf Soldiers told me that he was taking it in his teeth."

"I didn't see him doing that," Shela admitted. "When he killed his second rider I should have."

"Second rider?" Melissa exclaimed. She dropped the plate down in front of Bill. "How many did he kill?"

"Um—am I Bugs Bunny here?" Bill looked into a plate more fit for Little Storm than for him.

"He killed four," Lupus admitted. "But he didn't stomp them, they just fell off and were dragged."

"Whoa—when were you going to tell me?" Bill asked.

"Never," Lupus said. "You'd have been afraid of him."

Melissa took Bill's beer out of his hand and replaced it with wine. He scowled and she said. "Empty calories."

"He was right not to tell you," Karel of Stone said. He'd been seated on Bill's other side. "It would have made you shy of him."

"Power help you if the horse smells that," Shela said.

"Grandfather is going to let me ride him," Vulpe said.

"I get to ride him, too," Lee protested. Vulpe stuck his tongue out at her - Shela put something that looked like yellow mashed potatoes on it.

"Eat," she warned.

Lupus looked to the corner of the room where Nina stood, back on duty. "You're clear as to that, right?"

She nodded, then resumed her vigilance.

"You handled your time at sea passing well," the Scitai said to Melissa, looking over Bill's belly. He had to sit on a board that crossed the arms of his chair, much as a young child would. His blue eyes seemed almost hawkish as he assessed the girl. "Are you of a sea-faring people?"

"I grew up in a port," Melissa said. She picked greens for Bill, and he started to think this had been a bad idea.

"We had a skiff," she said. "One-master, low and fast."

"A—I'm sorry, a what?" Karel said.

Shela said the word in the language of Men, then in Uman for Bill's benefit. "Like Volkhydran raiders use."

Karel smiled. "In with the wind, out with the tide," he said. "You weren't the daughter of a pirate, I hope?"

Melissa smiled. "Not much of a pirate, no," she said.

"Perhaps of a Wizard?" Glynn asked, picking pieces of meat and vegetables from where the court barons had raided the platters on her side of the table. "That would explain the incident in the stables."

It turned out Lupus had ordered that no man touch the Princess. Some males, such as Karel of Stone, one of the palace wizards and other members of what he called 'the Free Legion', and what others called 'Daff Kanaar,' had been excluded from that. Nina had sworn a blood oath to protect the girl, and she took it seriously.

No one knew what had happened in the stables. Nina's energy had been drained to only a sufficient amount to keep her alive. She hadn't passed out; she had been sleeping, regaining her strength. Even now she could do almost nothing magical.

Bill didn't understand it entirely. It seemed to him as if these people who cast spells had batteries.

"I had never seen a Wizard before—" Melissa began, and Bill nudged her. She caught a look of warning on the Emperor's face, and Bill had already been told not to talk about their home planet.

Glynn seemed willing to let it pass. "I wish I had been there to observe their exchange," Glynn said. She wore a gorgeous green dress, strapless, its neckline plunging down almost to her navel and the back up past her neck, fanning out into a starched collar that expanded past her ears. Its skirts billowed out, in the current fashion. Her hair hung green down to her shoulders, curling inward.

"You tried to kill him, correct?" Glynn said, looking at Nina.

Nina looked back at her, unimpressed. "Yes."

"Does anyone *not* want me dead?" Bill asked the room.

"And it required the touch," Glynn continued. The rest of the room grew quiet, interested in this exchange.

"It did," Nina said.

"I have cast spells on her," Shela said. "I was successful each time, and in fact was not weakened."

"Raven," Glynn said, looking at Melissa. She had already gotten used to her new name. "I want you to listen carefully."

"Okay," she said.

"This will hurt you," she said, and she raised her hand, glowing white with power.

"Glynn," Lupus warned her. A trail of white rose up like a cloud from Glynn's hand, arced over the table, and reached for Melissa.

Stupid trick, Bill couldn't help thinking. Glynn wouldn't kill her, she would just create an illusion to see what happened. Melissa waited for the arc to come close to her, then she batted it with the back of her hand.

"Please," she said.

Glynn flew backwards out through the bay windows, with a crash of glass and a sound like metal tearing. Melissa watched with her mouth opened as Glynn sailed out over the palace wall, and dropped behind it.

"New rule," Lupus said. "No more spell casting at dinner."

***

It took a few moments before Glynn realized what had happened to her. She had heard the sound of metal tearing. She had heard the crash of glass. Her reality couldn't immediately adjust to accept that she still sat in her chair, traveling backwards through the night sky.

The cold air slapped the sense back into her, as she sailed over the palace wall, and watched it seem to rise, meaning she fell and would soon hit the ground.

Levitation had been the first feat she had ever mastered. She tried it now, and found the strength within her to impede her progress downward, slowing gradually as the chair continued to fall.

"Hey," she heard below her, in the language of Men. She

could do nothing but continue to descend. In several minutes she felt her toes on the ground, her dress in tatters and her delicate skin cut in a dozen places.

"So women just drop out of the sky in Eldador?" she heard from behind her.

Glynn turned and saw a Man, taller than she, stocky, dressed in the shaggy pants and overcoat of a Volkhydran, a sword on his hip and a pack on his back. He had brown hair cut above his ears, brown eyes, and a nasty scar down his left cheek, similar to the Emperor's.

"Actually we are shot out of windows," she said. "I don't suppose you know the fastest way to the palace gates?"

"The palace gates?" he repeated. "I'm not sure. If you don't hit me with another chair, I suppose I can escort you until we find it." He punctuated the remark by spitting on the ground.

"I really don't require an escort, Sirrah" Glynn said. "However I would welcome the company."

"Good enough then," he said. He started down the road they stood on, stone buildings lining either side. His boots banged the cobblestones in a rhythm she knew well enough. She straightened the moment that she heard it.

"How long were you a Wolf Soldier, Sirrah," she asked him.

He didn't stop, so she had to quicken her pace to keep up with him, tripping on the hem of her ruined dress every third step.

"What makes you think I was a Wolf Soldier?" he asked.

Glynn smiled. "You march when you walk," she said. "I know that tread from the sack of Outpost IX, the Battle of the Two Horses, and the second invasion of Thera."

"I had heard it was the Uman-Chi who financed the second invasion of Thera," he said, not looking at her. "There were no Uman-Chi at the Battle of the Two Horses."

"Thera happened in the days when we thought we could defeat the Empire," she said. "All Uman-Chi know better than that now. As for the other, I happened to be in Volkha."

He laughed softly. "The Uman-Chi were never too quick to learn," he said. "It doesn't matter, though. I'm not a Wolf Soldier."

"You just have the walk?"

He kept looking forward. "I'm not one any more," he said.

"Might I ask your name, Sirrah?" she asked.

He walked for a while, and didn't answer. She felt tempted to repeat herself, when he said, "Jerod. Jerod the Bold, of Volkhydro."

"I am honored, Jerod," she said. "I am Glynn Escaroth, of the family Escaroth, and now the Baroness of Britt as well."

"An Eldadorian barony?" he asked, looking sideways at her.

"Indeed, Sirrah," she said.

"I don't suppose you expect me to call you m'lady or anything, do you?" he asked her.

"Whatever your manners and your common courtesy demand, Sirrah" Glynn answered him.

She felt she should know this one, but she couldn't recall him. She'd listened to his voice, watched his manner, and marked his stride. He came of Volkan-kind, the bigger, meaner Men who lived along the Confluni boarder. A city dweller, not one of the tribesmen—she could tell by the hard soled shoes, the way he walked, the way he spoke. He used complete sentences and his diction seemed good. He had seen the inside of a school or been tutored.

She didn't need the company of a Man, but an escort meant less chance of some ridiculous peasant or city rogue bothering her. "What path brings you to Galnesh Eldador?" she asked him. She tried to reach out with her mind to the Empress or to the palace wizards, but her magic seemed indeed weakened.

"You wouldn't believe me if I told you," he said, and spat. "Doesn't the Emperor say, 'All roads lead to Galnesh Eldador'?"

"The Emperor boasts many things," Glynn countered him. They came to a crossroads and the Man turned to his right. She would have chosen that direction herself. In fact, looking down the road, she could see the palace spires, several hundred yards away.

An impressive distance, she noted. There could be more to this Raven than she had assumed.

"You don't believe you can trust me?" she asked.

“I know people,” Jerod said. “I know Uman-Chi.”

She smiled indulgently. “You are welcome to your secrets.”

He remained quiet for a bit, his boots staccato on the cobblestones. Say what you would about Men, Duke Hectar and the Emperor kept a clean city. Even in Outpost IX one saw a little slop in the street. Not so, here.

Jerod sighed. Glynn made her face blank, suppressing a smile. *That is a Man,* she thought. *They cannot bear their own secrets.*

“A month ago I argued with my father, and I decided that I should see the rest of Fovea,” he said. Glynn already knew he lied. He wouldn’t look at her, his inflection showed insecurity. His thumbs in his wide belt and the hunched shoulders testified for him.

“I was going to come here eventually, but I wanted to see Andoron. I had just stepped off of the boat in Chatoos when I couldn’t get it out of my head that I wanted to be in Outpost IX.

“And no sooner did I leave for there, then the Port of Eldador seemed better. I’m here now, and I don’t want to be anywhere.”

“Just so?” Glynn said. Certainly this seemed too convenient for comfort.

“Just so,” he said. “I am going to see some friends, I think, and maybe replace my sword with Eldadorian steel. I’m told the Emperor employs Dwarves at his forges.”

“Uman trained by Dwarves,” Glynn commented. They fast-approached the palace gates. Glynn could see horses there already, one of them a huge, white stallion.

Jerod stopped dead.

“You know the Emperor?” Lupus didn’t want for enemies.

“No, and I am going to keep it that way,” Jerod said. “He kills a lot of people.”

“Precaution is a better armor than steel,” Glynn quoted.

“What?”

“I agree with you,” she said.

He nodded. “Be well, m’lady,” he said, and spat again.

“Might I inquire to your lodgings?” Glynn pressed him.

She saw nothing wrong with being forward with a Man. They knew nothing else.

"I'm told that 'The Rider's Inn' is owned by Men. Uman in Eldador think all Men are rich. Others of my kind know better."

"I should like to inquire after you, Sirrah," she said.

"You would?" he seemed amused. The Emperor had marked her already and his stallion approached with a riderless palfrey and three score Wolf Soldiers.

"Be it to your convenience," she said.

Jerod looked to the approaching Wolf Soldiers, then to Glynn. "Tomorrow night," he said, and turned on his heel. He disappeared down a side street without a backward glance.

"Are you well?" Lupus asked as he approached her, from atop his stallion, in his usual flawless Uman-Chi. The Wolf Soldiers fanned out around them.

"I am injured, and I am drained, but I will recover," she said. "I was aided by a good citizen."

"We saw him," Lupus said. "He was polite to you?"

She knew what he meant—had a rogue pressed his fortune? "A good citizen, to be sure," she said. She didn't want them chasing the man down. She reached for the stirrup of the palfrey and pretended her knees were giving way.

"Perhaps I overestimated my well-being," she sighed.

Three Wolf Soldiers stood by her side faster than she would have expected. With strong but gentle hands they helped her into the sidesaddle. She expected a hand on her breast or buttocks, but they respected her dignity. For criminals, killers and rogues, the Wolf Soldiers kept their discipline.

She sat the side-saddle and pretended to swoon. "If we may, your Imperial Majesty?" she asked.

"At whatever speed you can manage," he said, and turned the great stallion to hover protectively over her.

They returned to the palace in good time, making no conversation along the way. Glynn found her way to her bed, claiming to be best fit to take care of her own needs. She would rather sail back to Trenbon than submit to a local healer, although she doubted she would be given the option.

Once alone in her chambers, she stripped off her dress, her

Uman serving girl sponging her wounds clean and then washing her body and brushing out her hair.

She fell asleep just as she realized how relaxing it all felt.

* * *

"If that's what I get, you should ride every day," Melissa said, her face buried in his shoulder, his bear arm wrapped around her.

"Maybe it's all you," he said.

She bit his nipple. "Maybe," she said.

They lay quiet, naked, buried deep in another goose down mattress, in another palace, in another person's custody. *The gilded cage,* Melissa thought. *I'm a Raven in a gilded cage.*

"You thinking about dinner?" Bill asked her.

She kissed him. "Yeah."

"Lupus told me she came back okay," he said.

"I was there," she said.

"Oh, right."

She kissed him again. "Its okay, Buh—Mountain," she said. It killed her to call him that. It was like she'd lost part of him. "I'm not freaking out, and it didn't hurt me at all."

"What does it feel like?"

She shrugged. She ran her fingernails over his belly, and said, "The first time, I got the pins and needles in my arm. You know, like when you sleep on it?"

"Yeah."

"This time it was—hmmmmmm—it felt like when you hit your funny bone, how it starts at one point and jolts through your whole body? I felt that until she flew out through the window.

"I'm not crying for the rude bitch," she finished. "You know Shela is going to have her scrubbing dumpsters tomorrow?"

He laughed. "I heard Lupus threaten that. She liked the idea, huh?"

"She smarted off to Shela in the wagon," Melissa said. "Glynn seemed so nice, too."

"At least we know the magic here can't hurt you," Bill said.

"Do we?"

* * *

Shela found her White Wolf where she knew she would find him, where he always went when he felt troubled.

She saw it as a comment on him that this gave him solace.

"If you stand the ritual, Nina will feel as if she isn't needed," she said to him in Andaron.

"I don't care what Nina feels right now," he said to her. His eyes flashed stormy, his jaw set. He wore his house robes and sandals, his arms crossed over his chest. He stood in the doorway to the children's rooms, his shoulder on the jamb, watching them sleep.

"Where is she?"

"Not here. Somewhere else." His scar twitched.

"She left?" Nina didn't leave Lee for any reason.

"She had a few bruises she needed to tend to."

Shela watched him quietly.

"I wasn't in the mood to discuss it; she wasn't in the mood to listen. I won."

"Nina has been a loyal—" Shela began.

"You want some, too?" he asked without looking at her.

"No, my Emperor," she said, and pressed her body up to his, his good slave girl, his loving wife. "I do not."

"It isn't like I can take it back now," he said.

"If she misspoke, then she is lucky to be alive."

"That she is."

They stood quiet. The children breathed, Lee and Vulpe in their separate beds, little Angry at the Sun in her basinet. Shela had seen him watch them until the sun rose. After certain battles, after attempts on their lives, after he had personally carved his way through a troop of Confluni at the second Battle for Thera, he had found comfort here with his children, his woman at his side.

She had kept them inside of her for ten months. They were of her. He had kept them inside of him since.

"I don't want to have to kill Raven and the Mountain," he said, finally.

"Nor should you," she said, wrapping her arms around him.

He still didn't look at her. "You saw the girl," he said. "Glynn barely challenged her, and she went airborne. Nina was completely knocked out. When we move, that girl is going to be standing right in our way, and if you challenge her—"

"If I challenge her," Shela said, daring to interrupt him, "it will be with a dagger in my hand. Let her try to counter that."

"Her 'Mountain' might," he said.

"He's no match for you," she said.

"He was today."

She pressed her chin into his upper arm and gazed up at the side of his face. "Is that what is bothering you?" she asked. "Are you worried for your stallion?"

He looked at her across his shoulder with cold, blue eyes.

"You and I both know we tried a snaffle in Little Storm's mouth," he said. "That horse couldn't be ridden."

"In honesty, Yonega Waya, he just couldn't be ridden *well.*"

"I doubt this Mountain has any magic touch," Lupus said.

"I sense no magic in him," Shela said. "Raven brings that."

He thought about that. One of the things she loved best about him—he looked to her opinion. All her life, her breasts and body had brought in suitors. She'd won this man with her mind.

She held him, and she waited. The children breathed, and he watched them. Her feet grew tired and she ignored them. Her knees and back had stiffened before he finally decided he would sleep.

She could have used her power to relax her muscles, but he wouldn't, so she didn't. She made it another of the many gifts of herself she had given him, and of which he would never know.

Chapter Fourteen:

A New Boss, Same as the Old Boss

Melissa awoke before Bill, as she usually did, and slipped quietly out of from between the goose down mattress and the pile of quilts on their bed onto the green, thick pile rug that bed sat on. Past that, more towards the door, lay another, more ornamental green-blue rug with a sofa by it, a few leather over-stuffed chairs and the armoire where they kept their clothes and their few possessions. Bill had carved a little wooden figurine on the voyage between Outpost IX and Galnesh Eldador, for example, and she'd painted a couple pictures she wanted to keep.

She padded naked to the armoire and found a robe she liked—white terry cloth with red tooling on the hem and cuffs. She slipped into it and belted it around her waist, then stepped off the carpets onto the cold, wood floor, to their window.

The window didn't have bars but it had to be fifty feet from the ground, set in stone with cherry-colored shutters banded in black iron. There would be no escape from here, if she wanted to escape. If she wanted to say, "Screw it," and head out on her own, not that she would, she'd have to ask permission, and frankly that took the fun out of it.

She watched the morning breeze roll the long winter hay on the fields to the west of the capitol city. Once again something seemed 'not-right.' There was something there to see, and she knew she was missing it, but missing something she couldn't identify was like craving food she'd never eaten. Even if she found it, how would she know?

If she didn't watch it with Bill then she might have to deal with that, too. Shela had warned her it was her fertile time just five days ago, and Bill had been so excited and passionate last night she'd nearly forgotten herself in their mutual climax. It wasn't like she could run out to *Ye Olde Drugge Store* or whatever passed for it here, either. She'd have to either have more caution with Bill or *the Mountain* was going to have some hills.

The thought made her smile. Seeing Shela with her children lit something off inside of her. Shela had confided that she thought she was around seventeen when she birthed her first (Andarons weren't big on calendars). Melissa could be a spinster by local standards.

She had to ask Bill about this subject, she resolved.

Beneath her, on a walkway along the palace walls which connected the tower where they were staying to a different tower, she saw Karel of Stone scurrying away from her. She wanted to think the other tower was what was called 'the family tower' where the Emperor and his wife slept. Their children resided in a whole, separate wing of the palace, under heavy guard and with Nina of the Aschire in the next room.

She'd been told this but she hadn't seen any of it.

Because she was a prisoner. A pet. She was a Raven in a gilded cage and, no matter the gilding, it was still a cage. She was waiting to find out what a song meant, and what it *could* mean was that she'd just be staying here forever, if she was lucky. Somehow Lupus didn't strike her as someone who'd keep her around if he had no use for her, or that he'd let her go if she could hurt him. No, that didn't sound like the Emperor of Eldador at *all*.

Bill slipped up behind her and wrapped his arms around her middle, saying nothing. She pressed her body back against him and closed her eyes, feeling the warmth of his body through her terry cloth, then the reason for his affection against the small of her back. She unbelted the robe and let it fall to the ground. His hands ran over her breasts, down her abdomen to her thighs. She sighed a little sigh as he pushed against her.

Yes, she thought—there was a conversation that needed to be had with this man.

* * *

Nina looked into the mirror and didn't like what she saw.

Mirrors. The first time she had seen her own face was in Galnesh Eldador, at the armoire in her personal chambers, in the room alongside the Emperor's before there'd been a royal nursery. It had amazed her how much like her father she looked.

Like him, but softer. Soft body, soft face, soft look in her eyes, the softness would be what she fought from that point in her life to this. Nina of the Aschire, like her father Krell before her, became a person of decision, and she'd decided to be the first of her kind to make her mark upon Fovea, not just on the forest called 'Aschire.'

An Uman called Drekk had told her once that she had the hands of a thief. Long, dexterous fingers that never shook—perfect for picking pockets, locks or fights if she wanted. Shela had informed her that she had the natural gifts of a plains witch, a sorceress. The Aschire considered both gifts uncommon. She could find no one there to teach her, to help her, to guide her in developing or at least controlling her power.

She looked into the mirror and she saw the eye swollen shut, the puffy lip, the purple swelling at her jaw where her long hair wouldn't hide it. What she saw didn't look soft, neither did it look very pretty.

She had come here to have Shela Mordetur teach her something of sorcery, in return for protecting the girl Lee, her daughter, from all harm.

For fourteen years she had done so. For over a decade she had been the last voice in the safety of the children. She ruled the nursery and, if she said, 'Go away,' then even the Emperor went away.

She stood naked at a basin of cold water at her toilet stand in her spare room in the nursery wing. She dabbed her lip with a clean, white cloth and winced. Last night the Emperor had wanted to be alone with his children, and for a reason even she didn't understand, she had told him, "No."

"No?" He had looked right into her eyes.

Many said, "Fear the Emperor in his anger, be terrified of him in his calm." He hadn't shouted, he hadn't scowled, he had just…looked at her, and she had held her ground and stared defiantly into a storm coming over the Iron Mountains.

"I need to talk to you about—" she had begun. She hadn't finished the statement. She'd been caught entirely off-guard when the back of his heavy hand caught her underneath the jaw and flipped her head-over-heels. The back of her head had hit the stone floor before she even realized she had been struck.

A natural acrobat, she had leapt to her feet, to her defense, and looked the Emperor back in the eye.

A Man would not put down the daughter of Krell so easily, she'd thought. However Rancor Mordetur was no regular Man.

She went for her knife. A fist took her in the stomach, another in the eye, and sent her back down to the floor. She raised her hand to exercise her power, and she spoke the words to raise fire.

He had picked her up like a rag doll from the floor, taking her by the belt, and heaved her against the stone wall. That he could do so with one hand spoke of might that no one Man could have, but again, Rancor Mordetur was no regular Man.

She used her power instead to cushion the blow, to survive. In that moment, for some reason, she remembered the first day she had lived here, the only Aschire, missing her father, missing her forest, surrounded by cruel stone and hard beds. The Emperor had held her all night, listened to her, let her cry, let her hold him, pressed his lips to her forehead for hours. She had not been born his daughter, but he had fathered her from that moment on. When he spoke of 'his kids,' as he did, Nina of the Aschire felt herself included.

She thudded against the wall, fell to the floor, and lay still.

"More?" he had asked her.

"No, my Emperor."

"Out."

And she had left, found an empty linen closet and folded herself beneath its lowest shelf. Her knees to her breast, she had been there all night, weeping, wishing he would come to her, and take her into his lap, and love her like the father he had become to her.

He hadn't. The mirror told her why. Men didn't like to look at their handiwork, not like this.

"Nina!" Shela appeared behind her, Chawny in the crook of her arm. Already the child reached for her, her face alight.

"My Empress," Nina said, not turning. She hadn't called Shela that for years.

Shela knew it as well. Shela's hand found Nina's shoulder and squeezed it. Nina had thought herself alone in her rooms. She stood naked, but Shela was a woman and like a sister to her.

"Yonega Waya told me he had struck you," she said.

"I misspoke," Nina admitted.

"Unless you had a knife to his throat, you didn't deserve this," Shela said, looking into her eyes in the mirror.

Nina looked away, and dipped her clean, white cloth into the basin before her.

"Oh, Nina," Shela said.

"I should consider myself lucky," Nina said, and tried to smile. It hurt too much. "There are not many alive who can say they attacked Rancor Mordetur."

"No, I suppose there are not," Shela said. She pushed the washcloth back into the basin, and turned Nina to face her. Nina complied. She had been mentored by Shela for over a decade and grown accustomed to her direction.

Shela reached out her hand to Nina's eye, then her lips, then to her jaw. Her eyebrows dipped in concentration. Nina felt the painful tingle of her skin knitting, the blood flowing freely through bruised flesh, now restored.

"At least you won't scare the children," Shela said. She had other marks on her, she knew. Her shoulder where she struck the wall, her head where she struck the floor, the purple welt around her waist where her belt had cut her. Shela left them. She didn't have to tell Nina why.

The Emperor was her man, and Shela knew the truth of this. Nina had defied him, and gone for her knife. No one took Nina of the Aschire less than seriously, and *no one* raised a hand to the Emperor.

"You have been angry since Raven and the Mountain arrived," Shela said to her. "I hope you don't feel threatened by them."

"She could be your twin," Nina blurted, her eyes welling. "Already Lee is certain she is an aunt, even though she's been told otherwise. All talk is about this 'grandfather,' who puts his hands on Lee as if he were the Emperor."

"And no one took the time to explain to you what was going on," Shela said, stroking Nina's purple hair with her free hand.

Nina's gaze fell, finding her feet on the floor. The stone felt cold on her toes; the air chill on her back and tender parts. Normally she would use her magic to warm herself, but she still hadn't fully recovered from Raven's touch.

"I love those children as if I bore them," Nina said. "If I am to be replaced—"

"You are *not* to be replaced, Nina," Shela said. "I am not done with you, and Lee and Vulpe would be heartbroken."

She handed Chawny to Nina, and the infant immediately sought a nipple. Both women smiled.

"Can I replace that?" Shela said. "Can anyone?"

* * *

Karel of Stone was waiting in the Emperor's sitting room, just outside of the Imperial bed chambers, when his Daff Kanaar ally emerged from his sleeping quarters, his blonde hair a tangle around his head and neck, his eyes pinkish and the beard stubble barely discernible on his fair chin.

"Got in past the guards again, huh?" Black Lupus grunted. Karel thought of him that way, as every member of the Daff Kanaar identified himself by the color of the strange hook-symbol emblazoned on his breast.

Karel had a silver symbol on the bear skins he wore as armor. If he hung it up and wore a regular shirt for long enough, that symbol would appear there.

"Yeah," he said. "I wanted you to know that Xinto is bound up in your dungeons still."

Lupus crossed the sitting room to the small dining area reserved for the Imperial couple. Half the time he ate here, the other half in the palace dining rooms with the palace nobles and whatever dignitaries were visiting. Lupus called them 'moochers' sometimes—that word didn't mean anything to Karel but he still liked it.

"Didn't you do that yesterday?" Lupus asked him, pulling out a chair at the table. An Uman servant appeared from a corner of the sitting room and entered the dining room. There was a tiny cooking brazier here and she stirred a stand of coals. When it glowed red she placed a copper kettle over it.

"Yeah, but if you don't check on Xinto regularly, you won't know when he's escaped," Karel said.

He jumped up into a chair by Lupus, one reserved for him when he came here. Lupus had re-engineered it personally with a false back. He pulled on the top corner of it, and it bent at the middle to the level of the arms, resting across them and making a padded seat for Karel.

The thing looked like all of the other chairs. If he marked it, then sometimes Lupus would remove the mark to another chair and chuckle when Karel picked the wrong one. Karel wouldn't have found that funny if it wasn't the exact kind of thing he would do.

"When he escapes?" Lupus repeated.

"Yeah," Karel said. Suddenly he was hungry. The Uman at the kitchenette fished underneath the counter where the cooking coals were smoldering.

"You can't keep a man like that a captive for long, not with your facilities," Karel said. "Wizards and foreigners you don't like—yeah. A Bounty Hunter, on the other hand? I was actually surprised to see him there this morning."

Black Lupus grunted. "Maybe we need to beef up the security, then?" he said.

Steam had already begun to drift out of the copper tea kettle's spout. Lupus had designed some of these to whistle when they were ready. Karel had always thought that clever and actually sold them in other countries.

Karel could point to a lot of things like that. There were people he'd met in Volkhydro who swore a younger Rancor Mordetur had taught them the secret of the carpenter's plane, who sold it as fast as they could produce it. There were Eldadorian merchants selling little vials of alcohol to soldiers throughout Fovea, alongside vials of witch hazel extract, which they used to treat wounds.

Now the Emperor was producing steam plants, and these plants were turning out clean water and compressed air cylinders. Those cylinders were attached to what the Emperor called 'nail guns' and, using these, a worker could drive 100 nails before another worker with a hammer could drive three.

His own Scitai would buy these cylinders and were using them to power a crossbow that could fire one bolt after another. It was the most guarded secret the Scitai had, but when perfected, woe be to those who thought to oppress them!

"I don't think feeding your guards more beef will help you," Karel said.

It wasn't what Black Lupus meant and Karel knew it, but it was just too funny to not understand him and see him try to explain himself.

Lupus sighed. "We need to make the security stronger," he said. "You understand that?"

Karel nodded. "I agree," he said. "I'm doing what I can, but the people who are best at this are the Bounty Hunter's guild, and frankly that's not going to help you with Xinto.

Xinto was a Bounty Hunter. In fact, he was the Bounty Hunter who'd set the whole guild on Lupus about fourteen years ago. That had resulted in a lot of assaults on Lupus, and a *lot* of dead Bounty Hunters.

Lupus had come to terms with the guild, but not with Xinto—not until now.

The Uman servant served them tea in ceramic cups. Lupus preferred the blackest of black teas, the ones loaded with what he called 'caffeine.' Too much of it would fill Karel with nervous energy. A Scitai's metabolism ran faster than a Man's already, so

Karel had to be careful drinking it.

The smell of eggs and ham cooking filled the room of a sudden as the Uman servant broke them over a pan on the brazier, replacing the tea kettle.

"You need a solution to keep your man a captive while I work," Karel said.

Lupus sipped his tea and Karel imitated him. It burned the end of his tongue and made him shudder. The Man smacked his lips and sighed.

"We can keep him under constant observation," Lupus asserted.

"That should help," Karel said. "You should have someone watch the watcher, as well. If the one closest should catch an escape beginning, you don't want him to have to leave to find someone to tell you."

Lupus nodded. They sat quiet for a while as breakfast cooked.

"Where is your Empress?" Karel asked him, finally.

Lupus sighed. "Probably with the children," he said. "We sent Glynn Escaroth out to clean dumpsters this morning. It was Shela's decision and she wanted to see to it. Glynn decided to mouth off to—she decided to voice her opinions too blatantly to Shela when they were in the carriage."

Karel nodded. "That won't sit well with the Uman-Chi," he said. "And rest assured, it will get back to them."

"I'm not real worried about the Uman-Chi," Lupus said.

The Uman servant flipped the eggs she was frying. The smell of some sort of spice filled the air. Lupus liked his eggs hot with flavor. The Scitai did as well, however perhaps not as hot as the Emperor.

Karel shook his head. "You'd be well advised not to discount Angron Aurelias," he said. "The man has nearly one thousand years behind him. I don't care what your race you don't live that long stupid."

"Noted," Lupus said. "He's pretty much concerned with being my ally right now, though. I don't think he's out to—"

Karel was already shaking his head and Lupus stopped. He cocked an eyebrow and his scar twitched. He waited.

Karel sighed. “You’re dealing with Uman-Chi. I’ll allow that you’ve been able to defeat them up to now. The sack of Outpost IX, the Battle of the Deceptions, the second attack on Thera. But you’re thinking in terms of actions, of years and of decades.

“Uman-Chi think in terms of generations,” he said as the Uman servant delivered their breakfast to them. “They think in terms of centuries, they think your life and mine are the blink of an eye. If Angron Aurelias has conceded something to you now, or given you *anything*, it’s because he has a plan that maybe doesn’t even kick in until a decade after you die of old age.”

“They tried that,” Lupus informed him. This came as a surprise to Karel. “The first year of my reign, just before the Battle of the Deceptions, they kidnapped my wife.”

“I remember that,” Karel said.

“They offered her back to me,” Lupus said, picking up a fork and knife. Karel did the same. “They said that all it would cost me is Vulpe.”

“They wanted to foster your son,” Karel said. “I remember that, too. That’s about the same time you developed Eldadorian Fire.”

Actually, Karel had developed Eldadorian Fire, truth be told. The Emperor had given them a basic formula, and Karel and a group of alchemists and distillers had gotten together and refined it into the most devastating weapon of its time. More deadly than magical fireballs or a Wizard’s lightening, Eldadorian Fire could even reduce stone to dust. Eldadorian Sea Wolves often carried it as a weapon.

Tech Ships, the warships from Trenbon which used to rule the waves, would see the ships that bore Eldadorian Fire and surrender or flee. Pirates wouldn’t attack Eldadorian merchants for fear Sea Wolves would visit their home ports.

Lupus nodded and took a bite of fried eggs and ham. He chewed and collected his thoughts.

“I know Angron Aurelias is smart,” he said, finally, “and I understand he’s going to make some kind of plan, some kind of deep plan, that I can only guess at.

“But Uman-Chi think in long terms, Silver Karel, and

that's their weakness, too," Black Lupus said. "Sometimes they think so long, they're still thinking when I run right past them. Sometimes they think they've planned so well they don't even consider the idea that things changed while they were planning. That's how I beat them in Outpost IX, that's how I beat them at the Battle of the Deceptions, that's how I beat them in Thera."

"And that's how I'll beat them now."

Karel nodded. He took a bite of ham. He didn't care for fried eggs—the grease would make him slow. You had to be fast to keep up with Lupus the Conqueror.

* * *

The Uman servant excused herself and left the room where the Emperor and his Daff Kanaar ally spoke of battles and futures.

Like all nobility, Rancor Mordetur couldn't see the servants around him. He was grand and they small, and too tiny for him to see from the top of a throne.

The Uman servant, a woman named Kakira, didn't do much more than pull a piece of parchment from her sleeve and wipe the sweat from her forehead on it. She tucked the piece of paper into one of dozens of books on one of dozens of shelves in the Emperor's sitting room. She then went about her duties as a loyal Eldadorian servant.

Another would come and take the parchment. Another would deliver it to a Wizard. The Wizard would know what she was thinking when she imprinted the parchment. Then her message would be delivered.

Kakira went about her duties and, once in a while, she remembered the sweet young man who'd been her brother, who'd fallen to the Sarandi when Lupus' Daff Kanaar allies had decided to raid up and down the Llorando River, as payback for some slight against an Eldadorian queen.

* * *

Jerod awoke in the morning in a decent bed, in a decent room, where he could put his pack and armor down and be reasonably sure they would be there when he woke up in the morning.

Galnesh Eldador had been a scum hole once, but not now. There were cities in Volkhydro he liked less than this one.

He washed himself in clean water. A rare luxury of these Eldadorian cities—the water moved through the ground in pipes, running from towers built throughout the city into peoples' rooms and hotel bathrooms like this one. Clean water—if he looked into a bowl of it, he saw nothing but the bowl. Some steel and wood edifice within the city walls took water from Tren Bay and turned it fresh. The magic required must have taxed a hundred wizards.

From there he went to the common room, where mutton turned on a spit. At this time of year, just before the spring, vegetables of any kind became scarce and expensive. Mutton and warm ale or fresh water made up the simple fare of common folk in Eldador.

"Might I join you?" a woman asked.

He looked up from his place at the board—an actual rough-cut board set on hand-turned wooden legs, benches running alongside. He recognized the woman as the Uman-Chi whom he'd met the night before. He felt his scar twitch in irritation.

"Suit yourself," he said. "You don't care what I say, anyway."

"I apologize for not waiting, Sirrah," she said. "But mine need is urgent."

"Were you followed?"

"Sirrah?"

"*Were you followed?*"

He didn't like stupid people, and he didn't respond well in the morning. The woman sat daintily, showing those phony manners that Uman-Chi saved for their inferiors, meaning everyone not their own.

"I feel certain I was not," she said. "I would know if anyone were interested in me now, and no one is."

"Would you know if the one following you were protected, perhaps by a sorceress?"

The Uman-Chi girl—Glynn Escaroth, had she said?—frowned beneath the hood of her cloak. He didn't need to know any more. His head rose just in time to catch the hem of a cloak as a man stepped out the tavern door.

"War's beard," he swore, and leapt up from the table, his body twisting like a dancer's as he leapt between spilled food and angry people. He slipped out the door, his sword already drawn.

To his left, nothing. To his right, that same cloak, flared out from the hem, its owner taking long, fast steps towards the palace.

He sprinted after the fleeing cloak, peripherally aware of the girl who followed him. So be it. He didn't have time to stop her and he could think of worse things than having an Uman-Chi at his back, even one interested enough in him to get him killed by the Emperor.

Hard-soled boots like those he wore worked great for the outdoors and horrible for sneaking up on someone. He ran without dropping his heels but didn't get within twenty feet of his quarry before the one he chased turned around. He recognized an Uman in light Wolf Soldier armor—a leather breast guard, and sword on his hip, tied down.

Jerod knew if he killed the man or attacked him on the street, then a swarm of Wolf Soldiers would be on top of them both. As the Uman fumbled for his sword, Jerod closed the distance to him and, without slowing down, took him by the right shoulder and spun him around in a half circle. He heaved the Uman like a sack of grain down an alleyway, past one of the 'dumpsters' where Eldadorians liked to keep their great mass of garbage.

Jerod turned on his left toe and sprinted after his victim. A few passersby took notice—no doubt one of them would make mention to the next Eldadorian guard he saw, but it wouldn't be the sprint for aid a swordfight with a Wolf Soldier would bring.

The Uman lay on his back, getting up from the ground. Jerod leapt and landed on his shoulder with his left heel, feeling the collarbone snap beneath him. The man groaned in pain, Jerod spun again and had his sword at the Wolf Soldier's throat before he could cry out.

"I have no trouble with killing you," he said, spitting to one side. "I've killed Wolf Soldiers before."

Glynn marched regally down the alley, past the dumpster, her cloak billowing out behind her. She'd thrown her hood back so her hair trailed out green behind her shoulders, her face looking pale and stern, her ambiguous silver eyes seeming fixed on him and unfocused at the same time.

"This is not wise," she told him simply.

"What wasn't wise was you leading *this*," and he emphasized his point by jabbing the Wolf Soldier with his sword, "right to me."

"He was following me, not you," Glynn protested.

"And yet, he left you the moment he saw me," Jerod said. "Why do you think that is?"

Glynn had no answer, which left him nothing else to do.

"Stand back so you don't get blood on you," Jerod said, and raised his sword over the man's heart with one hand.

"No!" the Wolf Soldier and Glynn said together. Glynn followed it up with, "I can block the last hour of his memory. He will be drunk in a bar and not missed by the Emperor."

"And in a week he'll remember," Jerod said. He knew this Wizards' trick.

"And you will be a week farther from the Emperor than you would be now," Glynn said. "Unless you can hide the body, and you cannot, the Empress will read the corpse and know you killed him, and then if ever she has met you—"

"And we both know she has," Jerod said. Glynn was right. A dead man needed to be kept away from the Emperor, and toting around a corpse wouldn't get him quietly out of the city.

"I am going to sing something to you, Jerod the Bold," Glynn told him.

"We are going to sing?"

"I will sing, you will listen," she told him, and in a moment, she sang to him, in his native Volkhydran.

That surprised him—the song seemed familiar, but at the same time he knew he had never heard it before. The man at his sword point stared at the Uman-Chi as if he had no idea *what* she was doing.

"The coming day?" he asked her.

She smiled, a cryptic Uman-Chi smile, and took a step closer to him. She reached out toward the Uman, and he simply closed his eyes.

“He will sleep, and mend,” she said. “When I am ready, he will awake inebriated in a tavern and fear for his poor judgment.

“You, meanwhile, will go to the next Eldadorian hostel on the way to Steel City. You will wait there for a week and I will join you with three friends.”

“I will, will I?” he asked her. Uman-Chi, they are so typical! They thought of the world as theirs to command.

Jerod the Bold didn’t take commands.

“Or I shall invoke my right as an Eldadorian Baroness, and I shall procure thee to the Emperor, Sirrah,” she said, and took another step forward. “Or didn’t you say you would rather not meet him?”

Jerod the Bold wasn’t stupid, either. If nothing else, then she would get him out of the city and to somewhere safe.

“Your word on it warrior,” she said, her face close to his. He looked into her silver-on-silver eyes, assuming she looked into his. “Your word, you will wait for me.”

“I will wait a week, no longer,” he said. “After that, I will assume the Emperor was smarter than you thought.”

She smiled. “Fair enough.”

Chapter Fifteen:

We Are the Young Americans

As promised, Shela took Raven out to the Imperial stables and picked her out a sturdy mare for riding. She'd lent the girl a pair of leather trousers that no longer fit her and a yellow cotton blouse that tied up in the front. She already had proper riding boots from the Uman-Chi.

Shela herself had would have preferred her leather skirt split up one side and her halter, but an Empress simply couldn't be seen in public dressed that way. Instead she picked herself out soft black leather trousers like the ones she'd lent Raven and a red top with frills around the neckline and cuffs.

Her Uman servants had decked her hair out with green and blue gemstones. She brought her children in tow, Nina watching them. The children both would want to ride, of course, however she planned to take Little Storm once around the city walls and she didn't want to have to mind them.

A smile split Raven's pretty face and highlighted her naturally high cheekbones as she held the mare's headstall in her hands. "She's beautiful," the girl gasped.

"She's Angadorian," Shela informed her. "I've a friend in the Duchess of Angador and she does a wonderful job breeding these there. You'll find no horse with a longer wind."

Raven knit her thin eyebrows and deciphered Shela's words. Being able to learn languages quickly wasn't a trait of her husband's people, she surmised, although in fact these newcomers didn't do too badly.

"And you're not going to make me ride her side-saddle?" Raven asked, a smile on her lips.

Shela clicked her tongue. "You're no blushing virgin," she said. "I don't suppose you think that it will rub off?"

Raven laughed and Shela laughed with her.

"I want to ride!" Lee protested.

"I want to ride, too!" Vulpe joined her. He was already running toward his gelding, Marauder.

"You will *not*," she informed them. "Nina!"

"Mind your sister, Lee," Nina ordered the young girl. At her fourteenth spring, Lee, stiffened as if she meant to defy her nanny. Shela expected the girl to assert herself—she'd never be a proper sorceress if she couldn't be her own woman. However Lee's upbringing hadn't made of her the equestrienne her mother was and one bucking stallion could start a whole herd.

"Ninaaaaaaa—" Lee whined.

"Ha ha!" her brother tormented her.

"You can't ride either," Lee shot back at him.

The boy bridled and Nina stiffened.

"There's an Uman-Chi scrubbing dumpsters, young ruler," Nina warned him. "She could use someone to help her."

Vulpe's eyes widened and Shela pressed her lips together to suppress a smile. Nina always came up with ways to discipline the children that would never have occurred to her. She turned her back on the group of them and went searching for Little Storm.

An entire section of the Imperial stables were reserved for Blizzard and his get. Another open-air corral outside of the city walls served for those they'd given up on. Right now there was a grey stallion belonging to young Hectaro Gelgeldin, a chestnut mare which Shela herself had hopes for, Blizzard and Little Storm.

Shela crossed the stables to that section. The horse she sought stood still as a statue in his paddock. All of these horses were over-large and had stalls and paddocks twice the size of other horses. All of them were steel-reinforced, and in each case it was pointless. Any of them could leap their paddock wall without trying hard.

"He's such a magnificent animal," Raven sighed, leading her mare by its halter. Nina followed behind with the children, Lee now carrying little Chawny.

"Mmmm," Shela agreed, studying the stallion with the trained eye of an Andaron plainswoman.

She knew this horse. Where some saw a sullen animal, she'd always seen a coiled spring. When he'd dragged his first rider to death, Shela alone hadn't been surprised. She'd wept for that man, a brother Andaron who left her own tribe to be a Wolf Soldier. She'd known him for a long time and he'd been a great rider.

Little Storm's eye, black against his black coat and black hide, watched her. This animal seemed to know neither joy nor kinship. It waited for her to do whatever it was she planned to do.

She plucked the horse's harness from a hook on the bare steel gate and she pulled open the latch.

"Keep the children back," she ordered Nina absently.

"Behind me," Nina ordered the children in turn. Raven backed her mare up.

Little Storm didn't move at all as Shela approached him. It made her very wary. A horse should react to her; sniff her, step away from her. She reached up and took a handful of his thick, wild-cut black mane and pulled his head down to her. She slipped the harness over his head, behind his ears, and snapped the buckle under his jaw.

Still—nothing.

She clucked to him. "C'mon," she said to him, pitching her voice softly.

Without a moment's warning, the horse kicked out with both back feet and launched himself out of the paddock, Shela yanking her hand out from between the harness and the horse's cheek before he dragged her. She clutched ineffectively for its mane as it shouldered past her and the freedom of the stables.

"Horse free!" she shouted automatically, Nina echoing her.

Lee called out the same a moment later, back-pedaling to safety with her sister in her arms. Raven's face turned from left to right, trying to figure out where to go, what to do in the chaos.

And like a lone tree on the plains, little Vulpe stood stock-still outside of the open paddock gate.

"Vulpe!" Shela shrieked.

The stallion barreled out of the gate right at the boy. Vulpe didn't freeze, his eyes didn't go wide. He simply drew himself up, so much like his father, and refused to give ground.

The mighty stallion reared before Vulpe, pawing the air with front hooves as hard as stone and larger than the child's head. Still the prince didn't move, his feet apart, his face set in the same scowl his mother had seen on his father's face a dozen times.

The stallion took a step back and began to descend, crashing back to earth directly into the same space Vulpe occupied.

Raven swept in from the child's right, abandoning her mare. Tackling young Vulpe, she took the boy to her breast with her left hand and raised her right above her, rolling onto her back, warding off the stallion as he righted himself.

The giant hooves changed direction in mid-air, sliding along an invisible wall to its left. It was a tiny change, the great beast didn't stumble. As the stallion stepped back and bobbed his head, Shela sprinted to his side, to take hold of the halter and drag him back into the paddock before he could strike again.

The stallion launched itself again, kicking out with both back hooves and leaving a giant divot in the ground behind him as he shot past Raven and Vulpe into the open aisle between the stalls within the stable.

Three Uman stablemen in the white and brown livery of the horsemen appeared before the stallion. The beast reared again, pawing for them, terrified and angry as only a stallion could be. One held a head tie and the other a crop. The third, the senior man, called out to Little Storm by name, trying to quiet him.

Shela knelt down by her son's side, reaching for him. She didn't miss the ozone stink that hung in the air after a spell of protection.

She took Vulpe to her breast, her fingers in his short,

brown hair. Her eyes finding Raven's as the girl pushed herself off of the ground and ran fingers through her dusty tresses.

"Mamaaaaaa," Vulpe complained.

"Shush, you," she warned him. She wanted to whip him but she couldn't. The boy had stood his ground. This was second only to taking first blood among Andaron men. In her home tribe he would already have been pulled from her and his name shouted in triumph for such courage.

Or buried, of course, another dead warrior. The boy struggled and finally subsided, taking his mother in his arms.

Shela saw the stallion was letting the stablemen connect the head tie to his harness. They would take the horse to their arena and work him to stumbling now. Pointless to beat a horse for being a horse, however as her father had told her growing up, ground work is everything and no horse ever suffered from a firm, fair hand.

Nina took hold of the mare's reins, watching Raven as if expecting her to leap off of the ground and bite them. She must have smelled what Shela had.

It wasn't Nina of the Aschire whose magic had warded Vulpe and Raven; who had created a shield wall between their bodies and Little Storm's hooves.

There was work to be done in learning of these new comers.

* * *

Bill, who was still having trouble thinking of himself as 'the Mountain,' walked the passageways through the palace of Galnesh Eldador with his hands in his pockets, trying to think of something to do.

Lupus was conducting court. That was pretty boring, and done in Uman, which wasn't a language he could follow easily. Melissa—Raven now—was off riding with Shela. He'd have liked to go with them but he wasn't invited and he didn't want to horn in. He also suspected Shela wanted a crack at Little Storm and he didn't think he should be there for that.

Karel of Stone was kind of an interesting character but he was in and out and hard to keep up with. He wasn't overtly friendly and Bill didn't want to press his luck there. It might be interesting to hang out with that senior Wolf Soldier guy, J'her, but again, that guy seemed pretty busy, and Bill didn't want to impose.

In his life, he'd never felt more useless.

"Mountain!" he heard from behind him.

He turned on his heel in a darkened passageway with steel-banded doors to either side and a single torch burning in a wall sconce next to him and found himself almost face-to-face with Nina of the Aschire, Lee and Chawny with her.

A smile cracked his face. Lee ran to him and leapt up into his arms, her arms around his neck and her face in his beard. Nina held Chawny, who gurgled and shook her fists at him.

"Grandfather!" she said in the language of Men.

"He isn't your grandfather," Nina admonished her, the Aschire's lips set in their usual thin line, something close to a scowl on her surprised-looking face. Her long, purple hair had a strip of birch bark braided into it on the left. The young woman moved somewhat stiffly, her body unnaturally straight compared to the lithe, dancer's movements he'd seen in her. Whatever Melissa—Raven—had done to her must have had lasting effects.

"My Lady," Bill said, and dipped his head.

He turned to face the young girl in his arms. "My Ladies," he said, putting her back on her feet.

Lee, dressed in a blue palace dress with a white sash that tied up in a bow on the side, dipped a curtsy to him. "My Lord," she said, and smiled.

Nina didn't stop scowling.

"Your horse tried to trample the prince," she informed him. "The stablemen are working him now."

"Whu—what?" Bill stammered in English, then caught himself. "Kak etot?" he responded in the language of Men. *What is this?*

"It was scary," Lee informed him, taking his forearm in her left hand. "Mama was going to ride Little Storm, and he broke free, and she couldn't hold him, and he started runnin', and there was Vulpe, and he didn't move, and Little Storm reared up, and then *boom!* Raven tackled him out of the way!"

Bill needed that repeated to him a couple of time, but by then they were all moving back to the stables, Bill in the lead and Lee beside him.

He found Raven and Empress Shela leaning on the fence alongside of a covered arena where the stallion was running on a long rope, called a lead-line, an Uman holding a lunging whip cracking the air behind him.

Bill knew what they were doing. The stallion had done something they don't like, and they were going to exercise it out of him. Lots of people did that.

They were wrong.

"Hey!" he shouted, and found himself angrier than he'd have thought. "Hey, you there! Bring me my horse."

Melissa jumped, the Empress turned on her heel with her eyebrows knit in curiosity, tossing her thick black hair over her shoulder. Bill could see dirt smudges on Melissa's blouse and the thigh of her pants. When they moved, he could see Vulpe was standing in the arena, a few feet past them.

"Mountain," Shela addressed him, straightening. "I sent Nina to find you—I assume she's told you—"

Bill waved his hand and cut her off. The surprise on her face was plain for anyone to see. He was probably pushing his luck here but his temper already had the better of him.

Americans don't have nobility, and it was hard to keep telling himself that so-called 'royals' could do a lot of things to him for mouthing off.

He looked past the two women to the Uman, one of them watching him with the lead line in his hand, and shouted, "I said, '*Stop!*'"

The Uman shook the lead line and the stallion trotted, then slowed down to a walk, cooling off.

"I know what you're doing," he informed Shela. "Don't do that to my horse."

She straightened. He heard Lee gasp behind him. Vulpe was already climbing the fence and Melissa's look of actual fear was unmistakable.

"My Lord," she said, her voice icy, "you have that horse for my husband's good graces, and you have your *freedom* for the same reason."

"And I know you can take back both," Bill said, stopping a foot from the dark-haired Empress. "But until you do, your Imperial Majesty, that is still *my horse* and I don't want him treated that way."

"Your horse struck out at *my son*," Shela informed him.

"And you think you're going to work it out of him," Bill challenged her. "But the problem is that he's a *horse*, and he doesn't even *remember* what he did with Vulpe, and he has *no* idea what you're trying to teach him now."

"My people almost live on their horses," Shela answered. The anger on her face was clear now. "This is how you handle a stallion who strikes out."

"Oh, I'm not saying it won't work," Bill said. "You do this enough times, and he'll be jaded, and he won't act up. He'll be about worthless, too. Let me show you how to do this right."

Shela's eyes widened, then narrowed with rage. Bill knew right then he'd gone too far. Lupus had reminded him there was nothing more important to an Andaron than horses, and Shela was no exception.

"Buh—Mountain," Raven whispered.

"No," Shela took a step back where she could see the both of them. "No, Raven—let us learn from this old man. Teach me, please, the ways of horse flesh, Mountain of Another Land."

Bill stepped away from her while he still could. Now there were a dozen people gathering around them at the stable. It must not be every day that some stranger challenges the woman who called herself *The Bitch of Eldador*.

A sack of carrots, their green stems protruding from the bag, hung from several walls and from the railing along the arena. Bill grabbed one up and put a hand on the upper railing to the arena. He leaned back and then pulled himself up over the fence, the bag in his free hand.

Vulpe leapt right up next to him.

They both launched over the fence together. Shela called her son back but the boy didn't react.

"How old are you, boy?" Bill asked him.

"I'll be twelve," Vulpe informed him, his face upturned.

Bill nodded. "You know your mother's not going to like you coming out here."

"I want to learn this," he answered.

Good enough.

The Uman who held Little Storm's lunge line offered him the end, but Bill grabbed the whip out of his hand instead. He handed the bag of carrots to Vulpe and said, "Wait here," walking the length of the line.

"We've barely worked him an hour," the Uman warned him.

An hour, Bill thought. This horse had been going too long already.

Little Storm stood stock still as Bill approached him. He had to wonder how many times he'd been through this, how many times these people had run the poor horse to exhaustion for no reason.

He reached up and rubbed the stallion's nose. The horse lowered his head and he rubbed the flat space between its eyes. He dropped the whip and unbuckled the line from the halter, dropping it on the ground. Without turning, he said, "Coil that line up and leave here with it."

"My Lord," the Uman said. Bill didn't know if it was an affirmation or a question. He *did* know better than to take his eyes off of a stallion in his care.

"Just do it, Elleck," he heard Vulpe say. The rope dragged away behind him. Shela called for her son again.

The stallion took a step away from Bill. Bill put himself back in its path. The horse stopped, bobbed its head and tried to take a step past Bill to the other side. Bill moved again.

Now I have your attention, Bill thought.

He squatted down and picked up the whip. Using the butt end of that, he kept the stallion face to face with him. The huge animal, as much as seven times Bill's weight, started to become frustrated. It wanted to wander away from Bill and he couldn't.

"Bring me the carrots," Bill commanded Vulpe.

He heard the boy approach from behind him. He held his left hand out toward Vulpe and felt him shove the carrot bag into it. All the time he kept his eyes focused just past the stallion, not making eye contact.

He waved the carrot bag under the stallion's nose. Little Storm lunged for the carrots and Bill pulled them away. He did this two more times, and then he actually put his hand on the bridge of the stallion's nose and pushed the huge animal back.

"These are *my* carrots," he informed Little Storm, more for himself and his audience.

The stallion pawed the ground. Bill tossed the bag into the arena sand behind him.

Now the stallion saw that all he had to do was move the man and he could have the carrots. He tried to shoulder past Bill but Bill put his hand on the stallion's jaw and turned him. He backed up, bobbed his head, pawed the ground and snorted in frustration.

Bill held his ground.

"That's what *I* was doing," Vulpe informed him.

"Just watch," Bill said.

The horse started pacing to either side of the Bill. He ran around the carrots in a circle, Bill standing next to them with the lunging whip. He snorted, he reared, he pawed the air and called out his challenge.

Bill kept his eyes just to the right of the stallion's head, or focused on his legs. He didn't give any ground and he didn't take any.

Finally the stallion broke away, trotted about thirty feet from Bill, wheeled on his back legs and came at him at a dead run.

This is it, Bill told himself. Make or break.

Bill held his ground. Melissa called out to him from the fence. He heard the Empress say something but he couldn't be sure what.

All focused on the charging stallion.

Little Storm stopped dead in front of him. He batted him with his forehead. Bill chuckled and rubbed his ears.

He took a step back, bent down, and pulled a carrot from the bag. He held it out and Little Storm reached for it. He pulled it away. Little Storm stopped. He held it out again and when the stallion reached for it again, he pulled it away again.

When the stallion stopped reaching for it, Bill held the

carrot under Little Storm's nose and let him have it.

Some of the stablemen actually applauded. Vulpe stepped up next to him.

"Mama's smiling," he said.

"Your attention should be on the horse," Bill admonished him. "You want to train a stallion, you have to keep your focus on him. Your mama has a lot of smiles for you, but a stallion only needs to hit you once."

"Yes, grandfather," Vulpe informed him.

Bill nodded. He took a step back from the stallion, put his hand on the boy's shoulder, and then handed him the lunging whip.

"Okay, now," he said. "You do it."

* * *

Melissa watched Bill train the stallion from the fence, Shela on one side of her, Nina on the other, Lee standing just inside the fence where Vulpe had been, the hem of her palace dress already smudged either from climbing the rails or from leaping into the arena sand.

Melissa bounced Chawny in her left arm. The baby was highly interested in the consistency of Melissa's hair, and how many strands she could rearrange.

Shela at first criticized Bill—the Mountain—then became more curious. When the stallion trotted away from him, she said, "See—this doesn't work."

Then the horse wheeled and stampeded toward the one man. Several of the stablemen leapt over the fence, but Shela ordered them to stand fast. Melissa called out, "Bill!" without thinking.

"Stop using his name," Nina admonished her. She didn't like Bill, Melissa knew. She wouldn't care if he died.

But he didn't die. The horse slammed to a halt right in front of him. It was a bluff charge—a tactic by the horse to see if he could take over dominance. Bill had taught him otherwise. Now he was teasing the stallion with a carrot.

"Is—what?" Melissa didn't understand. "Is that a game?"

"No," Shela said, and sighed, turning to face Melissa. "He

won't let the stallion have the carrot until the stallion stops trying to take it. In that way, Little Storm sees the Mountain controls the food. In the herd, the one who controls the food is the leader."

"Lead the herd, lord the horse," Lee said from within the arena. Shela smiled and turned to her daughter.

"You're an Andaron daughter, aren't you?" she asked. "A true Waya Agiladia."

"I am," Lee said, and turned her attention back to the arena, where Bill was handing the lunging whip to her brother.

"Hey!" she protested. "I want to do that, too!" and she was hiking up the front of her skirts and charging across the arena sand.

Shela laughed and shook her head.

"Should she—I mean, is it safe?" Melissa protested.

"Hell, no it isn't safe," Lupus informed them, emerging from a row of stalls to the east of the arena. "When are my kids ever doing something safe?"

Stablemen and women bowed to the Emperor as he approached with a squad of Wolf Soldiers. Shela smiled and reached for him.

"My husband," she said as he took her hand.

"My wife," he responded, and kissed the back of her hand. He turned to Melissa. "My child?"

She laughed and handed Chawny to Lupus. The baby gurgled and beat his face and chest with her tiny fists.

"Ah, this one is her mother's daughter," Lupus said, between pummeling.

Melissa turned her attention to the arena and saw Nina was already shadowing the two older children as Vulpe fended off the stallion and Lee held Bill's forearm and tried to tell her brother what he was doing wrong.

"Let him do it himself, girl," Bill told her. "You don't want him telling you."

"If *that* works I'll make him an Earl," Lupus chuckled.

"You almost had to dig him a hole," Shela informed him.

Lupus laughed again. "Why do you think I'm here?" he asked. "The stableman sent three apprentices to fetch me."

Shela turned her attention back to the arena. "I wouldn't

have hurt him," she said.

"You wouldn't have hurt him *badly*," Lupus corrected her.

"Well, I can't hurt him at all, now," she said. "He was right. I like this way, with carrots. I'll send this method to my father."

Lee opened her mouth to say something, looked up at Bill, closed her mouth and clung to his arm. The stallion reared up on Vulpe and the young man held his ground.

"Now *that* is something you can tell your father," Lupus said.

"Vulpe's courage?" Melissa asked him.

"Mountain shut Lee down," Lupus said.

"I'm seeing it, but I can't believe it," Shela agreed. "She's actually obedient to that old—she's, um—"

Shela shot a guilty look at Melissa.

A smile curled one side of Melissa's mouth. "Every kid is better for someone else," she said, finally. "It'll wear off when she gets used to him."

Shela laughed, kissed her husband's cheek, then reached out and squeezed Melissa's hand.

"I think I will enjoy this while it lasts," she said. Then, with a sideways glance at her husband, she added, "And I think you should pick out a portion on a map of Eldador before my husband forgets his promise."

They all laughed as Vulpe fed a carrot to a much more compliant Little Storm.

* * *

Later that night, they all sat at dinner in the Imperial dining room, Melissa now seated next to Shela, and the children on either side of their adopted grandfather.

"And he bolted at me, and I watched him, and he kept coming, and I was *so scared*, but I didn't show it, and he stopped a *second* before he was gonna hit me, and I fed him a *carrot*," Vulpe was informing all of them.

"He was quite brave," one of the palace barons chimed in. He was a Man whom Shela recognized but didn't really know. "A warrior so fearless should lead a life full of adventure."

Vulpe beamed. His sister, of course, couldn't have it.

"I did it, too," she complained.

"Of course you did," another of the palace barons, this one a hanger-on she remembered as Dellick Jarves, a youngish Man whom Shela had always thought should be doing something more useful with his life, said. "My Lady, your bravery is *already* legendary. Did you not ride your first horse at two?"

"Yeah, I remember when I caught her grandfather helping her out with that," Yonega Waya drawled.

Shela rolled her eyes.

"Is it always like this?" Raven asked her.

"Too often," Shela informed her. She plucked a pile of vegetables from one of the platters and dumped them on her children's plates.

"Mamaaaaaaa," her daughter complained.

"Eat," the Mountain ordered her. "You can't work horses if you don't have the right…um, what's the word for 'Nutrition,' he asked, looking to her.

"Peetanya," her husband informed him.

Shela hadn't known that. However her daughter made a face and immediately started in on her vegetables.

Vulpe actually did the same without being told.

"Never has a man more rightly been named an Earl," Lupus noted.

Shela couldn't say she liked it. She took a sideways glance at Nina, and her protégé also seemed wary.

"How does he *do* that?" she demanded of Raven.

The other woman shrugged and took a sip from her own glass of wine. "It's a grandfather thing," she informed Shela. "They're trying to impress him. It won't last."

"To his Excellence," Dellick Jarves said, raising a bowl of mead. "Long may he…do whatever it is Earls do!"

"What *do* Earls do?" the Mountain asked her husband.

The Emperor was drinking, the rest of the room with him. When they lowered their glasses and bowls, Raven leaned against her, "Does this make me anything?" she asked.

"Are you married to him?" Shela asked her.

Raven sighed. "I don't think officially, no," she answered.

"Then it makes you lucky," she said, glaring at her children.

Raven chuckled, Shela with her.

Dinner dragged on. All Lee wanted to talk about was horses, so all her brother wanted to talk about was horses. Chawny had been in the sun all day and fell asleep into her mashed vegetables, so Nina took her to bed and remained there to guard her.

As the meal broke up, the children insisted that their 'grandfather' take them to bed. When it was revealed that he couldn't read them a story, it was decided they would read him one.

Shela watched them leave. "Are you right to bed?" she asked Raven.

She shook her head. "I think they'll keep him away from me as long as they can," she said.

"As long as Nina will let them," Shela said. "Come with me."

Raven followed her obediently out of the dining room, where her husband was engaged with his Oligarchs and Duke Hectar, out to the stables.

"I'd like to finally ride that horse," she said.

Raven nodded.

They found their way to the stables. There was a light mist of a rain—not enough to inhibit riding, but enough to keep the moon hidden and the torches out. Magical light was preferred in the stables, open flame being a danger to the hay.

Shela focused her power, and these lights glowed brilliant around the arena fence. She walked past them toward Little Storm and Blizzard's paddocks.

"Did you do that?" Raven asked her.

"Yes," she answered. The horse had bedded itself down for the night in a pile of hay. Its sire, Blizzard, stood at its paddock's steel gate. He nickered a warning to the other horses as she approached.

"What's it like?" Raven asked her.

Shela turned on her. "What's what like?" she asked.

"Your spells, your—um—casting? Is that the word?"

Shela nodded. “It’s an expenditure of energy,” she said. “It’s sometimes like being angry at a man, then realizing that you still love him.”

“Do you get a lot of practice at that?” Raven asked her, smirking.

Shela turned on her. She reached behind her and pulled the laces from her palace gown. The string came loose and the top dropped to her waist.

“No,” she said. “In fact, I don’t. I’m blessed with a husband who loves me, and I love him.”

Raven blushed and looked away. “My—my apologies, your Imperial Majesty,” she stammered. “I meant no—um—insult to you.”

Shela sighed. She pushed the dress down past her hips and handed it to Raven, standing in nothing but her leather harness, that with the breast straps around her hips. She reached down and took the strings to the straps in her fingers and reached them up behind her neck.

“No,” she said to Raven, “you’ve done nothing. I’m not a happy woman tonight, Raven. My husband has informed me he’s out to campaign.”

“I’m sorry, your—Shela. What means…campaign?”

“You understand army? Wolf Soldiers? Elddorian Regulars?” Shela asked. Raven nodded.

“He’s leaving with them all,” she said. “And he’s raised his Daff Kanaar allies, and they’re all meeting in Uman City, which is another city like Galnesh Eldador.”

“Why?”

“Because of this prophetic song,” Shela said. “You understand ‘prophetic?’”

“Yes.”

“He believes it’s finally time to push our fortunes, and to conquer the rest of Fovea.”

She led Raven to her personal stalls, where she kept her riding equipment. As a younger woman she’d needed nothing more than this and a skirt. As a mother of three, pants made riding much more comfortable.

She stepped into a pair of leather pants the same color as

the ones her husband liked to wear and a white cotton blouse with a tight middle that pushed up her breasts. It made riding a lot easier if they, as Yonega Waya put it, couldn't "Do their own thing."

Raven's face was knit in concern. She probably feared her Mountain would be leaving with them, and she was right to fear.

"The rest of Fovea?" Raven asked. "Can—can you do that?"

Shela shrugged and plucked her boots from where they hung on a hook. "I have to assume they can," she said. "My husband is undefeated in battle, and he's been in many."

She placed a hand on Raven's shoulder and stepped into her boots. Raven placed a delicate hand on her hip to help her balance.

"How long will this take?" she asked. Yes, she was worrying for her man. She remembered her first time at home while her husband campaigned. She'd wept and wept, worrying for him constantly.

"Years," she said. "If you want his children, now that he's an Earl, I'd advise you to apply yourself. You *do* know how to get yourself pregnant?"

She looked into Raven's eyes.

"Yeah," Raven said. "Been thinking a lot about that."

"I'm thinking I might want another," Shela admitted. She started down an aisle in the stables. The light mist seemed like it might be tapering off.

"Wouldn't it be grand to be pregnant together?"

Chapter Sixteen:

Time for a Change

For five days, the Mountain exercised his stallion with the Emperor's eldest children, their nanny and his wife in attendance. Glynn would watch them from a proper balcony, in a room assigned her by the Eldadorian Emperor, befitting a landed baron of that nation.

A simple suite of rooms with a bedchamber and a parlor. Not nearly as grand as those she'd become used to in Outpost IX, but enough room for her meditations and her slumber. She admitted she enjoyed the balcony which overlooked the stables. She'd feared the room would fill with the stink of manure but in fact the Emperor kept a remarkably clean stable and instead, even in spring, the only smell that filled the place was that of fresh cut hay.

Compared to the smell of Men, she found that odor delightful.

She still reflected on her single day of scrubbing dumpsters in the city proper. The Eldadorians maintained these huge, metal monstrosities for the collection of common refuse, and then would cart them away one day per week to other carts, which would carry this refuse to an open pit past the hills to the west of the city. Here the refuse could be tilled back into the earth, planted over, and new pits dug.

In Trenbon they would cart waste into Tren Bay, and often times it would wash back up onto the shore. Then it was a villain's job to pick it up and remove it.

At least there were no slops. In the rest of Fovea, common persons relieved themselves into pots kept in their bed chambers, and then cast these onto their personal property if they had it, more often into common streets, to mix with the excrement of horses, dogs and other persons. In Eldador it wasn't uncommon at all for a home to have fresh running water flowing into it, and for persons to relieve themselves into water bowl receptacles which carried their refuse away.

Glynn Escaroth didn't understand the purpose of the system, but she didn't have to see it, neither did she have to clean up after it, and for that she was grateful.

Below her the Man called 'Mountain' was running his stallion through a series of poles. The purpose was the horse should switch leads as the pole ran to his left or right, and then stay on balance. This Mountain would do this, and then his woman, now called Raven, would do the same thing, either in a man's or in a proper side saddle, and then the children would follow suit. To one side Nina of the Aschire, called among other things *The Emperor's Watch Bitch* for her unnerving dedication to the children's safety, oversaw everything, usually with little Chawny in her arms.

"You know we've got to get them away from the Emperor," Xinto of the Woods informed her.

Poor Glynn nearly leapt over the balcony rail! She turned to see the little Scitai in his rumpled over cloak, with his rakish hat with the long, orange feather, standing in the doorway behind her, grinning up a storm. He bowed to her and added, "My Lady, Baroness."

"My Lady *Duchess*, if you please," she corrected him, drolly. "I see you've finally relieved yourself of the Emperor's hospitality."

Xinto clucked his tongue and stepped back into the room. Glynn followed him. "The Emperor's dungeons were designed by the Bounty Hunter's Guild," Xinto said, "although he doesn't know it. I could have left sooner, except Karel of Stone kept watch over me, and still is by proxy."

"Ah," Glynn said, smiling. "The flaw in his plan. You bribed or slew the ones sent to watch you."

"Nothing so common," Xinto informed her. "The Guild does not kill without cause. No, I slipped out when a bored watcher fell asleep, found my cloak and some extract I keep, and now the two of them will sleep, each with a dart in his neck, until relief comes. I suspect I have another half an hour to leave the city."

"So little time," Glynn noted.

"True," he said, "and having had time to consider this song of yours, I have to believe it would be best for all of us to leave Galnesh Eldador, your foreign charges with you."

"Easier said than done," Glynn complained. She crossed the room and sat on the corner of her bed. Xinto leapt up next to her. "The Emperor loves his countrymen, his children no less. This woman who calls herself Raven now actually saved the life of young Vulpe. The other, calling himself the Mountain, tamed one of Blizzard's get and has been named an Earl of estates outside of Angador."

"An Earl?" Xinto parroted her. "And yourself, a Baroness?"

Glynn waved her hand. "Don't remind me, not that I care," she said, although in fact the treatment stung. "I'm not surprised the Emperor would use title to ingratiate his countryman."

"So they *are* from the same lands?" Xinto said. "I'd thought I saw a similarity between them, and they're both giants."

Xinto's nature was to collect intelligence. Time, however, was fleeting. "Regardless of this," Glynn informed him, "we must needs away from here, I agree, and our charges with us. There is another I would meet upon the road, another mentioned in my song, no less, and after tomorrow I think he will move on from whence he's waiting."

Xinto nodded. "I could go find this person for you," he offered. "Inform him that you need more time."

Glynn shook her head, her green hair waving underneath

her chin. Outside she could hear the Mountain telling Vulpe to keep his heels down.

"He's a Volkhydran, and a Wolf Soldier deserter, I fear," she said. "He has no trust in him. I think he will not speak with you."

Xinto shrugged. "I've dealt with Volkhydrans before," he said. "He could even know me."

Glynn smiled. "All the less reason to trust you," she said. "No, we must leave together, and anon."

Xinto nodded. "How to convince your former charges, then?" he asked.

Glynn sighed. "They'll stand by each other and do nothing, if we ask the two of them together," she said. "We got to get them apart, and then perhaps by guile or by force—"

Xinto was already shaking his head. "You don't want to bully them out of the city," he said. "They'd escape the first opportunity they saw, and I don't want to sleep in shifts watching them. Some spell to convince them, perhaps?"

Now Glynn shook her head. "Another development anew is this Raven's immunity to normal magix," she said. "We'd noted among the Uman-Chi her abnormal resistance and resilience to magic, now it seems to absolutely evade her. Young Nina was rendered unconscious for hours and powerless for more than a day when she tried a spell on Raven. I myself was thrown from the Imperial dining room over the palace wall, merely floating a glamour toward her."

Xinto frowned, impressed. "No magic, no force. Too bad they're Men, or we might try to reason with them."

Glynn sighed again. "Too well is it known that reason eludes the capabilities of Men," she said.

Xinto smiled. "Reason, yes," he said. "But not raw emotion."

Glynn nodded. "It is ever true the way to engage Men is through their hearts," she said. "Get their blood pumping and they might do almost anything."

Xinto smiled a wolfish grin. "Yes," he said to her, leaping off of the bed and walking to the doorway to the open balcony.

"Properly motivated, or properly engaged, I believe it's

safe to say Men might do anything, indeed."

* * *

Shela entered the nursery to rouse Chawny from her nap. She'd just come from a meeting with J'her and a Wolf Soldier she'd assigned to follow the Baroness Glynn Escaroth on her dumpster-cleaning duties. He'd ended up drunk in a bar with no excuses for his action, and truth-saying revealed he honestly didn't know. There was something wrong with that man, but whatever had been done with him had happened days earlier and was now too faint to sniff out.

Now she didn't sense one of her children, and that was strange. Normally her babies were like bells in her head, always ringing. Chawny's bell had rung silent.

She shook her head as she pushed open the door to the children's bedroom. Strange, strange happenings.

Her next annoyance came in finding Chawny's bassinet empty. If Nina didn't watch her closely, Lee liked to take the baby out and mother her; normal for a young girl but not good for Chawny.

"Lee!" Shela called for her daughter.

"Yes, mama," her eldest daughter emerged from the playroom alongside the nursery, her brother in tow.

"Lee, do you have your sister?"

"No, mama."

"Do you know where Nina is?"

Both children looked at each other, then at her, a warning signal to any mother.

"She's sleepin'," Vulpe said.

"Sleeping?"

"She was crying," Lee admitted.

"Oh, no," Shela said. She didn't think it would be so easy for the girl to get over her conflict with White Wolf. He'd become a father to her. "Did she take the baby?"

"Chawny is in here," Lee said, and ran to the bassinet. She looked as surprised as Shela to find her missing.

Nina's room lay opposite the nursery, on the single hall to this place. Glynn burst through the door in a moment, to find Nina in a fetal position on top of her covers, and no Angry at the Sun.

"Where is the baby?" Shela demanded.

Nina leapt up in a moment, reaching for her knives. Shela didn't need to ask again to know the answer.

She summoned Power's might and reached out with her mind for her youngest daughter, and found nothing on this hall.

Nothing on this wing of the palace.

Nothing within the palace walls.

Nothing within the city of Eldador.

"Alarm!" she called out. Behind her Lee started crying, so Vulpe of course joined her. "Alarm, the Guard!"

Nina sprinted past her without asking—Shela bolted for her private rooms where she kept a large portion of her best materials and tools. Nina would protect the children and maintain contact with Shela. She dragged Lee and Vulpe into their room, and activated the wards that made them impervious.

Shela found the Wolf Soldier guards who stood at the one entrance to the hall, a full squad. Shela had its sergeant by the collar before she stopped running.

"You," she commanded the soldier next to him. "Alarm the Guard. Chawny is missing and not within the city."

"*You*," she addressed the sergeant, the other soldier already sprinting off with two of his fellows. "Who has been down that hall?"

"N-no one, m'lady," he said. "Yourself, Nina, the children."

"Raven, the Mountain, Glynn Escaroth?" Shela demanded. Her magic reached into his mind, finding the answers before he uttered them.

"No," he said. "And none asked."

"On your *life*," she told him, "no one but myself or the Emperor past these doors."

"On my life," he said, and made a fist over his heart.

* * *

"I am so sick of your asking—" the Emperor complained, and a squad of Wolf Soldiers burst into the throne room.

J'her knew the Emperor's foul mood. He could likely lose

this squad if this interruption proved frivolous.

"Alarm," the sergeant shouted. "Alarm the Guard!"

The throne room erupted into chaos. J'her raced Lupus to the Wolf Soldiers.

"What is this?" Lupus snarled, pounding across the throne room.

"Lupus," the man said. J'her recognized Thek Mandin, a Volkhydran, already ear-marked for captain. "From Shela—alarm the guard.

"Your youngest daughter is missing and not in the city."

A momentary look of shock crossed Lupus' face. No one expected those words.

The look that replaced it spoke of an anger that actually made them all step back from him. When old King Glennen had died, J'her had seen Lupus on the verge of berserker rage. This seemed worse.

"Seal the city," he commanded, and turned to J'her.

"Martial law," he said. "Right now. Raise the whole Pack. I want a door to door of every room in the palace and every house in Eldador, and I want it now. Use Eldadorian regulars if you have to—Hectar has a thousand, they are yours."

"Lupus, Shela said—"

In a moment, the Emperor's face was inches from J'her's, his eyes fixed on his Supreme Commander. J'her actually felt the huge Man's breath on his cheeks and nose.

"*DID YOU HEAR ME, SUPREME COMMANDER?*"

"*I HEARD YOU, SIR!*" J'her responded immediately, a reflex. He was a Wolf Soldier.

Lupus took J'her by the shoulders in his hands, the grip painfully tight, the Emperor's eyes almost burning into J'her's own.

"Every room, every house, make it happen."

"I will," J'her promised him.

Lupus turned on his heel, J'her turn on his. The four majors whose Millennia were stationed permanently in Eldador the Port already waited for him at the throne room entrance.

"You saw that?"

Dev Nevala nodded, an Uman with scars on her face, the

Mark of the Conqueror received for her bravery at the Battle for Wisex and the second invasion of Thera. Agtar and Belmar, both Volkhydrans—Lupus called them 'the bookends'—nodded after. They were all muscle, with the stupid look of muscle men. In fact these were brilliant men whom the Emperor had saved from hanging in Ulep for running some kind of protection scam.

"We saw," answered M'den Grek, another Uman, from Sental, his ever-present smile pointed at his Supreme Commander. "I've never seen him that angry."

"I have," J'her answered him. "You know the situation?"

"Hard not to," Dev said. "What are your orders?"

"Shut the city down," J'her said. "Martial law—everyone off the streets. Dev, your Millennia and Duke Hectar's regulars will search the city house-by-house. What you can't enter, break down."

She turned on her heel. That would be a mean job. Eldadorians were used to a certain level of independence.

"Agtar, your troops have the palace. Start with the dungeons and work your way up."

Agtar left. Since the inauguration when a Bounty Hunter had almost escaped from Eldador through the tunnels beneath the city, Wolf Soldiers had maintained squads who were specifically responsible for them. Agtar commanded these men.

"Belmar, the wharves," J'her said. "Every ship and, if any have left today, run them down with our Sea Wolves. If you have to leave the city, take one of our *barely gifted* messengers, every ship."

Belmar made a fist over his heart and left. During the day when the Empress bore Angry at the Sun, Belmar had personally stood watch outside of her rooms with three of his captains. He had wanted to be the first Wolf Soldier to salute her.

If Belmar caught the man or woman who took her…That was a thought for another day.

J'her stood alone with M'den. M'den was the best of them. If J'her should die tomorrow, M'den would have the Supreme Commander's job before laying J'her to rest.

"Shela said that Chawny isn't in the city," J'her said.

"I heard. Which roads?"

"All of them."

"I think not," M'den said. "Free Legionnaires will be in the city of Metz. Let's have a wizard tell them to secure the east, and have Thera come in from the West with two thousand Lancers. I'll go south."

J'her nodded, recognizing the better plan. "I'll let the Emperor know," he said. He took M'den by the shoulder, just as Lupus had done with him.

"She doesn't disappear," he said, looking into M'den's eyes. "Chawnaluh Nanahee Nudageehay sleeps in her own bed tonight, no matter the cost."

* * *

Shela in her room searched for the personal signature which marked her daughter's aura, as only a mother could know it. Her identity, her being, her smell. She'd expanded her search from Galnesh Eldador and moved to the roads and outlying villages.

"Where are our troops?" Lupus demanded.

"We have a thousand searching the palace," J'her told him, "and a thousand at the wharves and marketplace. Two thousand are searching the city, Wolf Soldiers and Eldadorian regulars. Another thousand went south with M'den."

"East, west?" Lupus said. Courtiers put his armor on him, Blizzard had already been saddled. Wolf Soldiers buzzed in and out of the Empress' rooms like bees to a hive.

"We have confirmation the Free Legion has mobilized one hundred squads from Metz. Duke Two Spears has sent two thousand lancers east. Andurin is already searching their city, in case this is the work of a very gifted wizard."

"Check the other kids, Shela," Lupus said.

"I just did—they're fine," Shela said. She checked with Nina every fifteen minutes. It wouldn't be the first time that someone came after them one way, to get at them another.

Dev returned, and made a fist over her heart. "They aren't in the palace, they aren't in the tunnels," she said. "They didn't leave through there—the passages are secure from the inside.

"But Lupus," she said, and she waited for the Emperor to

look into her eyes before continuing, "Xinto of the Woods is missing."

"War's beard!" J'her swore. They'd kept a watch on the Scitai, and a watch on the watch. Shela couldn't imagine how he'd snuck past *that*.

"Take your Millennia southwest," Lupus said. "Go as far as the Lone Wood. Search everything you—"

"Got her!" Shela shouted.

She had gone northeast on a hunch. Someone might think to leave the country on a fishing vessel. Yonega Waya had used them to invade Trenbon long ago.

Sure enough, halfway between Tonkin and Eldador, she detected her daughter, moving fast.

"The shore road, half way to Tonkin," she said. "I can't see her, but I can sense her movement. One of them must be a wizard, trying to mask her essence from me."

"I'll go on Blizzard," Lupus said, as the squire attached his breastplate to his black plate. "Dev, your Millennia will cross south of me. If they detect me and turn south, you'll catch them."

"J'her you'll catch M'den's Millennia and divert them south of Dev's. If they get in front of or behind Dev, you will catch them."

"I'm going with you," Shela said.

"You're staying here to coordinate," Lupus ordered her. She knew he would, even when she opened her mouth. She knew the decision made sense, too.

Yonega Waya would more likely catch them if he could go as fast as Blizzard could take him.

"You can't go alone," J'her protested. "Lupus, be reasonable—they know who you are."

Lupus nodded. He searched out Shela, and their eyes met.

Only one horse could keep pace with Blizzard.

"Fetch the Mountain to me," he ordered J'her. "Tell him we'll be riding fast. There's a breast plate and greaves that used to belong to Glennen—they should fit him close enough. There's a falchion the Volkhydrans made for me in the armory."

He turned to Shela when J'her saluted and left.

"Contact Ancenon and let him know what you know. Tell

him to cut them off from Tonkin."

"I will," Shela said. He stepped down from the dressing stand, and she ran to him.

"And as for Xinto—he's yours. You can do whatever you want to him, I don't care. He wants to run; you make an example of him—a *scary* example. If he has anything to do with this, you make it worse."

Shela nodded.

He kissed her and he gave her a squeeze. "She will sleep in her own bed tonight," he told her.

"Just bring her home safe," she said, and she felt the tears on her cheeks.

* * *

Melissa sat alone in her rooms on a stool by their one window, a paintbrush in her hand with the paint drying on it, a blank canvas in front of her. She smelled the oil in the paint, the salt air coming off of Tren Bay. A breeze blew in through the window, caught her hair and the ruffles at the neckline of the purple blouse she wore.

They'd come for Bill an hour ago. Might be more time or less—there wasn't a clock in this room. The sun hadn't moved very far or the shadows on the floor lengthened much since then. Lupus was leaving because someone had kidnapped his daughter, and he was going after them. He needed Bill, because Little Storm could run with Blizzard.

They'd dressed him up in a leather vest and a breast plate over it and strapped steel shielding to his shins and arms. They'd pushed a huge sword into his hand, and then given him a sheath for it that he could wear over his shoulder. Finally they'd pushed a helmet over his head and guided him out the door.

She'd wanted to kiss him before he left, to warn him to be careful, to wish him well. The Uman J'her and his Wolf Soldiers weren't having it. They'd burst in with the armor and weapon and told him what was going on as they dressed him. They weren't asking him if he would help, they told him they were going. The princess was missing and this was serious.

People who'd take a princess from an emperor would kill

to keep her. Supposedly the Emperor could handle himself, but Bill wasn't a warrior. He could die in a fight.

He could die without her ever getting to tell him that she loved him.

"My Lady, Raven," she heard behind her.

She spun around on her stool to see Glynn standing in her rooms, her hands held one-in-the-other before her, dressed in a heavy cotton blue dress with bows on the skirt and white lace at the neck and cuffs. Her green hair hung loose at her shoulders, the breeze not affecting it.

"Oh, Glynn," she said, and couldn't help bursting into tears. She didn't run to the other woman because, even though she was really more than a century and a half old, she looked sixteen, but she felt the tears run down her cheeks and her nose fill up. "Glynn, someone took Chawny, and now Lupus took Buh—took the Mountain to find them."

Glynn smiled a smug little smile and Xinto stepped out from behind her. He was wearing the same cloak he'd had when she first saw him, and a pointed hat with a rakish, orange feather.

"The princess is fine," he said. "Your man is going to go on a hard ride, but he's in no danger."

Melissa straightened. Xinto was a prisoner. If Glynn released him…

What was she getting into?

"What's going on?" she demanded.

Glynn smiled that irritating little smile again. "Raven," she said, "You've heard my song, and you know Lupus is the One about whom we were warned," she said.

She shook her head. "Oh, Glynn," she said.

Xinto stepped forward. "Believe me when I tell you," he said, "I am no more anxious than you to make an enemy of the Emperor Rancor Mordetur."

"*You*," Raven said, and wiped the tears from her cheeks and eyes with her blouse's cuff, "are just afraid of him."

"Of course I'm afraid of him," Xinto said. "I'm afraid of him, she's afraid of him, most of Fovea is afraid of him. You'd be afraid of him, too, if you knew him."

Raven shook her head. "He's been nothing but decent,"

she began.

"You mean, he gives you things," Xinto interrupted her, "but you've spoken to him, just as I have. What does your countryman want, Raven?"

Melissa had been thinking a lot about this. She reflected on that conversation she'd had with Shela after dinner one day, when she'd learned that Lupus planned to go conquer the rest of Fovea.

Forget the fact that he was probably going to take Bill with him. He was going to go *conquer Fovea.* He was going to do it because he felt like it. They hadn't done anything to him, they didn't have anything he needed, he just *wanted to.*

Whose side was she actually on?

Glynn stepped up next to Xinto. They were closing in on her. "What do you think he wants, Raven?" Glynn repeated.

Melissa leaned back against the stool.

"He wants more," she said, finally. "He wants more land, more followers, more power. He thinks he can change the world, and he hasn't even explored it all yet."

"And what will the world be like, with a man like that running it?" Xinto asked her.

Melissa had never liked history. She'd never liked the human sciences. But she wasn't stupid, either; she could see what was right in front of her. The Emperor of Eldador, fellow human or not, wanted to be the emperor of a bigger empire, and he was pretty-much convinced he could do it. More importantly, these people were likely in no position to stop him.

Lupus liked to call himself 'the Conqueror.' More importantly, he liked other people to call him that.

Melissa sighed.

"What do you want me to do?"

Chapter Seventeen:

Free as a Bird

Side by side, Blizzard and Little Storm pounded out the distance between Galnesh Eldador and the little sea village called Tonkin. There'd been a spring rain and the roads were wet and slushy, barely graveled and mostly mud. Spray from the horses' hooves coated their sides as well as their riders from their feet to their noses.

Lupus leaned into his saddle and rode with his head close to the horse's neck. Bill tended to want to sit back more, move with his hips, flow with Little Storm's natural motion. More used to Appaloosas, a destrier like Little Storm gave a whole other ride. The stallion's natural power surged through him, travelling up to Bill through his loins, letting him feel the raw energy of a tireless mount.

Lupus rode grim-faced and didn't speak. Blizzard cantered along the road without as much effort as Bill would have expected. Normally he wouldn't run a horse flat out like this—he'd want to trot and walk as well as canter so as not to leave the horse jaded.

Both Blizzard and Little Storm seemed to thrive on the punishing pace. Bill's legs and butt were already burning, his back and shoulders aching from the effort. Three hours into the ride he was ready to call a halt when they saw wagon on the horizon.

Lupus turned to him and grinned. It was an almost evil sight. Right then, Bill saw his priority was not to save his daughter as much as it was to punish the people who'd dared to offend him, who'd dared to challenge him.

Bill's heart constricted. Someone was going to die in a few minutes, he knew. He didn't want to kill anyone, and he didn't want to join them, either.

Lupus touched his steel heels to Blizzard's sides and the stallion pressed on to a speed even faster than Bill had experienced during their race. Little Storm bore down and silently matched his sire. Side-by-side, they closed the distance between themselves and the wagon.

"I'll take them head-on," Lupus told him. "You ride past them, turn around and just block their horses. I don't expect you to fight, but don't you expect that you won't have to. They have my daughter—they'll know what I plan to do them."

Bill nodded. His heart raced. He was sweating in the cold.

Someone stood up in the wagon. It was a simple, four-wheeled, open-topped flat wagon with at least two people in it. Bill imagined that he heard a shout, and then the wagon picked up its speed.

The horses pushing faster than he thought a horse could move sensed a race was on and pushed faster still. The wind actually stung Bill's eyes and made his tears run.

Lupus had a long, shiny sword out. Its surface was so perfect it almost gleamed. Bill thought maybe he should pull his own sword, but drawing it over his shoulder on a moving horse, he was afraid he'd cut his own head off.

The person in the wagon stood back up and waved his hands over his head. Lupus didn't slow down so Bill didn't. The horses thundered on. It wasn't long before they were less than a stone's throw from the wagon.

The teamsters on the wagon reined in. Bill flew past them, then yanked the stallion's reins to the left, turning the horse in front of the wagon.

Bill nearly sailed out of the saddle, his legs throbbing and almost too weak to grip the stallion's barrel. He righted himself, the horse bobbing his head and pawing the graveled road. Bill pulled his sword out over his shoulder and faced the two steaming draft horses that had been pulling the wagon. Both were black in rope harnesses.

Lupus was speaking to the drivers in Uman. Both were clearly terrified. Either they knew him on sight or they saw the armor and weapon and knew they were no match for him. They were two Uman men with long white hair, dressed in white homespun over shirts and cloth pants, both with old, worn boots. Their eyes were wide with fear and they were speaking too quickly for Bill to follow.

Melissa—Raven—was the one who'd focused on Uman.

Lupus raised his head up and regarded Bill. "They say they don't have her," he said.

"Maybe they're behind the ones we're looking for?" Bill suggested.

Lupus nodded. He spat on the ground. "Shela wanted to come and I said, 'No.' I should have brought Nina. We could have asked her—she knows Chawny as well as anyone alive."

Bill kicked Little Storm and the horse walked the distance to the wagon. The wind changed and Bill got a whiff of something he hadn't smelled in a long time.

"You smell that?" he asked Lupus.

Lupus straightened and sniffed the air. Another father, he knew the scent right away.

"What do you two do?" he asked the Uman.

One of them responded, "As we said, your Imperial Majesty, we're simple porters. We've a load, we're paid to move it—"

"They've got a load alright," Bill said. He pushed the horse a little farther forward, past the drivers to their wagon's bed, and pushed an old, worn tarp aside from what it covered in the back.

Two baskets, each full of diapers.

No baby.

"War's beard!" Lupus swore.

"What?" Bill said.

"I'll bet those are Chawny's diapers," he said. "Someone

paid these two to move them. That comes from Chawny—Shela detected it."

Bill nodded. As much as anything that was magical made sense, that made sense.

Lupus sighed. "There's a town near here," he said. "I know its Baron. He has a wizard. I need to coordinate with Shela. You watch these two. I'll be back in a bit."

Bill nodded. He needed a rest. Lupus kicked his horse into motion and Bill had to rein his own horse in to keep him from following.

"A noble steed, my Lord," one of the Uman porters said. "Is it one of Blizzard's get?"

"I'm not a lord, I'm called 'the Mountain,'" Bill informed them in Uman, even as he realized he *was*, in fact, an Earl. "And yes, this is."

"You must be an important Man," the other said. "There aren't many who ride so well."

Bill shrugged. He saw how nobility was treated here—they'd be more honest with him as a common. "He seems to like me," he said. "I'm told, um, no one else can ride him."

One of the Uman turned to the other. "The same as the Emperor's Blizzard," he said.

"I don't understand," Bill said.

The other turned back to him and said, "It's said the Emperor was chosen by his horse, and not the other way around."

Bill nodded. These men were afraid. They were making small talk out of nervousness. They didn't know what was going to happen to them, and they had decided, as people would, that if they made a friend of him, then he'd have a harder time hurting them.

That wasn't up to him, he knew.

"You're porters," Bill said, finally. "You move stuff with your wagons?"

"One wagon," one of the Uman said. "It's all we have. We've worked hard and earned these horses. Now we move larger loads, farther, and make more money."

"There's much trade in Eldador," the other said. "More every year. There are so many in the capitol it consumes more than it can make for itself, so there is always a need to bring in more."

Bill nodded. Probably true of every capitol.

"You—my Lord, you don't know, I mean, can you?" one began, alternately trying to look him in the eye and looking down.

"If you were just moving a load with no idea why, I don't know why the Emperor would hurt you," Bill said, having a little trouble with some of the words.

They seemed openly relieved.

"You were afraid?" Bill asked them.

They looked like they couldn't believe the question. "The Emperor is terrible in his wrath," one said.

"There are a thousand stories of what he's done to his enemies," the other informed him. "You are his associate, you do not know this?"

"No," Bill said. "What has he done to his enemies?"

They turned to each other. Scared, Bill thought. They didn't want to say anything about the Emperor. This could be a trap.

"On my honor," Bill said. "I'll repeat nothing you say."

"On your honor?" one repeated.

Bill nodded.

* * *

"I'm bored," Lee complained.

"Me, too," Vulpe agreed with her.

Nina paced the nursery. Stupid, how could she be so stupid?

She hadn't proved herself worthy, this much she knew. She'd betrayed Lupus and Shela and lifted her hand against them. Now Chawny had been abducted, and who knew what would befall her.

"Nina?"

Nina immediately alerted to Shela's voice in her mind.

"Yes? Does Lupus have her?"

"Lupus has overrun them, and found porters with dirty diapers."

"Dirty diapers?" That made for an interesting trick. What

the body left behind came of the body. As far as a spell behaved, one could be fooled, especially a mother desperate for her child.

"So, now we don't know—"

"Lupus wants me to ask you if anyone has had interest in the disposal of our diapers."

Nina knew the wet nurse, whose family made a few extra coins removing such things, supplying toys, weaving clean linens for the baby. She gave Shela their name, and dreaded their fate if they made more coin giving what they thought of as worthless to some enemy of the Empire's.

"Baby's cryin'," Lee told her.

"Take care of—what?"

She turned her attention to the room around her, and sure enough, she heard Chawny's plaintiff cry. A sound she knew as well as her own breathing.

Nina ran to the nursery from the playroom, and sure enough, she heard the cry from the empty bassinet.

"Oh, I don't believe it," she said. It seemed too simple.

"Edvagietye," she said, and snapped her fingers—the simplest of all spells to dispel magic.

Angry at the Sun lay wailing in her bassinet, her diaper heavily soiled.

"Shela!" she called the Empress in her mind.

* * *

"We've found another of the people mentioned in the song," Xinto informed the young girl.

Her eyes were red-rimmed from crying. Say what you would, this girl loved that fat old Man for some reason, and she was very dedicated to him. That was Xinto's way in.

People in general, no matter the species, wanted to feel like they were moving forward. Xinto had learned this as a child more than one hundred years ago, in his village in Conflu, playing with other children, both Scitai and Men. If they wanted to play a game Xinto didn't want to play, it was always more effective to give them a better game than to refuse to play. If they wanted to go somewhere he didn't want to go, he quickly learned to posit a more interesting place than simply to criticize their decision.

That simple philosophy and served him well from then to now. Not that this Raven could admit her benefactor might not be the best caretaker of her future, it was time to suggest a better one.

"Where?" Raven asked, and sniffed.

"To the south," Glynn said, stepping forward. Xinto wanted her to stop crowding the young girl but couldn't think of a way to tell the Uman-Chi to stop. Men were especially aware of their personal space and would react unpredictably if trapped.

He finally stepped to one side, away from the girl toward the bed she shared with the old man. The quilt stank of the smells of Men, but he ignored it.

The girl sighed, a little more relaxed.

"We must go ourselves, and find this one," Xinto informed Raven. "We need you to come with us."

"Why not just tell the Emper—tell Lupus?" Raven argued.

Xinto looked into her brown, doe eyes. The girl had already answered this question in her own mind. Xinto just needed to reinforce it.

"Because if we tell the Emperor, he'll send one thousand Wolf Soldiers and capture this person," Xinto said. "Most likely, he'll kill the man. We can go ourselves and speak with him. He's already identified himself to Glynn—he knows her and he'll trust her."

Melissa sniffed again. "So we'll bring him back?"

Xinto and Glynn exchanged a glance. Raven saw it and stiffened. She wasn't foolish, this one, she could at the very least keep up with them, if not exceed them.

"We need to know what this new person can tell us," Xinto said. "The addition of a new member to our group has brought another member each time. You arrived and added Glynn. Glynn identified you and added me. I was brought here and this new person arrived."

"He's here?" Raven asked, squinting her eyes.

"He was," Glynn said.

Xinto wanted to curse her into silence. The girl might have the wisdom of a century and a half, but she had been taught to be so self-assured as a Caster she couldn't believe the whole world didn't see things her way, if properly educated. This made for an ally who could undo his plans without trying.

"He left, from fear of the Emperor," Xinto said, covering for Glynn. "We suspect he could be a Wolf Soldier deserter."

Raven nodded. She looked past the two of them to the door.

"How can we get out of here?" she asked.

* * *

The Andaron warhorse Melissa rode was nothing like the palfrey she'd ridden in Outpost IX. For a week she'd been trying to get used to it; its fearlessness, its tendency to want to put its head down and push things out of its way. A mare, it didn't know a lot of fear and it relied on a lot more attention from its rider. A twitch to the reins could have it wheeling to one side or charging—responses that could save a warrior's life but which came as a huge surprise to a novice rider.

Xinto rode behind her, his hands on his waist or creeping to other parts of her anatomy. He complained about every bump in the road, every quick turn, start or hesitation. Her father would have described him as a guy in an expensive car complaining that the radio was too loud.

They'd informed her they'd found another person mentioned in the song, and Glynn had arranged to meet him in the south. The Emperor would *never* allow them to leave on their own; he'd prefer to send a thousand Wolf Soldiers to the place where Glynn knew he was hiding and capture him. Melissa knew Lupus well enough to believe Glynn and Xinto on this. She needed more information on these people mentioned in the song; she needed time away from the influence of the people who would cage her.

With the Emperor chasing after his own daughter and the palace and the city already having been searched, it wasn't all that hard to get out of the city through the Imperial stables. They acted as if they were doing what they were told to do, and they kept Xinto out of sight. They rode out of the gates with nothing more than a wave to Wolf Soldier guards.

No sooner was Raven out the gate than she saw that same movement in the winter hay to the west of Galnesh Eldador again.

Her 'not there,' a whisper through the hay where there was no breeze, gone before she was really sure that she'd seen it. She rode her mare with an eye to the left as both horses moved south, but never saw it again.

They travelled less than an hour before they met the first Wolf Soldier patrol; fifty warriors with an officer on horseback leading them. They marched north along the road to the capitol and met the three of them moving south.

"My Lord," Glynn said, inclining her head to the mounted officer.

"My Lady," he said. He was a Man, dressed in Wolf Soldier greys with steel sleeves on his upper arms and steel greaves on his shins.

"What is your purpose on this road?" the officer demanded.

"We were bound for the capitol but were turned away at the gates," Glynn lied to him, her face unreadable. "I'd thought to be received in the High Court."

The officer tipped his head to Glynn. "I apologize, my Lady," he said, "however the capitol is closed for at least the day. I believe there are estates to the south…"

"Yes, yes, Sirrah," Glynn assured him, and painted on a smile. "We stayed at one last night and will be returning, I fear. Perhaps better luck to us on the 'morrow?"

Melissa and Glynn reined their horses over to the side of the road and let the Wolf Soldiers pass. A few looked curiously at the pair but most simply stared straight ahead. Xinto kept himself hidden behind Melissa the entire time.

When they passed, she said, "Little man, if you like those hands attached to those wrists, then keep them out of my lap."

Glynn sighed and Xinto chuckled. They kicked their horses and pressed south.

* * *

Bill returned to the capitol with Lupus, their horses lathered, just as the sun was setting. The Empress met them with a compliment of Wolf Soldier guards, her children and Nina.

The latter seemed shy around the Emperor. M'den Grek

knew why.

He'd had a report made to him, as J'her's second in command, that the Emperor's Watch Bitch had actually snapped at her master last week, and he'd rewarded her with a beating. He'd asked about this when he saw her limping, and seen bruises under her clothing when she moved, which could only come from combat. In general even Wolf Soldiers feared the purple-haired guardian whose gaze found anyone within a stone's throw of the children. Behind her back, they often called her 'Mistress of Pain.'

She stood back from the Emperor now as the Empress threw her arms around her husband, still clinging to their youngest child.

They spoke softly as man and wife will. M'den stood the guard over the royal family with six squads. Part of him would have liked a hundred, his entire Millennia on watch and alert now. Part of him, the part that made decisions, knew better. The walls and the city stood armed. No one would come here for them through all of that. Even six seemed excessive.

The youngest of the Emperor's children had been thought gone. They could be excessive.

Chawnaluh Nanahee Nudageehay hadn't left the Empress' arms for hours. Of all of the things she'd become, Shela Mordetur called herself a mother first. Her child had been used against her—she wouldn't put that baby down for days.

"Nowhere to be found?" Lupus demanded of J'her.

J'her had been one of the first Wolf Soldiers. J'her had become a legend among them. He had protected the Conqueror from the Battle of Tamaran Glen, through the Sack of Outpost IX, and in many major battles until becoming Lupus' Supreme Commander of the Wolf Soldier guard, responsible for the security of the palace and the training of all new recruits.

"Gone, Lupus," J'her told him. "Two mounts are missing from the royal stables, a gelding and a mare. Xinto of the Woods disappeared earlier in the day, even though under double guard. Glynn Escaroth is gone with this Raven."

The Mountain, this kinsman of the Emperor, looked gravely concerned. M'den would, too, if he lost such a sweet young wife at this gaffer's age.

"Did they leave or were they taken?" he asked the Imperial couple.

Lupus shook his head. "I'd be guessing if I told you," he said. "Someone knew right where to hit us, right where we were vulnerable. Even Shela didn't know her own magic wouldn't work in the nursery. This is Uman-Chi cunning. Glynn might have done it, or her countrymen might have wanted her back."

"Lupus," J'her said, "I don't think Trenbon would take us on now—"

"No?" Lupus turned on him. His temper, M'den Grek thought. That was his failing - his temper. Lupus acted from his heart. Lupus would have had the whole Millennia turned out to protect them now. In fact, Lupus had turned out the whole Pack to recover his daughter, and left the city defenseless.

Lupus had never found himself in a situation he couldn't get out of. He put his head down and charged in, and he won, or he backed out, charged back in and won.

"If Trenbon had arranged this, then they would have the city," M'den said, and every head in the stables turned to him.

They stood in the half-light, enchanted orbs lighting the rafters where it wasn't safe to use fire. It would have been better to have this discussion in the war room, but the Imperial family would want to cling together after such a shock. Horses neighed, Blizzard was munching grain and groomsmen were currying Little Storm. Others put the two horses' tack away and hung their saddle blankets to dry.

"Meaning?" Lupus demanded.

M'den looked him right in the eye. "Meaning we turned out the whole city. Trenbon wouldn't have wasted an opportunity like that. If it killed half of their Wizards, they would have moved enough troops here to overwhelm the guard while most of our strength was out. Why else do it? Because they want to save a woman they abandoned to us?"

"Uman-Chi think on more levels than that," Lupus said.

"But not fewer," Shela said. "He's right. Trenbon would have taken the advantage. They would be drinking our wine now in our throne room to toast us and their own victory. This was not Angron Aurelias."

"Having spoken to him, this sounds like something Xinto would have found hilariously funny," the Mountain said. "I don't know the Uman-Chi like you do, but it's too big a coincidence that he escaped with the others."

"I should have killed him—" Shela began.

"Where are they now?" Lupus interrupted her.

She focused, and she shook her head. "I cannot see them—any of them. Either they are warded, or my strength is gone. I did everything I could to find Chawnaluh Nanahee Nudageehay."

"Another guarantee this was not the work of Trenbon," M'den said. "It would be the highpoint of his thousand years if he found you like this now."

"You sound like a man trying to make a point, M'den," Lupus said, his voice almost sinuous now. The Emperor squared off on the Major, searching his face, searching it. "What would that point be?"

M'den looked Lupus right in the eye. The first Wolf Soldiers had been convicted criminals. Now there were vagabond swords, or a loser in life's game. Every one of them had come to Lupus' Wolf Soldier guards and pledged his life for three years, to get a second chance, to make something of his or her future.

Over 95% didn't leave after three years. And of those who did, most came back in a few months. Of those who didn't, they were statesmen, military minds, warriors of repute.

Because Lupus let them be what they could be, not what they'd become. When Lupus asked your opinion, you got to give it—and that was rare on Fovea.

"This was terrible, and it was despicable, and someone should die for it," M'den informed him. "But this is the type of trick our enemies should use on us, because it will work. And even if Trenbon is not pursuing us, their spies are here, and the spies of other nations are here, watching us, because how else would they know and exploit our weaknesses?"

"I would not send one less man—" Lupus began, but stopped when he saw not only M'den but J'her shaking their heads.

"Nor should you," J'her said. "But if it happens again, then we hide reserves in the city. We know what our enemies know, and we let them think us vulnerable when, in fact, we are not."

Lupus thought, and then he smiled. He nodded and turned back to his wife, and took Chawny from her. He nuzzled his daughter in his arms.

"If there is a next time, we'll send out seven hundred and fifty of each Millennia, and retain the rest at the walls in the city," he said. "You're right, M'den—we went too far. We were lucky we lost as little as we did.

"But then," the Emperor asked them, "what did they gain?"

Chapter Eighteen:

An Emperor, An Empire

Bill hadn't slept alone in what seemed like a very long time now. In fact it had just been a couple of months, but he'd grown used to another body in the bed. He hadn't realized he'd reach for Melissa in the middle of the night until he reached for her and she wasn't there.

The guy with salt-and-pepper hair had charged him as her guardian protector. He needed to protect her from harm. How the hell was he supposed to do that if she was going to take off without him?

So, after a long night where sleep usually eluded him, Bill came to a conclusion in the dark and rose up before the sun. He donned a tough pair of trousers and a blue shirt and undershirt that fit him right for riding, sturdy boots they'd made for him, and the falchion and scabbard they'd let him keep. As quietly as he could, he exited his personal rooms and beat a path for the stables.

He found Little Storm waiting for him. The stallion had curled up in his stall in a pile of straw he'd collected against a wall. Bill pulled a carrot out of one of the bags they kept throughout the stables and held it out for the stallion. The giant beast rose up out of the straw and crossed his paddock to the gate where Bill waited. He sniffed the Man and batted his chest with his nose, then took the carrot in one mouthful and crushed it in his powerful jaws while Bill stroked the side of his head.

"Planning a trip?" Bill heard behind him.

Bill didn't turn. No matter how much you trust or love a stallion, you don't take your eyes off of him; you don't turn your back on him, not for a second. That will be the second when he wonders what the back of your head tastes like, or gets playful and kicks you.

Besides, Bill knew that voice.

"You're not invited, Karel," Bill said.

The little Scitai stepped up to the gate and leaned against the lowest rail. He'd dressed out in his bear skins with a silver question mark turned upside-down on the front. He bore a rapier over his shoulder much as the Emperor wore his own sword, and looked up at Bill with eerily similar blue eyes.

He laughed. "I don't think I'd like to go," he said.

Bill nodded and sighed.

"You going to try and stop me?" he asked.

The Scitai frowned and shook his head. "Nah," he said. "I had a woman like that; I'd take off after her, too."

Bill nodded. A sleepy groomsman emerged from the hay barn. It wasn't abnormal for the bachelors to sleep there. It was warm in the winter, cool in the summer and free. Their presence kept the rats away and if there were ever a fire, always a fear with so much dry hay, they were right there.

"M'Lord," he said, rubbing his eyes. "Are you in need of your horse?"

Bill sighed. This was supposed to be a secret.

Karel stepped in. "Saddle up Little Storm," he said. "Pack him with food for a week. Be quick about it."

The Uman scowled, then saw who'd given him the command and his eyes widened. "Fast as light," he said, and turned on his heel, running toward the tack barn.

A moment later another Uman scurried out of the barn in his undershirt and boots with an over-large halter for Little Storm.

Bill stepped back from the gate as the small Uman opened it and approached the stallion.

Little Storm didn't react to him. He allowed the halter to be put over his head, and he allowed the Uman to lead him out.

"Include a hoof pick in the supplies, and a brush," he ordered the Uman.

"Of course, m'Lord," he said.

He led the horse into the barn. Bill regarded Karel.

"Why are you being so helpful?" he asked.

Karel smiled his wide, Cheshire cat smile and said, "You don't think I'm just a good person and a fast friend?"

"Not to me, you aren't," he said. "You barely know me."

Karel nodded. "True enough," he said.

The Scitai walked away from Bill toward the barn. Bill followed him. He stopped at the barn's open double-doors and watched three Uman curry and prep Bill's horse, tied by two lines between his halter and opposite polls inside the barn.

"You know big things are coming," Karel said. It wasn't a question.

"Yeah, I kind of sense that."

Karel grunted. "You have no idea," he said. "I never heard that song when Glynn sang it. I've had it explained to me, but when she opened her mouth to sing, I heard nothing."

"That's strange," Bill said. He honestly didn't know what to make of it. "I heard it in my native language, and I guess everyone else does, too."

"Yeah," Karel said. Just then an Uman entered the barn from a side door with the huge saddle designed for Little Storm, much like the Emperor's. It was outfitted with a forward crest rather than a saddle horn, and a sling on one side by the stirrup for a lance. A front brace and a bucking strap made for a saddle designed to stay on no matter what the rider went through.

The Scitai turned and faced Bill. "I can't help but feel you'll play a big part in this, you and your woman," he said. "Black Lupus thinks the same. He thinks he needs to keep you close, monitor what you see, make sure you stay on his side."

"And you don't?" Bill said.

Karel smiled that smile again and shook his head. "No," he

said. "I think you need to get yourself out of here, and see what he thinks he has to fight for. I think you need to get your hands dirty, if you want to call yourself a farmer."

"What?"

"Sorry," Karel said. "He speaks in allegories and I've developed the habit. If you don't know Eldador, then you'll never feel you're fighting for Eldador. You already know the Emperor. You need to know the Empire."

Bill nodded. The Uman were already cinching the saddle to Little Storm. The stallion didn't react to any of them.

"Can you get a message to the Emperor for me?" Bill asked.

Karel shrugged. "It's not like I'm not going to tell him this happened," he said.

"Let him know I'm not abandoning him, I just need to find Raven."

Karel nodded. "Probably a good thing for him to know," he said.

Bill looked into Karel's eyes. "You're afraid of him, aren't you?" he asked.

Karel smiled. He pointed to the question-mark turned upside-down on his breast. "You see this?" he asked. "That's the mark of the Daff Kanaar. People with this mark, they can't hurt each other, and they can't allow anyone *else* to hurt someone wearing this mark, so no, I'm not afraid of Rancor Mordetur, Emperor of Eldador."

Bill nodded, knowing he hadn't gotten the whole story yet. "Okay," he said.

Karel took a step back from him. Two Uman were picking Little Storm's hooves while the third was feeding him his bit and settling his bridle.

"That said," Karel added, "if you want to know how I feel about a Man who was able to take over a nation and turn it from a backwater into the top power in Fovea in a handful of years, and who did it pretty much by eliminating anyone who stood in his way, maybe starting with one of his best friends in the world? Well, I can tell you that I wouldn't cross *that* Man without more than a real good reason, and I wouldn't be the one to advise anyone else to do it, either."

Bill nodded. Pretty much the same story he'd gotten from the porters, without the warning.

"You have a safe trip," Karel said, turning on his heel. "Come back real soon."

* * *

"You miss your Mountain," Glynn asked, urging her mount up alongside Melissa and disturbing her musing.

They'd found a place to camp last night, a small town with a small tavern where travelers sometimes stayed on their way to Galnesh Eldador. Glynn paid for each of them to have a private room and for each of them to eat breakfast this morning. None of them had thought to bring food for the journey.

She nodded. "He is a good man."

"I don't see how he is your guardian protector, however," Glynn continued. Melissa couldn't tell where the Uman-Chi's ambiguous eyes pointed, and it immediately put her on her guard. "In fact, had he not mastered that stallion, I would not know what to make of him."

"Why is that such a big deal?" Melissa asked.

Glynn thought for a moment, either choosing her words or framing them simply enough for Melissa to understand them.

"Do you understand why Blizzard is so special?" Glynn asked.

"Only Lupus can ride him," Raven said.

"No," Glynn corrected her. "Blizzard is of a clan of horses far to the north, known as the Herd that Cannot be Tamed. They are larger and stronger than any other horses on Fovea, and they are sacred to the goddess Life. They will bear the touch of no living thing, and there are many Uman-Chi, as well as Uman and Men, whose deaths or injuries prove they cannot, in fact, be ridden."

"And Blizzard actually loves Lupus," Melissa concluded. "And Life is probably not on good terms with a god called War."

"Yes, precisely and astutely, Raven," Glynn complimented her. "Lupus, we fear, is the champion of the god War, and to have mastered one of Life's sacred is to say the wolf has surely bedded down with the lamb."

Melissa really didn't understand what that meant, but she got the feeling Glynn didn't feel sure, or her people couldn't be sure, who fought on whose side when it came to their gods.

"Now here is Little Storm, and he is sired of Blizzard and, like his sire, he will let none master him," Glynn said. "However he is not his sire, and thus he can be ridden, if not tamed."

"Until this Mountain leaps onto his back and humbles Blizzard," Xinto added from his seat behind Melissa, "and the invincible Lupus."

"So now you want to know who is letting Little Storm know that the Mountain is okay," Melissa said.

"Again, astutely measured," Glynn said. "We Uman-Chi have made record of the forty sired of Blizzard. First we know that Blizzard rejects most matings."

"Or it would be more like four hundred sired," Xinto said.

"And so. Next, we see only a handful that could be ridden. These all remain under Lupus' control with the exception of Little Storm. Of them, only Little Storm, another stallion named, 'Bastard,' and three other mares show any likeness to Blizzard. The rest are either overlarge draft animals or too wild to be useful."

"So perhaps the goddess Life doesn't want her sacred animals mixed in with regular horses," Raven said.

"Or perhaps she is using them for very specific purposes, meaning our Mountain has more to him than we have thought," Glynn said.

"So what does all of this mean, Glynn?" Melissa asked. "We let him keep doing his thing and watching him, or we do more to protect him and hope for some 'sign.'"

Glynn sighed. Melissa had come to hate those sighs. To her they meant, "Stupid human." Glynn would smile in a person's face, but no one ever forgot for a moment the Uman-Chi thought of everyone else as inferior.

"I believe it means we must first find what god favors our Mountain," Glynn said. "Then we must encourage the Mountain to that god's will. If we are to follow the prophecy of Eveave, as I think we are, then we must seek other allies for our advantage, for Eveave will give us only balance, where we seek purchase."

Raven digested that. She hadn't been a church-going Christian since her childhood, but that didn't make her ready to change her religion, either. She had a lot of questions she didn't have the language skills to ask, and she didn't know if she trusted Glynn to give her the right answers, either.

"The gods are important here?" she asked, finally. "They get right down into your lives?"

Glynn sat her mount silently for a minute or more. Both sat sidesaddles, their dresses' skirts draped over their mounts' butts. The plains stood open and the day quiet, the cool breeze in their faces.

"It is forbidden by Adriam," Glynn said, finally, "for a god to touch the life of a mortal born on this world. With what we know now, there are some Uman-Chi who believe this is why the god War sought the Conqueror. War can direct this 'Lupus,' this wolf, directly, and break the rules."

"So the Mountain and I?" Melissa couldn't finish the question, for all it implied.

Glynn nodded. "You have not, then, been contacted, heard any voice in your head, directing you?"

Melissa shook her head. "How would I tell?" she asked. "I mean, what would it sound like?"

"Honestly, I have no idea," Glynn said. "The Emperor would know, if I am correct, but then how would one ask him?"

"Yeah," Melissa said. "Kind of late for that now."

They continued in silence. A cool breeze blew from the west and tugged at both women's hair. She'd been forced to take a side-saddle because all of the ones for men were in use when she was leaving. She shifted on it, giving Xinto the opportunity to move his hands on her waist.

"The Mountain hasn't told me anything about any voices," she said, finally.

Glynn nodded, and said nothing.

"Maybe we have to—you know—pledge ourselves to a god first?" Melissa asked.

"Would you do that?" Xinto said. "Forsake your deity, who created you, who cared for you, for another, whose intentions you do not know?"

Melissa thought of the ones who had created her—a mother who had made her life hell, and a father who had let her down, chosen her loser sister over her, trashed her chances at college.

She considered the god who had let them.

And in the end she said nothing.

* * *

Little Storm's hooves drummed the plain, faster than any horse should move.

The Mountain—he had to force himself to think of himself as that now—had spent his time on horseback before. Growing up on a farm, he'd enjoyed the Appaloosa ponies his father raised as a side business, and had broken many of them to saddle himself.

Appy's were a great breed, but they didn't run this fast. Thoroughbreds ran fast, but the fastest of them wouldn't have kept pace with Little Storm, and none of the fast ones had his stamina.

The Mountain turned his head and looked back down the road, no longer able to see the markers for Galnesh Eldador, much less the city spires. That shouldn't have happened so soon, he thought.

It was another two hours before he came to a decent-sized town, if you could call it that, the Mountain thought to himself. Approaching from the North, he saw a few sod houses dug up out of the dirt and, past them, a central building made of dirt and sticks. They kept a few horses and a few cows that he could see, the cows looking bushier than the cows of Earth. Domestic bovines had been bred thousands of years ago from aurochs, and he wondered if he saw that now. He didn't see a bull.

He slowed the horse as he found what was likely a market. It consisted mostly of Uman and a few swarthy Men, their wares on blankets before them, and children of both races running between. To their west, a solid wooden building had to be an outhouse from the reek coming off of it.

The swarthy Men turned out to be Volkhydran immigrants. Bill walked himself right up to them, staying on his horse, and introduced himself.

"Mountain—there is a funny name," one said. "There is no

Volkhydran called that."

"What's a common Volkhydran name?" the Mountain asked.

"Krell—that's common," one woman said, a toothless grandmother with children at her feet. Lupus had explained the Eldadorian custom meant keeping your fields away from your home. Farmers staked a claim and declared it to the Empire, and farmed it, but walked to the farm and lived on land that wasn't as fit for farming.

"Nantar, too," another woman, just as old, said. They dressed in loose fitting cotton dresses, died in purples and blues. They kept their hair loose behind them. "Because of Nantar of the Daff Kanaar. Agtar, Kafar—those are good Volkhydran names."

"Jack," the first woman said. "I know a Jack from Kendo."

"Jack?" the Mountain asked. He could live with Jack. He had an uncle named Jack.

She nodded. "You see these furs?" she pointed toward the piles on the blanket before her. Flies buzzed around them. "These are Hydran furs, but Volkans wear them. You put these on, you look like a Volkhydran."

The Mountain put his hands to his wide belt, about to explain that he didn't have any money, when he found a bag attached to it that he didn't remember putting there.

He pulled it from his belt and it jingled. He opened it and found a collection of gold, silver and copper coins, which the locals called 'Tabaars."

"Got anything an Andaron girl would wear?" the Mountain asked.

"Do they wear anything?" the first old woman joked. The second sniggered. "I thought they didn't waste time with clothes. Took too much time to take off."

"Isn't the Empress an Andaron?" the Mountain asked.

"What of it?" the second asked. "All that means is Lupus is insatiable."

"He *is* insatiable," the first old woman said. "He has an appetite for everything."

"He does?" the Mountain asked.

"Well, he doesn't tax as bad as our old lord," the first said.

"But you have to pay it all—I don't know that we are better off. I lived in Alun, and our lord demanded half of our planting. I don't think we ever gave him more than a tenth part, though. We knew how to hide it. Here, they take fifteen of a hundred, which is hard to figure out. We grow a lot of corn—you have to actually take a hundred ears to get fifteen. Same with spuds, same with squashes. The magistrate comes 'round with the local bull—he takes one calf in seven."

"It's a game—the game here is the same game as the game there," the second said, and took a fur back from Bill. "I didn't mean to have that one in the pile."

"But it was in the pile," he said, his salesman sense sparking.

"But I didn't mean to have it there," she said. "That's a nice fur."

"I want a nice fur."

"Well, it's more."

She and Bill began to haggle. Bill didn't know the local currency, but a good rule of thumb was to ask for twice what you expected to get for your wares. The first old lady turned behind her and pulled out a tangle of leather.

"I can let you have this for a silver," she said. "It is off of an Andaron woman, I know it. Put a skirt on your girl and a horsehide robe, and she'll look like any Andaron."

"Do you have the skirt and the robe?"

"I know someone who does—can you wait?"

"I can wait."

"Will you be wanting a girl?" she asked him.

Bill straightened. "What?"

"Oh, don't be embarrassed," the old woman made a 'shooing' motion with her hand. "Man comes off the trail, come to a town, he'll eventually look for a girl."

Bill sighed. "Well, I *am* looking for a girl, actually a couple girls, who may have come through here."

The one old woman poked the other. "He's chasing a girl," he said.

"*That* is more like a Volkhydran man," the other answered.

"Was a young girl came through here with an Uman-Chi

and a Scitai feller," the first told him, squinting into his eyes. "But unless you want another daughter, she's too young for you."

"Where were they bound?" Bill asked.

The two women exchanged a glance.

Bill leaned forward. "She *is* my daughter," he said. "And the Uman-Chi thinks she looks like the Empress. I don't think they have any good plans for her."

"Knew that Uman-Chi was a liar," the second woman said.

"Was with a Scitai," the first agreed. "You know they do nuthin' but steal."

"Your daughter went south to find Brinn's Hostel," The second informed him, laying the Andaron clothes out for him. "They'll be there the end of the day if they go a normal pace. I don't know as you can push that draft to catch 'em."

"Overland he could," a man said from behind them.

Bill turned to see another Volkhydran, probably his own age but looking *much* the worse for wear, with grey-shot hair and puckered skin. He dressed in worn leathers and sandals.

"The road takes a gentle curve," he informed Bill. "You take the straight, keep a point on the south, you'll save yourself three *daheeri*, like as cut them off."

The Uman-Chi had educated Bill and Melissa on standards of measure. *Daheeri* were each a tenth of the distance from one horizon to the next on a flat plain, or about 1.2 miles, if this planet was about the same size as Earth. The gravity didn't make him think otherwise.

"Is there a point you know of?" Bill asked him. It wasn't easy to keep your bearings when you travelled, less so when you went fast. Any animal tends to want to circle to one side or the other.

"I can sell you a comm—pass," he said.

That word was just too similar.

Sure enough, the Emperor had introduced the compass to these people, along with the secret of making them. Bill spent six silvers on clothes for himself and for Melissa, for the compass and a meal while he was here. They threw hay to his horse for free. A couple Uman whores presented themselves to him but he declined their services. They were more persistent than Bill would have liked.

* * *

Glynn and Raven arrived at the Eldadorian hostel as the sun set. They unsaddled their own horses in a public stable, with plenty of hay and grain, outside of a big, stone holding, three stories tall, with a gigantic tub in front and a fire next to that.

Dark skinned Men, no less than six of them, filled the tub, laughing and splashing each other. One stood beside the tub, stoking up the fire under an animal like a deer turning on a spit cranked by two children.

Raven laughed to herself. Glynn turned her nose up in disgust.

"I know, I know," Raven said. "Men acting as the animals they are. Keep reminding yourself, Glynn."

"I am reminded sufficiently, thank you," Glynn said. "I think that we must needs wait here for my friend to find us."

"Why?"

"Because we have no males," Glynn said. "And I don't fancy my breasts to be pawed by a flock of rude Men."

Raven covered her breasts reflexively. "They would do that?"

"Draw near them and find out," Xinto said. "And don't think I'm going to fight ten Toorians for your honor."

Raven straightened. "I think there's a male already here," she said.

"What?" Glynn said, and looked into her face. The ambiguous eyes turned different colors in the twilight. "You sense him, or you see him?"

"I see Little Storm, in the stable," she said. She pointed to a stall on the other end of the stable.

The Uman-Chi turned her head to where Raven's outstretched finger pointed, but Raven didn't. Once again, by the scrub grass past the far barn door, she saw the swish, the 'not there.' This time she saw something like a serpent's tail, with green scales, appear for an instant in the grass.

Glynn sighed. "For whatever reason, your guardian protector has found us," she said. "Let us pray he didn't bring an

Eldadorian escort with him."

"I don't see Eldadorian livery," Xinto said. "I'm surprised to say, I think your warrior came alone."

They approached the hostel. The Men in the tub went quiet as the women approached. Two started licking their lips—a bad sign.

"Dahara," one said.

"Jumbo," Glynn answered.

"Faharra mtisaa?" he said, and stood, showing that he was naked in the tub. Raven blushed and looked down.

"Dem zakahi," Glynn said. "Jang daheeri, tafooza gaballa Mountain."

The Man shook his head. "We saw an old Man," he said, in thickly accented Uman. "A Volkhydran, but he calls himself 'Jack.'"

"Jack?" Raven said.

"It is a common enough Volkhydran name," Glynn said.

The dark-skinned man picked up a robe from the side of the tub and put it on. It hung on his muscular form, drenched with water, but he didn't seem to care. He stepped out of the tub toward them.

"Forgive me, please," he said. "But I cannot help to mention, I have seen you before."

"You have?" Glynn asked him.

He nodded. "In a dream, I called you Magee—a singing woman. You sang of my destiny and then floated into the sun."

Raven straightened, and Glynn sang to him:

> "On Fovea, on Fovea, find a noble young and old,
> A foreigner among his kind
> A hero, fate foretold
> One who fights as does the Sun
> Waits in a sacred place
> A guardian will bring you there
> With a devil born and raised"

He nodded. "I know these words, and yet I wonder, I cannot sing this song."

"Might I ask your name, Sirrah?" Glynn asked him.

"I am Jahunga," he said. "I am come north from Toor, to see the people from the Silent Isle, and ask them why I dream of them."

"If you would escort us to our male friends, then I would explain it to you," Glynn said.

Raven found herself speechless.

Chapter Nineteen:

An Untouchable One

The ale was warm, the meat was tough, and the vegetables were soggy. The rough stool he sat upon teetered precariously on three uneven legs, but it was the only one close to a wall, and Jerod wasn't here to rearrange the future.

He sat hunched over the table—a long, wide board, rough cut and gouged from a thousand knives and forks, placed on saw horses and stained by the overflow of plates and mugs.

'Why not just eat on the dirt?' Jerod wondered, licking the sour foam from his lips.

"Do you like this?" an old Man pretending to be a Volkhydran asked him.

He called himself, 'Jack.' Common enough name; Jerod knew a share of Jack's, Jehk's, Ju'huks and other names to confuse this one with.

"I like it better than being sober in my hunger," Jerod said, and stabbed at the thready beef on the wooden plate before him. "I like it less than what I got from sailors when I travelled here."

Jack chewed and chewed, taking beef and vegetables in the same mouthful. An auroch with a cud made for more appetizing company.

He swallowed forcefully and said, "I was thinking the

same thing. It isn't good, and I don't like beer this bitter."

"Then maybe you should shut up and go to your rooms," Jerod growled at him. He dressed in furs almost the same as Jack's, but wasn't as large or as tall. He felt the scar on his face twitch in irritation.

He'd been waiting here for days, and he'd be leaving in the morning, his time wasted by an Uman-Chi. They didn't think of anything but themselves, and that left Jerod irritated.

"Maybe you should make me," Jack returned immediately. "Or maybe I should teach you some respect for your elders."

"You want to see my sword in your guts?" Jerod pressed him and stood, his hand on the hilt of the weapon at his hip. "Curious to see what that looks like?"

He might not *be* Volkhydran, but the gaffer knew how to *act* Volkhydran, anyway. He stood up on the other side of the table.

"If you want to get kicked out of the hostel for sword fighting," the older man said, in Uman. "If you want to fight bare-fisted, I can take you outside and beat your ass for you."

"Gentlemen, please," an Uman woman said in Uman. The hostel staff consisted entirely of Uman, and they had already started clearing plates. Eldadorian hostels had a no-swords rule, and you took your fights outside. If you tore the place up, sometimes they kept your horse as payment for the damage, and sometimes they sent you to Eldador. A good many Wolf Soldiers had gotten their start right here.

"With fists, then," the Jerod said, in Uman this time. "I'm fine with fists. Want to make it interesting?"

"I'm going to hit you until you apologize," the old man said. "I'm interested in that."

"Two Tabaars on the gaffer," a Scitai said, entering the room as others filed out. Jerod didn't know him. "If you show them to me, first."

"I will take that," another Uman said, from a different board. Everyone started standing now. Plates vanished and chairs followed them—if the fight didn't make it outside, there wouldn't be as much to keep it going in here.

A waif-like Uman removed the old man's chair as he

turned and marched out of the one door to the hostel, the Scitai behind him. Jerod watched them both. The old man's anger surprised him, but the Scitai made him suspicious. As he followed them out the door, he wondered that this might be a set up of some kind.

Travelers needed to watch their fates on the road, or have them made for them. Still, what threat could come from an old man and a Scitai? Most likely the Man had been a warrior once, and thought he still had fight in him.

* * *

Outside, Melissa started when Xinto entered the hostel, and a flood of people came running out of it.

Among them she saw Bill and Xinto, and people were approaching Xinto and showing him their gold and silver. Men and some women were collecting around a circle, and Bill pulled some furs he was wearing over his head as he stepped into it.

More than a handful of naked Toorians climbed out of the communal tub, pulling on the thick white robes they wore and stepping into thonged sandals, the laces dragging behind them. Men and Uman filed from the hostel to the circle where Bill was waiting. Xinto seemed to be taking wagers from more than a dozen spectators.

Bill sported a big stomach covered with thick, gray and black hair. Another Man stepped into the circle opposite him. He stood smaller by a head, but Melissa saw no fat on him. The abdominals, the pectorals, the biceps looked pronounced, and all smaller than Jack's. The younger man would have speed, but the older probably strength.

"I think my father is younger than you, gaffer," the brown-eyed one said.

"I think he should have done to you what I am about to, and made you a better man," Jack returned, and threw his furs behind him.

"What is going—is that our Mountain?" Melissa heard Glynn's voice behind her.

She turned and there stood Glynn and Xinto. Glynn actually had to put her hands on Melissa's shoulder to keep her from bolting into the ring that had formed.

"Ware, Raven," she said. "This is between the males. You cannot stop it now, and you cannot change it. This is in—"

"If you tell me this is in the nature of Men, I will stick you," Raven hissed at her with uncharacteristic anger. Xinto actually chuckled, like this was funny.

"Once one Man started fighting, they *all* want to," Xinto said to Glynn, then he turned to Melissa.

"She is right," Xinto said to her. "He is an older Man, and he is finding himself, Raven. He called for this, not the other. Even if he loses, he will have fought. Do your best now, as a woman of Men would, and support him, and clean his wounds if he fails."

Melissa looked down at Xinto, and she felt her brown eyes brimming.

"You—um—believe this?" she asked, stumbling on the language.

"I do."

She straightened. Bill stepped from his furs, toward the younger man, and the younger came to meet him.

Melissa straightened. "Kick his ass!" she shouted.

Bill turned, surprised. He searched the crowd and found the three of them.

"Kick his *friggin*' ass!" she shouted. They wouldn't know the expletive here, but Bill would.

He grinned wolfishly and charged.

Melissa could hear her heart pound in her ears as the two Men closed.

Bill was bigger, but older and slower. The other seemed to be a Volkhydran with a terrible scar on his face, and just looked mean, like a killer or a judge. He fought stripped to his leggings, his feet and chest bare, revealing the dimple between his hipbone and his abs. The waning light gave his skin a ruddy hue, tight over a hard body, marked here and there with scars less severe than the one on his face.

Before meeting Bill, this would have been 'her type,' rugged and gorgeous, mean and handsome, the kind of man who would love her and hurt her at the same time.

Bill let him close. The younger man moved deliberately, his face unexpressive, his almost beautiful brown eyes focused on measuring the distance between them, trying to get Bill to strike first.

Bill didn't fall for it. He held his fists before him—no karate or kung fu or anything else—a bare-knuckle fighting stance to hold the other at bay. The males, and a few women, who gathered to watch started shouting for action.

Finally, the smaller man did some sort of head-bob, then ducked under Bill's fists to deliver a punch, another, and another into Bill's exposed abdomen. Graceful as a dancer, he skipped away from Bill and then ducked back in, under his guard, jabbing away while Bill swung on air again and then again.

Bill's belly shook but it didn't seem to faze him. A half-smile twisted his beard when the younger man made a third attempt. Just as the other man's fist touched him, Bill hammered down into the side of his face with a meaty left, moving him to line up with Bill's right. He took the younger Man straight between the eyes with a heavy right, the 'thud' resounded through the suddenly silent crowd.

The younger Man stepped back and shook his head to clear it, a look of surprise seeming out of place alongside the scar. Bill followed up with a swing at the jaw. The younger ducked at the last moment, then caught Bill for one, two, three to the ribs with a firm right fist, holding Bill's arms at bay with his left.

Or so he thought. Bill reached a long arm out past the younger man, and wrapped up his head and one arm under his own. Now the younger man's face was pressed to Bill's flabby stomach, his arm pinned, and Bill started pounding the back and kidneys with his free right hand.

Melissa saw the stress on Bill's face, the sweat streaming into his eyes, his beard, running like a river down his belly. The blows were telling but the other's body was hard—his knees might be shaking, but he dug his toes into the ground, trying either to break free or to bowl the older man over.

The crowd roared its appreciation.

Finally a hand came up, and Bill gave a shout as the other man turned the fight dirty.

"Oooo," Xinto winced. She heard other sympathy groans, even from the women. Bill gave something like a roar and, changing his grip; he reached out and took a fist full of the back of the other man's pants.

Melissa couldn't help thinking, 'Kind of stupid to give him a wedgie,' before she realized Bill now had the man by the back of the neck as well. With another roar, Bill raised the struggling man over his head, took a step forward and slammed him like a rag doll onto the ground.

The younger Man moved to get a foot underneath him, and Bill lumbered forward to kick him in the ribs, flipping him onto his back. The younger Man looked up wild-eyed, not knowing what had happened, and Bill seated the instep of his boot on the other's neck.

"Had—had—had," he panted, and squatted down, getting his wind, putting his elbows on his knee, his weight on the Man's neck.

"Had enough," he asked finally.

"Uck, uck," the younger gasped. He reached for the boot, tried to punch the leg, but found nothing. He arched his back, his abs straining as he tried to reach for purchase with his feet. His face had turned purple when he finally slapped the ground three times, counting himself out.

The crowd cheered. Bill stepped off of him and magnanimously reached down his hand to the younger. That one rubbed his throat for a moment, looked grudgingly up at Bill, and finally took the extended hand.

Glynn gave Melissa a gentle push in the back. "Go," she said.

She turned. "What?"

Xinto intervened. "Run to your champion," he said, "throw your arms around him and give him a victor's kiss. It is what a woman of Men would do."

Melissa didn't need to be told twice. She hiked up the front of her skirts and ran to her sweating guardian protector. Not even giving him time to let go of the other man's forearm, she threw her arms around his bull neck, lifted up her heels and rammed her tongue into his mouth, tasting his sweat and his hair and some dust from the ring, and every bit of Bill that she could swallow.

He swung her, and despite herself she felt like a little girl—a very excited little girl, at that.

He broke the kiss and she looked into his eyes, feeling his breath on her face, the stink of beer and the sweet smell of victory. "My hero," she swooned for him.

He grinned like a little boy, his arm around her waist now, her feet still off the ground.

"Your woman?" the younger asked.

Bill looked away and put her down on the ground. She clung to him, his sweat soaking her bodice. "Mine," he panted. The younger, though beaten, seemed less winded. Bill's face stood out redder.

"Explains plenty," he said, in the language of Men. "She is no Volkhydran, but then I never saw a Volkhydran who looks or fights like you."

"In Uman, if you can," Bill said. "I am trying to learn the language."

"In Uman," the younger said, "because you can't speak Volkhydran, can you?"

"I think you know he cannot, Sirrah," Glynn said, approaching them. Xinto had been left behind, running between Men and Uman, collecting coins. Jahunga approached from the opposite direction, a smile on his face and a spear in his hand.

"So he is one of yours?" the younger Man asked. "I should have known."

"I assure you, Sirrah," Glynn began.

"You know him?" Bill asked. He didn't look happy, but the color started returning back to his face.

"He is Jerod the Bold," Glynn told them. "And I am told you are Jack, now?"

Bill – Jack - nodded. Melissa had just gotten used to the Mountain, but this fit him better. He looked like a Jack.

"Another one running from that friend of ours?" Jerod asked.

"Indeed."

Jerod extended his hand, and Jack tried to take it. Jerod

reached past the older man's hand and took Jack by the forearm. Jack did the same, and Jerod looked into his eyes.

"You remind me of that mutual friend," he said, in the language of Men. "And I got to know him pretty well. I think you need to tell me more of what I am involved in here, Uman-Chi, or I might have to leave you."

"Well, if you do, then I'm going with you," Xinto said. "Because you just made me a lot of gold."

"I think I made you that money," Jack said, his arm still around Melissa. She couldn't help feeling ten feet tall right then. He'd become so *vital* now, so alive. It may be a stupid, girly thing to feel, but for whatever reason, her man would have a hell of a night tonight.

"You will get your quarter," Xinto said.

"My half, you mean," Jack said.

"Half?" Xinto gasped. Glynn turned to the hostel, the rest of them, Jahunga included, following. Jerod looked Jahunga up and down once, then shrugged and followed, scooping up his clothing as he went. "Why would I give you half?"

"Because I can smash you," Jack said.

"He *can* smash you," Melissa noted. "Where we are from, he would get eighty-five coins of a hundred."

She didn't know how to say 'percent.'

"Remind me not to go there," Xinto said, and handed a fist full of coins to Jack. One of Jack's possessions now was apparently a coin purse, because he emptied them into it.

Raven watched Jerod using his furs to blot the sweat gleaming on his chest and upper arms. The leggings twisted on his hips, revealing first the left then the right dimple between his groin and abs. He shook his hair once, and sprayed them all with his sweat. Two tiny drops landed on her lower lip and, holding the image of him in the corner of her eye, she swallowed them rather than wiped her mouth.

He ignored her, another man's woman. That might be the proper thing to do, she supposed, but it made her hot as a June bug.

* * *

Glynn just sniffed at the idea of eating at the board in the common room. They took a room for her, and Xinto and Jack each secured their own.

"We could get by with half the rooms, or a single room, even," Xinto complained. They had collected in Glynn's room, the largest of the three. Jahunga would stay with the other Toorians, and Jerod had his own room as well.

"Um…no," Raven said. She had loosened the back to her dress and was pulling on the bodice, letting the cool air find her skin. The males peeked guiltily down her bosom.

Glynn shook her head. She'd sung her song for Jerod and Jahunga, and they had made the obligatory 'why is it in my native language?' comments.

"And you think we are each some part of this song?" Jahunga said. "I see no place for me, nothing about it that says, 'Jahunga.'"

"I don't think you are the one who fights as does the sun," Xinto said. "I am the foreigner among his kind. Glynn is the noble, young and old."

"I'm the Hero," Jerod said, almost sullenly.

Glynn watched him. She'd known the truth of that already, but that he should know it surprised her.

"You're a hero?" Raven asked him, with the bluntness of Men.

"A person's privacy is their own," Glynn reprimanded her gently. "It is sufficient that he is the Hero."

"Do we not want to know why?" Jahunga asked the rest of them. He seemed an acceptable Man. His muscles stood out carved like a statue. He bore his spear with him, a wood and steel device common to his people, and a three-pronged piece of bone through a piercing in his left ear. She'd been mildly surprised that 'Jack' could defeat Jerod, she'd be stunned to see him humble Jahunga.

"You probably already know why," Jerod said. "It isn't important—I'm the Hero."

"And I?" Jahunga pressed. "I have led a heroic life, and my fate was foretold by the seers on my birth. They told my father that I would be everything that is Toor, but that I would not die there."

"That must be a comfort to you, now that you're here," Xinto noted.

Jahunga shrugged. "Death is the only promise Life keeps," he said, philosophically. Glynn had to admit the statement as profound, coming from a Man.

"I don't suppose you elude prying eyes," Xinto asked him.

"I know nothing past the stealth of the forest," he said. "Keep low, move quiet."

Xinto poked Jahunga in the upper arm with his finger. "Not the untouchable one, then," he said.

Jahunga smiled, and he pointed to the tiny knife in the top of Xinto's boot. "Try with that thing, little man."

Xinto shrugged. He pulled the dagger and he pushed it at Jahunga.

The point of the dagger stopped at his skin. It didn't leave an indentation, it just stopped there.

Xinto leaned his weight against the blade. It made no difference.

"The bone in your ear?" Glynn noted. Jahunga nodded.

"The kafeara bird, which is in deep Toor," he said. "It cannot be struck by any implement crafted by living hands."

"Then how did you kill it, or did you find it dead?" Jack asked.

He called himself, "Jack," now. Glynn approved of this change. Mountain was just too strange—a name that others would remember. Jack was common enough where others wouldn't recall it if asked.

Jahunga grinned a wide, jovial grin. That he'd trained as a warrior there could be no doubt, but she didn't see warrior meanness in him.

"When they die, the light of the next dawn burns them to dust," he said. "I caught the kafeara in a net, and then drowned it in a shallow pool. When the sun struck it on the next day, the water took the heat of its burning, and the bones partly survived. I drove this one through my earlobe, and there it remains."

"And now you're invincible?" Raven asked him, the innocence of short-lived Men on her.

“I am unbeaten,” Jahunga admitted, and didn’t look at her. “I don’t know that any warrior is invincible.”

“And that is what we must remember,” Glynn said. This, she felt, was the time to rally them to her cause, to get them to the revelations they must make to follow her.

“The Emperor is powerful, but in the end, nothing more than a Man,” she told them. “And like any Man, or Uman, or Uman-Chi, he can be defeated, if we are but to learn how.”

Jerod sighed and threw her a dark look. “It’s not a matter of defeating the Emperor,” he told her. “That’s pretty obvious.”

“It is?” Xinto asked him. “Because, I didn’t see it.”

“Your own song says we’re too late for victory,” Jerod said. “Our goal is to win, but we don’t know what we’re winning yet.”

“You claim the Emperor plans a conquest?” Jahunga asked. Xinto nodded.

“The Trenboni are so convinced of it, they are siding with Eldador,” the Scitai said. Glynn looked sideways at him.

“The politics of the Silent Isle are not a part of this discussion,” she informed him.

Jerod laughed. “And there you are, claiming to be so focused on this mission, still trying to keep secrets.”

“So sayeth the hero, reputation unknown!" she cast the accusation back at him.

He turned sullen and crossed his arms over his breast.

This went poorly. She’d seen a day when the wisdom of an Uman-Chi would have been enough to rally them. That day had passed.

“*For Fovea, Fovea, then must they live and die.*
Fight the battle from within
With a champion from outside.
You shall be the weapons
The tools of men and gods
Who come too late for victory
And win despite these odds.”

Raven sang the words, and sang them sweetly. She almost

seemed to choke on the last line, and could not continue to the refrain.

She stood, and she looked out the window while their eyes followed her. She seemed to focus on something outside for a moment, then she turned and faced them.

"I'm the champion," she said.

"A woman?" Jahunga scoffed.

Jerod just snickered. Bill straightened and Xinto's eyes searched all of them.

Glynn had seen more than sixteen decades of males who believed they were the source of all great deeds and she'd learned to accommodate them. Males were most easily handled when they thought they had the right of things, regardless of the truth, however glaring.

"I'm the one from outside," Raven said. She seemed almost distracted now. "I don't even come from this world."

"A goddess?" Jahunga asked, looking at Glynn.

She shook her head. "I summoned her here with Jack the first time I sang the song. Nothing like it has ever happened since."

Jerod was leaning back against the room's single bureau, his arms crossed over his breast, shutting them all out. "He doesn't fight like a god," he said.

"I fought well enough to humble you," Jack said.

"Maybe you'd like to go another time around," Jerod snarled at him, putting a hand on the floor to push himself to his feet.

"Gentles, please," Glynn began.

"Stop it," Raven said, stepping away from the window, turning to face them. She didn't shout it like an order, she barely asserted herself, but both Men subsided. She crossed the room and put herself between them.

"We agree we have a battle to fight?" she said, and swept the room with her eyes.

Jahunga nodded, Xinto sitting next to him did the same. The other two males looked on and Glynn said nothing.

"But while we're too late for victory, we can win," she continued. "So…there is a difference between winning and victory."

"Not when you lie stinking on a battle field with your guts beside you," Jerod said to her. He shook his head and he stood.

"People like you," he said, and then pointed at Glynn. "People like her, like the Emperor, they speak lightly of battle and war. But those of us who fight it, whose taxes pay for it, whose *blood* pays for it—to us, there is no difference between winning and victory."

"But to the gods—" Glynn began.

"And you think you speak for the gods?" Jerod said, cutting her off.

Ill-mannered Man, Glynn couldn't help thinking, but she held her tongue.

Yes, she thought, *I speak for the gods, but no, you could not understand it.*

"It doesn't matter," Raven said, pressing on. "We have to decide what that means, victory and winning. We have to find these other weapons, this devil, born and raised; this one who eludes prying eyes, and the one who fights like the sun."

Jerod shook his head. "I don't have to do anything," he said. "I think you're all fools, and I don't see why I should leave with you."

"Nor I," Xinto said. Glynn was surprised—she thought she had an ally with that one. "I'm sorry, but if the Emperor wants a war, he'll have it, and I say, 'Why fight, if we can't win it?'"

"Gentles," Glynn said, "you *cannot* defy a prophecy from the gods."

Jerod just smiled. "Watch me," he said.

Chapter Twenty:

One Who Eludes Prying Eyes

The sun rose up warm and inviting over the plains. The pink light touched Raven's face, too weak to warm her in the cold morning air, as she stretched and smiled in the uncomfortable bed.

Bed: uncomfortable. Man: *very* comfortable. She'd let herself pretend Jack was a barbarian Volkhydran, and inspired him to ravage her, whispering into his ear how he'd fought like a hero and had vanquished the younger man.

Her behind still stung from his slapping it, her hips throbbed dully from his weight. Not just her hips, she thought, smiling to herself. Knowing he would sleep for at least another hour, she slipped silently out of bed and padded naked across the cold wood floor.

The room had a little heater, but they hadn't used it. She slept better in the cold. She found her new Andaron clothing, quite a change from her Uman-Chi dress, ruined now by Jack's sweat stains.

First she donned her black leather harness, essentially a few strips of horsehide that tied behind her neck and held her breasts in place with two diamond-shaped cuttings. Below them it became one wide diamond that traveled down her stomach, narrowing as it passed between her legs, then up her backside like a thong, breaking off once again into two pieces that tied across her belly. She adjusted the front with the excess behind her neck, making it truly a 'one size fits all'.

Over the halter went a black leather mini, slit up the side. That she liked—in fact, she'd had one like it once upon a time. It came with a long leather duster's jacket, open in front with narrow lapels, its back with tails running almost to her knees, with three quarter sleeves. It moved with her so it felt light, but kept her warm as well. Finally she put on black, thigh-high, calfskin boots, flat-heeled, rounded in the toes, and a sheath on the inside of the right one for her boot knife. Dressed like this, no wonder an Andaron woman needed a hidden weapon! She tossed her hair over her shoulder and she looked at herself in the room's one cloudy mirror.

And there stood Raven; the champion, come from earth. She left Jack to his dreams, his beard flat from sleeping on it and wet from his drooling, and slipped out of their one door like a soft breeze.

She'd been given a room on the hostel's second floor. She clunked down the narrow set of hardwood stairs to the common room, where the good smell of roast meat mingled with the sour smells of ale and old milk. She'd never been one for breakfast, although she'd found herself eating it here. This was one of those times when she'd *really* have gone for a cig.

No one had come down to eat yet, so she didn't stay in the common room. She didn't want to eat alone, and she didn't feel that hungry yet. She had work waiting for her in the stable.

She swept out the door into the compound, her jacket billowing out behind her. The Toorians camped now on the edge of the hostel's compound, wrapped in their robes around the smoldering remains of their night fire where the ribcage of some animal still hung spitted.

The tub they had enjoyed stood empty, tiny ripples running in the morning breeze across its black surface. She flirted with the idea of a quick bath, but discarded it. She didn't want to be surprised by drooling men with an eye for her naked body, and she didn't want to see 'Jack' in another fight so soon.

It had left him sore, she thought, as she walked to the barn. The boots had her taking long steps, her back straight, her bust out. As much as he had done a good job with her the night before, she could see the pain on his face, felt the hesitancy in his muscles, seen the bruises on his stomach and his groin. She smiled to herself that she had let him spank her, first tentatively and, as he decided she liked it, with more authority.

It got her juices flowing just to think about it now.

She tugged the barn door open and found the horses munching on their morning hay. Glynn had mentioned that they'd likely be fed early for those who planned to leave with the rising sun.

She stepped into the barn, dust hung in motes suspended in the air. A huge pile of hay sat rounded at the top to her left, stalls lined the right. Tack hung from pegs on the left wall past the hay.

Something wriggled in the hay stack. She stepped back from it, fearing rats, but received a bigger surprise when an actual lizard emerged before her.

The lizard was as big as a man; green skinned with long, black claws, a small ridge running down its back, a flat saurian snout and yellow eyes with black slits looking up at her, its tail whipping to the left and right.

She took a step back and saw it clutched a spear made of bone in its right claw between webbed fingers. All of a sudden it rose up before her on its hind legs, facing her and revealing a white, scalloped belly.

It stood a little taller than she. Its nostrils had scales which opened and closed when it breathed. Teeth like an alligator's protruded from under thin, black lips.

"Ray—en," it hissed at her, and approached without being asked.

This had to be her 'almost there,' the thing she felt had been following her since Galnesh Eldador. She'd caught a glimpse of it in the bay when she'd stepped off of *The Bitch of Eldador*. She recognized it now.

"That's right," she said, as if to a child. "I'm Raven. Do you have a name?"

She spoke in Uman and it didn't respond. She tried again

in the language of Men.

"Slurn," it hissed at her. He tapped his scalloped breast. "Slurn."

Raven nodded. Her heart was bounding in her chest. This thing could tear her apart with those claws or spit her on that spear. She couldn't imagine what it wanted.

"Are you hungry, Slurn?" she asked him. He looked at all of the horses, then back at her.

"Eat," it hissed.

"Oh, don't eat the horses!" she insisted. "I will bring you—um—meat. You want meat?"

"Hish," it said, and tried again. "F—f—f—ish."

"I'll try, Slurn," she offered. "You stay hidden, I'll be back."

"Ray—en," it hissed, and walked back to a pile of hay. It slithered into it, and disappeared as if it had never been there.

'One who eludes prying eyes,' she reminded herself. Her horse bobbed its head, skittish from being close to him. Little Storm stood stock still in the next stall. She left the barn and closed the door behind her.

Time to call for backup.

* * *

Jerod took the same place he had taken the night before, in the hostel's common room, and called for meat, bread and ale from the Uman servants.

He liked the spot. No one could get behind him. He could see the one exit without putting his back to the stairs, and the common boards and seats around them made an obstacle for any attackers.

He'd lost a fight before, but it hurt him a lot to lose the one last night. He looked into the wooden bowl of ale in front of him before he drank it. That gaffer had a fist like a hammer, and a belly so fat that Jerod couldn't punch through it. If he'd been thinking, Jerod would have danced around more and made the gaffer chase him before engaging. At the end of the fight he left the old man panting, and Jerod on his back, but he could still have gone for more.

"You look angry," Jack said, approaching him.

He hadn't noticed the big Man and hadn't heard him walking down the stairs. That made Jerod cranky. A man that large shouldn't move that quietly, and no one should get that close to Jerod the Bold and not alert him.

"Sit," he said.

The gaffer sat. He had to move the stool back from the board to accommodate his belly. He had a half-smile showing through his beard, so he wanted to pretend that last night hadn't happened.

Jerod could play that game.

"Is that good?" Jack asked him.

He looked at his meal. "No," he said. Stabbing his meat with a hunting knife. "And if you are going to complain about it, sit somewhere I can't hear you."

The gaffer smiled even broader. "I just wanted to know if I should try the oats."

"Uck," Jerod shuddered. "No way for a man to start his day."

"You don't like oats?"

Jerod stuffed a wad of meat into his mouth so he didn't have to answer. He had the bread right there as well if he needed to stall the answer further. He didn't like to talk in the morning and even if he had to, he wasn't in the mood to play nice with the man who had just bested him, after insulting him to his core.

As if to rescue him, the gaffer's woman walked in the front door to the hostel—another one who had gotten past him.

She dressed like an Andaron woman on a raid. Riding boots fit for scrub, skirt slit up the side for riding, raider's coat cut long in back for the warmth, open in front so she could shed it if she had to, tight on her arms so it moved with her. All she lacked was a bow.

She stomped in, making too much noise with her boots, and smiled when she saw them. She cuddled up to Jack and nuzzled his ear in greetings.

"I thought you would still be asleep," she told him.

"Bed got cold," he told her. She hooked a stool with the toe of her boot and dragged it next to him. Sitting on it, she looked for the Uman servants.

"No caw-fee," she commented. He didn't know the word.

"No," the gaffer said. "Ale, though. And milk."

"Have milk," she said. Jerod swallowed and shook his head.

"You do what she tells you?" he asked the gaffer seriously.

The old man bristled. He liked that better. He looked Jerod straight in the eye and said, "She didn't tell me to beat you last night."

"You want to try and do it again?"

"I could work up an appetite," the gaffer warned him, which probably meant yes.

Jerod put his hands on the board to stand, the old man with him, and Jahunga's spear inserted itself between them.

He hadn't thrown it—that would have gotten them all kicked out. He held on to it, and laid it down on the board. He meant to get their attention, and he had. That meant that another person who had gotten too close to Jerod without him noticing.

He could forgive himself the Toorian—they moved like cats. Jahunga had a ready smile and already wore his robe and sandals. His wooly hair, still matted from sleeping, said he'd just gotten up.

"You two complain like old men at a fire," he told them, keeping the point of his spear on the board as he circled to sit next to Jerod. "And at least one of you has no excuse for it."

Raven laughed. The Uman staff had already started watching for the fight that might break out, but Jahunga put up his spear and sat next to Jerod. The old man took his hands off the board and settled down, so Jerod let himself relax a little.

Just a little.

"I was just in the barn," Raven informed them, "and I found something in there."

"Horses?" Jack asked her. She struck him on the shoulder with the back of her hand. That was more of a Volkhydran response than an Andaron. An Andaron man would have slapped her if she'd done that in front of his friends.

"No, some kind of lizard thing," she said. "It's hiding in the hay. It stands up like a man if it wants to, and it called me

'Raven.'"

Jerod leapt back up onto his feet, Jahunga with him. "A Slee?" he demanded of her. "A Slee is in the barn with the horses?"

"I don't know what a Slee is," she said.

"Half of a man, half of a lizard, mouth like a crocodile, webbed fingers and toes?" Jahunga asked.

Raven nodded. Jahunga turned to Jerod.

"We must kill it," he said. "I will gather my men. There must be more of them—"

"Just the one, Sirrah," Glynn's voice trailed down the stairs before her. She entered the room in a faded blue riding dress with little bows on the skirt, cut high for the cold and long in the sleeves. It wasn't fit to fight in, but she likely had him here for that.

Seeing no room next to Jerod, she pulled a chair up next to Jahunga. No Uman-Chi would sit on a stool. She daintily placed her ass on the chair's edge and called for clear water, then informed them she had taken breakfast in her rooms.

Raven shot her a dark look. Jerod noted bad blood there. Well, no one liked Uman-Chi, and being around them too long usually put a normal person off. Jerod saw some real animosity here though, and it interested him.

"You knew that thing was following us?" Raven asked her.

Glynn put her nose in the air. Uman-Chi did that, too. She elevated the tip a hair's breath, and it seem like they soared over you.

"No, dear Raven, I knew that thing was following *you*, and that you'd seen it debarking from our ship in Galnesh Eldador. I don't know where it hid when we were in the palace, but it left with us for here from Galnesh Eldador."

Xinto leapt up onto the stool next to Raven, appearing from nowhere as Scitai will. "In case you're wondering," he said, "that thing *is* a Slee, and it won't touch the horses."

Glynn raised an eyebrow at him, and Raven smiled. Jack's oats arrived with a pitcher of milk. The greasy Uman set another of water between them.

The Scitai looked once around the table. “I heard her rise and followed her to the barn,” he said. “When she left, I spoke with the thing. It was drawn to her, it doesn’t know why, and it’s hungry.

“I feel the same way,” he added.

Jerod stabbed his hunting knife into the board, picked his meat up with his hands, and tore a healthy bite out with his teeth as he sat.

“I can’t be rid of you people soon enough,” Jerod said.

“Nor I, except that I’ll be staying,” Xinto said, and banged on the board with his tiny fist. “Ale, woman! I am sober in the company of Men!”

Jerod called for more meat, and Raven poured milk for her man and herself, calling for melon and oats.

“You changed your mind?” Raven said, looking directly at Xinto.

“I have,” he said, “no thanks to your speech.”

“What swayed you then, Sirrah?” Glynn asked him. Jerod could see the curiosity on her face, beyond the unreadable eyes.

“Last night I looked at a collection of Men in a land ruled by Men, to fight another Man, and I asked myself what a Scitai would be doing in it,” he said.

“This morning I see a Slee in a barn, waiting for a woman,” he continued as an Uman servant girl laid a plate and a mug in front of him.

“If this song has a power to draw Slee out of their swamp, then it speaks of divinity, especially considering this one’s special skill. This is the ‘One who eludes prying eyes.’”

“I still don’t know about this common goal,” Jerod said, finishing his meal. “And even when I agreed to meet you, I didn’t agree to travel around with this carnival. That mutual friend of ours spends a lot of resources to know what is going on here, and if he doesn’t know exactly where we are, he will soon.”

“Jerod speaks true,” Jahunga said, stabbing at his meat. “The Emperor’s spies are in every village and hostel in Eldador, Andoron and as far away as my own Toor.”

They sat quiet. Jerod got his second helping of meat and took a long drink of ale. Glynn sipped her water and made a face.

"I think they dipped this in the bath," she complained.

"I know they did," Raven added. "You can see the hairs in it."

Glynn pushed the cup away. Raven couldn't have possibly seen through the wooden mug's sides, Jerod thought.

He liked this girl.

"We must create a base of operations for ourselves, where we can further our studies and be safe," Jahunga said.

Jerod nodded. That made sense to him. "We need to do it outside of Eldador," he said, "but close enough to watch Eldador."

Xinto turned to him. "You mean Kor?" he asked.

Jerod nodded again. "Kor is a lawless port city," he said. "We can hire a ship from there; we can escape to the outer islands if we need to. The Emperor had shown almost no interest in Kor—it's a good place."

He shot a glance at Glynn. She hadn't put forward the idea, so he expected her to oppose it. She was receiving another mug of water from an Uman, and she turned to face the rest of them.

"I concur," she said, surprising them. "No matter what our needs, I think we'll find them in the free city."

"City of pirates, you mean," Xinto said. "They'd as like to cut our throats as help us, in fact more probably just skip to the throat cutting. Why can't we go to your nation? I'm well liked in Outpost IX."

"I'm sure you are, Sirrah," Glynn said, "however King Angron Aurelias would not like to know that I am estranged from his new ally, the Emperor, and would most likely return us to his mercies."

"I don't want to go back to Outpost IX," Raven said.

"Because you have not been to Kor," Jahunga informed her. "However, we'll find my countrymen there, and I think we will find friends."

Jerod sighed. He didn't know what to make of Glynn agreeing with him so easily. The Uman-Chi would have her own motives, and they were unlikely to be his.

Nothing for it now. He couldn't argue against the idea if it was his. The others sparred over how likely they were to go but

Glynn had made her mind up, and he had to think she'd win out.

He turned his head and spat where a spittoon might have been strategically located, but hadn't. One of the Uman servants saw him and made a face, but the Volkhydran didn't acknowledge her. He focused on his meal and ignored the conversation until they all stood up, ready to meet this Slee.

* * *

Bill, now 'Jack,' pushed the barn door open and grunted at the pain in his belly the effort brought with it. Jerod might be six inches shorter and two thirds his weight, but he was almost solid muscle and he could *really* pack a punch. Bill hadn't been in a fight in thirty years and hadn't actually won one in longer.

Dust hung suspended in the air, shining in the sunshine that streamed in through the door behind him. The horses were snorting and stomping in their stalls to his right, a giant pile of hay to his left, reaching two thirds of the way to the ceiling—with two eyes in it, staring at him.

His heart might have actually skipped a beat.

"Well, hello," he said to the eyes.

Behind him he felt Melissa—Raven—put her hand on the small of his back. He could hear Jerod and Jahunga to either side behind him.

Xinto stepped past him, and hissed something at the pile of straw. He dropped a leather sack in front of them—even Jack could smell the red meat. The two eyes blinked, regarding the bag, then the hay moved.

The lizard-thing that called itself Slurn slithered out of the hay and into the open. It was exactly as Melissa described it, except it also wore a belt of shells around its waist, bound with some kind of black wire.

Glynn hissed something at it from behind them. It turned to her, standing upright, its back straight and its shoulders held back.

It hissed something and made a sweeping gesture with one hand. Bill turned to Xinto.

"He says he felt an irresistible curiosity about Galnesh Eldador months ago, and left its people to travel up through

Andoron and along the shores of Tren Bay to get there. When he finally arrived in the port, he was swimming under the ships in the port and saw Raven."

"Ray—enn," he hissed, and pointed at her. She stepped up next to Bill.

He hissed more, and Xinto translated, "He saw Raven with the sun behind her, and he knew he'd found whom he was looking for. He's heard Glynn sing her song—where?—when she sang it in her room for Jahunga and Jerod."

Bill nodded. "If he can hear the song," he began.

Glynn interrupted him. "We know only a select few can hear it."

"Xinto speaks true," Jahunga said. "He *could* be the one who eludes prying eyes."

Jerod nodded. Bill found himself agreeing with them.

He didn't like this sound of this place 'Kor.' He'd studied enough history to know what pirate towns could be like—order by the strongest strong man, lives sold cheaply. Even if they could get there, it didn't mean they'd be safe, just that they'd face newer dangers.

Slurn hissed again. Glynn said, "He'll go with us to Kor. He's not asking me, he's telling me. I believe, my compatriots, that we have another."

"And a devil of a time getting there with him," Xinto said, turning. "Every peasant farmer who sees us travelling with a Slee will tell everyone else he meets, and then the Emperor will be right behind us."

Slurn hissed again, turned on his heel and dove back into the hay. The pile shook once and then was still.

"I don't think we'll find a series of giant hay piles for him to hide in between here and Kor," Xinto protested.

They heard a hiss behind them. They all turned to see Slee in the doorway to the barn, the light behind him. A moment later he hissed again and slipped off to his left.

"Well, isn't that a trick," Jerod said.

Bill found himself agreeing.

"I believe if we set out for Kor, then it will be as a collection of travelers, and no mention of a Slee," Glynn informed them. “Let us away without delay, then.”

Chapter Twenty-One:

A Devil, Born and Raised

Jack rode into the east on Little Storm, Xinto sitting behind him. Raven rode her Angadorian mare beside Jack, Jerrod and Glynn behind them.

The ten Toorians and Jahunga loped along in a circle around them. They shunned horses and preferred to feel their feet touch the face of Earth. Xinto knew this was typical of their people—they rode no horses in their jungles.

Eldador had been a collection of city-states once, loosely ruled by King Glennen in Galnesh Eldador. Dukes and Earls built walled cities and raided each other, paying taxes to the capitol when forced. The country had seemed too large for the capitol to manage, especially from its remote port location. There had been a time when a person could do almost anything he or she wanted to in Eldador, if his or her sword arm was strong enough.

The Emperor had changed that, even before becoming the Emperor. In his early days as a mercenary for hire, Lupus had ingratiated himself with Glennen somehow and become the Earl of Thera. As an Earl he'd worked some magic he called ech-nomics, and figured out a way to tax peasants less and get more gold and silver from them. A lot of commons became fantastically wealthy in Thera under Lupus' rule, and the King had named the

Earl a Duke.

With peasants flocking to Eldador from all over Fovea, as more and more Duchies and Earldoms and baronies adopted this ech-nomics, a decision was made between high-ranking persons in Trenbon, Sental, Dorkan and Volkhydro that Eldador had become too dangerous, and that Lupus and his allies needed to die.

Lupus' allies were called the 'Daff Kanaar,' a strange expression in Uman which meant a union of allies, entered into freely. Assassins had been assembled to eliminate the lot of them, starting with Lupus himself in his home.

Something had gone wrong, and the assassins had killed the queen of Eldador instead. No sweeter soul had ever walked the face of Earth, Xinto knew from personal experience. Rumor had it the assassins had tortured her for information on where to find Lupus and his allies, and had done so in Lupus' own home.

The berserker reaction to that assassination had rocked Fovea. Members of the Daff Kanaar had sailed out and sunk Dorkan ships, marched up the Llorando and destroyed every bridge between Sental and Volkhydro, killing every armed warrior they found along the way, and Lupus himself had sacked the unsackable Outpost IX, killing members of the Fovean High Council and destroying the city's gates.

That sort of attack would become characteristic of the Emperor. Don't just strike, crush. Don't just kill, slaughter. Plow the bodies of the dead into the ground so that the bones haunted the survivors' children. Don't settle for a statement where an atrocity will do.

Now Eldadorian duchies ruled earldoms which ruled baronies, and no one city thought to raid another. The major cities in Eldador were surrounded with smaller villages, towns and even smaller cities which had no walls, which were little more than collections of farmers and their local markets, with roads stretching clean between them. Now none of the people in Eldador ever feared that their neighbors from another duchy would come surging over a hillside if their crop was bad—they just sold them their excess goods.

Xinto had crossed the nation of Eldador twenty years before and not seen a person for a week at a time; had seen gazelle running wild across wind-swept plains, had surprised a covey of rabbits or come across a lonesome hawk's nest on the ground.

Now they travelled a flat, cobbled road from one village to the next. They moved quickly and stayed in hostels. People greeted them, Uman and Volkhydran and Confluni and even the occasional Scitai.

For a week they pressed on, closing on the port of Kor and the Salt Wood which completely enveloped it. As they drew closer to the wood, the villages became more sparse and more likely to be logging camps, wide farms and open spaces. On the seventh day of their journey, and the 21st day of Weather's month, they actually found themselves having to camp outside at night.

They slept in bedrolls because the nights were warming. They had a cook fire made from local scrub. They picketed their horses together, Little Storm at the center of them, and they chose a watch consisting mostly of Toorians.

Xinto piled his own bedding and laid down on top of it as the sun was setting. The members of their little band who were Men, the Toorians and Jack and Raven and Jerod, would talk their idle nonsense as Men would. Glynn kept her own council most of the time, and that left Xinto very little to do.

She'd sung her song a few times, and they all speculated on it. None of the Toorians except Jahunga could hear it. They had argued as to where the Sacred Place could be, as to what the missing weapons were, and where they might find them. Once in a while Slurn would show his face, but it seemed mostly to want to check on Raven and then he would slither away.

So double Xinto's surprise when it found him lying on his bedding.

"There is danger," the thing hissed at him.

There had been a time when the Slee had wanted to push past what was called the Black Lake now, the junction between the Safe and Mid Rivers where the Emperor was building a city called 'Wisex,' into southern Conflu. The Confluni didn't want that, and they'd enlisted Xinto to convince the Slee to stay in their swamp. Because the Slee actually ate Men and Uman, Xinto had found the greater challenge not to be eaten by the Slee than to negotiate with them.

He'd satisfied that challenge by ensuring them of his hatred for another species.

"There is a Swamp Devil stalking us," Slurn said.

That was the other species.

Xinto sat up and scanned the horizon. His hearing, much more sensitive than that of most other races, told him nothing, but that didn't mean much. He'd met with Swamp Devils as well, and even though they ranged between eight and ten feet tall, they could move as quiet as mice if they wanted to.

"Where?" Xinto asked.

"To the south, against the blowing wind," Slurn said. "He's hunting us."

Xinto nodded. The Devil wasn't within sighting distance yet, or Xinto would have marked him. He pulled a collapsible bow from his voluminous cloak and then knocked a dart to it. He pulled a vial with hemlock essence in it from a pocket and dipped the dart.

"Track him," Xinto said. "Don't fight him. Let me know when he's close."

Slurn hissed and turned on his heels back into the scrub, disappearing almost immediately. The grass was short and most of the large weed growths and scrub brush were brown. The thing would have a hard time getting close to them. When it was ready to strike, it would come at a sprint.

Xinto trotted over to the fire, where Jahunga, Jerod, Raven and Jack were talking.

"There's a Swamp Devil stalking us," he said.

Jahunga and Jerod were both on their feet, the Volkhydran with his sword out.

"Put that up, you thick-witted Man," Xinto said. "Do you want him to know we know *of* him?"

Jerod made a face and sheathed the weapon. Hopefully it was fast enough.

"Where?" Jahunga asked.

"To the south, against the wind," Xinto said. "The Slee marked him and he's stalking him. I told him not to attack it, but a Slee won't tolerate a Devil for long."

Jahunga nodded. "I'll tell my men," he said, and left the

fire. Jack and Raven stood. Glynn approached the fire from where she'd been meditating, in the shadows away from them.

"I don't sense this Devil," she said. "If he has magic, he is making an effort not to use it."

"He's deep into Eldador," Xinto said. "He probably has magic. You sometimes hear of them raiding into Angador, but never this far north."

"If he has magic and he's not using it, then he knows we have it," Jerod said. "So he's been following us."

"A devil, born and raised?" Jack asked. Leave it to a Man to announce the obvious.

"I'd feared this," Glynn said. "A Swamp Devil is a poor ally. He'll kill just for the pleasure of another's suffering. His words are mostly lies. They'll swear an oath and keep it, but then look for a way to turn it on the one they made it to, just out of their own meanness."

"Won't the song…" Raven said, looking from face to face. "I mean, Slurn, he wouldn't normally—"

Glynn nodded. Jerod answered her, "The song brought me in, and Jahunga, too. He wanted to be a part of it, I still don't. Maybe it will make him join us, but maybe he'll kill half of us before he figures that out."

"If he's stalking us he means to kill," Xinto said. He looked out over the horizon. "He may have already."

No sooner had he said that then Jahunga returned with nine warriors. No need to ask them about the tenth.

"This thing is coming," he said. "Our southern-most guard can't be found."

Slurn appeared as if from magic out of the scrub. "It approaches," he hissed. Xinto translated.

They lined up to the south of their fire, the Toorians at their center with Jahunga leading them, Glynn actually to the north of the blaze standing in its smoke.

That made more sense. If she needed to use her magic, then the fire might give her a few more moments.

"I know you've seen me," something growled from the south, out of the darkness. Xinto could see its red eyes now. It was tenth of a daheer or less away, laying on a rise, its body pressed into the dirt. Its skin was black as night; the moonlight glinted on its horns.

"I have it," Xinto whispered to the others.

"Send me one of your horses, and you can go," it informed them.

"Why would it want a horse?" Jack asked them. "Do they ride?"

"We're supposed to think he wants to eat it," Jahunga said. "If we send it, he'll kill it and eat some of it, but he'll torture it first where we can hear. The horses will be skittish and we'll fear him, and then he'll come again, and we'll have one less horse."

"Send it now," the thing roared. It voice was baritone and gravelly, dripping with evil.

Glynn drew herself up to her full height and straightened her back. She inhaled and Xinto knew she was going to make the greatest mistake she possibly could.

She was going to negotiate with it.

"I advise against that," Xinto said, interrupting the Duchess.

She pressed her lips together and regarded him. Jahunga was speaking in hushed tones with his warriors, Jerod with them. Jack and Raven kept to each other's company alongside the fire.

"It's pointless to negotiate with him," Xinto informed her. "His word means nothing unless he takes an oath, and he won't do that just to please you."

"Sirrah," she said, her deprecating tone not lost on the Scitai, "I have, in my century and a half, in fact met Swamp Devils before."

She probably had, Xinto knew. But she'd met them in the company of other Uman-Chi with more experience than she, and under better conditions than this.

This banter, of course, distracted Xinto, which was unfortunate because that left the thin-brained Men to their own devices and, left to their own devices, thin-brained Men do only one thing.

Three Toorian warriors crept off to the east, four more to the west, leaving two with Jerod and Jahunga, who began to march south, bold as a brass penny and no more valuable. Jerod took a moment to spit to one side as he walked alongside the other warriors.

"War's beard," Xinto swore. They were going to engage it, and they thought with twelve they had enough. They didn't know Swamp Devils.

"Wait here," Xinto commanded Jack and Raven, who as like would have done nothing else. He adjusted his overcloak and trotted out after the Men. If they were willing to die, he might as well use the opportunity to put an arrow in this thing's eye, if it presented itself.

The Devil didn't say another word, and Xinto didn't see it where it had been last. Challenged, it would fight, Xinto knew, and it was cunning enough not to give its position away. Swamp Devils are ambush hunters and it would press its body to the ground and wait until an enemy was almost upon it, then rise up bellowing and strike.

The Men pressed forward. Xinto could see that Jahunga and Jerod wanted to draw the thing out and let the other warriors flank it. They counted on their superior fighting ability to be able to hold the monster long enough for the Toorians to put a few spears in its back.

But those spears were metal-tipped and most metal weapons would bounce off a Devil's hide. Their swords would likely be no different. If a person could penetrate an ear, or an eye, or the mouth, then one could damage a Devil, but then, the Devil knew this, too.

The night fell deadly quiet. Xinto could hear the Men's feet shuffling in the loose earth and scrub. He could smell the swamp stink off of the Devil and, to his west, that of the Slee, who was closing in like he was. Slurn had also likely guessed what the Men were doing and would wait for them to entangle the Devil, then strike.

His mind racing, Xinto waited for the explosion of violence that a mixture of these three species was guaranteed to deliver.

A moment later a roar like an angry lion's ripped the night and the Devil rose up before the four Men moving south, his red teeth and eyes gleaming in the moonlight, his arms spread wide and his talons bared. His muscles stood out gleaming and black. The thing's long, black hair almost touched the ground behind it, waving to the left and the right as it slashed with one claw, then the next at the surprised Men.

It wore a steel breastplate. Xinto stood stunned for a moment. He knew this Swamp Devil—he knew it well.

The two Toorian warriors drove forward with their spears, stabbing for the legs and groin, trying to avoid the claws. The Swamp Devil stood nine feet tall and his arms reached over five—he caught one Toorian on his right along the side of the face and peeled the skin and flesh away from his skull. The Toorian fell screaming, a hideous site out of nightmare, one eye gone and the other exposed in the socket, the jaw bone visible all the way around as choking voice screamed and teeth chattered.

Jahunga leapt forward, driving his spear two-handed at the monster's throat. Jerod swung his sword in a great arc and connected with the Devil's thigh, his steel sword clanging against Swamp Devil hide. Toorians charged in from the southeast and southwest, driving their spears like battering-rams toward the Swamp Devil's exposed back.

For any other creature it would have been a slaughter. The Swamp Devil back-handed the Volkhydran, then dragged his left claw down the front of the Toorian beside him. Jahunga stabbed again and his spear snapped as the head connected with the Devil's breastplate. Seven Toorians stabbed again from behind, their steel spear points clanking against Swamp Devil skin and steel breastplate as the creature raised two giant claws into the air and, screaming his rage, drove them toward the helpless Toorian.

Like a green blur, the Slee sprinted in and tackled Jahunga from the side, driving him out of the way of the claws that dragged two divots into the ground. The Devil roared in anger and stood up to his full height, dirt clods dripping from his claws, looking for an enemy to kill.

"Hey!" a woman's voice called out behind them. The Devil turned to see who called him out. Xinto dreaded it. Sure enough, putting herself in front of the fire, there was little Raven, the night breeze catching the tails of her Andaron raider's jacket, drawing the monster's attention.

"Mel—Raven, no!" Jack shouted. He'd moved next to Glynn for some reason and was now sprinting 'round their fire. Raven stood there, fifty feet from the Swamp Devil with nothing between them, not knowing he could cross that distance in a breath of time.

She jabbed her outstretched palm at the Swamp Devil and shouted, "Feel my power!"

For just a second, Xinto wondered if the girl had been hiding some sort of magical talent. Swamp Devils could be deceptively gifted spell-casters, and Xinto knew this one certainly was. The creature threw up his hands in front of his face as if to block some bolt of energy then, realizing nothing was coming his way, dropped his left hand and took a step forward.

"Feel mine, daughter of Men," it snarled in that same, gravelly voice, and pointed the claws on his right hand at the girl. Green energy crackled in the air around his fingertips, then flew in a long, emerald arc toward Raven.

She stood her ground. The energy almost touched her.

Then, seconds before Jack could knock her out of the way, there was a bright flash and the Devil roared in pain. The creature actually flipped over backwards, his clawed feet rising higher than his head for a moment, as the back-surge from the attack struck him no differently than it had Glynn weeks before, and the Swamp Devil crashed into the ground.

A moment later a satisfied-looking Raven did the same as her overweight lover leapt for her. Xinto saw her body shimmer for a moment as the two of them fell in a tangle in the dirt.

The screaming Toorian stopped screaming as the goddess Life took him. His compatriots and Jerod slowly approached the Devil as it lay unconscious on the ground, its head turned to one side, its forked black tongue lolling from its open mouth. Slurn and Jahunga stood together from a tangle in the scrub.

"Well, I guess now that would be something," Xinto said to no one in particular.

* * *

Part of the training necessary for the Emperor's children was to watch their father in court. Lee at fourteen and Vulpe at nearly twelve both hated it. They sat in the gallery on hard wooden benches and kicked their feet and scuffed their shoes, complained the court was boring and that the petitioners made no sense, and eventually got to noticing that their bottoms hurt.

Stern looks from Nina of the Aschire were usually sufficient to quell them if court ran less than three hours. More than that and threats could buy her another hour, and finally actual, physical harm to these children whom she loved as if she'd born them could keep them for another two.

She wasn't above a slap to an over-used mouth to quell a petulant child, much as if any other than then Imperial couple did the same in her presence she wouldn't hesitate to leave in a dagger in that person's heart. It was Nina's job to ward these children's lives and she took it seriously.

She loved them. She'd make future Eldadorian statesmen out of both of them, given the opportunity. That was sometimes funny to her, who'd grown up living in a tree.

"We call Nina of the Aschire," the court squire announced.

Nina looked up in surprise. She'd been called up to court twice in her entire life—once to officially bestow upon her the title of guardian of the Emperor's children, and once on her birthday when she'd been presented with four dwarf-made daggers the Emperor had ordered for her, because he loved her.

She stood, she straightened her skin-tight leather pants and black leather vest, she shot a warning look both at the children and those around them, and she left the gallery for the long, red carpet that ran from the wooden double-doors to the throne room, to the raised dais where the white marble throne of Eldador held the Emperor, Rancor Mordetur the First.

She walked to the circle carved in the stone floor at the end of the red carpet. She stepped into that circle, her heart pounding, and she tilted her head back, her long, purple hair cascading back over her shoulders, and her eyes found those of the Emperor.

They hadn't spoken since she'd defied him, since he'd struck her and she'd pulled her knife on him, and raised her hand in Power to him. He'd been busy, first with his lost daughter, then with finding his lost countrymen. Still, it was the longest week in her thirteen years at court, where she'd gone without a word from him.

She readied herself for the worst. She failed him. This was it. She was being sent back to the Aschire.

"Nina of the Aschire," the Emperor said in Uman, the language of the Eldadorian court.

He waited. She just stared into his blue, blue eyes. His lips were set in a thin line, his face dour, accentuated by the scar on the left side, the Mark of the Conqueror.

"Come to me," he said.

He'd never done this. She took a step toward the throne. It was like being lost in a foggy field in the morning. Her feet found the way for her, up the steps, balancing on the balls of her feet, looking him in the eyes, his face all she seemed able to see.

She's miss those children. She'd miss the Empress, almost a sister to her.

She admitted to herself she loved this man. He'd been more of a father to her than her own.

Finally she stood before the throne. Still, she hadn't said a word.

"Clear the court," the Emperor ordered.

She heard the commotion behind her as people stood and shuffled out. She wondered if the children remained. She wondered who'd watch over them. As shuffling feet found their way farther and farther behind her, she wondered what kind of man Vulpe would become. Would Lee be a mother? Would she herself be one now? Who among the Aschire would want her?

The throne room fell silent. The Emperor stood to his towering height. The only other Man she'd ever seen who approximated his size was this new countryman of his, and that man was gone.

"Nina," he said, finally, "I need you."

"M—my Lord?" she asked him. This made no sense.

"I don't think the Mountain and Raven are coming back," he said. "And I don't trust that Uman-Chi whore as far as I—well, I don't trust her."

She looked down, then looked back up. "I," she said, and swallowed. "I don't trust her, either."

“I want you to take twenty Wolf Soldiers and find them,” he said. “I know you haven’t done anything like this before, but I think it needs to be you. You have magic, so you can communicate back to us, and you can counter Glynn if you need to.

“But I want to send someone who’ll do it right, someone I can trust,” he said. He reached out and he took Nina’s hands in his, and he looked into her grey eyes with his blue ones.

“I think you’re ready for this,” he said. “Will you go find them for me and, if you can, bring them back?”

Someone I can trust. The words ran over and over in her mind.

He still loved her. He wasn’t sending her away; he was trusting her on a mission.

Almost before she realized it, she had her arms around his neck and her feet off of the ground. She heard his deep chuckle and felt his arm around her waist. For a moment she was the little, lost girl on her first night here, with him holding her until she fell asleep in his arms.

“I’ll do it,” she whispered into his ear. “I’ll do it for you.”

Chapter Twenty-Two:

Missions and Contracts

Zarshar the Swamp Devil awoke with the sun shining in his eyes, trussed up on the ground with his face in the dust, a pair of feet in front of him. He instinctively lashed out and found his arms bound behind him, bent backwards to prevent him from struggling against the ropes they'd used. If he flexed hard enough, he'd break his bones before he broke the ropes.

He lurched to one side in order to leap to his feet, and was rewarded with a painful tug on his hair that bent his neck back. They'd woven rope into his long, black mane and then bent his legs back and bound them together and to his hair. If he fought to straighten them, he'd snap his neck before he was free.

Something wanted him for a prisoner. He remembered coming across this strange band—Men, a Scitai, an Uman-Chi caster, female, no less. They rode horses and walked, and were moving in the direction of Kor.

They looked like fugitives, and fugitives are always easy prey. Well, almost always.

He turned his head in the dust and looked skyward to see the owner of these feet, and saw none other than Xinto of the Woods, the Confluni Ambassador he'd met years before.

“Hello, rat,” he said to it.

It smiled wide and bowed, the ridiculous orange feather in its ridiculous hat touching the ground before it.

“I knew I should have eaten you,” Zarshar said.

“My friends,” Xinto said, “I introduce you to Zarshar, the Black Adept, one of the most feared of the Swamp Devils.”

“I know of Zarshar,” someone with a Toorian accent said behind him. “He’s killed many.”

“I’m not done yet,” Zarshar promised him.

“You may be,” Xinto said. “I’m going to introduce you to a Lady, a Baroness in Eldador and a Duchess in Trenbon, and she’s going to sing you a song. I’d like to know your opinion of it.”

Zarshar chuckled. “Then untie me,” he said. “I like songs.”

“You like nothing but other beings’ suffering,” Xinto challenged him. Behind him, the green-haired Uman-Chi in a blue travel dress stepped up with her hands clasped before her, at her waist. “And I’m not foolish enough to untie you.”

“So sing,” Zarshar said. If they wanted his opinion, they wanted him alive. If they wanted him alive, he’d escape.

His own kind would be scooping his heart of out his chest by now to ingest his courage.

The girl sang, her eyes always on him. Other races supposedly only saw silver when they looked into Uman-Chi eyes. He saw hers were an off-violet at the cornea; rare among her people.

At first he was surprised she’d bother to sing this song in his own language, seeing as he clearly spoke the languages of Uman and Men. Next he was a little interested in the story of the song, the combat, the champion, the idea of weapons—all were good to a Swamp Devil.

Then he heard of ‘a Devil, born and raised,” and his mind stuck on that.

They thought this song was about him—about them meeting him. Zarshar’s magic wasn’t great but he sensed the power in the song. They thought this was a prophecy, and they thought he figured in it.

Other races were so stupid, most of the time. He’d enjoy

pretending to play along with them and then betraying them.

"Very well," the Swamp Devil said, a moment after the song ended. "You need a Devil to guide you to a sacred place. You think that providence has brought me to you. Where's the place?"

"More than providence, Sirrah," the Uman-Chi informed him. "Fate, destiny, a purpose divine. Your very essence has brought you to us—"

"We don't know the place," Xinto said, interrupting her.

Zarshar grinned a wide, evil grin. Uman-Chi hated being interrupted, even when they go on and on. He could see the anger in the girl's eyes. He liked that.

"Well, I don't know it," he said. "But, I suppose if you untie me, then I'll have to help you find it. The song is a spell and now I'm compelled to obey you."

Xinto chuckled. "You're not even trying," he said.

Zarshar grinned even wider. Of course they weren't going to believe him, so why waste time with a good lie? Use up the predictable lies now, and then come up with something good later.

He'd tried that with this one before. The Confluni had wanted the Swamp Devils to swarm up into Angador as they attacked Thera for the second time. Xinto had come with the gift of this very breast plate to bribe him to collect the hundred other Swamp Devils who'd sworn fealty to him and catch Lupus the Conqueror on his softer side.

Zarshar had negotiated for five hundred Confluni archers, marched north with them, set upon the Angadorians and abandoned them to Tartan Stowe. He'd learned a lot about Eldadorian defenses watching them die. He knew he'd need even more Swamp Devils before he actually *did* take the south of Eldador.

"What do you think you have, that I want?" Zarshar asked Xinto.

"I have your life in my hands," he said, holding his palms up before him. He clapped them together, and added, "And I can take it."

"So take it," Zarshar said. "Everything dies eventually."

They wanted him alive. They'd talk and talk. Eventually

they'd start to concede things to him, looking for something he wanted or would trade for his freedom. Zarshar knew these weaknesses. He could exploit them with patience.

Xinto turned to the Uman-Chi, who stepped forward to begin negotiations.

At the same time, a male of the race of Men stepped over him and placed himself between Zarshar and the negotiators. He turned, and the Swamp Devil saw the grey in his beard, the fat on his belly. He stood taller than most Men, but he was old.

"This is pointless," the old Man said.

"Sirrah," the Uman-Chi sighed, but the old Man held up his hand.

"I am called, 'Jack,'" the old Man said.

"Good for you," Zarshar growled.

"Jack," the Uman-Chi said, stepping up next to him, "the Swamp Devils are a cunning race—I think you'd do best to allow the Ambassador and myself to negotiate here."

Jack made a strange face and shot a glance at the Uman-Chi as if she were crazy. This was interesting.

"Can you think of anything in your song that says this Devil can't be scarred, crippled, maybe missing its teeth or an eye?" he asked the Uman-Chi.

The Uman-Chi frowned but didn't answer.

"Thought not," he said. He looked past Zarshar and said, "Come here, Slurn."

A Slee leapt over his shoulder, turned and hissed at him, its tail waving behind him, its claws bared.

Zarshar instinctively roared and tried to leap to the attack. He failed—the bindings that held his arms and legs and hair simply wrenched at his bones. He tried to invoke his magic but it failed him.

What had these things done to him? He wondered.

"Slurn," Jack asked the Slee, "how would you like to show this Swamp Devil what you think of him?"

The Slee hissed appreciatively. It gripped the air with its long, white claws and took a step toward Zarshar.

The Black Adept was no coward, but certain indignities could not be suffered. He wouldn't let his body be the play-thing of a Slee.

"Enough!" he demanded. He turned his red eyes to the Man. "What do you want?"

Jack shrugged. "What can you give me?"

Zarshar could appreciate this—put the onus of a deal on the one in the weaker position.

"I will swear not to harm you, or yours," he said. "Unless of course you first harm me, in which case all deals are void."

"Nah," Jack said. "That's too convenient. You'll just swear to that and leave."

Zarshar couldn't hold back a wicked grin. Yes, that is what he would have done.

"I will travel with you to this sacred place, as well," he said.

"You'll travel with us to this sacred place," Jack repeated, "and you will not harm us, or lead us into harm, or contract with others to harm us *and* if we are attacked, you will defend us to the best of your abilities."

"Unless you first harm me—" Zarshar repeated.

"Unless we *intentionally* try to harm you," Jack corrected him.

The Swamp Devil sighed. The Uman-Chi and Xinto were looking on curiously now. He could have negotiated a better deal with these. Men could be cunning, but this one seemed quite smart, and that made the dealing harder.

"Agreed," Zarshar growled.

"This to include our horses, or any other animals or other persons which we may need to join our group," Jack said.

Blast! Zarshar swore in his mind. He'd just realized he could attack the horses and goad at least one of them into fighting.

"Agreed," Zarshar growled again.

"And afterward," Jack continued, "you will leave us, and never come looking for us, or come seek any of us out to harm us."

This thing's negotiating skills were maddening. Yes, Zarshar would try to get them to harm him in some way but, that failing, the moment they achieved their 'sacred place,' he could have fallen on them.

"Agreed," Zarshar growled.

"Everyone in front of him," the old Man commanded the rest.

"Sirrah," the Uman-Chi began.

He turned to her and said, "Otherwise he's going to say, 'I didn't know *that one* was a part of your group' after he beheads one of us."

The Uman-Chi looked to the Scitai, who nodded. As a group they lined up where he could see them, including their horses.

"Now swear it all, at the same time," Jack instructed him.

They had him. For a moment he thought it might be better just to kick his own legs out and break his neck, but that would be admitting someone from the race of Men had bested him, and that was almost as bad as being torn apart by the Slee.

He swore.

"Happy, lummox?" Xinto chided him.

"No, but I can live with it," Jack said. "Untie him."

"With your permission, of course," Xinto inclined his head. Jahunga ordered his men to approach him, and Zarshar had to wait for the hour it took to release him.

In that time, the large man left with a Volkhydran. As his legs were being unbound, they returned with a raw haunch, large enough to be from a stag or a young horse.

"Feed," the Volkhydran, Jerod, said, and tossed it on the ground before him.

"You are kind," Zarshar inclined his head.

"Thank this one," Jerod corrected him. "He said you were going to tell us you had hunger pains, it was our fault, and then attack us."

Jack smiled a satisfied smile. Xinto rolled his eyes. A dark female in Andaron clothes walked up to this 'Jack' and kissed his cheek, bending her left leg at the knee as she stretched to his height. She perhaps enjoyed him—it was impossible to say.

Zarshar hadn't thought of that, but he would have. Hunger would have pained him, and he would have struck without explanation. He could not claim now their causing him the pain of hunger was intentional. Power was not so naïve a god.

"You vex me, Man," he said to Jack. "I like you, but I assure you that, when the time comes, you will be the first to die."

This Jack didn't seem scared, but the female clearly felt threatened. "You can't tell me—" Xinto began.

The last knot came untied, and Zarshar leapt to his feet as fast as any of them could follow. Slurn had his spear in place as quickly, the Toorians only slightly slower. The dark-haired female gripped Jack's belly and the Uman-Chi raised a hand white with power.

Zarshar had the Scitai in his grip in one sweep of his hand. Xinto's head emerged from his thumb and forefinger, his legs kicked free past the heel of his hand, as Zarshar lifted Xinto from the ground.

"Rest assured, I would have marched to your picket and killed every horse you own," he said. "I would have forced you either to attack me or watch them die horribly.

"Your Man is someone you are wise to listen to. He knows my mind, and I do *not* like to be bound."

He expected the usual complaints of Men, the irritating reasoning of Uman-Chi, the Slee to threaten and the Toorians to argue to attack him—which he would have considered an assault.

He got none of these. Instead, the female Uman-Chi sang her song again.

* * *

Glynn sang, and Jack listened to the now familiar lyrics.

He almost liked mentally sparring with this Swamp Devil, much as it was a lot more serious than negotiating with a stubborn client. Zarshar had been right in that Jack knew its mind. Xinto thought he had history with this thing, and that it knew him and liked him.

It hadn't killed the Scitai when they met before, but that didn't mean anything to it. Zarshar knew it could kill Xinto later. Jack saw the truth in its red eyes, the way it licked its lips, wanting to fight. Jack had seen Zarshar's type in sales people who ripped their clients off because they liked it, not because they needed the money—people like that don't take a vacation from it.

Jack watched Zarshar, and Zarshar watched Glynn. The

Devil's red eyes first widened, then narrowed, and all the while the hand that held the struggling Scitai lowered until finally the song was over and Xinto stepped out of his grip to the ground.

Xinto fussed and straightened the lumpy gray robe that never actually fit straight, and altered the feathered cap on his head. He made sure to step away from Zarshar and in among the Toorians where he wouldn't be snatched up again so easily.

"I heard your words in my native language," Zarshar said, predictably, "but your lips moved in yours. If I had more of my power I would know for sure, but I think you are not the originator of this magic."

"I am not, I swear it, Sirrah," Glynn said. Jack didn't know how much that would mean to the Swamp Devil, but he knew how little it meant to him.

He hadn't considered that this Glynn used her magic to trick them, but what if the real magic was her making them believe her? Could she have fooled Shela? He couldn't ask her now.

"And I can tell you do not lie," Zarshar said. "For the now, I will accept that this song of yours is prophecy, much as it upsets me a great deal."

"Then you aren't here to wage the war against the Empire?" Xinto asked him.

Zarshar shook his horned head. "I honestly can't say why I came here, except that being here is all I could think about for all of the last month and, having resisted it as long as I could, I departed for here, and came across you."

"I know the feeling," Jerod grumbled, looking at no one.

"I am familiar with this as well," Jahunga admitted. "I left everything I had accomplished, everything I was to be here."

"And now one of you—the guardian—must guide me to 'the sacred place,'" Zarshar surmised.

The thing showed intelligence, Jack admitted to himself. He put his arm around Raven, already stuck to him like glue. She feared that they would be separated, but she needed time away from him to reconcile for herself why she felt so attracted to him.

If she left him now, he would miss her. At the same time, it would hurt less than when he finally let his guard down, as he knew he would soon do.

"Clearly, we have two goals," Glynn informed him. "The one is to collect this last part of the prophecy—the one who fights as does the sun. The other is to commence to 'fight the battle from inside.'"

"We must move on to Kor," she said, "and from there, we must lay plans against the Eldadorian Empire."

* * *

Melissa sat at a counter, in a dinette, on a vinyl-covered stool. The place was familiar, but she knew she hadn't been here in a very long time. There were laminated menus and stainless steel knives and forks, cheesy linoleum counters and tiny white coffee cups.

The whole thing wasn't right, she knew. She shouldn't be here. She had something else to do.

"Back she comes, like a bad penny," an older woman told her.

She turned to her right and saw a woman with silver hair, wrinkled skin, dressed in a yellow sundress and white shoes. She smelled of Sunflowers perfume.

She hadn't smelled that smell since…

Since…

Since that night in Augusta, when she'd done the worst thing she'd done in her whole life, ever.

"You picked you a hard row to hoe, missy," the older woman told her.

Eve, Melissa remembered. She called herself Eve.

That name meant a lot more to her now.

"My, look how you've growed," Eve commented, her face lighting up in a smile. She reached out and touched the back of Melissa's hand. "You were barely a girl when we first met. Now you're all a woman."

Melissa looked down and saw that she was dressed in her Andaron leathers, all boobs and belly. The back of her jacket hung over the stool. Her black leather mini rode up on her.

"I wanted to thank you," Melissa said, finally. She looked into Eve's eyes. "That money you slipped me, in that pack of cigarettes—I used it to start a new life. I—well, I think you kind o' saved me."

Eve made a shooing motion. "You was too pretty a girl to be turned out on the streets," she said. "I jess did for you what you'lda done for yourself, but faster."

Melissa smiled. She hadn't heard a real Maine accent in a long time, and she hadn't realized how much she'd missed it.

Of course, this wasn't a Mainer—this was a goddess, and her name wasn't 'Eve,' though it was close.

"Am I doing what I should be doing now?" Melissa asked her.

The waitress behind the counter, a middle-aged woman who had also been here that day, came and set a cup of coffee in front of her, cream and two sugars. It smelled wonderful, and Melissa couldn't resist it. They had nothing like it here.

"I think you know the answer to that," Eve told her.

Melissa did, but she still wanted to ask. They were stuck. Glynn had decided they were going to some pirates' den named 'Kor,' and the closer they drew to it, the more certain she was that this was the wrong direction.

"We can't figure out what to do next," Melissa complained. The coffee cup was warm in her hand, she steam rising up into her face. She'd left lipstick on the rim, but she didn't remember putting on lipstick.

Eww, she thought. *Dirty mug*. But no—it wasn't. She'd left lipstick on it herself—she touched her mouth and came away with pink fingertips.

She looked up at Eve—the goddess Eveave. This meant something, she knew it did. Eveave wanted her to make a connection.

"That doesn't mean anything to you, does it," Eveave said.

"No, ma'am, I'm sorry. I—it—I don't want to seem stupid."

Eveave shook her head. "Stupid is pretending that you know when you don't. You've got friends of yours, *they* are the ones being stupid, heading off into creation with no plan and no plan for a plan."

Melissa smiled. She thought the same thing. Taking off

with no plan was worse than doing nothing.

She looked back into the cup, and the lipstick had vanished from its rim. She pressed her lips together and could still feel it. She couldn't have drunk the lipstick from the coffee cup rim—it didn't work that way.

There wasn't a trace of the lipstick—she didn't see it on any part of the rim.

The lipstick that had been left there had been removed. Or maybe it still remained, and something hid it from her?

She didn't have enough information to solve this puzzle—but she could ask her new friends. As likely this would mean something to one of them.

She saw Eveave nodding. The waitress took her coffee.

"You're the taker and the giver," Melissa challenged her. It occurred to her that this didn't necessarily come free.

"What I gave, you have," Eveave told her. The goddess looked Melissa level in the eye.

"And what I'm taking, you lost already."

Raven awoke with a start, Jack next to her. She could still see the darkness of the plains, the night sky dotted with stars above them. The Swamp Devil was crouching by their one fire, far too close to it for safety, staring into its depths. She sat up and it turned to her with evil red eyes, and flashed its red teeth in what could have been a grimace or a smile.

Chapter Twenty-Three:

Teamwork

Glynn shook her head. "What you describe cannot happen," she informed them.

Raven had awoken Jack, frantic, demanding that he raise the rest of their little party. Jack admitted to himself he had done it more to quiet her than because he believed her story, and here he saw he wasn't the only one.

"It violates the Rule," Xinto informed her.

"What rule?" Jack asked him.

Xinto sighed. They sat around the campfire. At the head of their meeting sat Glynn, Jahunga on one side of her and Xinto on the other. Next to Xinto sat Zarshar, and next to Jahunga, Jerod. Next to Jerod sat Slurn, then Raven, then Jack between her and Zarshar.

Jahunga's Toorians stood out on the plains, all of them roused, ensuring that no one listened in on them. They'd already conducted a service for their fallen, committing them back to the Earth they believed had born them. Like Men, they'd wept openly for their lost allies, extolled their virtues and made promises to them in their afterlife.

"The Rule of the Gods," Glynn informed them. Jahunga and Jerod both nodded. "Set forth by Adriam to protect the children of Earth and Water, he decreed that no god or goddess can affect any of Earth's children directly in any way."

"We aren't Earth's children," Jack said immediately, before thinking.

All heads turned toward him. Most didn't know this, and Lupus had warned him to be jealous of his secrets.

Lupus wasn't here, though—and this was an Uman-Chi secret.

"We weren't born here," he said. "We were brought here from another world, possibly even another reality. We are from a world entirely different from this one. Raven, me, and the Emperor."

"Another…world?" Jerod seemed skeptical.

Who could blame him, Jack thought. It sounded like something a crazy person would say.

"There are those who believe," Glynn told them, "that there are worlds like balls, that circle the sun, and other suns, and there are people living on them, just as people live here."

The rest were quiet for several minutes. Then Jerod broke out laughing.

"How could people live on a ball?" he demanded. "The ones on the side—"

"At the bottom would fall off," Jack finished for him. "When we have more time, I'll explain it to you, but for now just pretend that it's right. Where I'm from, the moon is nothing like yours, the people are nothing like the ones here, and there is no magic."

"There are people with no magic," Jahunga said. "The Confluni have very little. My own people—"

"They think of magic, like you think of the Earth being a ball," Raven told them.

"And if that is true," Zarshar said, "then they are not of Earth, and the gods can speak directly to them."

"And if they are the Emperor's people…" Jerod let the idea trail off.

They were quiet for a long while after that. Jack had felt the same way when he'd seen Shela levitate glasses for them, back in Outpost IX. It violated fundamental reality.

Slurn hissed something, and Xinto translated it.

“If the Emperor is advised by War, then what possible chance could we have against him?”

“If that is true, then we are advised by Eveave,” Glynn said, “and She is a greater god.”

“Eveave, you say She tried to show you that something right in front of you can be hidden?” Jahunga said.

Raven nodded. The rest fell quiet again.

“A cup,” Xinto said. “A circular rim, paint on it, then gone.”

Jack knew it was lipstick, but paint would do.

In sales, he had learned to ask interrogative questions. No one could know enough about a client before they met to make a sale so, in essence, a good sales person asked the client how to sell him, and the client then told the salesperson, never himself the wiser.

“Tell me something,” he said, and all eyes turned to him. “How can you tell a sacred place from, say, a normal place?”

Jerod sighed. Jahunga tried to look into his eyes, to read him. Zarshar’s red tongue ran over his red fangs—Jack noted that the end was forked.

“You know,” Xinto said, poking the embers of their fire with a stick, “that is a pretty good question.”

“It is?” Jerod asked him, his eyes narrowed.

“Indeed,” Glynn answered. “We take these things for granted, but Eveave wants us to see through new eyes. How do we know that the Tears of the World, for example, is sacred to Earth and Water?”

“That’s easy enough,” Jerod told her. “If you approach the Llorando, you hear that crying sound—a man on the Volkhydran side, a woman on the Confluni.”

“And it tastes of tears,” Xinto added, and shuddered. “I couldn’t drink from it—it wasn’t even fit for my pony.”

“Well enough,” she said. “And the shrine to War at Thera, installed by the Emperor. How do we know it to be holy?”

They were all quiet. Jack thought it figured that Lupus would build himself his own shrine.

“I’ve seen it,” Jerod admitted. “It’s huge, with that rare black marble from the Ogre lands. I’m for Adriam, not War, but I looked at it and I didn't want to go in there."

"So you had a feeling that it must be holy," Jahunga said. "In your heart, you knew."

Jerod nodded. Jack thought Glynn must be moving somewhere with this.

"I myself have seen it," she said, "and seen the Tears of the World, and I can tell you the Tears of the World is the first place where the Emperor's boots touched Fovea."

"Well, that makes sense, with his horse and all," Jerod said.

"But the Emperor, then Rancor, didn't know the Tears of the World is holy," Xinto said. "I know this right from him. He thought it just another polluted lake."

"Hmph," Jerod said. Zarshar put his hands on his hips and chuckled.

"How about a holy place, at the center of Eldador, just like this cup, where anyone who went there would know, 'That is a holy place,'" he asked.

Xinto's shoulders slumped, then Jerod's. He turned his head to Jahunga, looking on curiously, but even as the Volkhydran opened his mouth, Jahunga came to his own conclusion.

"The Lone Wood," Glynn said for all of them. "Of course—the home of the Druids, a place that even the Emperor will not invade."

"Druids?" Raven echoed her. Jack felt her hand take his upper arm. "I know that word. We come from a place with Druids."

"In truth?" Glynn pressed her. She seemed more interested than she usually allowed herself when it came to the two humans. "But you claim to have no magic."

"That's why the Guardian must go with me," Zarshar said. "Only I could hope to protect him inside the Druids' domain."

"The Druids we know had no magic," Raven said.

"Well, in their time they claimed to," Jack added.

"No one goes in there," Xinto informed him. He stood right next to Glynn now. "It is forbidden—"

"Not true, Ambassador," Glynn informed him, taking back

control of the conversation. "In fact, some Men and certain Uman have entered and returned, as has one Swamp Devil, if I am not mistaken."

Zarshar nodded. "I have been within the Lone Wood, and I have spoken to Druids," he said.

Glynn nodded. "Then some of us to the Lone Wood, and others to where?"

Then Glynn smiled and straightened her back. Zarshar stood, towering over all of them.

They'd both gotten it, Jack realized. Raven had been right. Eveave hadn't meant for her to find the answer, she wanted her to convey the question.

The Scitai sighed now. "So you're saying we should all go to the Lone Wood?" he asked.

Sitting with the butt of his spear in the ground before him, Jahunga turned it against the dirt as he thought. "No," he said, "I think the song would tell us all to go, if all of us were needed. The Guardian must lead the Devil, that is plain.

"I think that Eveave tells us about Kor," he continued. He took a moment to look once at the rest of them around the fire. Jack met his brown eyes for a moment in passing. "Kor, on the rim of the cup. Kor, on the edge of Eldador."

"Kor was always the right idea," Jerod informed them. "Its resources, its location, the fact the Emperor has no leverage there."

Slurn hissed something, Xinto cracked a smile. Jack looked into the little man's eyes, feeling his brow furrow.

"Just a clever observation," Xinto told him. "He can be quite sarcastic."

* * *

Raven stood a few feet behind Jack, watching him saddle up Little Storm. The latter just stood at the picket with his head down, as if it didn't matter to him what they were doing.

"I'm going to miss you," she told him.

Her lower lip wanted to tremble, but she had a handle on it. She still didn't know for sure where she stood with him, for all they had been through, and she didn't like him going where she couldn't keep an eye on him.

"I'll miss you, too," he said, but he didn't turn around, and didn't take her in his arms like he should have.

"I wish there was a way we could communicate," Raven complained. She knew she sounded whiney but she didn't care. She needed to say this and he needed to listen to it.

"Glynn said that if we did, it would take no time for the Eldadorians to figure it out—hey!"

She had kicked him in the butt, and she felt glad she had done it. "Don't logic me, Bill," she said.

"Jack," he corrected her.

"Bill," she repeated. "Bill, Jack, Mountain, fountain, I'm just getting sick of it. I am getting sick of having to be a good girl and smile, and act like this isn't all as screwed up as it is."

"Well, this isn't the TV, Raven," he told her. He turned back around now with his face all bunched up in a scowl, his beard bristling like it did when she pissed him off.

"Don't call me that," she said. She ran to him, put her arms around him, pressed her face into his stinky furs.

"Call me by my name," she whispered.

"Melissa," he said. "This is real, and the danger is real, and we have to be smart now if we want to get out of it."

"Did we do the right thing?" she asked, not because she didn't know, but because she needed to hear it. "Should we go back to the Emperor with our apologies—"

"You'd spend the rest of your life in a cell if they even listened to you," Jack said. "We had no choice, and there's no going back."

"He's from Earth," Raven said.

She could feel him nod. "And he is going to use the advantages of our world to rule this one," Jack said. "He isn't doing it to enrich lives or make anyone happier or anything better. He is doing it because he wants to be a conqueror.

"We know enough history to know what conquerors do."

She squeezed out a tear for him—just one. A man like Lupus wouldn't sit idly by and wait for them to do what they wanted. With his resources and his power, he would already be looking for them, and he had the means to find them.

And Shela seemed pretty smart.

She broke the hug and she took his beard in both hands. She looked into his eyes and said, "I want you coming back to me, Jack. And not on a slab."

"Ok, I was going to come back on a slab, but not now, thanks to you."

She kicked his shin and hugged him again.

* * *

Jerod watched their ridiculous exchange from where his own horse was picketed. Good to get them away from each other, he thought. No Volkhydran ever slobbered over a woman like that, and an Andaron would stab him in the heart for trying it.

Glynn prepared a beacon for them, praying by their fire. He would carry it himself, and had been warned several times he shouldn't let this 'Raven' near it. She could discharge it without knowing, and then they would be lost, and have to try to find the three of them, while they themselves worked hard not to be found.

"You are not a good spy," Jahunga said to him, from behind his back.

He didn't turn. He had heard the Toorian coming, knowing him from the soft shuffle of his sandals on the dirt. Slurn watched the pair from a pile of hay, as well. Jerod could smell him. Zarshar had gone off into the plains to hunt for food for their journey.

"Just waiting to see if they need me," Jerod said.

"I think they know what they are doing," Jahunga chuckled. Jerod could imagine the smile on his face without seeing it.

Raven planted her lips on the old gaffer's, and slid her tongue into his mouth.

"You leave a woman behind?" Jerod asked, finally.

"More than one," Jahunga said, "and many good sons, and fertile daughters, I am sure. Jahunga's seed will spread throughout the people of Toor."

"Not me," Jerod said. "Never found the right one. My father tried to match me off a couple times—never felt right."

"Volkhydran parents often arrange marriages," Jahunga commented. "You say you had some choice in this?"

"I chose to run south while I could," Jerod said, and smiled. "A wise man told me once that discretion was the better part of valor."

"And what does that mean?" Jahunga asked him.

He turned. There stood Jahunga, in his white robes and with his spear in his hand. His men waited by the fire for them, and the sun had climbed high enough to be hot in the sky.

"I don't know," he admitted. "Guess I'm not a wise man."

* * *

At a dead run, Little Storm chewed up the miles, pounding across the Eldadorian plains where the winter grass crunched underfoot or, more commonly, had declined into mud and slop that flew from his hooves, behind him or into Jack's eyes.

At fifty, Jack never knew that he could love anything so much. He'd ridden for pleasure, but like this, these long rides, watching the miles go by, he became a part of the world he lived on—felt like he had a stake in it. He existed as a part of Little Storm, and the world moved around him and through him, the air crisp with the promise of spring in his lungs and in the lungs of his mount.

As it had done three times already this day, the Devil bellowed out a cry of rage to tell him that he had, once again, drawn too far ahead of them. He needed to be more aware of that, he knew. He was no fighter—he kept his falchion but he could barely use it. If someone ambushed him then he had only Little Storm's speed to save him, and he knew of one out there to whom that speed wouldn't matter.

He slowed, and he could feel the stallion balk beneath him. Little Storm wanted to *run*—as fast as he could go, wild and free.

Glynn rode side-saddle on her Eldadorian war horse. Even now it fought to keep pace and failed. She rode it with her back straight and her green hair flying out behind her. Alongside her, loping like a wolf with its tongue lolling, Zarshar's long paces devoured the daheeri. Jack watched them follow his trail across the plains, waiting until they came close before he kicked his mount into motion again. By the time he was up to a trot, they ran beside him.

"You stray too far, Sirrah," Glynn chastised him.

"You will find yourself spitted on a pike like a hog," Zarshar informed him, gleeful at the prospect.

"We're east of Thera," Glynn said in Uman. "This is the land of Theran Lancers."

"And if you find them?" Zarshar asked. "What will you do?"

Jack had no answer. They were right.

Glynn shook her head. "They employ good scouts, even in fair lands as these. If they are to war, then they are to war readiness, and this means they will be looking for just such a thing as our trail."

"We wait," Zarshar growled. He looked at Glynn, almost eye-to-eye with her sitting her mount. "In fact, we cut east, and then north. Anyone finding our trail thinks we're one of those scouts."

Glynn nodded. "Sage wisdom. But that our compatriots are so fortunate."

One of the reasons Jack had been letting his horse run out so fast: it distracted him from worrying about Melissa. That little girl about broke his heart as he was leaving. He could only hope they were doing a good job taking care of her.

* * *

Nina of the Aschire knelt low to the ground, the wetness of overturned earth soaking into the knee of her leather pants. Ten Wolf Soldiers knelt and waited two hundred paces behind her—what remained of her guard. She'd sent more back to Eldador when she'd picked up their trail at a hostel, and more when the two forces had split.

It had been tempting to follow the enchantress and her two friends east, toward Thera, but she knew better. Glynn would go to Trenbon—a predictable move. She would try to get a ship from Uman City, and she would be caught.

But the rest headed for Kor, and from Kor they *could* escape, either south with the Toorians or north to Dorkan, two lands where Eldador held little sway. They couldn't be allowed to do that—couldn't be allowed to get away.

Xinto and his people moved slowly east across the flat plains now, just outside of the Salt Wood. It would be easy enough to pass them in a wide arc, to cut them off in just two days, and then appear between them and their goal. Then it would be nothing to obtain the Scitai and Raven once again.

Nina grinned to herself, pulling back, confident she hadn't been spotted. Calling for her Wolf Soldiers, she began to set her trap.

* * *

"Where does the power go?" Raven asked Xinto, although the question was good for anyone.

They'd spent three days on the road, and she was bored and tired of her own thoughts. None of them were talkers, unless they had some stupid question about her and Jack that made her miss him.

"What power?" Xinto asked her. She could almost feel his eyes on her ass. He had reduced himself to copping a feel about once an hour, be it to stroke her skin as he shifted on the horse's butt, or pulling himself closer and incidentally getting a hand on her thigh. In the beginning he had gone for the goodies about three times in fifteen minutes, but then she had had this accident involving her elbow and his forehead.

"The power that goes into me," she said. "Shouldn't I—ummm—have to expel it, shoot it out, jump in a bath and have it go into the water or something?"

"I think I will not be bathing with you," Jahunga quipped.

"I would risk it," Jerod grumbled without looking at her. He spat to one side from atop his horse, then wiped his lips with the back of his hand.

The horses plodded on, the Toorians loping along between them.

"You can't feel it in you?" Xinto asked her.

She thought about that. Did she? She felt restless, she blamed it on not having Bill there, but even when she had him, she hadn't slept well since the incident with Nina.

"I am kind of—I don't know the word—antsy," she said.

"I don't know that word," Xinto admitted.

"Can't rest, too much energy for no reason," she said.

"Ah," Xinto said.

"I don't know where an enchantress gets her power," Jerod said, still not looking at her. "I know a sorceress like Shela is gifted it from her god. Shela claims she's fed by the desires of her enemies."

She could feel Xinto turn behind her. Incidentally again, he put his hand on her belly. "I didn't know that."

Jerod just nodded and said nothing.

"So, maybe I get my power from the people who attack me," Raven said, removing his hand.

"I suppose that's reasonable," Xinto said, "if you are a sorceress, or an enchantress, which you are not."

Raven sighed. This was frustrating. They passed a bush, just beginning to get its spring budding.

She pointed at it. "Burn!" she commanded.

Nothing.

"I am reasonably sure there is more to it than that," Xinto said, his hand on her hip now.

"That hand finds anymore to it and you will be wearing it on a rope around your neck," she said.

He took his hand away, but she could feel him chuckling.

"Scitai have bad manners," Jerod said.

"Not like Men," Xinto returned.

They started in on the faults of each other's races, Jahunga offering his pieces of information, and Raven looked at another bush.

"Fuego," she said. "Enflame. Ignite."

Nothing.

How did Glynn do it? When Glynn had wanted to make her feel threatened, she hadn't said anything, she had just made it happen. Some kind of white energy snake had jumped from Glynn's hand to Raven, and she had smacked it away, and then the energy transfer.

So she thought about a plant burning. What it would look like burning, how it would be hotter and smokier.

And she saw the next bush, actually more of a weed, and she thought about it being on fire.

Nothing.

Maybe she only had the energy for a little while, then. Or maybe she couldn't do this at all.

"Mark it," Jerod warned. She looked up from the bushes and saw a band of warriors on the eastern horizon, in metal armor, the sun shining from their weapons.

She felt Xinto's body move as he nodded.

"Got it," he said.

"Turn?" Jerod asked Xinto.

Jahunga shook his head. "Better to meet them head on," he said. "My men can run all day, but these want to meet us, and I think that, eventually, they will."

"Agreed," Xinto said. "You Toorians won't ride, or we'd out run 'em. On the plains like this, we can't lose anyone."

They drew up closer. The warriors waited there, ten strong in their armor, in Wolf Soldier formation of four shield men, three swordsmen and three with pikes.

"Someone else hiding among them," Xinto noted.

"See her," Jerod said. "Purple hair."

"Nina of the Aschire?" Raven gasped. That wasn't good. Nina had cruel eyes and, if she wasn't with her kids, then she wouldn't be happy about it.

"The Aschire—I don't know these people," Jahunga said. Another of his men perked up, running next to him.

"I do," Jerod said. "I wanted to go to Andoron three years ago, and they would not let me through their woods. They wouldn't fight me, they shot arrows."

"That's them," Xinto said. "They love Lupus like he's a god, and they are the best archers on Fovea after my own people."

"We need to be farther apart then," Jerod said. He looked down at Jahunga. "Divide your men in two, half to the left, half to the right. You go right; I'll go left with the others.

"Raven, you stay with Xinto, and if you see your lizard, keep him close. We don't want to fight before we're ready."

Jahunga nodded and his men broke off. Jerod looked at Xinto.

"You talk," he said. "Get in front of Raven so she can see you."

"You might have used that Volkhydran brain of yours to think she and I are the ones Nina are after," Xinto complained, as he stood up on the horse's butt. He managed a hand on either of Raven breasts as he moved to sit in front of her, to plant his butt in her lap.

"You think I didn't?" Jerod grinned, and kicked his mount to their left.

"He's a take charge kind of guy," Raven commented.

"Isn't he, though?" Xinto said. "How much do you think this girl hates you?"

"I humiliated her," Raven said, casually moving his hand from her thigh. In the same motion, she checked the dagger in her boot. "She wanted to kill Buh—Jack, for touching Lee. She must have something in mind if she let him go."

"Or she got him already," Xinto said. "I know her reputation, Raven—cruel and fast. She learned at the knee of the Imperial couple. Even Wolf Soldiers fear her."

Raven sat quiet. When the Toorians broke off from the two of them, Nina stepped out from among the Wolf Soldiers. She had her bow out, an arrow knocked in it.

"How good is she with that thing?" she asked Xinto.

Faster then her eye could follow, Xinto's hand flew in and out of his robes, and he was aiming at the Aschire with a cross pistol.

When she'd been a little girl, Raven had seen boys make these. Not quite a crossbow, not quite a pistol, mechanisms from both that shot a dart, usually in some random direction. She had seen them kill a cat with one once, and she had seen a boy sent to the hospital with one of those darts stuck in his shoulder.

Xinto fired, and the dart whipped over 100 yards across the plain. It didn't hit Nina.

It hit the string on Nina's bow, and broke it. The whole thing flew from her hand and she jumped to the left.

"Not as good as I am," Xinto said, casually loading another dart, pulling it from within his robes.

"That was—I mean—oh, my god, Xinto," she gasped. She would have called that shot impossible. She couldn't even see the bowstring from this far away.

Neither Nina nor the Wolf Soldiers ran for cover, not that there was any. Nina drew the slim sword from her hip, leaving her daggers on her arms and thighs and the bow on the ground. She probably felt afraid to use her magic around Raven, and Raven couldn't help thinking what good sense that made.

"Being a good archer isn't hitting a target," Xinto said, and grunted as he cocked his pistol again. The dart seated with a click.

"Anyone can hit a target. Being a good archer is shooting where the target is *going* to be. That's hard—because you have to understand what you're shooting at, and you have to be right."

"That must be Xinto's philosophy on life," Raven said, grinning.

Xinto turned to look up into her eyes. "No, daughter of Men" he said. "My philosophy is, 'Don't be a good target.'"

They were close enough to see the gray in Nina's eyes, about forty feet away, when Nina held a hand up and Raven reined her mount in. To her left and right the men kept moving until they formed three corners of a triangle with the Wolf Soldiers and Nina at their center.

"The Emperor misses you," Nina called out to them.

"Well then, by all means, bring us to him," Xinto said, standing on the saddle.

Raven turned slightly to keep the little man's butt from right in front of her face, and to see what was going on.

"I didn't think you would be so cooperative," Nina said. "Dismount and we can begin the journey back to Galnesh Eldador."

"I think we will stay mounted," Xinto called back. "Scitai have *such* difficulty staying out from under the feet of Men. However, you begin the journey, and we will be right behind you."

"I am afraid I cannot accept your terms, Xinto," Nina said. Raven saw the leering grin on her face now. She wanted this fight.

Jerod must have as well because he kicked his mount into motion and approached the Wolf Soldier guard from the side opposite Nina.

One of them, a Man with three scars on his face a lot like Jerod's, turned to his right for just a moment, saw Jerod, then turned back, only to whip his head around again in double-take, his mouth open. He stood in the middle with the swordsmen. He closed his mouth and narrowed his eyes, then turned to Nina.

He said something to her, she turned and snarled something back. He said something similar, his tone more insistent, and Nina looked past him to Jerod.

"I don't know you," she said to Jerod.

"That's right," he said. He turned his head and spat on the ground, then turned back to her.

"You don't."

"You don't want to be between me and—"

"Save it."

Nina's eyes narrowed.

"You've heard him use that expression before, haven't you?" Jerod said. "You know he says that, and 'skip it.'"

The Wolf Soldiers had already begun to waver, turning their heads, lowering their weapons slightly. Jahunga and three Toorians approached quietly from the right, behind Nina and her distracted, single squad.

She said something too soft for Raven to hear. She could see Xinto strained for it, too. She wanted to urge her mount closer, but she didn't want to spoil what Jahunga and Jerod were doing, whatever that might be.

"Who or what does he want her to save?" Xinto asked her without turning.

"What?"

"He told her to save something," he said.

Raven shook her head despite herself. "No, it's an expression," she said. "Like, 'never mind.' It means not to continue talking about something, to save your breath."

This time he did turn to face her.

"How do you know that?" he asked, his brown eyes finding hers.

"I say it all the time," Raven said. "Everyone does."

"Everyone, at this place you are from," Xinto said. "This place where you and Jack and Lupus come from."

"Yes."

"So," Xinto asked her, and she saw a grin bristling his

beard, "how do you suppose our Jerod knows it?"

* * *

The spring wind caught Glynn's hair in its chill grip, running its fingers across her dainty skin like some depraved old man, even through the thick cotton travel dress she wore. Atop her mount, still sitting a proper side-saddle, she kept her posture straight, her hands in her lap, the reins to her mount held in them, and looked to the West, to Thera, and the setting sun.

For three days they'd stayed off the road, and this had slowed them. Zarshar had run regular reconnaissance and told them he'd seen many patrols, some with dogs, clearly looking for them, as well as companies of Eldadorian Regulars, the cavalry and foot soldiers of the Empire.

For over a decade, when the Emperor had sought to expand or express his power, he had used Wolf Soldiers. They were the most feared troops on known Fovea, having defeated many times their number in enemy warriors.

Eldadorian Regulars were simply clean up, maintenance, border guards. Even as their ranks swelled, the Emperor had demonstrated no respect or even any real interest in them, leaving them to his Dukes, his Barons, his Counts and Earls.

But now they marched to Thera, and now that she could see the outlying villages surrounding the historic port—the first duchy on the Conqueror's road to empire—it became clear they marched here.

"There must be thousands of them," Zarshar informed her. It wasn't common for the Devil to be so plainly surprised.

"Tens of thousands," Jack added, astride Little Storm. Their campfires had begun popping up across the plain at night. They were in their *jess doonari*, the little cities on the plains from which they could either fight or project their positions. At the infamous 'Battle of Tamaran Glen,' as few as 200 had defended themselves against thousands.

Eldadorian Regulars with Wolf Soldier training, perhaps? Tens of thousands capable of defeating hundreds of thousands?

Glynn hated to admit it to herself, but Angron Aurelias had been vastly mistaken in his decision to turn over everything they knew to the Emperor. It had clearly inspired him to mobilize, and to ready Eldador for war.

"This must have taken years to assemble," Zarshar informed them, still taken back by what he saw. "He must have planned this, even before he became a king, much less an emperor."

Jack shook his head. Glynn noticed him from the corner of her eye, the blank expression followed by the anger.

"What is it?" she asked him.

Jack turned to her slowly, as if he had to peel his attention away from the collected warriors. As if looking away were painful.

"I've seen this before," he said. "Well, not seen it—heard of it. Someone who did something like this before."

Now he had Zarshar's attention, too.

"And?" the Swamp Devil asked him.

"And if Lupus is emulating *him*," Jack said, "then we *really* have a lot to worry about."

Chapter Twenty-Four:

It Begins

Nina of the Aschire had never really gotten her mind around the concept of what made Wolf Soldiers any better than any other kind of soldiers, other than the simple fact—they were.

She knew they wouldn't survive an hour among her Aschire, no matter their numbers. The Aschire would pincushion them before they could have their precious shields up, or their pikes out, or whatever else they did.

Except the Aschire loved Lupus as they did the very forest, and wouldn't raise a hand against him. In that, the Wolf Soldiers could in fact walk through Aschire unmolested, if unwelcome.

Now she had a troop of these 'invincible warriors,' and here they were telling her they couldn't fight.

"You can do whatever I tell you," she told their sergeant. "Or you will be dead, and the one who replaces you will do it."

Their sergeant looked her right in the eye, his expression flat. The three scars on his cheek, the Mark of the Conqueror, made him look slightly crazed. Nina had never seen a Wolf Soldier so highly decorated, who didn't command at least 100.

"You weren't at the battle," he told her, "but I was. I recognize him and neither I nor any among us will lift a sword against him. Not on your order."

"You have a real problem," the Volkhydran informed her from his horse, a half-grin on his scarred face.

"I can deal with *you*," she told him, and reached within herself, finding her power as Shela had shown her.

Her mind took on the spontaneous calm that came with years of training; the calm of an experienced sorceress, capturing the moment, embodying the *thing*, calling what she needed.

In this case, she sought the fire—she would eradicate this Volkhydran in flame.

"'Ware, Nina," the Wolf Soldier sergeant told her. They remained in their formation, and would do so until she ordered them otherwise. Nina allowed the smallest portion of her attention to waver, and became aware of more than saw Raven's mount, bearing Raven and Xinto, pounding the plain directly toward her.

"Protect me," she ordered them. That order didn't bother them. Raven and Xinto meant nothing to the Wolf Soldiers, other than another enemy to kill.

Her mind saw the flame, felt its power, knew its heat. She called forth the element of flame, and in her mind's eye she saw fire, cupped it in her unburned hand, willed it like a living thing from the source of its being to the place where she wanted it to be.

The Wolf Soldier squad moved as one being, picking up on the left foot, marching from between her and the Volkhydran to between her and Raven, in three smart steps, their pikes lowered threateningly. If Raven made it through that, it would be flying from the back of a dead horse.

She made herself the conduit between the place where she stood and the home of flame, and she willed the energy transfer, exhilarated by its power. Balled fire blossomed in her hand, a living rosebud, hungry to return from whence it had come.

She reached her hand back over her shoulder; she saw her target, seated on his warhorse, smiling at her with his arms folded over his breast.

She had time to think, "Why would he be doing that?" before the dark green blur from the plains grass knocked her from her feet.

* * *

The Man was becoming irritating, and Zarshar prided himself on being dangerous to irritate.

They had needed to take a wide route around Thera in order to avoid the Emperor's troops and his outlying patrols. Easier said than done on wide Theran plains, where one could be seen for a daheer or more, and where the noise from the horses carried at least as far.

He tolerated the horses—without them, the Uman-Chi and the Man would slow his pace considerably. Zarshar had no desire to spend any more time with these creatures than he had to.

The horse's speed became useless if it took them to an Eldadorian dungeon and, although Zarshar could handle ten times his number in Eldadorian soldiers, he couldn't beat them all, neither did he want to suffer the whim of an Emperor notorious for his effective methods of torture.

"Stop," the Man commanded them.

Zarshar caught himself as he obeyed. He hadn't expected that tone of command from this one. He's never made it a practice to follow anyone else's leadership. He hesitated, and that gave him the moment to see what he should have detected before the Man had.

A dog, on a hill a tenth of a daheer before them, stood looking right at them, wagging its tail.

"It's seen us," he informed them unnecessarily. He flexed his talons. He'd catch the beast in a sprint, but not with too much of a head start on him. Four legs still moved faster than two.

"Don't frighten it," Jack warned him.

Glynn regarded him from her sidesaddle. "You can't think to want it, Sirrah," she said.

Jack dismounted. The dog's ears lowered and its tail dropped. Zarshar recognized the signs of an animal ready to run, probably to the patrol it served.

Zarshar suddenly realized it hadn't bayed. The Confluni employed dogs along their borders and, when they either saw or scented a stranger, they howled to bring troops.

Jack seemed focused on the animal. "Is that a common dog here?" he asked them.

Zarshar turned his head to Glynn, just slightly above his eye level in her saddle. He recognized that *look* that Uman-Chi wore—as if it actually pained her to have to tolerate the company of inferiors, but they were trying to *hide* the pain.

Zarshar would show her *real* pain when this was done.

"Sirrah, what would constitute a common dog?" Glynn asked.

Jack sighed. "Have you seen that breed before?" he asked her.

She closed her eyes. So stupid, Zarshar thought. It was a dog, and Zarshar meant to kill it before it drew other dogs. He took a step forward and the Man actually dared to place a hand on his hip.

"You go too far," Zarshar warned him, turning his head to meet the Man's eyes.

Most Men would look away—not this one. Jack didn't look away from Zarshar because his eyes had never left the dog at all. Zarshar hunted his mind for a way to call this an attack, in order to finally turn on these two and be free of them.

Glynn recognized the situation and, like a good princess, stepped in to defuse it. Placing a delicate finger on Jack's shoulder, she said, "If you would unhand the Black Adept, Sirrah, then yes, I've seen such dogs in Conflu, however not so large, nor so wrinkled."

Jack removed his hand from Zarshar and took a step forward, lowering himself to one knee. The dog ducked his head and took a few cautious steps toward them.

This was progress. If Jack could lure the thing in, then Zarshar could have its head off and make a meal of it.

"That's a mastiff," Jack told them. Zarshar didn't recognize the word. "We have them on my—where I am from."

"Sirrah, I saw no such beast—"

"Shh!" he commanded her. Zarshar grinned wickedly at the look of shock on her face. No Uman-Chi wanted to believe the rest of the races didn't hang on their words.

Jack snapped his finger, and the dog ran right to him. As it drew nearer, Zarshar noted it was, in fact, a good deal heavier than other dogs he had seen—perhaps the weight of a grown Man. Its skin hung loose in dewlaps—as an aurochs might have, or a very old Man. Its gray coat flashed almost blue in the sun.

It bore its heavy teeth plainly, with a wicked under bite and pronounced canine fangs. Saliva ran freely from its lips, forming liquid ropes at its jaw line. Zarshar wondered at that until he realized the lip had evolved to stay clear of the teeth when it attacked.

The creature's eyes struck the devil as it drew closer. Neither kind nor cruel, it took them all in, focused mostly on Jack. Zarshar had killed smaller animals his whole life, and had learned to read them, but this one had the look of a beast that would as quickly tear the Man's throat out as lick his hand.

The former would solve many of Zarshar's problems.

It ran to Jack and lay at his feet, looking up at him. Jack reached his hand down before it, far too close to those slavering teeth, and let it smell his fingers, then rubbed its head until its tail wagged.

"You can't think to retain the creature?" Glynn asked him. Zarshar planned to kill it, no matter what the Man wanted.

"We need to keep this dog and see how it was trained," Jack informed them. He looked up into the Devil's eyes. Zarshar had already decided where to take the head to pull it off cleanly.

"Where I am from, these dogs were used in war in different ways," he said. "And the Emperor has gone to a lot of trouble to recreate them here. If you just kill it like you're planning to do, we won't know what they're for, and we'll give up a tactical advantage.

That gave Zarshar pause. If the Emperor's plans depended on some new breed of dog, then they should know of it.

"Sirrah, such beasts are used for guarding—clearly this one is lost form a patrol," Glynn informed them.

"No," Zarshar said. "It didn't howl, and it didn't attack us. A patrol dog is trained to let its master know when it sees something like us. This one is trained to be quiet, and it doesn't attack on sight."

He squatted down beside the Man, now vigorously rubbing the animal's belly. It had eight teats, all oversized, marking it as female. It hadn't had a litter yet—it might not even be full-grown.

He held his claw out for the animal to smell. It playfully took his forefinger in its mouth, its tail thumping the ground. It surprised Zarshar with a jaw strength that might have broken a Man's arm.

"If it betrays us," Zarshar informed Jack, "I'm going to gut it and leave you behind, old Man, to satisfy whoever follows us. But you have me wanting to know what the Emperor is doing with this thing."

Jack grinned to himself, his eyes focused on the dog. *It would have been better if it had bitten the old man,* Zarshar thought.

* * *

Raven could keep her seat when the horse plodded on, and with a little more difficulty when it trotted. She knew to keep her head up, her back straight, and her heels down as she rode.

On a dead run the mare bounced her like a doll on its back, and in a few moments Raven's feet had come out of the stirrups and she clung to the saddle horn. A warhorse ran completely differently than the Andaron horses she'd learned on, used to a heavier rider, built to sprint and charge.

She yanked on the reins when the Wolf Soldier squad marched between her and her target. That turned the horse toward Jahunga and threw Xinto from the saddle in front of her. She reached for him and without thinking pulled the reins to the other side, sending the mare racing for Jerod and leaving herself tilting halfway from her seat.

The Wolf Soldiers did a smart job of keeping themselves between Raven and Nina, which is how they missed Slurn entirely.

Raven hauled herself back into the saddle in time to see Slurn leap from the scrub where he had been invisible, into a clinch with Nina. At the same time Jahunga and his spearmen leapt from one side, Jerod and the two Toorians with him charged in from the other, and the Wolf Soldiers were caught between.

The Wolf Soldiers back-pedaled, trying both to keep the two opposing forces in front of them while protecting Nina, their sergeant shouting commands from their midsts. Jahunga cut behind them, moving for the shieldless pikemen. Seeing this, Jerod cut in front, trying to prevent the squad from turning.

It could have been anyone's fight if Raven had kept her mount under control. Instead she crashed into a shieldman, fell and landed in between Slurn and Nina, before Nina had the opportunity to dispel her energy.

The moment she touched Raven, Nina flew like a missile into the backs of the pikemen, limp as a corpse. Jahunga's Toorians advanced, Jerod with his own troops closing on the other side, but the sergeant proved to be a smarter man, leaping for Raven and taking a handful of her hair at the scalp, dragging her to her feet, his sword at her exposed stomach.

"You'll see her guts," he said, his shieldmen falling in around him, "if you don't stand back from me."

Raven reached reflexively for her hair, and he shook her. She knew she couldn't reach the dagger in her boot. Jerod made an exasperated face and motioned for his men to fall back.

No! Raven swore to herself. She refused to play the helpless girly. She wouldn't be the damsel in distress. That was Melissa—she was *Raven.*

She reached down to the man's thigh, felt the muscle through the leggings, took a firm grip and said, "Burn!"

With everything in her, she yearned for the man to explode into flames. She focused her mind on the burning, the heat, the screaming, the dread, even the smell of cooking meat.

She felt the wetness at her side from the edge of the blade at her skin. He kept his sword sharp.

But then it fell away, and he stood back from her. She turned to see his hands reaching for his face, the skin blistering, the eyes bulging from his head. He opened his mouth to scream, and flames licked out to singe his upper lip.

His eyes exploded, then his skin within his shirt, and he fell. Flame shot in two plumes from his ears, bathing the plains around him in steaming blood and cooked brains.

Raven's hand flew to her mouth as the guilt washed over her. It was horrible, unimaginable, to die that way. She looked for sympathy to those closest to her, and saw the horror on their faces.

Wolf Soldiers. One of them transformed before her eyes

from shock to rage. She had killed one of them, and now she stood *right there.*

"No," she said, shaking her head. She raised her hand between them and they flinched, fearful of receiving more of what their sergeant had received.

Nothing. Then four slow smiles.

They had her.

"Pain!" she screamed, pointing at the nearest of them. Nothing. He flinched for a moment and then advanced on her, hefting his sword.

Slurn swept in once again, quick as a flash, his spear prodding one man's shield. On the other side of the fight the Men with Jerod advanced, their spears finding Wolf Soldier pikes.

Raven's body had started shaking, full of energy, full of power, like a spring that had been compressed and released, but hadn't sprung yet. She'd cast a spell and expended her energy, but now she had more, and no way to expel it.

Jerod looked her in the eye, the concern plain on his face. The sergeant's corpse smoldered next to her—it wouldn't take long before those Wolf Soldiers decided that the sergeant had the right idea—that she was their weakness, after all.

No! She opened her mouth to try another word, but she couldn't form it. She worked her jaw, trying to overcome something that felt like a dam to her brain, and something else that made her feel like she would throw up.

"Are you alright, girl?" Jerod shouted at her. His voice sounded at the same time right in her ear, and a million miles away.

"*Girl!*"

She couldn't even tell who said it. She looked to her left, and a bush exploded in flame. Then to her right, where her eyes landed on the back of a Wolf Soldier. The warrior exploded, scorching the land around him, burning pieces of flesh flying out among them, the Man's terrified scream spooking the horses.

Her mind became a wash of red heat and angry flame. Suddenly too large for her body, her awareness fled out over the plains grass, scorching it in a blast pattern that radiated from her. Small creatures, rabbits and birds, flew screaming and burning into the air, fleeing her great wash of flame. Wolf Soldiers bolted from their formation, one after the next exploding in a ball of fire. The Toorians ran after them, even though her magic hadn't touched them.

She felt it getting away from her, and somehow she knew that, if she lost it, then the flame would eat her, and her friends, and run wild across the plain. She forced herself envision the flame dying, the smoke fading. Her mind took her from the burning plain to a dark place, quiet and tranquil, and then plunged her into cool, dark nothing.

* * *

Thorn sat his new mount, an Eldadorian mare with too much spirit and too little stamina, next to Nantar, who's shed his armor for soft leggings and an open cotton shirt.

Nantar rode a gelding. It had that lack of spirit geldings had—Thorn preferred the mare since his own horse had grown too old to campaign, and he hadn't had the time to go to Andoron for another.

He missed his home country. He'd planned to spend the War months with Nantar's daughters there, but this new plan had come and ruined everything.

"You sure you want to wait?" Nantar asked him.

He nodded, saying nothing, stewing in his own juices.

"How do you like the Eldadorian horse?" Nantar commented.

Nantar tried to draw him out. Nantar did that. He kept everyone around him and smiling. Sometimes Thorn expected him to joke with the corpses he made.

"It's not as good as ours," Thorn commented, peeking out from his melancholy.

They led five thousand. They'd marched out on the plains now, spread out in their squads, twenty-five across and twenty deep, with a gap between each as wide as a squad, making them seem four times their already enormous size.

Nantar's Sarandi, Thorn's scouts, they formed the vanguard for the Free Legionnaires, the fingers and the fist of their army, probing the land before them.

Not crushing—they were in Eldador. Supposedly friendly.

Thorn kept his eyes on the edge of the horizon. He'd seen some dust—not a lot, but there wouldn't be this time of year with the ground still wet. Just enough to tell them of the approach, and most would miss it.

Not Thorn. No Andaron, no Hunter, would miss something like that.

"You should ask for one of Blizzard's get, I think," Nantar said.

"About time a Daff Kanaar had one," Thorn agreed, his eyes straining to the horizon.

There! Topping the rise between them and the horizon, the flash of his armor. Thorn grinned, and it felt satisfying.

"Marked him?" Nantar asked.

"Halfway to us," Thorn said. He shifted on the mare. He didn't feel comfortable with her. Shela would have a better mount for him, he knew. As Nantar suggested, he'd ask for one of Blizzard's lot. Shela would understand.

"Where?"

"He cut between two rises, ahead of his army," Thorn said. "Look there for the flash of steel from his armor."

Nantar strained to see it. Thorn pointed an outstretched finger, not where the rider hid, but where he soon would be.

Sure enough, he saw the flash between two hillocks.

"He should have darkened his horse and his armor," Nantar commented.

Thorn shook his head. "He wants to be seen," the Andaron said. "He wants me to admit I taught him and he learned it.

Nantar grinned a big, furry grin. "Well, you *did* teach him."

"Never thought he'd learn it, though," Thorn answered. The flash came closer now—he would run out of places to hide soon and come at them at a dead run.

"He likes to pretend he knows everything already."

"That he does," Nantar agreed. "Mostly he likes to learn what you teach him and show you what you missed."

Thorn nodded. "I hate it when he does that."

Nantar laughed. "You hate it when it works," he said.

"And you hate it when it works with something you taught him, when you didn't see it first."

"Well, I see him coming this time," Thorn said, but he immediately became suspicious. He shouldn't be seeing this.

They heard Blizzard's challenge, not from before them where the rider approached, but from between them and their army, from a pit in the ground someone had covered with a mat and grass.

Lupus leapt from the pit on his horse, rearing and snorting, and then pounded toward them, his lance lowered.

Half the squads bolted forward, into the other half that didn't move without orders. The gelding Nantar rode reared and the mare bobbed her head.

He stood before them a moment later, his horned helm on his head and his childish grin on his face underneath it, offset by his cruel scar. Taller than Nantar, he seemed a big child sometimes, and Thorn faulted him regularly for not being serious.

"That wasn't bad," Nantar commented, reaching forward to clap the shoulder of his armor.

"It would have been bad if we had marched into that," Thorn argued. "And if we had kept marching, we would have."

Lupus shook his head. He still wore the same corrugated Dwarven armor he had on when they met, over a decade earlier. He still rode the same giant stallion, who should be getting too old to ride now but wasn't.

"My men on the other side of that ridge watched you coming. They started forward in time to bring you to a halt," Lupus said, still grinning. Blizzard stepped closer than most horses would, his instinct just as Thorn remembered it—to intimidate the other horses. It worked, and Thorn had to fight the mare as she tried to withdraw.

"I knew you would make me come to you," Lupus, said, looking directly at Thorn.

What could Thorn say? Lupus was right. It was irritating.

Nantar just laughed. Nantar always laughed. For a killer, he really had no bad side. As mean as he could be, there was no meanness in him. It made him a good best friend.

"How many of you are there?" Lupus asked, serious

without notice. He became the Lupus Thorn liked—the man who knew how to make war, who knew the gravity of the world.

"Five millennia of Sarandi in the van," Thorn said. "His warriors and my scouts. Another ten millennia of regulars in the main force, with five more of heavy lancers."

"Veterans?" Lupus pressed him.

Veterans were important. Lupus had taught them how to fight in squads, how to turn green men into soldiers in just eight weeks. But you had to mix them with veterans, or they could fall apart. The very worst mix was fifty percent, and usually they kept seventy-five percent.

"If we had moved last year as I wanted," Thorn said, making what he felt had to be the most important point, "we would have had five thousand less but moved with eighty percent veterans. We recruited heavily, but as you know the work for the Volkhydrans against those ogres—"

"We're at fifty-five percent," Nantar interrupted him, with a sideway glance at Thorn. Thorn scowled and bit the end of his own tongue.

"Fifty-five?" he looked out over the troops, struggling back into the rank and file. There would be a few bruises, both to eyes and to egos, as the veterans literally beat the *RIT* back into place.

'RIT.' That is what Lupus had taught them to call the new ones. Recruits in training.

"How are they?" Lupus asked Nantar.

He did that, too. He used certain of them for certain information, and he never asked Thorn about the quality of anything.

He didn't like Thorn's honesty, apparently.

"Bad," Nantar said, a grin in his black beard. "You saw. They came apart when one man surprised them. What do you think will happen when a few thousand shafts come over the horizon?"

"I was thinking about war games—" Thorn began, but Lupus waved one hand and nodded.

"Yeah, I can hit them with a few practice runs of Wolf Soldiers," he said, "but every nation has spies in Eldador. We don't want to make it too obvious they are as bad as they are, and we don't want to get that idea into *their* heads, either."

"So they walk confidently to their doom," Thorn challenged him. He kicked his mare forward. He was sick of waiting. They had a long march to Galnesh Eldador before them.

Nantar whistled for their sub-commander and kicked his gelding in the ribs. Lupus sighed and followed them on Blizzard.

"I have a whole millennium I can summon," Lupus said. "You can kick their ass."

"Wolf Soldiers?" Nantar asked him. Lupus laughed.

"You are dying to put your Sarandi up against my Wolf Soldiers, aren't you?"

Nantar just grinned.

"Ancenon informed us there is another Man who is actually from your home?" Thorn asked him, changing the subject. He'd heard this argument before.

Lupus fell quiet for a moment, and after a while, Thorn wondered that the big blond man wouldn't answer. He could be like that, one moment full of energy, the next full of melancholy. He would charge into the fray with his sword singing, and a day later weep for the dead.

"There were two of them," Lupus said finally. Their horses met a rise, and they began to climb it. The spirited mare snorted, wanting to go around, fighting Thorn's hand on the reins.

"And if you haven't already heard, yes, I am not only not from Fovea, I am not from this planet."

"That explains a lot," Thorn grumbled.

Lupus ignored him. "I hadn't really missed that place," he said. "Not until I could speak ang-lesh with them, hear it from them, talk about—" and then a bunch of words that made no sense.

The melancholy after the action. Lupus spoke more to himself than to them, Nantar and Thorn changing glances and listening politely, even though much of it sounded like blathering.

Lupus had always been hard to understand.

Chapter Twenty-Five:

Man's Best Friend

Nina of the Aschire awoke in the darkness, the pain in her wrists and her ankles telling her she'd become a prisoner, even before it occurred to her what had happened.

She remembered the stand on the plains, the trap, the confrontation. Something had attacked her from the scrub, held her until…

Until—something. Something, then sleep, and now she'd awakened.

"You lived," a gruff voice from the darkness informed her. She remembered fire. She lay on a blanket of some kind, still in her leathers. She could tell from the feel of them that she had been searched.

"Of course I lived, you fool," she said to the darkness. "Why not tell me how I fell, instead?"

A chuckle. Did she recognize…Xinto? No, the voice pitched too low. Certainly not Raven or her Mountain. She didn't hear the gravelly accent there.

Raven—she had touched Raven, and she had been casting a spell. She had called the fire on—

"If you're alive you should know how you fell," the Man said. "But it was Raven who disabled you. I don't know how."

"I was spell casting," she said. "Was it you I was going to kill."

Her eyes began adjusting. She saw Toorians in their white robes sleeping not twenty feet from her, and a picket with two horses. She didn't see her Wolf Soldiers, and she didn't see either the Scitai or the girl, Raven. The ground she lay on felt gritty and smelled scorched – fire had been employed here. Lots of it.

"If killing me is what you wanted," the Man said, "then that didn't work out for you."

She knew this person, without knowing his name. She knew his fame, a friend of the Emperor's. Troubadours sang of his deeds.

"You've fallen in with the enemies of Eldador," Nina told him. She doubted it would matter, but it could be worth a try. "I am on his official business."

"So I saw," he said.

She shook her head. "You are not a Man who should be killing Wolf Soldiers," she said. "If your Emperor needs you—"

"He is *not* my Emperor," he said. "He was a Duke when I knew him, and he wasn't my Duke then, either."

She felt her lip curl. "He is the Conqueror," she began.

"That he is," he interrupted. "I was there when he got that name, and I don't want to be conquered."

"You should be back at his side," she accused him.

He laughed.

"What is this, then?" that voice she knew. She recognized Xinto, right behind her. She strained her neck and saw nothing but a grey glob. "Are you trying to corrupt our poor Jerod?"

"Jerod?" she challenged him. She knew better.

"Leave it alone, little man," the Man warned the Scitai. "She's an Aschire, and they're crazy."

"Who did you think he was?" Xinto pressed her. She knew in a moment—the Scitai hadn't figured it out. The Man was a betrayer; he had betrayed these, too.

If she could divide them, she could escape. Her next action became obvious.

"I know who he is, one of my Wolf Soldiers recognized him," she said

* * *

Xinto approached the Aschire woman, her wrists and ankles bound, her weapons removed. Normally he would want to gag a witch like this, but Raven's power was to drain her victims dry of their magical energy. Nina would wear the gag tomorrow, but for now he considered her safe.

Now Xinto heard the kind of news he liked. He'd had no idea of Jerod's actual identity, although now it seemed obvious. Such a man would be a powerful asset; his secret even more. Right now only Xinto knew it, other than this plains witch who wouldn't be talking.

"Is that true?" Xinto asked Jerod, knowing the truth already. Too many things fit. The Wolf Soldiers being unwilling to attack him, his knowledge of the Emperor, his reluctance to be seen by him or his.

"It's true enough," Jerod said, a blob in the dark, his face unreadable.

"So that scar…"

"By the hand of Lupus the Conqueror himself, to reflect his own," Jerod said.

"We will wear our medals for our lives, for all to see," Xinto quoted the Emperor.

"Yeah," Jerod said. "He likes to say things like that."

"And you turned your back on him," Nina said, struggling in her binds. "You filthy traitor."

Jerod stood. Xinto sat, watching. Jerod's kept his emotions and his thoughts deep below the surface, so it was interesting to see—

The foot that caught Nina underneath the jaw interrupted Xinto's thoughts as well, knocking her onto her back. She made a sound between a snarl and whimper, and her teeth clacked together.

"You shouldn't kill her," Xinto said, as calm as he could be. If Jerod decided to kill the woman anyway, it wouldn't be Xinto who stopped him, and a race for Jahunga would assure her death.

"You scum," she swore, spitting out a gob of something that could be either blood, spit, or the end of her tongue.

The toe of his boot caught her in the side, lifting her off of the ground. Now Xinto stood—he had no doubt where this headed.

"We need her," he soothed the Volkhydran.

"We don't," Jerod argued.

"Our Raven…" Xinto began.

Jerod lifted his heel, held it over the Aschire's head. He regarded Xinto, his face unreadable in the dark.

"You think this one can help us?"

"I think she's our best chance if we don't hear from Glynn."

"You think she will?"

"If she doesn't," Xinto said, "she still has a head, you still have a heel."

Jerod put his foot down next to the other, towering over the prone girl. He turned his head and he spat to one side.

"Xinto is going to ask you some questions," he said. "Answer them. I don't want to hear anything more about the Conqueror from you."

She mumbled. It was a comment on her strength, Xinto couldn't help thinking, that she remained conscious.

Jerod's sword was out quick as a flash, its point at her throat. "I didn't hear you," he said.

Xinto had heard the same from what the Emperor called 'drill sergeants;' his trainers among his Eldadorian regulars.

"I said 'I will,'" she snarled. "What's wrong with her?"

"Of that," Xinto said, "we aren't sure."

* * *

Nina of the Aschire found herself hauled before a woman sleeping in her leathers on the plains grass, with the sun rising red and angry to her east.

She recognized Raven, but a different Raven than she remembered.

The hair remained black, but singed on the ends. The skin on her face was reddened, burnt by flame. She had no eyebrows. Her fingernails had been melted and scorched at the ends. She had been too near a fire, and she'd caused it. Nina knew the signs.

"She's been spell casting," Nina said, feeling her jaw thicken from where she had been kicked. Her stomach ached as well, but she didn't plan to give them the satisfaction of seeing it.

"She wondered where the energy she absorbed went," Jerod explained.

"So why not try to use some of it?" Nina let her tone mock them. Stupid people, what the Empress called 'mundanes.' People whose minds had not yet grasped the *ultimate truth*, or whose minds never would.

Invest yourself in politics, in armies, in worlds, and you will fall short. They are nothing, come and gone on whims. Even gods themselves could come and go.

The most powerful thing in existence is a thought. A thought births it all, and in the end a thought will finish it.

This Raven had thought wrong.

"She might have the black mind," Nina informed them. It wasn't unheard of. "She wielded power without being prepared for it. She might be like this for the rest of her days."

Jerod's hand immediately pulled back. Nina winced without wanting to. Xinto stepped in once again to rescue her from Volkhydran wrath.

"Can you tell for sure?" he asked her, painfully formal. He acted too friendly, too polite. Nina had seen the Emperor do this when he plotted against someone. He would be too kind, and then far too cruel.

"If you will unbind my hands, then I will touch her mind and see if I can rouse her," she said. "If she can be roused, then she doesn't have the black mind, and is merely resting."

"That would be real nice of us," Jerod sneered at her. "Letting you go and all of that."

Xinto shook his head. "She has no magic," the Scitai said. It was true enough. "She can't outrun your horse on the plains."

Jerod's scowl showed clear even through the dusk's beginning. "Wake your lizard and the Toorians first," he said. "If she wants it, then I don't want her to have it, no matter what 'it' is."

"Fair enough," Xinto said to him. Nina couldn't repress a sigh of relief. If she became useful, she remained alive. Jerod wanted an excuse to kill her and, given time, he would find one. Nina's mind already leapt to the next service she could provide, that would be too good for them to turn down, without betraying the Emperor.

Jerod's sword leapt out in a flash, and this time the point was not for her, but found its way to the Scitai's wiry beard.

"On your life, little man," Jerod told the Scitai, his eyes like steel. "If she deceives us and the girl suffers, then after I have her life, I *will* have yours, and this song be damned."

Xinto looked Jerod right in the eye, his jowl nestled against the steel sword. Nina knew the look of a man who had stared his fate in the face before and not blinked.

Xinto might be wary of the Man, but that was a far cry from being afraid. Nina wondered whom exactly she'd fallen in with.

* * *

Many tiny villages surrounded Thera, none of which could be trusted.

There were free holdings as well—persons from other nations, or from the cities of Eldador, having staked a claim to the land and registered with the nation. If they could get a writ from Galnesh Eldador and then could pay their taxes, they could keep the land.

Some peasants had made themselves fantastically wealthy on that plan. Glynn saw it as a travesty. Money to the commons fed their debauchery and their baser instincts. Money needed to be in the hands of nobles who knew what to do with it.

But then, Glynn reminded herself the Emperor had begun his life a common. He could be expected to know no better.

Jack had picketed their two horses and Zarshar had hunted down a wild antelope for them to eat. Their newest charge, this great, drooling beast, lay beside their tiny fire, its great head across the Man's leg, having already taken a haunch and crushed the bones in its great maw.

The race of Men used beasts for so many purposes—this skill had always eluded the Uman-Chi. In fact, the Cheyak's most favored people would have no beef were it not for the efforts of their Uman servants. Even their own gallant horses had to be trained by others.

It made no sense to negotiate with what had no mind for it, and yet here they came with a thing that Glynn would have, in her best judgment, allowed Zarshar to slaughter, wondering if they had the secret to a new warfare.

The Emperor had *not* become as intelligent or even as clever as an Uman-Chi, and yet he frustrated her people time and again, not with new knowledge brought from his world—that would have been exhausted long years ago—but with an uncanny ability to look at the world around him and see a path through it to victory.

Now things shone more clearly to her, kneeling in prayer to Eveave, secluded from the rest of them at the edge of the fire. Her head down, her knees protesting against the unforgiving dirt, Glynn fought to clear her mind of these concerns and did nothing more than unearth others, new fish for her stream.

War spoke to Lupus the Conqueror and advised him, step after step. Now Eveave had brought these new ones here, and would then do the same.

The gods had lost faith in the Uman-Chi as leaders of the people of Fovea. They had failed to step in where the Cheyak had fallen. Angron Aurelias himself had misjudged and worked against Her, in his ignorance, and now Eveave had clearly chosen.

What good, the salvation of the Fovean world, if the Uman-Chi are not to lead it? What good, the many centuries of Uman-Chi life, if it is spent on the knee to *Men*?

Glynn prayed into the night. Soon Jack fell asleep. Zarshar blinked in and out of the nervous rest of his kind. For hours she sought wisdom, solace and to renew her energy.

When she arose, not so much refreshed as renewed, Jack snored softly and the dog had wandered off.

Stupid, she thought. The beast had bided its time and slipped past all of them, in order to seek out its masters.

"Zarshar," she whispered. He might yet hunt it down.

"It's patrolling," he informed her, without opening his eyes. He lay on his back in his armor, far enough from the fire that his jet skin could be difficult to see. She identified him more by the ruddy glow from dying embers on his breastplate.

"The dog?"

"Well, I'm here, and so is the old, fat one, so yes, the dog," Zarshar rumbled. "Its hide - the brindle color - covers it as it moves, so it's difficult to see, but it gets up about once an hour, wanders out about a tenth of a daheer, and then comes back and lays on the old Man again."

"It's trained, then?" Glynn asked the Swamp Devil. As she spoke, sure enough, the dog returned from out of the night like a spirit, regarded her with a wag of its tail and, receiving no encouragement, returned to the Man's side.

Zarshar finally opened his blood-red eyes. "I suppose it is," he growled. "But there are dogs that do this out of instinct. In Angador, the farmers have a shaggy dog that tends herds against wolves."

She nodded—she'd heard of it.

"It loves him," she noted.

"It's a dog," Zarshar growled, and settled his shoulders deeper into the hard ground.

"They're stupid."

She had to smile, despite herself. The Devil may be evil, but not without his charms.

For lack of a better place, Glynn laid her bedroll down beside the Man and dog, and lay on it. His odor didn't reek as foul as the Devil's, and his body threw off plenty of excess heat.

Laying down, still in her dress, she watched Jack's simian face for a while, forcing her mind to rest as she prepared to take what sleep she could.

Kneel down before these? Never.

And yet, the goddess had spoken to their Raven, and surely War to the Emperor. Which of Adriam's children would address itself to Jack, then? Which would bless his mind with divine wisdom?

Perhaps one did so now.

The minds of Men had turned out to be a treacherous thing.

* * *

By a little stream in a *very* pretty meadow, Melissa dipped her toes (she had just had them done—they looked *gorgeous*) in the water and leaned back to let the sun beat down on her face.

Bliss she thought. What a perfect day. She had nothing to do and forever to do it—she couldn't remember the last time she had actually relaxed.

The birds started singing. Jasmine bloomed somewhere. She loved that smell. How strange for the middle of the day! Jasmine bloomed at dusk.

"Aren't you a picture?" someone told her.

She threw her hair over her shoulder and looked down the stream, where it flowed from between two grass-covered hill. She saw a doe on top of one of them, munching the clover. Down the other came Raven.

Uck, she thought. She didn't like this girl. She acted pushy and mean, and dressed in leather like some kind of super hero.

"What do *you* want?" Melissa asked her.

"Roust you up," Raven told her. Her leather outfit creaked as she walked, twisting on her breasts and hips. Melissa allowed herself the chick-on-chick mandatory check out. Had to admit—the outfit was working. She would turn heads anywhere.

"You're making a camel limp somewhere," Melissa sniped her. "You stole its toe."

"Nice," Raven told her. "Your boyfriend pay for those toes, or did he charge it to his wife's card?"

"I'm sorry," Melissa said, giving the toes a swish, "I didn't see the stripper bar down the road from here."

"You didn't see it or you couldn't read the sign?" Raven gave back.

The day began darkening. The doe looked up and seemed alarmed. The cool stream now felt too cold.

"Isn't there a pole you could be dancing on?" Melissa groused, pulling her heels underneath her butt. She realized right then that she was naked. Why would she be hanging out naked in a public place like this?

Raven walked right up next to her, stood there looking down at her. Melissa's eyes held level with the dagger in Raven's boot.

"You going to waste your whole day here?" Raven asked her.

"No," Melissa scoffed, and then looked up at her. "Why?"

"You have places to go," Raven said. "You have things to do."

"Do I?"

"You tell me."

For the life of her, Melissa couldn't think of one thing.

"Weren't you interested in something about fire?"

And behind Raven, both of the grassy hills burst into flame. Where the stream ran too cold, now the water began steaming.

"Fire?" Raven repeated.

"What is this?" Melissa demanded. She tried to stand but Raven shoved her back onto her butt.

"Don't you make *fire*?" Raven demanded of her. Her hair and her black leather outfit began smoldering. Her eyes looked wide and wild, and Raven's smile seemed almost gleeful as she started to burn.

"Fire?" she demanded again.

The flames swept down the hills and across the plain towards her. The doe ran screaming away from it. The stream boiled.

"What are you doing?" Melissa demanded.

"I'm waking you up, little girl," Raven told her. "Time for you to get your ass going."

The fire swept right up beside her, past Raven, whose flesh burned right off of her body as if it were tinder. The leather-clad skeleton stood over her, the flames like a crown around her head.

Melissa cringed back from her. An old song ran through her head.

I am the god of Hell Fire, and I bring you Fire!

"Roust, bitch!" the burning skeleton of Raven told her.

"Whoa!" Raven leapt up from the dirty plain. She had been laid down in her harness and pants, her coat turned around, covering her.

The first thing she saw was Nina, glowering at her with

some self-important smirk on her face. Without even thinking, Raven balled her fist up and punched the purple-haired girl in the mouth.

"You bitch!" Nina reached for her dagger, but couldn't find it in her arm sheath.

Melissa reached for her boot dagger, and found it right where she'd left it. Then she put it to Nina's throat.

"Stop it, both of you," Jerod snarled.

Nina's hand rose and did nothing, except to remind Raven of the day before.

She had intervened when Nina had tried to cast a spell. She had taken Nina's power.

Then Raven had tried to *make use* of Nina's power, to use it as her own. And it had worked.

Raven didn't drop the knife, but looked around her.

The grass looked black, the earth scorched. The scorched smell filled her nose.

She looked for Jerod, for Jahunga, for Xinto—she saw them all. The Toorians, the horses—they were there.

Then who…?

"Drop the knife, Raven," Jerod warned her.

Jahunga behaved more politic, but more firm. He put the head of his spear against the blade, and pressed it to the scorched plains. "Girl, you put that down, now."

Raven allowed the weapon to fall. She felt her jaw go slack, peripherally aware that her mouth lay open.

She had wielded magic. She had actually done it.

And more than anything now, she wanted to do it again.

She looked Nina right in the face. She felt the other woman's gray eyes search hers.

"You know, don't you?" Nina asked her.

"I know what?" Raven countered.

Nina just looked into her eyes.

Raven thought back to the deck of the *Bitch of Eldador*, alone with Shela, the conversation, the hug.

She had said, "I knew it." Once in a while, Raven had wondered about that.

"The most important thing in the world…" Raven began.

A slow smile crossed Nina's face, followed by the one on Raven's.

"I never would have guessed it," Nina admitted, shaking her head.

* * *

Glynn woke with the sun, the Devil already up and the dog gone. Jack slept the sleep of exhaustion, his old bones weighing on him, no doubt.

The lives of Men were fleeting and lived mostly in sickness.

She saw a portion of the antelope, still half cooked over the fire. She applied her will to drive the flies from it, then to heat it enough to be healthy. The aroma sufficed that hunger overcame sloth and awakened Jack.

"Hmmm?" he said, and rose up to his elbows.

She still felt unhappy with his kind and simply grunted at him. He stood and stretched, then made a low whistle through his beard.

The dog galloped out from between the surrounding hills to be with them, wagging her tail and bumping him for attention. One hand on its head, Jack drew a short knife from his belt and addressed the carcass uninvited. Glynn wondered at what may live in the dog's coat, which would now migrate to their meal, but said nothing.

"There's an army marching up from the south," Zarshar informed them, approaching from behind the dog. She saw dust on his forearms and leggings, and his hair had become tangled with grass.

"Another is coming from the north, and that one is Daff Kanaar," he continued. "We're leaving east, then we'll cut south around the Eldadorians. We don't want to face any Daff Kanaar."

Glynn nodded. "I agree," she said. "We leave as soon as we can pack the horses."

"What do we do with this?" Jack asked, his mouth around a half-cooked portion of meat. "If they have dogs, we can't leave this around—they'll be drawn to it and they'll know someone's watching. If I were Lupus, I would want to keep this quiet as long as I could."

Zarshar clawed a stretch of sod out of the Earth, large enough to cover a dwarf. "We'll bury it," he said. "Eat your fill while you can—I don't intend to wait on you."

Glynn, Jack and the dog made a quick meal, the dog once again crushing bones in its teeth. Glynn had to wonder at the purpose of the thing—too large to be controlled and too friendly to be trusted. She had begun to think it the pet of some dead farmer, his holding pillaged as forage for some army.

Zarshar made good his promise and they set off, walking their horses in order to make a smaller target for any scouts, the dog ranging out before them, then circling back to wag its tail at them before returning to its post. Occasionally Jack would rough its ears with his fingers and then send it back out on its way.

They had traveled as many as five daheeri before they saw it lay down in a crouch, its tail low and its ears forward.

"It sees something," Jack pointed out unnecessarily. Zarshar assumed a crouch and Glynn told him, "Hold, Black Adept."

His red eyes regarded her. "Make use your magic before your eyes, Sirrah," she told him. "What the dog sees may have already seen her."

Zarshar nodded. Being able to look through a hill, or through a portion of the Earth to see past the horizon, would be difficult. Every solid thing would have to be addressed and overcome individually—millions of millions of tiny grains of sand, even worms and such things as live in the dirt.

One might more easily make the sky to reflect an image, as a great mirror, but then of course anyone could see it. What is worse, they would see the caster.

What one would do instead, then, is to find which way the wind blew, and rob an image from that. It had been discovered long ago that the stuff that air was made from held a picture of what it passed by, and then could be read.

Glynn felt Zarshar reach out with his will and take hold of the wind, draw it into him, and then make a picture from it, bringing it before them so that all could see.

She saw files upon files of them, marching Daff Kanaari soldiers, having turned south for whatever reason, now moving west, directly for them, an army too vast for counting.

"There must be…," Jack began, but his voice trailed off.

"Too many to fight," Zarshar said. "We run—you better hope that thing can keep up, because I'm not leaving it to lead someone to us."

Jack whistled and the dog stood up and turned toward them. Glynn half-expected a flight of arrows to sail by it but none came. She mounted her horse, taking the sidesaddle, and Jack followed her example.

Zarshar set off south at his loping pace, running for a path between two low hills. Jack followed, and Glynn after him, her eyes to the east, waiting for what she had seen on the wind.

They ran another daheer before topping an unavoidable rise, seeing a great marching army, a vanguard formed in the squads of Wolf Soldiers, then file after file of trotting lancers, pennons snapping on the ends of their weapons, the hook-symbol of the Daff Kanaar.

Behind them marched orderly ranks of Daff Kanaari—their foot soldiers. Heavy armor, shields and short stabbing swords, spears over their shoulders.

Between the vanguard and the lancers, three Men in heavy armor, one each with the hook symbol on his breast: one scarlet, one brown, and one black.

No one could mistake the horned helmet, the fluting in the plate armor. No one could mistake the great, white charger.

"The Emperor," Zarshar growled.

"No, Zarshar," Glynn told him, softly.

The Swamp Devil's red eyes turned on her. It actually drooled in anticipation. Her horse took a nervous step and she had to tighten her grip on its reins.

It was the nature of a Swamp Devil to attack its prey, no matter what the odds. In fact, she would be surprised if it couldn't get within striking distance of the Emperor now.

However, their first priority needed to remain to find the 'One who fights as does the sun,' and they needed Zarshar to do it. Even if the Swamp Devil prevailed, it would never escape the wrath of the Daff Kanaar.

"We are not bound for this," she told him.

"If we kill him now, your prophecy can rot," Zarshar growled. "I can cut through the hills right there—"

"Zarshar, you'll be breaking your oath," Jack informed him.

The Swamp Devil straightened to look the Man directly in the eye.

"I made no such vow," he said. "In fact, if I charge him now, I could argue I am saving you."

Jack shook his head. "None of us are as powerful as you," he said.

"When they finish with you, whether you can take the Emperor or not, they'll back-track where you came from and find us. If you can't take them all, there's no way that we can."

The Swamp Devil became contemplative. Glynn found herself forced to admire the Man's grace. Cloaked as a compliment, the Swamp Devil could hardly take offense; neither would he ever deny his own superiority.

"It irks me to pass him so close," Zarshar admitted.

"Remember it, then," Jack said. "Savor it, and remember how sweet the chase is, over the kill."

Zarshar nodded. He took a longing look at the Emperor, and he started down the far side of the rise.

Glynn frowned appreciatively. She had to admit, she could have done no better.

Perhaps this race of Men had some small gift to offer?

Chapter Twenty-Six:

The Last Free City

Nina rode behind Raven now, her hands tied behind her. Xinto rode behind Jerrod, and Jerrod didn't seem all that happy about it.

"Oh, you disgusting Man," the Scitai complained.

The Volkhydran snickered. "Big breakfast," he said.

Nina chuckled to herself.

"All day long," Raven complained.

"He claims he used to sit behind you," Nina whispered into the other woman's ear.

She nodded. "Couldn't keep his hands off of me," she said. "Vile little male—whatever Jerrod does to him, he deserves."

All around them, Jahunga and his warriors travelled through the forest, making sure of their safety. That morning they'd buried the dead Wolf Soldiers or what was left of them. Now they pressed through the Salt Wood.

"I won't be putting my hands on you," she said. "But I will need to educate you in your new skills."

Raven turned half way around in the side saddle she rode. "You mean the magic?" she asked.

Nina snorted. "Of course, the magic," she said. "What else but the magic? You can't just start casting on your own. What you did—you have a strength, Raven. Shela saw it, so did I. You need to be *trained*."

Raven shook her head. "I'm not doing it anymore," she said.

Nina smiled. "You feel remorse for the dead soldiers?" she said.

"Don't you?" Raven countered.

"Do I wish they weren't dead?" she asked. "Of course. I knew those men, I shared a fire with them. Some had families, children. You made orphans, Raven. You made widows."

A tear ran down Raven's cheek.

"You think that's bad?" Nina pressed her. "You tell me this—did you mean to do it?"

"Of course not," she said.

"And yet, you did. You did it, unaware and out of control of your power. What do you think you'll do, the next time someone upsets you, now that the magic knows how to get free?"

Raven considered.

"How do you know what I did?" she asked finally.

Nina had been unconscious, of course. A last recourse of the uncommitted—find a technicality to disregard it all.

"I know because I saw the bodies," she said, "and don't forget who raised you from the black mind. And do not be fooled—you were on your way to the black mind. You'd have lived in that fantasy you'd created for the rest of your days, lying in your own wastes, if I hadn't roused you when I did."

Raven was quiet, looked down and finally whispered, "I didn't know that."

"I want you to think on that," Nina said. "I want you to consider what you might become, untrained."

The girl was quiet, and that was good, because Nina had something else to do.

They thought her stripped of her power, but what they hadn't realized was that she'd been able to rob a little of Raven's while she roused her. She used that now, and she reached out with her mind.

Not to Shela—the Empress was too far, and in fact while she was mighty, her might lay in the desires of others. She would be difficult to reach.

The Emperor's Daff Kanaar ally, the Green One, was closer, and that one, a Druid, always listened.

She reached out, and she found his mind.

"I know this girl," he informed her.

"Listen to me," she told him. "I don't have much time. Lupus' enemies are headed to Kor. You need to contact the Empress."

* * *

Northern courts were strange to him. Jahunga took it all in quietly, his men behind him, his friends Jerod and Xinto to his left and right, the women behind the other Man.

Jerod—he found it hard not to love this one, stern and cruel, his thin lips held in a line and his scar glowing on his face. Jahunga delighted in making him laugh, in making the Volkhydran admit to his humor. It is his humor that defines a man, not his spear. His humor, and the kind of children he raises.

To stand in a court like this one, a man needed to have his friends and his humor—they had taken Jahunga's weapon.

Northern courts had a *look*. Long, like a lodge, and narrow. The roof rose to a high arch in imitation of the sky. A gallery ran half way down the right side, half as wide as the right wall, and they liked pillars, gigantic columns to reach up to their artificial sky. Some were just poles, some had been carved. He'd been told the ones in Thera, in Lupus' personal estate, were carved as stallions, and yet the ones in Outpost IX were plain, because everything else there was so grand.

Here in the palace at Kor, the builders had carved the bases of their pillars as strange, furred creatures which stood man-like, their claws reaching up the pillar heights. They glowered up at the ceiling, as if they saw something above them which they wanted to kill. A bright green carpet ran down the center of the hall rather than the traditional red. Steel doors stood open at the entrance, opposite the throne of a Man called Xareff, the Duke of Thieves.

He looked stick figure skinny, his pinched face scowling into his audience. Jahunga saw no humor in this man. Experience had left him dry and brittle. Old man fingers with long, old man nails clicked on the stone throne's arm. He regarded them as if he saw some sort of trash, blown in by the wind, needing to be swept out.

"You are wanted," the Duke of Thieves said to Xinto, "and I see no reason not to turn you over to the Emperor."

It had taken them a week to get to Kor from the plains. Kor called itself the last of the 'Free Cities,' a port full of thieves and pirates, bad men and exiles, whores and schemers and those who didn't mind buying the loot of pillaged ships.

One could find every race here, even Toorians. Some men had noted him, walking in with this strange troop. Pressed up against both the forest and the sea, its shoddy rock walls were a brine-stained testament to what the race of Men would put up with to be free.

"You are no friend to the Emperor," Xinto countered. He looked comfortable in this element. Jahunga breathed freest when surrounded by trees, stepping on soil, a spear in his hand and a buck before him.

For Xinto, the court became his forest.

"I am no friend of yours, either, little man," the Duke said.

Nina had actually gotten them this audience. Nina and their Raven had become inseparable since discovering Raven had been gifted with the power to cast spells. They spoke in hushed voices, they traded secrets—Jahunga spent many waking moments wondering of what.

"You invoked the Emperor's name to get where you are," the Duke continued. "I thought it was to surrender yourselves. If you are who you say you are, then it is no secret to you how things stand between Kor and Eldador."

Xinto smiled. "The Emperor's unreasonable demand that you not sink or rob his ships," he said.

The Duke snarled. "I am no fool to take on Eldadorian Sea Wolves—but he extends his protection to any ship that flies the Eldadorian standard. That means any ship—"

"Would haul the Eldadorian standard the first time they saw your masts over the horizon," Jerod interrupted him. The Duke bristled. He wasn't born to this title, he had clawed his way to it, and he didn't do that with his humor.

Jahunga wished he had his spear in his hand—he would have gripped it harder. Now he could only flex his fingers and want it. His men, lined up behind him, probably felt the same way.

"And who are you, to complete a sentence for me?" the Duke demanded, leaning forward. "I don't know that ugly face."

The hair on Jahunga's skin rose as the Duke's personal guard put hands on weapons. No one could mistake that signal. The Duke intended to make an example.

Jerod had never been shy with his opinions; neither had he seemed to need to speak out unnecessarily. In a situation like this, those like Xinto would expect those who carried swords and spears to keep their own council.

Jahunga reasoned that, if Jerod felt he had to speak now, then something exceptional needed saying.

Jerod straightened. "I am Karl, son of Henekh, son of Dragor, warlord of Teher of the Volkhydran nation—and if I want to interrupt you, Xareff, I will. If you don't like that, pick five of your best men."

He turned his head to the right and spat on the green carpet.

The Duke leaned back and looked Jerod up and down, his jaw open and his lips closed. He transformed from angry to shrewd in a moment, and Xinto from shrewd to irritated just as quickly.

"I apologize for not introducing—" Xinto began.

The Duke waved the Scitai off, his eyes never leaving the Volkhydran. Jahunga couldn't decide if Xareff was considering hostages or guest accommodations.

"Your father seeks you," Xareff said, finally, "no less seriously than the Emperor seeks these."

"My countrymen come here," Jerod informed him, "and I'm sure they've marked me. If I don't walk back out of this palace, rest assured you will meet many—"

"Yes, yes," the Duke said. "Volkhydrans love a good fight more than a good thought. I have no desire to alienate your father, although rest assured he will be hearing from me."

Jerod nodded. Xinto stepped between the two of them,

trying to ease back into the conversation. "If we can speak of the Emperor for just a moment—" he began.

But the Duke had finished with them. "You will have no trouble with the Emperor from me," he said, "but know—you are marked, all of you. The Emperor has put great stock into obtaining Xinto of the Woods, and a woman called Raven, and an Uman-Chi woman. He has made it clear they are enemies of the Eldadorian nation, as are any who travel with them.

"And you," the Duke said, looking directly at Nina of the Aschire, "are known to me. The Emperor would not like to know you are keeping this company, and rest assured he will."

Nina nodded, and they were dismissed. Walking back down the green carpet to the throne room doors, armed Men waited ready with their weapons drawn to escort them from the palace.

"Well, aren't you a chirpy little bird," Xinto hissed at Jerod as they walked.

"Kept you alive," Jerod countered.

"You know, we Scitai have a saying about Men—"

"Make sure it's the last thing you ever want to say, before you speak it," Jerod said, not looking down.

Jahunga chuckled. His heart warmed with his love for these people and their ways.

* * *

"That couldn't have been what you hoped to accomplish," Nina said, a smirky smile on her face, sitting in a crappy little bar, on a dirty wharf, in what had to be the part of town where fish were gutted and then pissed on.

They all sat around a circular table, not a board like in the Eldadorian hostel. Tucked away in a corner, Xinto on a stool and Nina trapped with her back to the wall, a Toorian on either side, Raven leaned back and watched the play, a beer mug in her hand.

"Well, I didn't know I would have such good help," Xinto complained, sucking the foam from his mustache, a wooden mug in his hand as well.

"Be glad you did," Jerod countered him. "Because Xareff was going to put you in a cell and send to Vrekk for Wolf Soldiers."

"You don't know that," Xinto said.

"He is probably right," Jahunga said. They all looked at him. Jahunga didn't say a lot, which got him a lot more attention when he *did* speak.

"We Toorians know the Duke of Thieves," he continued, and one of his men nodded. "He doesn't negotiate unless he can't take what he wants."

"And he sure as Life's nipples had us," Jerod said, drinking mead from a bowl.

"I still don't know why he let us go," Raven said. This had been bugging her. Since she had woken up on the plains, and confessed to Nina she knew the answer to what Nina called 'the ultimate truth,' Xinto had been looking at and acting differently with Jerod, and she hadn't been able to figure out why.

Now he turned out to be some kind of warlord? That made no sense.

"Jerod's father is the most important man in Teher, which is a Volkhydran city on the border with Conflu," Xinto said.

"My father wouldn't sit by while some Koran trash put his son in a dungeon," Jerod added, looking into this mug.

"The Volkhydran people *are* quick to war," Xinto conceded.

"And he just took your word for it?" Raven didn't believe it. "Why couldn't anyone just say—"

"No one would just *say* they were Karl Henekhson," Xinto said, and took another drink of beer.

Jerod just kept looking down, saying nothing. Raven looked from face to face, and no one would meet her eyes.

"You know about the Battle of Tamaran Glen?" Nina asked her, finally.

Raven nodded. Shela had told her about it.

"You know about the Hero of Tamara, then?" Nina asked her.

"Some legendary warrior or something who turned the battle with the Wolf Soldiers," Raven said, dismissively. She really didn't believe it—every battle story that one hero that it turned on.

Jahunga laughed. "Even in Toor we know about Karl, son

of Henekh," he said.

Jerod stood, shifted his sword on his belt. He stood and walked away without saying anything. He shot a sideways glance at Raven—she caught his eye, looking more guilty than anything, then lost it.

Nina looked at her. "You really don't know?" she said.

Raven shook her head—she was getting sick of this.

"Jerod is the Hero of Tamara," Nina told her. "That man is one of the bravest who ever put a foot down on Fovean soil."

* * *

Jerod felt so sick of this crap that it burned him inside. Not a week went by when that day hadn't haunted him, and that had been a lot of weeks.

Stomping through Kor's stinking wharves, not really knowing where he was bound for, he relived it again. Lupus' small city, himself barely seventeen, never having killed a man before, the pampered son of a warlord whom people were wondering about—whether he had it in him to replace the old man.

Henekh had already taken another wife, to try for another son.

When those Confluni had swarmed out of the forest, across the glen and into their barricades, his Wolf Soldier guards, one hundred strong, had raised their shields, lowered their pikes and taken them, head on. What amazed him is that they held. Confluni died skewered on hand cut spikes in the dirt around their walls, then to arrow fire from their archers, hiding behind their barricades, then finally on the pikes of their men.

His first command, the Wolf Soldiers, one hundred strong, slowly being pushed back by thousands, and winning.

The shield bearers fell back as one, a wall over one hundred feet long moving in unison, then separating to allow swords to stab out and kill more men, then pulling back and closing, so pikes could strike again.

When it looked like the line would crumble, the Daff Kanaar flooded in from their flanks like water past a dam, taking the Confluni totally unaware, driving them until his Wolf Soldiers could advance back into the breach and stop the flood.

Precise as any machine, they did it over and over. Fall back, stab, push forward, slash. The Confluni hammered on them, trying to get around the sides of their barricade where the archers riddled them, trying to get over, standing on the bodies of their own dead. Trying to draw out the rest of the Daff Kanaar and failing.

The Confluni had retreated, and then they had come again, but this time with spears.

Not normal spears, but long poles born like battering rams held by as many as four men. They smashed through the shield walls, spilling the guts of the swordsmen, the spearmen, toppling the shieldmen as well. The Wolf Soldiers hung on only by the strength of their discipline, some still fighting with the splintered end of a spear protruding from a breast or hip.

He needed more, and he needed them now, and he knew where to get them, and that is what made him the Hero of Tamara.

They had walked here, and he had been interested in becoming a Wolf Soldier himself. They took anyone. He could join them, change his name, and he could forget about ever replacing his father, ever having to be the leader of his people—just fight and live and, someday, die.

In his cowardice, his weakness, he had asked them to teach what they did, and how. The Wolf Soldiers had thought it funny, their leader being taught by the troops he led, but they taught him to march, and the commands they used for advance, for falling back, to wheel to the left and the right. He'd marched as a shield bearer, as a pikeman, as a swordsman. At night when they drilled, he took all of the positions and he excelled at them.

And at the same time, other members of the Daff Kanaar, their foot soldiers, saw him, and joined him, and together they all learned the moves, and the basics of the discipline, and the regimen of Wolf Soldiers.

So when he needed them, he knew where to get them. He left the ranks, rallied those Daff Kanaar soldiers and lined them up behind his Wolf Soldiers. On that critical retreat, where it looked like the Confluni finally had the momentum to push them back into the small city, Jerod, then Karl, had given the order to wheel to one side, and Confluni crashed right into the ranks of those fresh soldiers.

They didn't fight as well as Wolf Soldiers. They weren't hard-core killers like Wolf Soldiers but they had the heart, the momentum, and as soon as he could, Karl replaced their casualties with his seasoned troops, interspersing experience where it was needed, taking the pounding from the Confluni and, again, turning them back.

"Can you hold them?" the warrior, his countryman, Nantar had demanded of him.

"For a while," he said. "Until these die."

And then the Confluni archers had engaged, and all of the men began falling, arrows raining in and striking them at random, Daff Kanaar and Wolf Soldiers trying to fight with shafts sticking into them, slipping on their own fallen, on their own blood.

They pushed the Confluni back. Some sort of spell casting was going on in and out of the little city. Karl remembered wiping the sweat and the blood from his eyes and looking past the Confluni horde to the troops beyond—seeing how many they had left to kill.

Like the god War himself, there rode the Conqueror on his white stallion, in the midsts of the enemy with the Sword of War cleaving down on shoulders and skulls.

Karl hadn't really believed it when he saw it—it came to him almost like a dream. Blood flowed down Lupus' face, oozed out of his armor—a dagger protruded from his ribs already. Karl had taken his sergeant by the shoulder and pointed out their commander.

"Can you believe that?" he demanded. "Am I seeing that?"

He and the sergeant both watched the invincible warrior pit himself against thousands with nothing but his sword.

"He's showing us!" the sergeant shouted, taking Karl by the upper arms. "He's showing us that we don't have to be afraid—that we can fight outnumbered, and we can win!"

If that had been his message then the Daff Kanaar lancers got it—they charged head-on into the Confluni and relieved him. Lupus had looked bewildered for a moment, as if this was his fight and they were intruding.

The Confluni soldiers at their front line hesitated, looking for orders, not sure whether to charge again or wait to see how things went on the flank.

Karl had raised up his sword with one hand and screamed his Volkhydran battle cry. It had energized the men around him, and the men next to them, and the men next to them as well. They started screaming, roaring, going wild in their eyes. They called out out for Black Lupus, started screaming things like 'He rides' and 'He conquers,' and the troops who had fallen back before demanded to push forward now.

Karl realized then the arrow fire had stopped. Lupus must have stunned even the Confluni. What madman would attack 10,000 troops like that, with nothing but a sword in his hand?

"At them, you bastards," Karl had roared, his own voice strange in his ears. "Save him! Save the Conqueror! *To his side*!"

And like a swarm they charged, the Wolf Soldier/Daff Kanaar mix in the vanguard, a howling mass of Legionnaires behind them. Karl saw a woman with half of her arm shorn off, a man with two arrows in his shoulder, charging, killing, holding up their position in the mass, refusing to die until they had done their share of killing.

Karl had been one of them. The sword his father had given to him, the two-handed behemoth that had always seemed too cumbersome to wield, felt light as a feather and graceful as a scalpel now. He caught the rhythm of the Daff Kanaari, his sword slashing down in momentum with theirs, tearing guts, spilling bowels, removing heads. The Confluni fell back in terror and found themselves trampled by the Daff Kanaar lancers.

The Confluni ranks broke, and from there it became just a matter of containing them. Karl had broken to the right with his men, the rest of the Daff Kanaar to the left, and together they had pushed the Confluni past their leader, their hero, him just staring at them as if Lupus had forgotten the Daff Kanaar had been invited.

Later, Karl learned it was Shela, not he, who'd turned the battle, but the men wouldn't have it. In the aftermath, they called him the Hero of Tamara, and Lupus 'the Conqueror.' He had gotten his scar and birthed some kind of legend.

Karl spat, walking through these stinking streets with these *stupid* people. He didn't feel like a legend, any more than he did with his father, who suddenly wanted his council on every move he made, and who had entrusted him with the military of Teher.

"I know you," Jerod heard behind him.

He knew he wouldn't be able to draw his sword in time.

* * *

Another of the Emperor's changes to modern society was banking 'skrits.' You could go to what was now the Bank of Eldador, and what had once been a moneylender, and you could access your account anywhere in known Fovea, if you knew your bank number and your password. A local truth sayer verified a client's identity, and then you got your money from the local bank.

If you used any bank other than the one where you kept your money, they transferred it for you. Meanwhile you paid only a small fee per month to them to hold it.

Those like Glynn with vast wealth could perhaps be paid to leave their silver in the Bank of Eldador, which is what Glynn did. If these Eldadorians found themselves hungry to give away wealth, she certainly found herself wise enough to take it. Every year, the bank took the average of her gold and added two percent to it.

Having crossed the Theran plains, they'd come across the city of Desdarre, just north of the Lone Wood. There she wrote an amount on the skrit, and she pressed her thumb over it. She handed the skrit to the Uman 'sayer,' whose job it was to manage the local accounts. He sought out a record and then returned to Glynn with a bag of coins.

Another miracle of the system was that it made use of those who possessed the gifts to use simple magic, but whose mind could not encompass the ultimate truth of things. Those *barely gifted* used to lead terrible lives, attempting on their own to explore their talents, usually until they killed themselves or fell to the black mind.

"This is drawn on a Trenboni account," he said to her offhandedly. "Are you a Trenboni Uman?"

She shook her head. That would be too obvious. Within her glamour, she opened her peasant-girl eyes up wide and put on the dumbest look she knew. “No, goodsir, I am from the city of Eldador and was paid by a woman to clean dumpsters.”

“Dumpsters?” the man looked skeptical, holding up the bag.

It would be like a male with a small job like this to use it for sexual favors. She pushed out her lower lip and let her eyes well.

He gave her the gold with a laugh. She put on a grateful look.

“You know,” he said, “I used to keep my gold in a jar, buried by a tree, and I used to check it every week. Once someone saw me and they stole my gold—then I had nothing.”

“I kept mine in the ticking of my mattress,” Glynn said. “Thank you, goodsir.”

She left and returned to where she had left Jack waiting, at a tavern on a street corner not far from the bank. He sat at a round table, his back to a wall, a wooden mug of beer before him and the dog at his feet. She sat beside him, kissed his cheek as a girl familiar with him would.

He looked surprised. “What was that?”

She did the little-girl look. “But goodsir, would you not expect this of your Uman girl?”

Jack laughed. “Want a beer, then?”

She nodded, and batted her eyes. “If I may, goodsir,” she said.

He raised his hand for the waitress. Glynn leaned forward as she had seen commons do at bars.

“This entertains you?” she asked.

Jack nodded. “Better than watching the grass grow, I suppose.”

She frowned. “And you discuss your ideas, your philosophies?” she asked.

“I suppose,” he said. “Exchange ideas, opinions.”

“To what end?” Glynn asked. “You discuss issues you can barely change. You may share you views—”

Jack waved her question off, as rude as any other Man, and

drank from his mug. Glynn tasted of her own bitter brew, wondering how the commons withstood it.

"You can talk and share opinions even when you can't change things," Jack said. "It makes you feel like you control your life. I don't suppose you would understand."

Glynn counted herself a rare enchantress, younger than her peers, learning a discipline whose methods had always been the province of males.

"I understand," she admitted. "Perhaps better than you know."

They sat quiet for an uncomfortable minute, and each drank.

Jack cleared his throat. It wasn't in the race of Men to keep their own company.

"Should we check on Zarshar?" he asked.

Glynn shook her head. They had rented a loft above the stable where they kept Little Storm, and hidden Zarshar up there. "He has been fed, he sleeps now," she said.

Another uncomfortable pause.

"They worship the god Power," Jack said, matter-of-factly.

Glynn couldn't help thinking how inane this seemed.

She sighed. "It was believed for a very long time they were the Cheyak," she said, and sipped the bitter beer. "But they are creatures no different than the Slee, and they are of Power."

"Were they around when the Cheyak ran things?" Jack asked.

Glynn looked him in the eye. "I couldn't tell you," she said. "What literature we have of the Cheyak does not mention them."

Jack frowned, as Men will do when pensive. "But the Cheyak worshipped the same gods as you do," he said.

She didn't understand why he would even ask that. "The gods are the gods," she said.

"But they don't all have a chosen people," Jack pressed her.

She shook her head. A child might ask such questions, but then isn't the child a beginner in this world, much as Jack?

"There are some races that favor some gods, but more

often there are types of people who look for a god's favor in his or her everyday life," she said. "So the thief looks to Eveave, the warrior to War, the farmer to Life and the fisherman to Water."

"And up north, there are Dwarves," Jack said.

She nodded. "They are Earth's chosen."

"And the Herd that Cannot be Tamed is sacred to Life," Jack said.

She nodded. He had some knowledge, anyway. He had clearly been thinking of this.

"Where I'm from," Jack said, "we had Druids a long time ago. They lived in a place called Europe, and they worshipped nature—natural things."

Glynn considered that, taking a delicate sip from her mug, then putting it down and running her index finger along the moist rim. She'd seen commons do this, as well, especially females with males they liked. Oddly, it made her feel sexual somehow—Jack clearly noted it.

"Those here are no different," she informed him. "They worship what they call 'the Trinity,' of Weather, Water and Earth—arguably the gods of nature."

Jack frowned again. "When we refer to our one God," he said, "we refer to a Trinity, but that is different manifestations of the same God."

"So it seems there are parallels between your religious beliefs and theirs," Glynn noted.

"That may be—and that's disturbing," Jack said. "Do you know what the odds are of two groups growing up independently like that, having similar beliefs?"

"The odds?" Glynn asked. "I don't know this word."

Jack sighed. He expected her to explain everything to him, yet when it came his turn, he became quickly exasperated.

He launched into a dissertation on what odds were, leaving her to think of gambling, which made more sense. In the end she had to agree the coincidence of these Druids seems somewhat incredible.

"That makes me wonder," Jack admitted.

She smiled. "And what do you wonder?" she asked.

At that moment they were fed, and Jack tore into his meal

as any child of Man could be expected to. He didn't bring up the topic again and Glynn considered herself glad to be done with it.

Chapter Twenty-Seven:

They Came and they Saw

"You're Henekh's son," the older man said. He had a few decades on Jerod, hair shot with gray, weather beaten skin and a jaw rough with stubble. Squint lines framed his probing brown eyes as he scanned Jerod's face. He had a look like he'd already been cheated.

Jerod counted fifteen warriors with him, all armed with belaying pins. Not most men's weapon of choice, but maybe not so out of place in a wharf, Jerod thought. They'd be easy to hide, easy to use, and they didn't leave a bloody mess.

Jerod knew of gangs that went out at night and way laid travelers, beating them unconscious and selling them to captains, mostly pirates, who needed to fill out their crews. Out to sea, you learned a job and did it, or you found yourself cut up for bait. Those men would prefer short wooden clubs like these to swords.

Jerod could draw his sword faster than the first of them could hit him, but he didn't think he could take fifteen ready to fight.

"What of it?" he snarled. He turned to put three men behind him. They stood in clumps, not circling him; meaning he could run between some of them and avoid the fight if he had to.

The old man put the pin in his belt and held up his hands,

palms toward Jerod. "No offense, no offense," he said. "We are countrymen, although I am from Volka, not Teher. You and I have a common friend, I think."

"Oh?" Jerod had no intention of letting his guard down. He listened intently for the soft steps behind him that would tell him that the rush was on.

"You knew him as Lupus the Conqueror," the man said. "I called him, 'Mordy.' Never knew that it wasn't his first name."

Jerod looked the man up and down, then turned his head and spat. "You weren't a Wolf Soldier," he said, matter-of-factly.

Jerod could spot a Wolf Soldier a mile away, even a retired one, not that there were many. They stood straighter than regular men. They looked right into people's eyes, as Lupus did. They never strayed far from a weapon; either a pike, a long sword or a short stabbing one, depending on the job they did.

And they walked with that timed step that Lupus drilled into them from the first day they signed on. These men moved like…

"We're sailors," the old man said. "I'm Forn, and I was captain of the *Sprite* until she went down just north of here. We walked in and ain't had no luck since."

"So how do you know the E—", Jerod began, and caught himself. "How do you know Lupus?"

No sound behind him, the men from in back had started circling around to get a look at his face. If they'd planned an ambush, they might have changed their minds.

"We ported him from Volka to Trenbon," Forn said. He shook his head and spat—a loose gob with more spray than anything else. The man had no teeth.

"Almost lost the *Sprite* right there, damn him," Forn continued. "He was a traveling emer-sary, or some such thing, and he didn't tell no one. That made carrying him—"

"Illegal, I know," Jerod interrupted. Volkan sailors were notorious chatterboxes, and this one was no exception. Before the rise of Eldador and the Daff Kanaar, they had moved most of the commerce on Tren Bay.

Daff Kanaar shipping moved more, charged less and any nation that interfered with them risked the attention of Daff

Kanaar. That made them about the safest shipping anyone could choose. Volkhydran ships suddenly found new opportunities in the islands past the shores of Dorkan, and with them new calamities.

"So you have no ship," Jerod said, and spat. His was cleaner.

"No," Forn said, "though if yer lookin' for some good men…"

Jerod let the smile cross his face. It felt good.

* * *

Slurn had never been to the Salt Wood before. He found it dry, filled with unfamiliar smells and unfamiliar prey, some of which he could barely hunt, and some of which he ran down almost too easily.

In the swamp, he could just lay in the muck and know everything he needed about the world around him. Here he had to use his eyes, his nose, his mind. Here things moved in straight lines along the ground, himself included, making his hunting style difficult.

The thing the others had called 'rabbit' still clung to the spaces between his teeth. He'd had to remove its bones—they were brittle and thick and could not be easily digested. He waited here, unwilling to enter the city they called 'Kor,' rank with the stink of Men and Uman. The Salt Wood pressed almost to the city walls, branches scraping her towers, beasts and beings both finding means in and out of the city other than through its battered gates.

The female had asked him to do this, in her way. He found the race of Men horrifying to look at—all angles and hair, smelling foul and tasting worse. It was odd for him to see this one and have the mating desire, but he could not help what he felt, and he felt this one would, if she were a Slee, be his, if she would have him.

As it was, there was no possible way for that to be, yet he felt the contentment with her that one feels with a mate. When she had been threatened, he had killed for her. She had rewarded him with a stroke of his snout that had sent his cold heart racing.

He'd crossed the Andaron plains, the Iron Mountains and the Eldadorian nation to find her, knowing her on site, and then followed her further until he'd seen her finally alone. Like a ripple through a bay, he knew her scent, her presence.

Now he waited in a dry, foul place, where he found water scarce and food vile, because she didn't dare walk beside him into a city filled with Men and Uman. Now he watched the sun set through slitted eyes, from beneath a pile of leaves and mud, and pined for that which, a year before, he might have eaten.

Contemplating the unreality of these thoughts, he felt on the scales of his belly the tell-tale tromp of creatures he had come to know all-too-well in the Slee Nation. He turned his snout to the north and waited, barely breathing, then to the south, doing the same.

The south—they came from the south, definitely. As stealthy as a whisper, he slithered southward to investigate.

He marveled at his own anger now—his instinct to protect her. If, in the days it would take him to know for sure, he discovered what he expected, then she would need protecting.

* * *

The candle's flicker in the dark could hypnotize—a red and yellow teardrop balanced on the point of a candle's wick. It stood between the two women, one of the race of Men, and the other an Aschire.

"The flame is the vortex," Nina told her. "The flame is the gate. It doesn't exist anywhere, and yet it produces light and heat in all of the places it doesn't touch."

Raven's knowledge of what flame actually was tended to interfere when Nina went on like this. Spiritually, maybe flame was a vortex and didn't really exist. Scientifically it was the result of a very predictable chemical reaction that—"

The flame expanded and swallowed half the wax on the candle. The flash had her seeing spots.

Nina looked exasperated. "You really need to not do that," she complained.

"I did that?" Raven asked. Her vision blurred, then refocused.

"Of course you did it," Nina said. "I didn't do it—you think it did that itself?"

They knelt alone in a hotel room that they both shared. The cramping in her knees told Raven they'd been doing it a long time.

"How—why?"

Nina sighed. "You are focused," she said.

"Yes."

"When you focus, your energy is right there," Nina said, indicating the flame. "It is a winged animal you have in the palm of your hand."

Raven considered that, imagined it—this flame bird that could sit in her hand.

The flame in the candle immediately took on the shape, exactly as she imagined it. She watched it, both knowing she was creating it and surprised it existed at all.

Nina shook her head. "Fine—yes, like that."

"I didn't mean to do that!" Raven protested.

"You did," Nina countered. "But you aren't controlling your thoughts and your emotions. You're focused on the flame, and now the flame is of you. If you don't want the flame any more, then release it."

She thought about that. The flaming bird was beautiful. It looked at her and tilted its head, flame dripping from the ends of its wings. It devoured the candle, and soon it would be scorching the table.

She forced her mind to release it, to let its energy dissipate. She thought about the heat being gone, the light being gone, the popping like a soap bubble.

Wrong allegory—the flame flew from the candle. Nina contained it with her own energy. The bubble that contained the energy she had released touched the tip of her nose.

"Not like that," Nina told her.

"No," Raven agreed. She shook her head, and the flame was gone. In a second they were in the dark.

"Like that."

* * *

“Is that it?” Jack asked her, pointing to the horizon.

Glynn nodded. She looked to her left, where the Swamp Devil ran doggedly on, its tongue lolling, its body wet with sweat. This Little Storm proved to be a remarkable animal, its endurance flowing like a river from it, pounding out the miles one after the other with no need for a rest. He own horse lagged alongside of it.

As amazing was the Swamp Devil running beside them. Without complaint or query the Black Adept, Zarshar, ran the same miles as the horses at the same speed.

“Zarshar,” she said, gently. “You have triumphed, Sirrah. That is the Lone Wood, as I know it.”

Zarshar’s red eyes looked out to the horizon, then back down. He didn’t respond and she couldn’t fault him. Each kept his or her own company until they achieved their goal and stood before the dense line of trees that abruptly marked the haven of the Druids.

Jack dismounted and, as ever, reached his hands up to her, to lower her to the ground. With his exertions, the Swamp Devil put his hands on his knees, panting, and just watched them.

As for the dog, it ranged tirelessly behind and before them. As often as they had outdistanced it, it had found them when they rested. Only rarely had Jack thought to pull it up beside him on Little Storm’s back, and then she had whined until he had let her back down.

Little Storm didn’t seem bothered by the animal or its weight. Of course, Jack had lost so much himself the horse might not have noticed the addition of the dog.

“I’ll rest before we enter,” Zarshar said simply. There was a haunch in a bag over his shoulder. He stood and pulled the strings open with his back to them before they could answer him.

“Is it safe to get wood from there?” Jack asked her, indicating the trees. “There looks like plenty of deadwood.”

Glynn shrugged. They needed to know how well the wood was protected. “Don’t touch anything living,” she said. “And don’t start your fire where the smoke will enter the forest.”

Jack nodded and walked directly into the wood. The dog stood at the forest’s edge, whining for the Man and wagging its tail. Glynn remained between her own mount’s and Little Storm’s head, her eyes pointed at Jack but her mind already focused on the wood, sniffing for anything that might be a welling of power.

She had been here before, decades ago, with her father. The Lone Wood existed as a place of raw energy, and so she had needed to see it as a part of her early training.

Jack's only problem seemed to be the plentiful scrub, soon encumbering his arms in a load that reached to his beard. He exited quickly, raising his nose to the wind to feel its direction on its face.

"Wind's blowing east," he said. "I'm going to go back north twenty yards."

She nodded, pressing into the Lone Wood with her mind, looking for some flicker, some indication of life, of magic.

Nothing.

"You hungry?" Jack asked, from behind her.

She nodded. "For anything but your bitter ale."

Jack chuckled. "What are you doing?" he asked.

She shook her head and turned to face him. He had piled his sticks into a pyramid, as she had seen him do. He would stuff the center with dry grass, and strike a spark from a dagger he'd picked up and a piece of flint.

She, of course, would use her magic—by why bother if the Man was content with this? He cooked for her, as well. She found that those times when he was occupied with something other than his endless string of questions were best suited to her need to meditate and to refresh her power.

"I am looking for our friends, the Druids," she said. She had found a patch of grass a little thicker than that around it, and thought she would be comfortable there. "I think we have caught them napping."

"Sending a Man to his death," she heard from behind her, "is not catching us napping. It is catching us forgiving."

She turned and there were two of them, dressed in white robes and brown over-cloaks. Both were Men, younger by the look of them, no more than two decades in age. They stepped out of the forest as if out of a fog, directly into the plain.

"Who are you to send others to defile this sacred place?"

Zarshar was up off of his haunches with a roar, his talons

and his teeth bared, taking on a fighting crouch. Comically, the dog took up a position beside him, her teeth bared and a growl low in her throat. Jack, a thick branch in his hand and the fire before him, stood and waited, looking to her for direction.

Glynn allowed her power to swell. Not flame, she thought immediately. They would have mastered flame. In fact, no elements at all—even calling down the lightning would be risky with Druids.

"I am Glynn Escaroth," she proclaimed, throwing her green hair back over her shoulders with a shake of her head. "I am Baroness of Britt, keeper of the southern walls of Outpost IX, Duchess Escaroth. I prithee, name thyselves, that I might know thee."

One looked to the other, then both back to her. Now she wondered if these were, in fact, Men. They were slight of build, and Men were burly. Their hair was brown in the tradition of Men, but their ears had no lobes.

Uman? No—they didn't *feel* like Uman.

She'd seen an Uman-Man hybrid among the Druids—she remembered him as Dilvesh, a member of the Daff Kanaar. Running into him wouldn't be good for them—but this risk had to be taken. These, however, could be his kind.

"We are of the Order," the one on the left said, meaning the Order of Druids. "We are guardians of the Lone Wood, and would know your business here."

Zarshar stood behind her now, still in his crouch, however still taller than she. The dog flanked him. A word from her and both would pounce. She had more to fear that one would do it anyway.

"We are summoned to the Lone Wood," Glynn replied, her left hand reaching out behind her to find the savage breast. She saw no point in lying—Druids were mighty. "If we may have the forbearance of the Druids, then we will be about our way quickly, we assure you."

"Druids?" Jack asked. He approached the three of them, looking at the two Men as if they were art on display."

"You are Druids? You—um—worship nature?"

Glynn shook her head—this wasn't going well and it

wasn't getting better. She held the Devil; Zarshar could be restrained against attack unless provoked. However Jack's questions couldn't be guarded against.

"We recognize the Trinity," one of them said, regarding the Man. "Weather, Earth and Water. We hold the power—"

Jack picked right then to do a curious thing: he stepped forward, and raised his right hand to his forehead, then to his belly, then to his left and right shoulders.

The stunned look on the faces of the Druids was unmistakable. They looked to each other, and then to him, and said a thing in a language she didn't understand.

He shook his head, and repeated something back to them, and they smiled.

Until Zarshar roared and fell to his knees, his hands to his ears, as if they'd gone aflame.

* * *

Slurn peeped out from the muck at the side of a stream he'd found. Although not as familiar to him as his home in the Slee Nation, he'd been able to make a decent meal for himself of frog and eel and, with a full belly, his outlook on life improved significantly.

That is, until he happened upon the source of his disturbance, two days hence. That rhythmic shake in the ground—the tread of thousands of feet, striking the face of Earth at the exact same time—brought back memories of home more realistically than any river could hope to.

The march of Wolf Soldiers—thousands of them—not from Galnesh Eldador or from Thera, but from Vrek, meant the Emperor's southern legions were on the march.

With the threat of Toorian renegades raiding up into much wealthier Eldador in the last few years, the Emperor had moved two thousand troops into Vrek under the command of Duke Ceberro. Men captured by the Slee had spoken of this, of the honor this meant for Ceberro, the only Duke alive to be given command of the Emperor's elite forces.

Since installing his Wolf Riders and their own Wolf Soldier troops on the plains of Andoron, Slee had become increasingly interested in Wolf Soldiers. Where Andarons had been somewhat easy to avoid and easier to prey upon, Wolf Soldiers had fortified their position at what his people called *His Jaws*, the meeting of the Great Mid and the Safe Rivers.

Slurn knew a lot about Wolf Soldiers—and one of those things was that, when they marched somewhere in this many numbers, it was to kill something. Once when there had been famine and the Slee had raided Wolf Rider cattle, fewer than this had marched on the Slee Nation and left a bloody wake behind them.

Slurn turned in the muck and tucked his arms and feet beneath him, clutching his spear. With his tail to drive him and his snout to steer, he slithered swiftly down the little stream, which he surmised would empty into the Forgotten Sea just south of Kor. From there it would be child's play to enter the city and find the woman he protected. She must know she lay in the path of Wolf Soldiers.

* * *

Xinto found it irritating that Xareff would simply snub him, as he had. In the back of his mind, he still blamed the air-headed Man, Karl, for bungling what would likely have been a smooth negotiation, at the first sign of trouble.

He sighed, as his legs carried him near as fast as a Man down one of the side streets in what could best described as a bad section of Kor. Considering what passed for a *good* section of this place, a bad section made for a place he was less likely to want to go.

However, if he couldn't have the Duke's help, then there were others who could be relied on.

He approached the green door as it has been described to him—an ill-fitted aperture to an ancient stone building. Xinto wondered who had originally put *such* care into these old stone buildings, these huge walls and towers, and what happened to them to let them fall to seed as these had.

The Man who stood at guard beside the door carried a battle axe Xinto doubted he could lift, much less wanted to be struck by, and so instead he flashed the secret sign of a Bounty

Hunter guildsman, his hand a flicker in and out of the sleeve of his robes.

The guard recognized him and stood aside, pulling the door open in its jamb. The will of Adriam himself had to keep the thing on its hinges, Xinto thought as he passed through it. He heard the huge Man wrestle it back closed behind him as he entered a gloomy room, very wide, the windows boarded over and light barely peeking in through the chinks.

"Those who die well," someone prompted him from within—a male voice, older, Sentalan Uman by its accent.

"Paid double," Xinto answered. He'd derived this challenge—it was one of his favorites.

"You always had a Mannish sense of humor about you," the other said, and stepped from the gloom to reveal himself. He wore the heavy leather cuirass and leggings of a Fighting Hunter—one who killed by challenge—rather than a Stealthy Hunter, like Xinto, who worked by guile.

He would lead here, Xinto knew. The Fighting Hunters did not number many, but were recognized simply as more fit to lead, for the nature of their business.

"Tagarag," Xinto recognized his old friend. His once-green hair had gone gray and left him with a widow's peak. His thickset arms and almost Man-sized hands combined with a jowly face to mark him for his farmer-heritage.

"Xinto of the Woods," Tagarag greeted him formally. "I was informed of your entry to the city, and disturbed you approached Xareff before coming to me."

"My apologies," Xinto bowed his head. "But these days I travel with air-headed Men, haughty Uman-Chi and even an Aschire, and I admit I am out of sorts."

"We saw Nina of the Aschire," Tagarag said, sweeping an arm backward to welcome Xinto into the lair. As his eyes adjusted, Xinto saw high-backed, comfortable chairs and newer caw-fee tables in the style of Eldador. For the squalor of Kor, this was a place where an outpost of the Bounty Hunter's Guild could be expected to do well.

Xinto entered and leapt into one of the chairs, settling himself. A young girl, of the race of Men, dressed in nothing more than a twist of yellow cloth around her loins, knelt down beside his chair and began to pull his boots off for him. He pointed his toes and allowed her. There was another, dressed similarly, here, and as his eyes became even more accustomed to the dark, he made out the shadowy figures of four more Men and two more Uman, all dressed in the robes of Stealthy Hunters.

A lot to be in the lair at the same time, Xinto told himself.

The girl had his boots off and began to work his feet expertly. Such girls traded their services to the Guild for their upkeep. Before the Emperor's economic changes, girls like these had been common as grass. Now they could find better employ, and some actually received a wage to perform their services at Guild Lairs.

"What news have you, then, Xinto of the Woods," Tagarag asked him, seating himself opposite the caw-fee table from Xinto, in another of the high-backed chairs. "I have never known you to enter a lair without some story to tell."

Xinto grinned within his beard. "Well," he said, "I could begin by saying the Eldadorians and the Trenboni have formed a secret alliance against the rest of Fovea, and even now the Emperor marches his troops to war."

Tagarag raised his eyebrows and frowned, nodding. "This is impressive news," he said. "I knew of the Emperor's trip to the Silent Isle to meet with Angron, but I had not guessed at that."

"Working for the Confluni Emperor," Xinto said, leaning back as the girl changed feet. "I eavesdropped on the Emperor himself, until I was captured by Karel of Stone and turned over to him."

"You didn't invoke Guild Sanctuary?" Tagarag pressed him.

Xinto felt his eyebrows drop. "No," he said, guardedly.

"Because you'd spied on a Guild member," Tagarag said.

The girl at his feet kept rubbing. The other Hunters stood as one; their weapons clear at their sides.

Many weeks had passed since that had happened, Xinto thought to himself, but surely not time enough for the Emperor to—

"One Ancenon Escaroth, formerly an Aurelias, approached

us on behalf of the Emperor," Tagarag informed him, interrupting his thoughts. "He brought us to light on that, and on your original report that the Emperor invoked the Guild."

Xinto's mouth dropped open. He'd been through the truth saying—no one had ever doubted Rancor Mordetur's guilt in having invoked the name of the Bounty Hunter's Guild on that fateful day, outside of Outpost IX.

"Apparently, only days before, Ancenon had, in your presence, called Rancor Mordetur a bounty hunter, and he had clearly demonstrated he had no idea what that title meant."

Xinto thought back to the dinner with the Prince and the Man who'd called himself Mordetur, then a vagabond in expensive armor.

Ancenon had sought his service—had Ancenon wanted a Bounty Hunter? Surely not!

"This is all to be properly inquired upon," Tagarag informed him, "at the Lair in Galnesh Eldador. There, three Masters will determine your fate—however, Xinto, were I you, I would make peace with Eveave in the meantime."

The other Hunters surrounded him—Xinto didn't kid himself into thinking he could fight his way clear. He might elude one of them, but with so many on his trail, in a place like Kor, he would be fortunate to make it to the nearest cross street.

Suddenly, it seemed very likely that this would be the end for Xinto of the Woods.

Chapter Twenty-Eight:

Sacred Places

If there was anything better than being the son of the Duke of Eldador under the most powerful tyrant in Fovean history, Hectaro wasn't aware of it.

The son of Hectar, whose health promised him *at least* another twenty summers, Hectaro drew on magnificent wealth and privilege, with the resources of a Duke and an Emperor at precious little cost to himself.

One of those costs approached him in the royal stables, even as he saddled *Bastard*, his own stallion. Little known to anyone outside of the royal family and his own, Bastard was a son of Blizzard, whose mother he had rubbed with wintergreen oil to make her more pleasing to the infamous brute.

Lupus had learned of it, of course. Mares don't seed themselves. Rather than the rage Hectaro had expected, he'd been labeled a 'clever little bastard,' and been allowed to keep the horse. Hence the horse's name.

One of those precious little costs for his many gifts for his life style, the Princess with her little brother in tow, found him musing as he heaved the saddle onto the grey, 17 hand stallion's back.

She'd watch him ride, she'd watch him fight, she'd watch

him eat dinner. If she could have arranged it, he felt sure she'd watch him as he slept, content to say nothing all the time.

She had a childish crush that entertained the whole palace and delighted his father no end. What better wife for him than the daughter of the Emperor, and a spell caster to boot? With such power, Lupus had carved himself out an empire.

"Whatcha doin'?" she asked him. Wonderful—she was in a speaking mood.

"Math problems," he kidded her.

"Nuh, uh," she told him, her nose in the air. She was as serious as her father when she wanted something.

"Nuh, uh," her brother repeated.

"You have me, my beauty," he told her, getting a giggle from the girl and a sigh from the boy. "I intend to ride while the spring weather holds."

"I want to ride," Lee informed him, her eyes already searching for the groom. Hectaro groaned internally. He wanted to *run*. He wanted the gasps of a crowd of peasants as his stallion ran impossibly fast past them all, then to bed the most comely among them.

"I've not seen the groom, your Highness," he tried to skirt out of the issue. "An it please you, I will keep to the wall until you can find him—"

"Pfft!" she made that noise her father made when he heard something that he considered stupid. "I can saddle my own horse. I'm an Andaron, you know."

"My apologies, your Highness," Hectaro said, the back of his hand sweeping the hay in the bow called 'the dying swan.' He knew from experience it was the Princess' favorite. "I am ever attendant—"

Then with the subtlety of a hurricane, the Empress burst into the stables, twenty Wolf Soldier guards behind her. She wore the voluminous skirts and tight bodice of court fashion, her hair decked with jewels and flowing out around her like a night sky. The look on her face spoke of fury.

When the Baroness of Britt had merely hidden one of her children, Shela Mordetur had vowed she would live an Uman-Chi's life covered in honey and buried to her neck in red ants. If she assumed impropriety with this daughter, Hectaro might dream of such a fate.

Shela had killed for her family before, and not cleanly.

"Hectaro, you're ready, good!" she informed him. "Help the children—I want fast horses."

"Your Imp—m'lady, but—what—" Hectaro was caught completely off his guard.

She stepped into the stall reserved for her personal gelding, an Andaron horse she'd had for over a decade. Without warning she pulled open the bodice, shucked the dress and had kicked off her shoes.

She turned and saw him standing with his mouth open, and the look of anger returned.

"You'll have weeks on the road to catch me naked, Hectaro," she informed him, "stop ogling me like an untouched virgin and *get those children's horses saddled*! I mean to ride to Uman City and I don't intend to waste this day."

"Uman City?" he wanted to move, but his feet were fastened to the dirt floor. "M'lady—my father—"

A saddle flew from the tack room, took a corner and struck him full in the chest. After it flew a bit and bridle, a blanket and a pair of boots. He found himself on his back in the straw and manure with a naked Empress looking down at him.

"Want the rest of the tack room?" she demanded.

"No, your Imperial—"

She turned, not needing to hear it. He stood as she stepped into some kind of one-piece leather thing that rode up her behind. The stretch marks were fine on her stomach and groin, but that unmatched beauty for which she'd been so famous was undiminished on her now.

Lee picked the saddle up from off of him. It looked almost as big as she was.

"When mama's like that, you best do what you're told," she commented.

"Salient advice, m'lady," he commented to her, almost as he would to any friend or ally when attacked.

"I can saddle my own horse if you can tighten up the cinch," she told him. "Want to get Vulpe's *Marauder* tacked up?

He rides cavalry."

Cavalry saddles rode high in the back and didn't have a horn. Hectaro rode the same himself. He had dreamed of riding with the Eldadorian Lancers some day, not as a career but to be able to point to a few military victories some day.

"Immediately, m'lady," he informed her. He looked into her eyes.

"She doesn't like men lookin' at her," Lee added.

"I'm sorry?"

Lee looked at her mother, pulling a tight leather skirt up onto her hips and shimmying to get into it. The Wolf Soldiers were all busy about getting mounts together and saddling. Two Uman were arguing whether a particular mare in heat was worth the risk of bringing.

Lee sighed. "She knows she's pretty, but papa's the only one who gets to look at her," she said, with the frankness of children. "If you go starin' at her like you just did, she'll probably just blind you so she doesn't have to deal with it."

Hectaro swallowed.

"She did it before to one of Groff's sons," she added, turning. "I don't think he got most of it back."

Lee took off for her own horse's stall and her own horse, *Singer*. Her mother was already dressed out in her black, leather Andaron raider's outfit, complete with thigh-high boots and leather overcoat. Hectaro tightened his own cinch and took Vulpe to the tack room to pick out his saddle.

He couldn't help thinking, *This was turning out to be such a good day!*

* * *

The Lone Wood reminded Jack of what some people called an old-growth forest. Ancient trees bigger around than he was tall, under a canopy that blotted out the sun, surrounded them and towered over them. The two Druids, Samhail and Haman, slipped between the trunks like ghosts, their white robes swishing between and over bushes, their feet hushed even in the crunching of the leaves.

Jack followed behind them leading Little Storm, the dog roving at his side. Glynn followed after him with her mount. Her ambiguous eyes didn't disguise the scowl on her face. The Devil trudged along last, crashing through the undergrowth.

Jack replayed the encounter with these Druids over and over in his mind. On a whim, he'd crossed himself, as he'd learned in catechism, and said the words he'd heard so many times from the priest at his first church.

"*En nomine patri, et fili, et spiritu sancti,*" he'd said. "In the name of the father, the son, and the holy spirit."

He'd seen the look on their faces, and he'd seen the words bring the Devil to his knees. His first thought had been that he'd violated their agreement—Zarshar would attack them now. Then he'd remembered the 'intentional' clause that he'd insisted on.

Thank god—he barely knew which one now—for an education in sales contracts.

He'd already asked once where they were going, and how long it would take to get there, and been ignored. The Druids had made clear only that they would make nothing clear.

The dog stayed at his side, and that surprised him. She usually ranged far ahead and then checked back with them. She loped along with her ears forward now, her eyes alert and her nostrils flaring.

He'd thought that finding a people called 'druids' made for an awfully big coincidence. For them to speak Latin, however, exceeded any chance of that. Either these people came from his Earth themselves, or they were descended from others who did, and maintained some of their traditions. Either way, they retained a language the Druids had in fact rejected, unto death.

That told Jack whatever game was being played here, it had been played before. He mulled this as he saw the forest open up before him, and then stepped out into a tiny glen.

It couldn't have been more than fifty feet across, one hundred feet long, centered around a shallow pool with lily pads at one end and a moss-covered boulder at the other. The dog immediately ran forward to lap water at its bank, while the Druids turned and stood between the rest of them and the pond.

"This is a resting place," Samhail told them. "Zarshar will remember it, I'm sure."

The Swamp Devil took a step forward. With one massive

claw he pulled his cuirass from his body and tossed it into a bush. "I'd wondered if you remembered me," he said, simply.

Haman smiled. He was of the race of Men, long brown hair and beard, brown eyes, deeply tanned skin. Jack had already noted something off about him—something in the eyes. They had that 'look' Uman had—that indefinable feral wildness, as if the bonds of civility only held them loosely.

"You are a legend," he said. "Neither of us greeted you, but all of us know of the creature that walked right into the Lone Wood."

"Creature?" Zarshar raised an eyebrow.

"I am certain they meant no offense, Sirrah," Glynn intervened. The Druids smirked and looked to each other, then back at Glynn. Jack knew that condescending expression and wondered if the Uman-Chi recognized it as well.

"As before," Samhail continued, "we'll want you to wait here. We must confer with the rest of the Brothers, and then return."

Jack frowned pensively and nodded, Glynn as well. The Swamp Devil simply leapt into the pond, one long, black streak slipping into the still water with barely a splash, then disappearing beneath it to emerge moments later at the far end by the boulder.

Jack pulled the headstall from Little Storm's head, freeing the bit from his mouth. Glynn dropped her own horse's reins on the ground, clearly expecting Jack to pull the tack from her mount, as well.

Jack shook his head and smiled to himself.

"Something amuses you, Sirrah?" she asked him.

"Hmmm?" he asked, pretending not to understand. "What? Oh – of course not."

"You can't expect *me* to put away its saddle," she challenged him.

"Of course not," Jack said. "You're a woman, after all."

Her eyebrows dropped over her ambiguous eyes. "If that is how you must justify your role, Sirrah," she shot back.

"My role?"

"Oh, just take the saddle off her horse," Zarshar intervened, leaping up onto the boulder at the far end of the pond.

He turned and scrunched his talons into its mossy surface. "I don't want to listen to you two arguing all day, and you already gave me a headache."

Jack felt his brows knit. "I wanted to apologize for that," he began, pulling the saddle from Little Storm's back. The dog had already left the side of the pond and had begun turning a circle in a puddle of sunshine next to the tree line. "I didn't mean to—"

"You'd already be dead if I thought otherwise," Zarshar informed him. "I'd never heard those words before, but they went through me like a knife."

"I would know how you knew them, Sirrah," Glynn pressed him. She had already reached behind her, to pull the laces in the back of her dress free. It didn't take long for Jack to realize she meant to take it off and jump in the pond, and that she meant for him to follow her.

Turning his back on her, his cheeks warming beneath his beard, suddenly it wasn't that big a deal to untack the horses.

* * *

Raven sat on the corner of her wood-framed bed, in a shabby hotel that represented the best Kor had to offer. Jerod—actually Karl—sat to her left, Nina to her right, a crowd of Volkhydran Men Karl had come across in the port at their feet on the floor and, in the center of them, Slurn.

None of them spoke the language of the Slee, other than Xinto, and Xinto had vanished without a trace.

"There is no spell," Nina explained to them, "that can turn one language into another. There is no element for language—language just is."

Raven had at first believed magic was *anything*, meaning that if she had magic and she wanted a glass of soda, then magic provided her with a soda out of the air.

She'd learned otherwise. Like the chemistry she'd studied in college, magic obeyed rules, contained formulae and used resources. She didn't summon fire from nothing—it came from an elemental plane of fire, and to have it from there, she had to will it.

She didn't know how to will a language out of or into something and, if Nina knew, she certainly wasn't going to explain it.

However she and Bill knew the Emperor had some magic that let him speak any language here, and that meant to her that it *had* to be possible.

Slurn didn't hide his agitation—he practically danced for them, his tail whipping back and forth, he himself pacing the room as if in a cage. He'd seen something that scared the hell out of him, and he couldn't communicate it.

"Uhl," he told then. "Uhl sochahs."

That sounded suspiciously familiar.

"A bad time for the bit to disappear," Karl grumbled, meaning Xinto. "I never trusted their kind."

Raven caught Nina's eyes regarding Karl, a smile on her lips before she made her face more plain.

She'd seen the Empress create an image on a wall, and she'd seen the Emperor and Jack appear on it, as if on TV. If images could be caught out of the air, then why not thoughts? Thoughts were real things, after all—alpha waves, electronic signals.

She focused her mind on an interface, a two dimensional plane, which could trap thoughts that touched it. If she couldn't understand Slurn, perhaps she could provide him with a canvas for his mental pictures.

"Think about what you saw, Slurn," she told him. "Think about the things you want to show us."

At first there was nothing, then wavy images. Raven concentrated harder, feeling as if there were a muscle in her mind she had never exercised. Slurn, realizing what she was doing, applied himself as well, reining in his imagination, forcing himself to relive the trip from Kor, through the mud, down small streams and then eventually, farther south, to what Raven expected he had seen.

She saw columns of Wolf Soldiers, marching north, a man in a white robe, on a roan charger, at their center.

"War's beard," one of the Volkhydrans swore. "Can you imagine the numbers?"

"It's the Emperor's whole southern guard," said another. He turned his face to Karl.

"He's moving on Kor," he said, "and we're right in his path."

Raven let the image slip out of the air, popping like a soap bubble. She laid a hand on Karl's shoulder without thinking of it, needing his support to keep her from falling off the side of the bed.

"Draining?" Nina asked her.

Raven met Nina's gray eyes and saw no sympathy there, more predatory hunger instead. Nina may have given her the basic knowledge to do what she did, but that hadn't made them friends.

"I'm alright," she said.

"We need Xinto," Karl said, and turned his attention to Slurn. "Can you find him by his scent?"

Slurn growled low in his throat, a frightening, saurian rumble. Clearly he could find them by their scent—he'd gotten himself here, after all. Raven knew he preferred to be at her side, guarding her, and he could in fact care less about the Scitai.

"It's important, Slurn," she said, softening her voice, forcing herself to stand, even though her legs wanted to fold underneath her. She stroked the scaly jaw, looked into the slitted eyes.

"We need him," she said. "Can you do it?"

He became still the moment she touched him, the agitated tail resting on the floor, the roar becoming almost a purr. Then like a flash he was out their third story window, into a tree that grew alongside the hotel.

"Gaah," one of the Volkhydrans said, "that thing makes me skin—"

"That *thing*," Raven said, turning on him, "is a friend of mine Volkhydran, and I owe my life to him. You'll respect him, or you'll get a taste of my power."

The Man swallowed and nodded. Nina had informed her of how the common people feared those with any magic talent, and she'd do well to cultivate it.

Another weapon to add to her arsenal.

* * *

And here you are, Xinto thought to himself. *Back in a cage.*

In Galnesh Eldador they'd put him in a cell, eight strides from one end to the other, with a cot and a bucket. The lock to the cell had been magicked to prevent picking it. They'd taken his cloak away.

Typical of the race of Men to put a spell on the bars but not the stone they were set in. It hadn't taken him more than a day to find a loose stone in the wall above the gate's hinge, to remove it and then to jar the gate just enough for him to squeeze out. In the end he spent more time finding his cloak than escaping.

Here they knew better. They put him in a cage, bars all around him, and every one of them enchanted against him.

But they'd caged him with his cloak still on him. Getting right to it, the Eldadorians had been smarter.

Xinto extracted a bundle of thin metal strands from one of his inner pockets, and set about braiding them into a tiny metal rope. He had enough to do a rope three stories tall, but he only needed this one to go to a window on the far side of the room.

He was alone in a dark, dusty room, three Man-heights by four. He'd heard them lock the door behind them. He hadn't heard a sentry in the hours that he'd been here. He didn't hear anyone talking.

He knelt on all fours in the cage. Nimble fingers braided the metal quickly, the product of his effort curling into a pile beneath him. If anyone entered, he could simply lay down and pretend to sleep, covering the evidence.

That didn't happen, and soon he had a coil that could reach to the base of the window.

The sun wouldn't be back up for hours, but he had other work to do. He spent long minutes twining metal threads around the gate to the cage, in and out of the locking mechanism and around the hinges.

With less than three hours until sunrise, he allowed himself a catnap. Nothing he could do now if he were discovered—he had to have this ready for the morning, and he knew he needed sleep.

The first rosy shards of the false dawn roused him, stiff and groggy in his cage. He'd kinked his rope where he'd lain on it and had to straighten it, then began the arduous task of snaking it straight out toward the window. It had been shuttered, of course, but there were chinks in the shutters that would provide him with the sunlight he needed.

Xinto had not been born with the gift of spell casting, however he'd been given an analytical mind instead, and with that he worked his own magic, including the ability to see how things worked, and how things interacted.

This skill made him an excellent ambassador, and over time had enabled him to learn how certain spells could be discharged, especially those used for warding.

The sunlight from the new dawn touched the metal rope, braided to be stiff enough to run from the cage to the window without touching the floor.

The sun's energy traveled up the rope and into the wire mesh around the gate and the lock. Its energy mixed directly with that of the spell that warded the cage and, with a blue flash, destroyed it.

Normal light wouldn't have done it, of course. It would make no sense that magic should require darkness. However the pattern of the wires on the bars, made to resemble a spider's web, got the spell energy flowing and drained it.

Xinto had seen this many years ago, when he'd watched a caster create such a spell. He'd spent long weeks figuring out the right method and the pattern, but it had saved him before and had just done so again.

Quick as a wink he had his rope tucked back inside of his robe and removed a steel hook from inside a pocket. The lock popped for him in just a few second, and then the gate swung open.

Free again! Xinto applauded his own intelligence and resolve. He'd slip out of the city, find Slurn, and then send him in for the rest of them, much more careful next time of his former guild brothers.

"Well done," a woman's voice purred.

He hadn't seen her enter, nor heard a door open. He knew

she couldn't have been there all night. He'd have heard her breath, felt the weight of her presence.

Xinto turned on his heel to see an old friend, whose acquaintance he had not made for over a decade. He might be, in fact, one of the few people who even guessed she was alive.

He bowed low, in the tradition of the dying swan, a private joke between them. She grinned, the green eyes hawk-like under a mop of untamed red and gray hair. She stepped to her left, taking an open stance, the bandolier of knives across her ample breasts showing one missing: the one in her hand.

Dressed in the usual tight-fitting black leather, she waited for him to make his move.

Xinto knew better than to pick a fight with Genna, the only Bounty Hunter alive ever to have crossed in and out of Conflu with a party of raiders, and to beat the Guard at their own game.

* * *

Glynn Escaroth sat naked in the tepid pool, the sun warm on her face and bare breasts, the Man they called 'Jack' sitting next to her with his hands in his lap, looking more than anything like a child caught raiding the larder.

The Swamp Devil perched like a living gargoyle on the boulder at the far end of the pool, clawing the tangles from this long mane. Their horses nibbled at the grass along the pond's end, the dog lay on her back, basking with the sun on her teats.

They'd sat here for over an hour, speaking very little. Glynn felt relatively confident Jack had peed in the pool beside her.

"How long will they make us wait?" Jack asked them.

"I stayed here for four days before they saw me," Zarshar said, not looking up from his hair. "I brought a haunch with me, though. I don't expect we should hunt here. If we're still here past tomorrow, you'll have to choose one of your horses or that dog."

Jack seemed appalled. Typical of the race of Men to form such strong attachments to the beasts around them. Well, she needed her horse and had no fondness for the dog.

In fact, she felt sure the Swamp Devil had only made the statement to torment the Man.

Jack, of course, sidestepped the issue. "Well, I doubt they'll just starve us," he said. "Be just as happy if they let me put my pants back on before they talk to me, anyway."

Glynn sighed. She'd bared her body in front of Uman-Chi when weakened after her song. The Swamp Devil saw her as nothing more than a food source, and she could barely differentiate between the dog and the Man on an intellectual level, making this seem less personal.

At the same time there was no point in making the Man uncomfortable, so without preamble she rose up out of the water and crossed to her saddlebags, withdrew a cotton slip and donned it. When she turned back around, Jack was out of the water and hopping up and down next to saddle, yanking his pants up to his waist.

At least then she understood what the young girl saw in him.

"You two make less sense to me than the dog," Zarshar said.

"That's because she's another fanged animal," Jack countered.

Glynn opened her mouth to respond when she saw the face of an Uman in the brush past her horse.

His skin looked pale, as if he rarely saw the sun. Her eyes adjusted to the shade and she picked out more faces, more eyes, those of Uman and Men, one Toorian and then a second. All of them wore white robes. She turned to her left, to her right, seeing no less than fifty Druids.

She had no idea that there existed so many. She searched for Zarshar and found his eyes.

"I smelled them before you put your clothes on," he said. "The dog had them before me."

The dog rolled back over onto her stomach, her ears up, her tail thumping the ground. Much as she acted as some kind of guard, she saw no threat from these.

"You are well met, Sirrah," she told the closest one, "and we are well convenienced in your grotto."

He smiled and stepped from the trees. True to her counting, forty-nine others did the same.

She looked for one among them whose reputation she knew, a member of the Daff Kanaar called, "Dilvesh," and did not see him.

Fifty-one druids then, no less.

"Your relation with the Emperor has you well benefited," she noted.

"An it be so," a young woman told her, of the race of Men, as tall as Glynn with glistening blonde hair down past her elbows and eyes blue as the sea.

"We are not met," Glynn said, extending her hand, knuckles up in the manner of the gracious guest.

Not because she expected the other to recognize the Uman-Chi form, but in fact to ensure she did not. The first rule of any new encounter was to establish the other's ignorance.

Her surprise was immeasurable, then, when this woman addressed her dainty fingertips with her own, in the manner of the welcoming host, in the feminine, and put her left foot behind her right heel, and curtsied.

"I am Vedeen, of the Lone Wood," she said, "first sister among the brethren, and keeper of the One."

"The One?" Glynn asked her. *One who fights as does the sun?* she thought. *Was this it, finally?*

She spread her arms wide and rolled her wrists in the manner of the presenter, in the feminine. "The One," she said. "This place, of course. The Lone Wood—One among the rest."

Glynn sighed. She would have been surprised to find it that easy.

"We would ask a boon of you, however, in return for your safe passage."

Glynn lowered her face and spread her hands, palms up, in the tradition of the humble supplicant. "If I can be at your service," she said.

Vedeen smiled. "Then I would hear your song."

Chapter Twenty-Nine:

Who Fights, as does the Sun

Slurn crept up out of the sewer into a crumbled courtyard surrounded by a battered wall. To his left he saw a window that someone had boarded over. On the other side of that window, he would find Xinto of the Woods. The scent wafted unmistakable from within.

She whom he yearned for, this child of Men, called Raven, bid him come here, bid him find this thing, this Scitai, who spoke his language.

Always, it surprised him that he loved her so much. Even now his cold heart warmed for her, his mind held in it to one side the image of her face, the feel of her fingers on the side of his jaw.

So he'd hunted through the night, followed false trails, even found another Scitai hidden in a hovel, a vile creature reeking of the alcohol Men and Uman drank. On more than one occasion he'd been seen by Uman, and once followed down into the sewer. He'd had to kill then, not that it bothered him.

He'd killed Uman before.

He slithered from the sewer grate he'd dislodged to the puddle of shadow at the base of the ruined wall. The ground felt dry against his scales, dead grass and leaves littering parched soil. He followed the wall to the stone base of the building, and that to the space under the window, ever watchful for some sentry or passerby who might see him. Sure he'd gone unnoticed, he raised saurian eyes to the base of the window, peeping inside through a crack.

* * *

Genna put her weight on the balls of her feet. She'd watched Xinto for hours, first wondering what he was doing, later marveling at his ingenuity. While he'd slept, she'd even gone so far as to obtain her own bundle of wire strands, storing them in the heel of her left boot. She could think of a million uses for them.

Xinto had expected someone to watch from a crack in the plaster or a peephole. He hadn't seen the mirror in the upper corner of the room by the door, or the groove in the wall beside it. Genna had watched him from three rooms away, through a system of mirrors, each larger than the one before.

Bounty Hunters, after all, had their ways.

Xinto had been brought here with a sword. He didn't have that now. As a trained Bounty Hunter, he could kill with his hands if he had to, however he wouldn't likely match a ready Master like her with a weapon drawn.

"You started all of this, you know," she told him.

She watched the startled reaction. She knew Xinto of the Woods. He never blamed himself for anything.

"I did?" he challenged her, the quizzical expression under his beard almost comical. "I suppose I should have left myself to the Bitch of Eldador—"

She shook her head, her long red hair brushing the naked skin on her back. "I don't mean this stupidity—this is nothing. This is a pretense to bring you home. Do you really think we care who spies on the Emperor?"

"Then what?" he began.

She wanted to *scream*. How could anyone be so stupid? Xinto was supposed to be one of their cleverest operatives, yet look at all of the trouble he had caused.

"He was a vagabond," she told him. "He was no one. So

you put him in the possession of an Uman-Chi Prince, and you set him on the road to be an Emperor."

"Mordetur?" Xinto demanded. His eyes opened up wide as saucers. "You think that I—"

"Did you, or did you not, take pay from Ancenon Aurelias to assemble that team he took into Conflu?" she pressed him.

He sighed. "Of course—I put you with them, didn't I?"

"And did you, or did you not, send him Lupus?"

Xinto's shoulders slumped. "You couldn't have expected me to know—"

"*Aiiiiii!*" this time she couldn't contain her frustration. "You spent a month with him," she said. "A month! I was with him less than a week before I knew there was more to him than a suit of armor and a sharp sword."

"Then why didn't you put him down?" Xinto countered, daring to take a step forward. She took a tighter grip on her dagger and he stopped, seeing the warning in her eyes, no doubt. "You had him—from what I've gathered, you had him naked and unarmed. You could have taken him at any time—"

"By then I needed him to stay alive," she hissed. "By then I'd fallen for his charm, his wit, his evil way. By the time I could have taken him, I was struck down and, after that, he had that *bitch* watching over him, and *no one* could get to him."

"And then you left," Xinto said, taking another step. He either had a weapon concealed or he thought himself fast enough to get to hers. "At the Battle of Tamaran Glen, you took to the trees, I assume, and you got out of range of his woman."

Genna remembered that day. The battle against an enemy that no one could have beaten, her elation when Shela fell, her shock and horror when Lupus charged out of the woods on his stallion, directly into the mass of the Confluni army, to kill himself without her.

That day she knew, no matter what else happened, he would never be hers. On that day, she realized how much love a man could have for a woman, and she herself would never experience it. Not from the only man she'd ever wanted it from.

She'd leapt up into a tree and traveled for daheeri through the canopy, leaving her allies to their fate. When finally she set foot on solid earth, she'd come to the gates of Tamara, where she took refuge in the Bounty Hunters' lair.

A month later, she learned he had survived, with *her*, and they'd had a daughter and named her Lee.

She'd stayed in Conflu from that time until this, because she couldn't bear to see him. It wasn't until she'd heard of Xinto's actions that she'd decided it was safe to emerge. Of all of the Bounty Hunters on Fovea, and of almost all of the people, Genna counted herself among the very, very few who knew what Xinto's actual crimes were.

"Yes," she said, finally. "I left. I couldn't get near him, and I knew what you'd unleashed.

"If you'd have stayed in your cage," she added, "you'd have lived, Xinto. You'd have been returned to Trenbon, and you'd have been tried and found innocent. We'd have decided you didn't know the nature of your assignment until you walked in on it. You were spying on the Uman-Chi, and no one would have guessed the Emperor could be there.

"But now that you've escaped, and so cleverly, you are mine, Xinto of the Woods."

She let herself lick her lips, watching his hips, his hands. He planned to reach for something inside of his cloak—being a Scitai, it would be some sort of cross-pistol or blow gun, no doubt. She'd have him before he could finish it. She just needed to be able to say honestly that he'd attacked her first.

"You know what we do to escaped prisoners."

Xinto planted his foot—he would attack now. She could tell any Wizard on the planet that what was about to happen had been done in self-defense.

She pulled back her arm, and the room's one window exploded in a mass of wood and splinters as some giant lizard leapt for her, fangs and claws bared.

* * *

Zarshar growled low in his throat. When he'd come here before, he'd seen, at most, five of these druids, and always smelled them coming.

This two-score and more had approached him from all four

directions of the wind and left him oblivious, until in fact the dog detected them and tipped him off.

He'd come to appreciate the dog. When he had stood to fight, she'd backed him, fang for fang and claw for claw. He'd told no one, but she had laid her great head across his lap one night, and somehow managed to touch him with those soulful eyes.

This time, when he'd missed the signal in the trees, she'd picked it up for him, and let him know without the pathetic lecturing he'd come to expect from the Uman-Chi.

Now the Druids wanted to hear their song, and it seemed to the Swamp Devil they wouldn't have asked if they didn't suspect already what it told of.

"It is my pleasure to sing it to you," Glynn informed Vedeen, "however it is my experience that—"

She nodded, interrupting the Uman-Chi. They hated nothing more. Zarshar did it as often as he could for that reason.

"If you would be so kind," the Druid said.

"Sing the damn song," Zarshar told her. "If they can't hear it, it does no harm. If they can, then we can leave this place."

Glynn frowned, then took her left hand in her right, before her belly, straightened her back, and sang the song from beginning to end.

The words rang in his ears. He'd already figured out what they would find—a dhar k'ten, one of the *old ones*, the fire-breathing, saurian menace from the Steel Mountains or the Great Northern Mountain Range. Wings, scales, fangs, terror—a close ally to the Swamp Devils, what Men called 'dragons.'

The Druids looked into each other's eyes. Zarshar smelled the magic flow between them. The dog's tail beat the ground, her ears up, her nose pointing first at him, then at the Man, Jack, then back at him.

Jack's eyes moved from Druid to Druid. Grudgingly, Zarshar admitted that, if any of them could hear the words, Jack would likely know it. The Man had a mind like a dagger, carving bits from his foes like an expert swordsman.

Glynn finished her song. Zarshar saw her aura waver. This effort drained her. If she were an enemy, he would attack her now.

He'd already reconciled himself that she was not. He wanted the Emperor dead and, on his own, he would have led two hundred Swamp Devils in an all-out assault against him on his next campaign, catching him unawares and unready.

He would have failed. The Emperor had proven many times that overwhelming force wasn't the way to take him.

"We are impressed," Vedeen told them. "For what few of us can hear the words, even we cannot pass them between us. It seems as if the All-Mother would keep her secret."

The Druids had discovered in moments more than the rest of them had in weeks. What this meant wasn't lost on the Swamp Devil.

"Then you can hear the words," Zarshar accused her.

She nodded. "Succinctly," she said. "A few of the rest, the melody and, of some of them, the intent.

"You have a dilemma, my friends," she said, sighing. "You must have this one who fights as does the sun, but yet you seek the answer before you fully understand the question."

Glynn frowned. "I am no one to deny the wisdom of the Druids," she said, and Zarshar recognized the condescension dripping from her words, "however I assure you, at the very least, all questions are understood."

A chuckle arose from the Druids. The dog's tail kept thumping.

Three long steps brought Vedeen to the dog's side. She knelt by the beast's shoulder and stroked the giant head. It laid its ears back and stilled its tail, the green eyes closing contentedly.

Vedeen turned her attention back to the Uman-Chi. Jack had stepped up beside her. Zarshar kept his place on the rock—if he needed to move, he'd rather do it from here.

"So you have your one who fights as does the sun," she said, squelching Zarshar's theory. "And now that you have her, what will you do with her?"

"Are you aware—" Glynn began.

"You face the Emperor," Vedeen told her.

"The One, who walks upon the Earth
The One, who is of War.

The One, who others wait upon
To fight forever more."

"In truth," she said, standing, "it could be no other, and none have been a better friend to our kind."

"Would you turn on him?" Zarshar asked her. All eyes turned to him. "Would you betray him, for a song you heard one time?"

Vedeen smiled to herself. "It seems an odd thing, put that way," she said. Another Druid opened up his mouth, but she raised her hand and stilled him.

"If you would have me as a part of your entourage," she said, "then I would travel with you. This will raise no enmity between Galnesh Eldador and us. The Emperor cannot think to tell us whom to travel with."

"And when it comes time to fight him?" Zarshar pressed her.

She smiled. The dog stood up next to her, pressed its body to her leg. The Druids, if nothing else, were dear to animals, and they to them.

"When that time comes," she asked, "then you should ask yourself, how does one fight, as does the sun?"

Karl Henekhson padded down a side street, as quietly as his hard-soled shoes could take him; his heels rapped the cobblestones deafeningly in his own ears, although in fact he knew at the same time he made less noise than a slippered priest in church.

The lizard had been gone too long. The sun had dropped and risen with no sign of him, although that came as no surprise.

The thing was barely more than an animal, and when did an animal ever care what time of day it was?

It hadn't taken much to track it. He'd found its marks all over the gutters and through what refuse piles he came across. Either the thing had no ability to smell the stink of such places, it didn't mind the reek or it actually liked it. Having come from a swamp, he might even consider it an improvement.

The thing had taken to a sewer near here—Karl assumed it

needed to get past a ruined wall that it didn't feel comfortable climbing over. Then he turned a corner and found himself not ten feet from a huge man with a battleaxe, standing in front of a battered green door.

No need to draw Karl a picture. Either Xinto had alienated the people who employed this man, or he'd joined them and done something to alienate them. Either way, they'd taken him, and odds were they'd made a carpet of the Slee by now.

So much for songs about prophecies.

"You don't need to be here," the Man told him; a Dorkan by the look of him, a big one, too. Most of them were dumber than the oxen that pulled the plows before them, but once in a while you got the cunning of a bull from one, and Karl saw that now.

"I'm here for Xinto of the Woods," Karl informed him.

The Man grinned. "I'd forget that name, were I you," he said, and turned the axe's wooden shaft in his weathered hands.

The axe would be too big to meet with his sword. When the man swung it, it would crush everything in its path. Many Volkhydrans preferred axes for that reason. Karl could fight that.

He whipped out his sword. The Man lunged with the axe, taking an over-hand swing, aiming straight for Karl's torso.

Three shafts protruded from the Dorkan's chest. His mouth opened wide, revealing rotten teeth. Karl recognized the shock in his eyes, the look of a warrior whose mind was telling him the body was already dead.

The weight of the axe dragged his whole body prone to the ground, snapping the shafts. He heard Nina swear behind him. She'd probably wanted those back.

His Volkhydrans melted out of the shadows behind him. A younger man picked up the axe and tried to heft it, but an older, larger man took it from him.

"Here, now," he complained.

The older man backhanded him casually. He parked the weapon on his shoulder as if War had grown it there.

"He *would* fall on his face," Nina complained. She kicked the huge man over just enough to retrieve the feathered ends of her shafts. With those she could fletch new ones, although as far as he knew, they only used wood from their forest.

More likely she didn't want her handiwork recognized. They didn't know yet whose home this was.

"I sense a whole crowd on the other side of that door," Raven told him. She'd put on her leathers and stood at his shoulder, her feet apart, the dagger still in her boot.

"Stop that," Nina warned her without looking up. "They'll sense *you*, and do worse if there's a caster among them."

"And there is," they heard from behind them. Karl turned to see none other than Xinto of the Woods, perched on the top of the ruined wall. Typical that he would show up right *after* the perfect moment.

"So much for saving you," Karl complained. He'd rather not have killed this man, and he already had a sneaking suspicion what sort of place this was.

"Slurn already did that," he told them, leaping deftly from the wall onto the street with them. "His timing couldn't have been better, either. Did you know that there's two Millennium of Wolf Soldiers bound for here from Vrek?"

Raven nodded. "He told us," she said, drawing a cocked eyebrow from Xinto. "Is he alright now—"

Xinto nodded. "He'll pop up in a moment," he said. "He took to the sewer to get out of there—like as he wants to finish something he killed. I saw no reason to watch that."

"Good sirs," Forn addressed them. The old Volkhydran seemed nervous. "As far as I know, where one guard's dead, there's twenty more to be upset about it—"

"Ha!" Xinto barked a laugh. "More like a hundred," he said, "and not guards, but Bounty Hunters, so why don't I get you thin-brained Men right out of this city before we have to decide whether to fight Wolf Soldiers, Bounty Hunters or both?"

Forn didn't miss the insult. "As like as we could, short sir, were we not so preoccupied with your pious arse," he countered.

"Enough," Raven told them. Fifteen Volkhydran Men, and as one they'd all fallen in love with her. Karl shook his head. Sailors did nothing but fight, drink and fall in love, or so his father had informed him, on more than one occasion.

"I think we've worn out our welcome in Kor," she said. Karl had never heard that expression before. "If the city's going to be overrun, then the best thing we can do is not be in it when that happens, so either we have to get ourselves a ship, or get out of the gates and head north for—what is it, Andurin?"

"Andurin would be the next city north," Xinto told her. "But stick your pretty nose in there and the Emperor's men will grab you by it and lead you to a waiting cell."

"If not me, then you," she countered. "But I didn't say we'd go in, just wait there for Glynn to show up, hopefully with the one who fights as does the sun."

Xinto opened his mouth, but Nina spoke next. "I can get you into Andurin," she offered. "I know Alekennen, who was Glennen's daughter—"

Raven spun on her heel and drove her fist into the Aschire's jaw. She'd been spending time both with the sailors and with Karl himself, learning how to defend herself with her hands, if her newfound magic ever gave out.

A woman of the race of Men could weigh as much as twice what the heaviest Aschire woman could rise too. Nina had been raised with Men, and had grown larger even than most Aschire males, but still was a fraction of Raven's stocky build.

Her feet left the ground as she flipped over backwards to the cobblestones. If the blow to the jaw hadn't silenced her, the rap she took to the back of her head would have.

A Volkhydran knelt at her side and put three fingers to her neck. Karl saw the pert breasts rise and fall and had his answer before the Volkhydran could deliver it.

"She lives," he said.

"Leave her," Raven commanded him. "The Bounty Hunters will want someone to blame for this, let 'em have the Emperor's nanny."

Karl and Xinto both grinned. The Bounty Hunters would have no trouble believing the Emperor had sent his troops in after Xinto, if it was Xinto he wanted. The invasion would make it seem only more likely.

"So to Andurin?" Forn asked.

Karl shook his head. "She said that for Nina's benefit," he said. Raven grinned up at him, her dark eyes sparkling mischievously. "We head southwest, for the Lone Wood."

Xinto barked a laugh and took off down the alleyway.

Chapter Thirty:

Back in Black

Back on the Eldadorian plain, the Lone Wood behind them and Little Storm beneath him, Jack ran the previous day's events over and over in his mind.

No, he kept concluding. *No way. Not buying it.*

They'd tromped up to the Lone Wood, were welcomed with open arms, here comes this Vedeen who hears their song, and then leaps on a horse and joins them—the one who fights as does the sun.

No, Jack told himself. *No way.*

Why did they need Zarshar for that? Why did they need him? Raven, Jerod, Jahunga—any of them could have come and had the same results. These Druids were supposed to be so xenophobic, and here they were all smiles and help?

Vedeen rode beside him now, long blonde hair and long white robes flowing out behind her, riding a roan stallion, reminiscent of a thoroughbred in height and power, pacing Little Storm, her eyes before her and that mention of a smile as ever on her lips.

She'd asked, "How does the sun fight?" Initially Jack had believed that meant with fire and overwhelming power.

But the sun knows that its planets are going to keep

spinning, and that they sure as hell aren't going anywhere without it. The sun hurtles through space and drags its system along with it—it is more concerned about what's before it than about what's around it.

Vedeen wouldn't even commit herself to being on their side. She'd said she was going along. That could be prophetic.

Jack watched their dog cross the plains before them, from his left to his right. She didn't usually get ahead of them but had been energized since leaving the Lone Wood. Behind him Glynn rode her own horse side-saddle, her thoughts her own, and the Swamp Devil loped along behind her, no longer sprinting as urgently as he had when they had come here. They'd been to the Lone Wood and decided they'd accomplished their mission. Now they ran to Kor to pick up the rest of their comrades.

Jack couldn't help thinking they'd seen something really important and missed it. It itched like a scab that wouldn't be picked.

* * *

Narem was an Uman who'd been born in Kor nearly one hundred years earlier, when there hadn't been an Eldador; much less an Eldadorian Empire, and Jark, a Man who called himself The Pirate King ruled the city.

His mother had been a whore and his father a pirate. He'd liked to think his father had loved his mother but because he was dead before Narem's 10th birthday it was hard to be sure. By his 20th birthday the pox that killed whores had taken his mother and Narem was alone.

He didn't want to be a pirate, so he'd joined the Koran Guard, the warriors who guarded the city when it was invaded, which happened now and then. The Koran Guard were the only police force the city knew. They kept fights from becoming riots. They made sure robberies didn't turn into massacres, and as much as was possible in this city they kept some semblance of order. Narem never thought he'd see his 30th birthday, but he justified that if he had to die that way, then he'd do it keeping another man alive, not robbing him for his treasure.

Eight decades later and he was still doing it. He'd seen

Jark the Pirate King fall to Tendehr, the Baron of the Forgotten Sea; him to Geler the Bloody, and him to another until twenty years ago Xareth had shown his wasted face and become the Duke of Thieves.

No matter who ruled the city, no matter who occupied what part of the tumble-down palace or who hung his banner on what was left of the walls, the Koran Guard persisted, it served and it lived on, taking a part of the spoils of every ship that pulled in here and a part of the profits from most of the crime, at least the major crime. In return they protected the city as best they could.

"Wolf Soldiers?" Xareff demanded, sitting on his 'throne,' a cracked marble edifice on top of a dais with chipped steps. Narem stood below him in a leather cuirass and steel greaves that didn't match; a sword on his hip and a crossbow over his shoulder. A few of his guardsmen flanked him, wearing what armor they'd come across in their travels.

"Two of what they call 'Millennia,' meaning fifty score each," Xareff informed him.

The scrawny 'Duke' fidgeted on his throne, looking to the two Toorian pirates who stood one to each side of his throne. Both were Xareff's trusted advisors—more trusted than the Koran Guard and Narem, anyway.

"Why so many, do you think?" he asked.

Narem shrugged. "They've not come to raid us," he surmised. "We've not done anything to the Emperor except to report on his nanny, and I think he'd hardly raid us for that."

Xareff shook his head and looked away. "You don't know that," he said. "It's impossible to know the Emperor's mind. He's crazy, he's just grasping and crazy."

Narem couldn't argue that he knew the Emperor's mind, however he'd seen crazy men before and they didn't tend to have empires.

"We don't have a lot of time," he commented to the Duke. "I've got five hundred men and women—you've got another three. I'll need them to hold the city."

"Hold the city?" Xareff exclaimed, standing. "Hold the city? Against that? Against one hundred score Wolf Soldiers? Are *you* crazy?"

Xareff thought a lot of people were crazy, Narem noted. What that usually meant was pretty clear.

"The Koran Guard will defend the city," Narem informed him. "If you don't want to stand with us, then you can step down. Others before you have tried. I can tell you the people who live here won't take it well."

Xareff looked to his two Toorians, heavily muscled males with blousy, cloth pants colored purple and bare chests. They both gave the Duke a sideways glance but said nothing. When Narem had been a captain in the Guard, Kraig the Beast had gotten Trenboni attention by slaughtering an Uman-Chi family on their yacht off of the coast of Dorkan, and when they'd come looking for him he'd tried to quit the city. The populace had caught him and presented his body to the invaders as a collection of parts in a wheelbarrow. That had satisfied the Uman-Chi and they'd left.

There was no way to know if that would work with the Emperor.

Xareff turned to one of the Toorians. "Are we still following that group with the Hero of Tamara in it?" he asked.

"We are," the man said in a deep baritone.

"Find them," he said. He turned to Narem, smiling.

"We'll see their appetite for a knife in the Emperor's nanny," he said.

* * *

People were scrambling, collecting what they could, making barricades in front of some buildings and collecting in alleyways and other places that seemed easy or at least easier to defend.

Jahunga led their mixed band through the streets of Kor to the stables where their horses were kept. From there they'd find a low-point in the broken down walls and leave while the Eldadorians and the Koran pirates fought for the gates.

"How much time do you think we have?" one of his warriors asked him.

Jahunga shrugged. One of the Volkhydran sailors chimed in, "The Koran Guard isn't more 'n a few hunnert. If there comes two thousand Wolf Soldiers, then they won't last long."

"A warrior behind a wall, even a bad one, can hold off

more than his own number of invaders," Jerod—Karl—said. All of them were looking to him now that they knew who he was. Jahunga had wondered why the Volkhydran insisted *he* was the hero, fate foretold, but now he understood.

A hero made by the one they were opposing. Fate may be foretold, but only the worst fate.

"If they don't just run," one of the Toorians, a warrior named Mfassa who'd been Jahunga's friend for years, said.

One of the Volkhydrans shook his head. "The Koran Guard'll fight," he said. "Some of the pirates, too. More, if the Emp'ror brought a few ships. I know as I'd ruther take my chances on the ground with Wolf Soldiers than at sea with Sea Wolves."

Jahunga nodded. He had to agree. Sea Wolves ruled the ocean and everyone feared them.

"Funny you should mention that," an Uman voice said from behind them.

They all turned to see a troop of warriors in various kinds of armor, watching them. They approached from behind as the group moved down a city street, now they were fanned out, thirty of them, most with clubs or rusty swords.

Jerod stepped out in front of the group, Jahunga stood up next to him, Xinto right behind. Raven kept back among the warriors and Slurn was nowhere to be seen.

"Doesn't seem funny to me," he said.

The leader of this new group, an Uman in a leather cuirass and mismatched steel greaves, with a sword at his hip and long, white hair, regarded them with flat, brown eyes. "I'm Narem of Kor," he said. "I'm Commander of the Koran Guard."

Jerod nodded. "Not easy to get that job," he said. "Guess you don't want me to waste your time any more than you want to waste mine."

"No," the Uman said, smiling. "That would be inconvenient."

"We know about the Wolf Soldiers," Jahunga said. "We did not bring them."

"Didn't say you did," Narem informed them.

His warriors had their weapons out. They were Men,

Uman, a couple Toorians that Jahunga noticed. All had long, unkempt hair and any of them could use a shave and a bath.

Jerod sighed. "You want to settle this, you and I, save your warriors to fight the Emperor?"

"I don't want to fight you at all," Narem said. "But Xareff believes the Aschire bitch with you will keep the Emperor from invading us, and if that's true I mean to have her."

Jerod nodded. "Would likely work," he said. "We left her outside of a building with a green door, in an alley back—"

Narem barked a laugh. "That's a Bounty Hunter's Guild lair," he said.

"We know it," Xinto said.

"So you know they'll quit the city, and take her with them," Narem said. His men were exchanging glances, working up their courage in case they were going to charge.

"That's what we plan to do, without the girl," Jerod said.

Narem shrugged. "Even if I were going to allow that," he said, "I think those Wolf Soldiers aren't going to."

"We're not worried about them," Jahunga said.

"Not too awfully worried about you, either," Jerod added.

* * *

Singer pounded out the miles, Lee on her back, her mother and a squad of Wolf Soldiers before her, her brother beside her and Hectaro and another squad of Wolf Soldiers to her rear.

She loved to ride, loved to feel the mare's power beneath her. Singer flowed like a river over the well-worn road between Galnesh Eldador and Thera. As her body moved with her mount, her mind sprung free to explore a world so new and fresh to a child.

Now and again she would look over her shoulder and smile at the handsome Hectaro. She'd imagined him a million times over as her husband, her protector, her hero with a bloody sword, as her father had been for her mother. She'd been raised on stories like the Battle of Tamaran Glen, where Lupus the Conqueror had charged ten thousand Confluni with his horse and his sword, and destroyed them all, to be at his wife's side.

Her mother had told her she was a daughter of heroes, of divine instruments, of legends. In her mind, Hectaro's victories rivaled her fathers as he cast down Swamp Devils and slew dragons while she supported him with her magic.

Now her mother had what she thought of as the 'Andaron Look,' that angry focus her people seemed to have. Like uncle Tali Digatishi when he fought, or her mother when she'd caught Bounty Hunters in the royal palace. When mother wore the Andaron Look, Lee knew that the best thing to do was to keep her whiny brother quiet and be what they considered a 'good girl.'

So now as her eyes drifted over the seascape, her mind creating great Sea Wolves packed with sailors, the decks slick with blood and her Hectaro battling a Confluni fleet with a sword in his hand, she had to give a start when one of those ships of Conflu actually sprang out of her fantasy and into her reality.

For a moment she wondered if she'd accidentally created a glamour. She'd done it before, when her father had told her of the 'unicorn,' a horse with a horn in the middle of its head, which protected virgin girls in their chastity. For a week she'd sworn one was following her around the palace, flowers in its mane, smiling at her, until her mother had reprimanded her for using her magic to such silly ends.

But no, she couldn't dispel the image and, in fact, the ship was there, and another on the edge of the horizon behind it.

"Mother," she spoke into Shela's mind, expending her power. Communicating this way when they rode was easier than shouting.

"Don't just use your power to be chatty," Shela admonished her immediately. As soon as she'd learned to do this, she'd haunted Shela's thoughts at night with idle conversation.

"Mother, to your right, a Confluni Ship of War."

Shela turned to her right and then immediately halted, the rest behind her. Bastard, Hectaro's mount, stomped and snorted and had to be reined in. Like his sire, he wanted to run, and didn't want to stop until he was too tired to go on.

"Hectaro, what is that?" Shela demanded.

Lee thought that a silly question, as she'd already said what it was.

"Hush, child," she heard in her mind.

Hectaro squinted and put a hand over his eyes to shield

them. Lee watched every move. Vulpe immediately imitated him.

"Confluni Ship of War," he verified. "Older one, bigger, pre-Empire, I think. Someone important on that. The one behind is newer, small and fast, to get out of the way of our Eldadorian Fire."

Shela nodded. She waved her hand before her, and the sky shimmered below the clouds.

The mirror image was dotted with Confluni ships. Dozens of them, followed by dozens more, all going east.

"Invasion force?" Hectaro asked her.

Shela shook her head. "Could be fifty ships, no more than one hundred to a ship—Conflu wouldn't invade with five thousand. Not after what we've done to them with thirty and sixty. They're going to Galnesh Eldador, but they're making a point, not invading."

"Shame no one's there," Hectaro said. "Although we could beat them—"

Shela shook her head. "Your father is more than able to handle either the defense of the city, or representing it to some Confluni rabble. If not, I can be back in an instant with the Emperor if I have to. There are still three thousand Wolf Soldiers in Galnesh Eldador. Even if they show up with one hundred thousand, the city would hold out for months."

"Will you at least warn him, your Imperial Majesty?" Hectaro pressed her. Lee knew he was angling to return home.

"I already have," she said. "While wasting time explaining to you. Hectar will put a few dozen Sea Wolves in their way and see what they do about it, and when we camp I'll find out what happened."

Hectaro nodded. Lee saw the disappointment on his face.

He hadn't learned to love her yet. He hadn't realized whom he was for. Nina had told her once that a woman waits for the right man, not because she isn't sure of herself, but because, like a good horse, a good man is slow to break.

She smiled to herself as, in her mind, Hectaro stood against the whole fleet of Confluni on the wharves of Galnesh Eldador, the bay around him red with the blood of the fallen, her magic destroying the missiles that the enemies shot at him.

Slow to break, she thought. *Not impossible.*

Chapter Thirty-One:

Reinventing Yourself

Dilvesh of the Daff Kanaar, whom Foveans called 'The Green One' for the green hook symbol on his breast and his being a Druid, sat a roan stallion from within the assembled squads of Wolf Soldiers he'd brought from Vrek to here.

He'd done so because Black Lupus' nanny, Nina, had informed him she'd be here, and that a group of Lupus' enemies were going to use this place to start plotting against him. Dilvesh had communicated with Shela in the capitol through a magic conduit they called 'Central Communications,' and then lead these troops here.

They'd always planned to take this city—it was a part of their long term plans. If it had become a liability, then there was no reason not to take it now.

Duke Tartan Stowe sat his own gelding next to him, of his new Angadorian breed. The youngish man, the eldest son of the old King, Glennen, had made a huge success of his duchy and supplied the empire with some of the best horses known on Fovea.

He supported Dilvesh with a thousand of his Angadorian Knights here, and another 3,500 on the Eldadorian plains.

Their instructions weren't just to sack the city; they were to crush it and everyone in it. An important move had begun in Eldador and the lives of a few dissidents didn't merit jeopardizing it.

"We could probably drive right in through the gates," Tartan informed him. "Their defenses are nothing. They probably have magic but if we drive in fast enough you'll have them before they're fully engaged."

Dilvesh nodded. "I agree," he said, "but I think we'll go slow."

Tartan sighed.

He was impetuous, this young man. He chaffed under the Emperor's guidance. Lupus had over-indulged him after his father's death, spent too much time with him then and not enough later. Tartan now wanted everything as fast as he could get it, and his successes fueled future failures.

"The Koran Guard defends this city," Dilvesh informed him patiently. "They've done nothing else for hundreds of years. They'll know nuances to that defense we could never guess at. Xareff, the Duke of Thieves, could afford to shore up these defenses if he wanted to, and hasn't. I think that makes this very obvious weakness a trap instead."

Tartan nodded. The young man wasn't a total loss, he was simply a challenge. Black Lupus had been right to send him to guide this one.

"I'll direct the attack," Dilvesh said. "Wolf Soldiers will take the gate and the plaza beyond, then reassess. You're correct in that I can handle what magic they might have."

Tartan nodded again. "And I'll handle the exodus that's sure to follow the invasion?"

Dilvesh smiled. "You'll make sure this exodus isn't an attack in disguise. It would be very clever of the Koran Guard to put a token resistance here, then hide among the refugees who'll quit the city, circle back and flank us," he said.

Tartan's eyebrows rose. His mount pawed the ground beneath him.

"Yes," he said. "Wouldn't that be clever?"

Dilvesh reined the horse away from the Duke, toward his

major. Some Aschire or even Eldadorian Regular bowmen would have been a nice addition to this invasion, but there hadn't been time to bring any. They were going to face losses in the initial attack on the city.

But losses are a part of war.

* * *

Nina awoke upright, her head lolling, her neck stiff, her jaw already swelling from where that black-haired bitch had struck her.

It hadn't taken much effort to contact the garrison at Vrek. She knew who was waiting there, and he was always listening. She'd told him of her dilemma, and who was holding her.

He'd told her to cooperate. Apparently, she'd done too much.

Being a nanny had made her soft.

"She's awake," some male said, a Volkhydran by the accent.

"Good," another voice, a woman. She knew that voice from somewhere, that jumbled accent. It had been a long time, the memory at the edge of her mind.

She raised her head, and looked directly into the symbol of the Daff Kanaar, its outline plastered across a red-haired woman's breast.

For a moment, she thought she had been rescued. Many of the Daff Kanaar had their personal troops wear their personal mark, in order to delineate them and express their personal power.

But none of them just wore the outline. Someone had done this to mock them.

"Someone's going to rip that right off of you," she told the red-haired woman.

The woman smiled. "I only wish they had," she said. "It would have made my life a lot easier."

Nina looked into this woman's green eyes. The room around them was dark, dust motes danced in the sunlight peeping in through cracks in the shuttered windows. She saw couches, and Men and Uman on them, and a couple of skinny girls, moving in between.

They weren't acting like people in a city, about to be

overrun.

"You don't remember me, do you, Nina?" the woman asked.

She did. Now that she mentioned it, Nina remembered those eyes, that hair, this woman in black leather, a warrior of some kind, someone who had come through the Aschire.

It was all too long ago, too fuzzy. She shook her head. This was too much to wake up into.

"I was there when a witch and an assassin decided your fate," she said. "Your father declared that you would have both worlds."

She leaned in closer. Now Nina saw the scars at her hairline, on her shoulder and her breast, barely treated but easily recognizable as the work of the Slee. Slurn had attacked her, but not finished the job.

But now Nina knew who held her. She recognized this dangerous woman, believed dead.

"Clear Genna," she said, looking into haunted green eyes.

"We're leaving here," Genna informed her. "The city will fall to the Wolf Soldiers. Already the city's 'Koran Guard' mans the walls, the Duke of Thieves' warriors are closing the gates, as if that can hold off thousands of the Emperor's elite troops.

"But I have a message for you, for him," she said, and leaned in so close, that Nina could smell her breath. "You tend his children, you have his ear. When you see him, you tell him this right in front of his bitch."

"I—I can't," Nina stammered.

"You *will*," Genna demanded. She took a hand full of Nina's purple hair, brought Nina's lips to hers, kissed her full on the mouth. Nina sputtered, never having been treated like this, never having known a male's kiss, much less a woman's.

The kiss was bitter—Genna's tears made it so.

Genna broke the kiss and pressed her lips to Nina's ear. She whispered a few words, dark and sinuous, looked into Nina's eyes, pressed her forehead to Nina's, and let her know the words were true.

Nina's blood ran cold. Such words—such darkness. The ramifications could shake the Empire, and at the worst possible time!

Genna pulled away and fled, the others in the room after her, and then the girls.

* * *

As the sun rose over the harbor, on the eleventh day of Earth's month in the 97th year of the Fovean High Council, the stomp of marching feet rang off of the walls of Kor as fifty squads of Wolf Soldiers marched out of the Salt Wood into the open glen before the shattered gates of Kor.

Arrows whipped out from the city and the warriors crouched behind their shieldmen. A few fell, most survived, pushing out more slowly, covered by their great shields as the squads closed, forming a block where the shieldmen in the second and third rows raised their shields over their heads and created a great wall to protect them.

The defenders peppered the Wolf Soldiers. As they crossed half way to the gates, another five hundred emerged from the forest, their shields already in place.

In the port, a ship was setting sail and others were trying to do the same. There were five Sea Wolves over the horizon to handle these.

Narem watched all of this with flat eyes, the Hero of Tamara standing next to him. An Andaron woman with dark hair stood next to this man, and spoke with a strange accent.

"I can throw fire," she said.

"No," both of the males said at the same time. Karl smiled to himself. "You'll give away our position to their casters," Narem added.

"The Emperor employs strong Wizards," Jerod said. "You wouldn't be a match for them."

The Wolf Soldiers were slowly but surely crossing the glen. When they came in through the gates, there were several mobs of warriors who'd attack them from their right hand side, where Wolf Soldiers were more vulnerable.

A runner, an urchin boy, charged up to where the three of them stood. Narem turned to meet him.

"They've horse in the woods," the boy said, gasping for breath. "They haven't found our tunnels yet, but they're close to the outer entrances."

"We can't flank them," Narem said to the open air. He turned to the battle. "Send a message to Xareff—we'll have to hold them at the gate if we can."

"That's it?" the female demanded of him. "That's your whole plan?"

Narem regarded her. "That's all of the plan we need. We catch them at the gate or fight them falling back into the city. We'll hold them if we can, but I've never fought Wolf Soldiers before."

"I have," Karl said. "You're doing the right thing. The best way to beat them is to wear them out. Make them move, make them march around without fighting. If you can get their leaders frustrated, it won't matter how the troops fight."

The female regarded him.

"So you think we can win?" she asked him.

Karl smiled a half-smile.

"No," he said. "I'd be very surprised if we could win."

* * *

Alone, Shela would have covered the distance between Galnesh Eldador and Thera in a week, maybe less. With her children alone, it might have taken her another day. She'd raised them in the Andaron tradition. Even little Chawny was accustomed to riding in a *kirruk* on her mother's back.

Hectaro wouldn't say anything, but the Duke's son lagged a few hours into the journey, even on a magnificent stallion like Bastard. In fact, they should all be trailing behind *him*.

The Wolf Soldiers also wouldn't *say* anything, but they had to keep fresh for fighting, meaning a slower pace and shorter days.

Eleven days into the journey, and they were just seeing the outer markers for Thera, meaning they still had a day's ride to get to the city, and the sun was already setting.

She reined in. "We stop here," she said. There was another camp to their east, and they'd been passing supply trains all day. "We'll camp at the side of the road and enter the city tomorrow."

"Is that wise, m'lady," one of the Wolf Soldiers, Meker,

asked her. Meker had been the captain of her personal guard for years. Of the race of Men, he'd been a Volkhydran miller whose mill had gone out of business. His wife was one of Chawny's wet nurses.

Shela swung her leg out of the saddle, feeling the good pull in her stomach and groin from a day's riding. Her belly had been softening of late and this excursion had given her that tone back. She'd noted that Lee, as well, had shed some baby fat, and little Vulpe sat straighter in the saddle than he did eleven days ago.

"We're tired, and we're almost here," she informed him. "The Emperor isn't going to march for another month. We'll see my brother tomorrow and leave the children with him, then carry on with fresh mounts for Uman City."

Meker nodded. "Mama," Vulpe said, "I'm going to take ten Wolf Soldiers and ride out a half-daheer."

So like his father, she couldn't help thinking. He wanted to know for sure they were safe. Meker had suggested that on the first night and, after a million questions, Vulpe had made it a part of his own routine.

"We'll care for him with our lives, Lady Shela," Drun, a Dorkan Wolf Soldier, said. Drun was built like so many tree trunks, all sewn together. If Drun couldn't protect the Prince, then all was lost, regardless.

"Come back when you smell the camp fire," Shela told him, turning her back to him to hide her eyes, wet with pride for her son. She listened to them gallop off as she pulled rations from her packhorse and the other ten Wolf Soldiers began to assemble camp.

"Shall I assist you, your Imperial Majesty?" Hectaro asked her. She shook her head, knowing her voice would crack. In fact she was weepy and lonely for her husband, and didn't want the bother of directing the young man. He *should* have either taken command of the Wolf Soldiers or gone off with the scouting party; however he seemed content to follow orders as she gave them.

Yonega Waya, her White Wolf, had high hopes for this one, but frankly she didn't see it.

"I'll see to your tent, then, and send a man to collect wood," he informed her. She nodded.

Some of her friends would have parked themselves on a comfortable pillow and watched all of these strong, young men take care of her. Shela Mordetur was no such Empress. Twenty-one men would find fifty ways to burn her food and build her tent on an anthill. She'd rather just do what women do, as Power intended it.

She pulled a cured haunch wrapped in spring leaves and leather from a pack, and then another pouch with some almost unbruised onions and peas. She was reminding herself where she'd packed the big, cast iron travel skillet she liked when she heard her daughter gasp, "Mother!"

She dropped it all and turned, summoning fire in her right hand, to see two of her Wolf Soldiers on their knees, Men behind them turning garrotes, and the other eight already engaged by four others in black leather.

She knew the stink of the Bounty Hunters Guild when she smelled it. Chawny still lay nestled in the kirruk on her back. As soon as she'd warned her mother, Lee had put up a defensive wall between her and the rest of them, as Shela had trained her.

"Khahen daharr!" Shela snarled, pointing her hand at the man behind one of the kneeling Wolf Soldiers. She needed numbers. The spell might not save him, but the explosion would draw the rest.

If they weren't caught already. She would have taken care of the outlying party before she worried about these.

The Bounty Hunter behind her kneeling Wolf Soldier exploded in flame. He screamed and released the garrote, the Man falling forward, dead already. Such weapons make quick work.

Someone leapt for Lee and bounced away from her defensive shield. Shela struck for the next Bounty Hunter, behind the other kneeling man, as one of her Wolf Soldiers fell, a sword in his guts.

Three of the horses reared, spooked from the screaming and the fire. Hectaro charged across the clearing where they'd planned to camp, toward her, to put his body between her and her enemies.

Right where he'd be in the way. The Bounty Hunter who'd been deflected by Lee leapt up and gave chase.

Lee gasped, "No!" and dropped her defenses.

"Lee!" Shela screamed, and extended her power to defend her daughter.

Hectaro fell to the tackle of the pursuing Bounty Hunter. Another of her Wolf Soldiers fell to his knees, no match for the Bounty Hunter training. The one garroting the other man dropped him and pulled a sword, coming for her.

Lee's power lifted the Bounty Hunter from the ground and flung her toward Shela. Shela barely stepped out of the way in time, and then found herself in the path of another Bounty Hunter. Two more of her Wolf Soldiers were down, the others sorely pressed and, now, outnumbered.

Someone struck Lee from behind. Shela saw her daughter fall. She felt her anger rise, Power swelled in her veins, her clutching hand rose to wield the spell that would burn them from the inside out.

A dagger flashed out of the darkness, nicking her upper arm. At first she considered it poorly thrown, then she felt her anger melt away and her vision blur.

Poison. She'd been poisoned. Bounty Hunters used it some times. She'd betrayed her husband, she'd damned her children. The Guild would use them to get Yonega Waya to surrender himself to them, and he would do it.

She tried to muster the energy to kill herself and the rest of them, but instead she felt a thud as her knees crashed to the dirt. The poison worked fast. She was swooning.

A face crowded into her cloudy vision before her. She wanted to recognize it, framed in red, green eyes. *Who is this?* she wondered. She felt she should know.

"Did ya miss me, baby?" it asked her.

She fell to her face.

* * *

Vulpe watched his mother fall, Drun to his right, Grelt to his left, mounted on their Angadorian horses.

He'd wanted to charge in and rescue them, but they

wouldn't let him. "If your mother can't handle them," Drun insisted, "what chance have we?"

Grelt, an Eldadorian Uman who'd been with his father for years, informed him, "If they don't know we're here, then we can rescue them. If we're found, then we join them. Which would you rather do, young prince?"

They'd been right, but still he'd watched his sister, Hectaro and his mother fall. He'd watched the Wolf Soldiers die, even Meker, who'd read to him when he'd been just learning.

Five Bounty Hunters, one of them a woman with red hair, strutting around, going through their things, tying them up in a circle, their backs to each other and piling the bodies of the dead.

They'd gagged all three. If they were smart they'd keep mother unconscious. She could cast without speaking a word.

"We have to get him to Duke Two Spears," Grelt told Drun.

Drun shook his head. "We wait, and when they sleep, we go in and take them back."

Dorkan simplicity and Uman caution, Vulpe thought. His father had taught him about these. Eldador reigned supreme because Eldador took the best parts of every nation and made them its own.

Meaning the Emperor took the best parts of the people around him, and made them work for him.

But the Emperor wasn't here, and Vulpe was only eleven years old.

But that was *mama*. That overruled everything.

"Send two men to Thera for reinforcements," he said. He turned his face first to Drun, then to Grelt. "My uncle has wizards who can find ma— who can find my mother. We follow them. If we see a chance to get them back, we'll decide then."

"Your Highness," Grelt began. Vulpe knew what came next.

You're a little kid. Do what the adults say.

But Vulpe knew what *one* adult would say to that.

He turned Marauder with his knee so he could face the larger warriors, and he put his hand on his sword hilt.

"I am Prince of the Empire, Heir apparent, and the son of

Lupus the Conqueror," he informed them, as he'd informed himself before a mirror in the nursery, a toy sword in his hand, playing whatever game his sister or Nina had invented.

But now the sword was real, and the woman who needed him was *mama*. He gripped that real sword's hilt, sheathed at his side.

"On your *lives*," he hissed, "you will obey me now."

They were Wolf Soldiers, and they did what Wolf Soldiers do. Supposedly, once, his uncle Two Spears had held up Lee and asked them, would they storm Outpost IX for her? They'd done so much damage to the city it was *still* being repaired.

"Aye, Vulpe," they said, calling him by his first name, as they would his father. Grelt sent two Men off to Thera, one of them an Andaron, like himself.

"We should get these horses out of the way," Grelt suggested. Drun nodded.

"Do it," Vulpe said, and dismounted.

He'd gotten them to do what he wanted. He'd save his mama, if he could.

At least he didn't cry.

www.ingramcontent.com/pod-product-compliance
Lightning Source LLC
LaVergne TN
LVHW010554100826
845148LV00014B/2715